Colby's gaze searched Anna's...

It was as if he were seeing things that had developed since the last time they had been honest with each other.

Anna let her thoughts grow and expand, knew they filled her eyes even as they filled her heart. She was being more open with him at this moment than she had been since his return...

"Would you mind singing it as I play so I can hear the words inside my head?"

Colby's voice seemed to come from a long tunnel, taking its time to reach her brain.

Anna jerked away and turned back to the piano keys. She must guard her heart. And thoughts. Hadn't she learned that lesson already?

So she played. He played. And she sang.

And despite her constant mental warnings, Anna let the music wash over her, numb her caution. She knew a height of pleasure so new and unfamiliar she didn't even know what to call it.

It was the music. That was all. Nothing more...

LINDA FORD

The Cowboy's Baby
&
Prairie Cowboy

HARLEQUIN® LOVE INSPIRED®CLASSICS

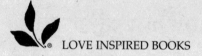 LOVE INSPIRED BOOKS

ISBN-13: 978-1-335-45467-6

The Cowboy's Baby & Prairie Cowboy

Copyright © 2020 by Harlequin Books S.A.

The Cowboy's Baby
First published in 2010. This edition published in 2020.
Copyright © 2010 by Linda Ford

Prairie Cowboy
First published in 2011. This edition published in 2020.
Copyright © 2011 by Linda Ford

www.Harlequin.com

Printed in U.S.A.

CONTENTS

Linda Ford lives on a ranch in Alberta, Canada, near enough to the Rocky Mountains that she can enjoy them on a daily basis. She and her husband raised fourteen children—four homemade, ten adopted. She currently shares her home and life with her husband, a grown son, a live-in paraplegic client and a continual (and welcome) stream of kids, kids-in-law, grandkids and assorted friends and relatives.

Books by Linda Ford

Love Inspired Historical

Big Sky Country

Montana Cowboy Daddy
Montana Cowboy Family
Montana Cowboy's Baby
Montana Bride by Christmas
Montana Groom of Convenience
Montana Lawman Rescuer

Montana Cowboys

The Cowboy's Ready-Made Family
The Cowboy's Baby Bond
The Cowboy's City Girl

Christmas in Eden Valley

A Daddy for Christmas
A Baby for Christmas
A Home for Christmas

Visit the Author Profile page
at Harlequin.com for more titles.

THE COWBOY'S BABY

They that trust in the Lord shall be as mount Zion, which cannot be removed, but abideth for ever.
—*Psalms* 125:1

I have been blessed by godly teachings from many preachers and teachers. Bill Gurnett and Mr. Fairholme played an important role in my early spiritual development but there are many, many more. I dedicate this book to preachers everywhere who faithfully teach God's word.

Chapter One

Steveville, Dakota Territory
May 1876

The pounding on the door threatened to bring down the roof. Twenty-year-old Anna Caldwell resisted an urge to call for patience as she raced to answer the summons before the racket woke the baby. Nothing made eighteen-month-old Dorrie crankier than having her afternoon nap cut short.

Anna paused long enough to take in a deep breath, lift her head and compose her expression to reveal none of her annoyance. After all, as the preacher's daughter and his housekeeper, she was expected to maintain a high standard of conduct. She pulled open the door and fell back half a step, gasping as her lungs spasmed so tight her chest hurt. "You. What are you doing here?"

Colby Bloxham stood before her, as handsome as ever. No. Even more handsome if that were possible. His dark blond hair fell past his ears, the ends faded by the sun. His blue eyes shone as bright as the sky behind him.

Her eyes stung and her throat burned as she recognized similar features she saw every day in the sweet face of Dorrie—his daughter. He'd left her—abandoned her—to Anna's care. Surely he didn't intend to upset the pleasant arrangement. He wouldn't dare.

He tipped the brim of his hat back with the barest flick of one finger. "Hello."

Anna stiffened her spine. "What do you want?" She kept her voice calm.

Colby's grin widened with confidence that she would welcome him again. His eyes smiled even more beguilingly than his mouth.

She didn't welcome him. She wouldn't. With a coolness she didn't feel, she ran her gaze up and down his length, hoping to convey how unwelcome he was. His grayish-brown trousers and tan shirt were faded in the areas that took more wear but surprisingly clean.

"I've come back."

"Didn't I tell you I never wanted to see you again?" It had been a year since he'd last entered this house, roaring with the effects of the contents of a bottle he still held, frightening Dorrie into hysterical screaming. It was the last straw as far as Anna was concerned. She'd had her fill of his carousing and having to listen to reports of his drunken behavior. She wanted nothing more than to protect Dorrie from such things. And perhaps shelter her own feelings, as well.

"I've changed."

She sniffed air surprisingly void of the repulsive smell of alcohol. "I can tell you haven't."

"You can help me."

"I've already tried. Several times." Each time her life had ended up more tattered than the last, her emotions shredded. She would not let history be repeated. "Not again."

The words were bravely spoken but forced with difficulty from her mouth. Her heart felt as if it had been rung hard by a strong washerwoman. She shuddered. Could she prevent him causing trouble over Dorrie? She should have gone to the judge and asked for legal adoption but as an unmarried woman, even with evidence of Colby abandoning his child… Well, she likely didn't have much chance of obtaining the necessary documents and she thought she'd never have to worry.

"You always help me."

She closed her eyes to his pleading tones.

"Anna, don't you give up on me. I've got nothing, no one else if you do." His voice rose with every word.

The commotion woke Dorrie and she cried.

"Is that my baby girl?"

"Colby." The feel of his name on her lips filled her with such sweet sorrow.

She swallowed hard and forced herself to speak his name again. "Colby, go away and leave us alone. I don't want to see you." She managed to slam the door and press her back to it. Her knees buckled. She slipped down the length of wood. Delving into her willpower, she stopped her descent and forced determination to her legs. Was he gone? She heard the thud of her heartbeat against her eardrums but no sound of boots marching away.

Go away, Colby. Leave us alone. Leave us in peace.

Dorrie continued to cry and call, "Mama." Anna had taught Dorrie to call her such, thought there would never be any question that she'd be the one to raise Dorrie, be the only mother the baby ever knew.

She never expected Colby to show his face in Ste-veville again.

For the space of several breaths, Anna could not move. Only when she heard Colby stomp away did she draw in a full-size breath, sending resolve clear to her toes.

"Mama." What a delightful sound that single word from Dorrie's mouth.

But knowing Colby was back forced Anna to face the truth. She was not Dorrie's mama and could lose the baby at the whim of a man who found courage and comfort from a bottle.

But he wouldn't take the baby without a fight. Anna wasn't much good at dealing with conflict. She'd sooner people just got along. But anyone trying to take Dorrie from her would discover the fury she was capable of.

Colby paused at the bottom of the steps and turned to face the door. "I ain't drunk." He'd made up his mind he wasn't going to be like his old man and drown in his drink. He'd tried that direction and finally got sick of it. Surprised him some, it had taken so long. He got sick of a few other things he'd been and done in the recent months of his life, as well.

He sniffed at his arms. Couldn't smell anything amiss but if Anna did maybe he should have spent more time soaking in the river before he came here.

The baby continued to cry. With a start, he realized she interspersed her cries with words. She could talk. Of course she wouldn't still be a baby. Wonder how big she was now. He couldn't get a picture in his mind of what this child of his would now look like. He had a hard time thinking of her as his child. He'd thrust the infant into Anna's arms shortly after birth and seen little of her since. He had only one memory of Dorrie, two if he counted clutching the newborn and rushing to Anna with her. The one time he recalled through an alcohol-induced haze was of the wide-eyed fear in the baby's face and her piercing screams of terror before Anna managed to shove him out the door ordering him to leave and never return. In hindsight he couldn't say he blamed her, though at the time he'd been plenty angry.

"I'm not going away." His voice echoed in his ears. He intended to be the kind of father to Dorrie he'd always wanted.

And never had.

He refused to believe Anna didn't want to see him. From the day he wandered into Steveville on the tail end of a cattle drive, only sixteen years old and already on his own for two years, he'd found a welcome with Anna that he'd found nowhere else. Not even with his deceased wife. He had married Nora for all the wrong reasons just as she'd married him for equally wrong ones.

He stared at the church to the right of the house, recalling in brilliant detail how he'd passed the building six years ago and seen fourteen-year-old Anna coming from the interior, beautiful as a western songbird and singing just as sweetly. Right then and there he'd decided he might give church a try.

From the beginning, he felt something special for Anna and she, he was certain, for him. She'd understood him, listened to him, encouraged his dreams and hopes just as he'd listened to hers. Mostly their dreams had been of a good solid home with a loving father and mother and several children. Funny how they shared similar dreams coming from such different backgrounds.

He wondered if she had the same hopes and dreams she'd once had. Or had they died along with the welcome he'd expected?

He continued to stare at the church. He kind of thought God would welcome him back, too. But maybe He didn't want to see Colby Bloxham any more than Anna did. *Go away. I don't want to see you.* The words banged against the inside of his head, filling his thoughts with old familiar feelings of being something from the slop bucket.

He swung up on his horse, his first instinct to ride the animal into a lather, straight down the road and away from all this. But Dorrie's cries continued. His child.

Somehow he would prove to Anna he had changed and could be a father to Dorrie. It was time. 'Course he could try and take Dorrie without her consent. After all, the little girl was his. But he suspected Anna might fight him and no doubt everyone would take her side. Besides, for some reason, it was important to him to win Anna's approval. A large ache carved itself into his heart by the words echoing through his mind. *Go away. I don't want to see you.*

But he was not going anywhere.

He turned to the left, and rode into the main part of town, glancing about as he passed the houses on each side of the dusty street. Things looked much as they had when he left. Somehow he'd expected them to be different. As if his own decision to be different would have changed everything else in his world.

The houses gave way to businesses—the blacksmith and livery barn set back from the street, the sounds of metal on metal ringing through the air, the smell of horses and hay filling his nostrils. The signs on each store were familiar—Mack's Mercantile, the feed store, the milliner, the lawyer. He stopped at the Lucky Lady Saloon and dismounted. His hands on the swinging doors, he hesitated. He'd had enough of drinking and so much more but he had friends he wanted to see.

He pushed the doors aside and strode in.

He avoided looking at the bright patch where the sun filtered through the dirty window as he gave his eyes three seconds to adjust to the dim light. A familiar figure nursed a bottle at the nearest table and he sauntered over. "Hey, Arty." The old codger had wandered into town a year or so after Colby had arrived. Arty had known both Colby and his old man way back when. Colby always wondered that they'd landed in the same place but guess all Arty had to do was follow any road long enough and he was bound to get somewhere even if only Steveville. At first he had resented the old man's presence, reminding him as it did of Pa, but Arty was harmless. He got sloppy drunk not fighting drunk.

"Colby? When did you get back in town? What are you doing with yourself?" Arty jerked toward the bar. "Sol, get us another glass. Colby here is going to share my bottle."

"Don't use that stuff anymore."

Poor old Arty almost jolted off his chair. "You're joshing. A Bloxham that don't drink. Ain't possible."

An old familiar anger at his upbringing seared through Colby like a struck match then died as quickly and harmlessly. "I decided I didn't want to turn out like my old man."

Arty studied the bottle regretfully and yet affection-
ately. "Wise move, my boy. So watcha been doing?"

He wasn't about to tell anyone the truth about where
he'd been and what he'd done since he'd last wandered
the streets of Steveville. Hopefully news of his doings
hadn't trickled back this far and never would. But Arty
waited, clutching his glass with both hands and studying Colby with the unblinking stare of a man whose
thought processes had been dulled by drink.

"Arty, I been wandering around a bit."

"Looking for anything in particular?"

Colby laughed. "Yup. Me."

Arty blinked, drained his glass, wiped his mouth and
tried to decide whether to laugh or sob.

Colby patted the older man's shoulder. "Never mind.
It don't make sense to me, either." He'd glanced around
the room when he first entered, noted several men but
paid them scant attention. Now he looked around again,
hoping to see a familiar face or two. He specially wished
to see Hugh, the only man who'd felt like a friend. He
used to come over and play cards with Colby and Nora
in the evenings and often stayed the night. Hugh had
been with him after Nora's death. Colby didn't know
how many times Hugh had dragged him from the bar
and made sure he got home before he got arrested.
Saved his hide on one specific occasion, yet last time
he'd seen Hugh, Colby had been fighting drunk and
accused the man of all sorts of horrible things. Even
accused him of having his eyes on Nora. Some way to
treat a friend who had likely saved him from the hang-
man's noose.

He didn't see Hugh but met the eyes of a bold

stranger, recognizing immediately a man itching for trouble.

The man left the bar and moseyed over to flick a finger at Arty's bottle, bringing a defensive grab from the older man. "This old drunk a friend of yours?"

There was a time in the near past when Colby would have jumped at the chance to respond. But no more. He thought of sweet Anna, who had once been his friend, and the way she'd looked at him, ordering him away like some kind of rabid dog. Yeah, she might have once had good reason to think so, but he'd win back her friendship if it took the rest of his life.

He hoped it wouldn't take near that long.

"Let the old man alone," he murmured in a soft, not-wanting-a-fight tone. "He ain't hurting no one."

"He hurts my nose." The dark-eyed stranger chose to flick at Arty's hat, sending it askew.

Arty clung to it with both hands like he feared further tormenting.

Colby pushed his own hat back so the man could see his expression clearly and crossed his arms over his chest. "I said leave him alone."

The man jeered. "Says who?"

Colby recognized the challenge. Hoped he wouldn't have to accept it. He gave the man his hardest look, one birthed before his sixth birthday and matured over the years. This past year had given it a whole new depth. He allowed himself a moment of victory as the annoying man shrugged and returned to his drink at the bar, muttering, "Ah, who cares? Just another old drunk. Seen hundreds of 'em."

Colby pulled his hat back to where it usually rode. Hugh wasn't there. He'd determined that. But he deliberately lingered in the saloon for a while longer, not wanting anyone to think he had reason to hurry away. But he knew if he stayed too long word would somehow get back to Anna about where he chose to spend his time. He knew small towns, knew this one better 'n most. Person couldn't so much as cough without it being reported and discussed freely. He knew her opinion about the evils of drinking. Had heard it many times especially after Dorrie was born. "Won't find any solution in the bottle," she said. He remembered the perverse pleasure he got out of asking her where she thought he'd find an answer for his loss. Always she said the same thing. *God is the great healer. God has a plan for your life. God loves you.* He almost believed. So many times he almost believed.

But how could God love him when he constantly found himself in one sort of trouble after another. Sure, anyone would say it was of his own making. For the most part, it was. But this time he intended to prove he was something more than a Bloxham living from a bottle. A better Bloxham than his father was or that he'd been in the past.

He waited a suitable amount of time then sauntered out the door as if it mattered not to him if he stayed or left.

He led his horse down the street, his feet aching to wander south toward the church and Anna. He didn't believe she truly meant it when she said she never wanted to see him again, but it might be wisest to give her a chance to get used to him being back in town and adjust to the idea he had changed.

He forced his steps to some of his familiar haunts, thinking he might find Hugh. But after an hour of looking he'd not seen the man. Likely he'd show up after he finished whatever job he currently held. Colby would make a swing by the Lucky Lady again later in the evening.

In the meantime…

Well, he'd give anything to see Anna hurrying between the house and the church like he had that very first time. Maybe he'd just ride on down the street, casual-like, no hurry, no destination in mind. Might be she'd have cause to cross the yard, perhaps carrying his little daughter with her. He wondered if Dorrie favored him or Nora. Or did she reveal a likeness to both her parents?

Anna carried Dorrie to her high chair. For a moment she held her close and buried her face against Dorrie's warm neck, breathing in the familiar scent. "My sweet, sweet baby." This child filled her with such joy. What if Colby had come back to claim her? Anger and determination drilled through her limbs and up her spine.

She would stand between Dorrie and her father, fight him like a wildcat, protect Dorrie from anything that would hurt her. No matter what. She loved this child as her own.

Dorrie squirmed. "Down, Mama."

Anna reluctantly ended her hug and put the baby in her chair. She'd brushed Dorrie's blond hair back and tied it with a white ribbon, letting little curls escape to frame the heart-shaped face. For the past year, she had allowed herself to pretend Dorrie was hers, allowed herself to believe Colby would never return, a thought that filled her with a strange mixture of relief and regret. She'd never been certain which was the stronger emotion.

Dorrie drank half her milk then threw back her head and wailed.

"Poor baby. You didn't get enough sleep, did you?"

And Colby was to blame. His loud intrusion had woke the baby. What did he want? Why had he returned? Her insides tightened until she wondered if something she'd eaten had been a little off. "Let's go find Poppa." She plucked the child from her chair, wiped her face and settled her on her hip.

"See Poppa?"

"Yes, pet. We'll see your poppa." She hated to disturb Father at the church where he went to meditate but she badly needed his counsel.

She ducked out the back door. The wall of the church was blackened. The sight still gave her heart a jerk. The fire had taken out several homes and damaged the church before it was quenched. Thank God the fire had stopped when it did. Thank God no lives had been lost, though a few families had lost homes.

Guilt weaved throughout her thoughts. She really didn't have time to wander around nursing her worries. Alex would soon be home from school, needing supervision. Supper needed making and she must finish sewing together the quilt top the women were making for the Anderson family who were among those who'd lost their homes. Tomorrow afternoon the sewing circle would gather at the manse to put together the quilt.

But first she would find some peace at the church and at Father's side.

As she crossed the yard she noted a saddled horse on the other side of the road, in the shelter of some trees where the road branched off to a pathway leading to the narrow river cutting past the town. Strange that a horse should be left thus. Then she saw Colby lounging in the shadow of the trees. Did he intend to spy on them, perhaps wait for a chance to snatch his daughter?

She clutched Dorrie tighter and raced into the shelter of the church. "Father," she called, her voice tight with unformed terror, "he's come back. What are we going to do?"

Chapter Two

Colby saw Anna look in his direction, noted how she jerked in surprise and likely a whole lot of anger, then raced into the church. She obviously didn't like the fact he was there. He doubted she wanted to know he intended to stay around. She'd hurried into the church so fast he'd gotten no more than a glimpse—just enough to make him want more. He recalled a time when they had spent many an hour wandering down the nearby path discussing anything and everything and sometimes nothing. It was the only time in his life he'd felt real and honest.

He'd run from that, driven by his own internal demons. But wherever he'd run, whatever he'd done—and he hoped no one would ever know what that was—a vast hollowness sucked at his heart. Only one thing had ever satisfied that emptiness—Anna's presence.

He'd seen the child perched on Anna's hip. Dorrie. Grown considerably. In the seconds he'd had to study her he could say she looked a sturdy child with hair somewhat fairer than his own with a big white bow in the back. He wanted to see and know this tiny bit of humanity he'd made with Nora. He'd come back to be a proper father but he knew so little about being one except to know he didn't want to be like his pa.

He guessed Anna wouldn't be leaving the sanctuary of the church while he stood there. "I'll be back," he muttered as he swung to Pal's back.

Several hours later he strode into the Lucky Lady and checked the occupants. No sign of Hugh. Was he still around the area or had he left for something better—or at least different? *Could save your energy, Hugh. Different ain't better.*

Arty sat at the same table, his eyes now glassy, his hat askew. Another familiar figure sat across from him—Tobias—neat and tidy as always, and rough shaven just as Colby remembered. He wondered if the man used a dull table knife for a razor.

He saw it all in a glance even as he watched the dark-eyed troublemaker nod to the men on either side of him who then slid away as the man slowly uncoiled himself from the bar to slither toward Colby.

"This the one who caused you a problem?" The question came from Colby's right.

He tensed, feeling as much as seeing, the two crowding close. He kept his attention on the man crossing the room. *Keep coming. Bring your trouble to me. Leave poor old Arty alone.*

But the man stopped and slapped the table in front of Arty. He jumped and half tumbled from his chair.

Colby eased forward prepared to help though he perceived it wasn't Arty the dark-eyed man wanted to tangle with. "Leave him be."

"Who? This old drunk?" He grabbed the bottle from the table and tipped it over. Only a few drops spilled out as Arty had already drained it, but the old man cried out and lurched to rescue it as if it held several generous drinks.

The man pushed Arty aside. "Sit down, old man. Before you end up facedown in the sawdust."

Arty stumbled backward, swayed and clutched at the stranger's arm to steady himself.

"Get away from me, you old bum." The troublemaker tossed Arty aside.

Colby saw Arty was going to land heavily and he strode forward to catch him.

He didn't make two steps before his arms were caught on each side. Helplessly he watched Arty skid to the floor and flounder for a grasp on something solid. He found the rung of the chair and started to pull himself back to its seat only to have the chair kicked away from him.

Colby growled. "Leave him alone."

The third man left Arty and marched over to glower into Colby's eyes. "You think you scare me?"

"Enough that you enlist two more the same as you to even the odds." He grunted as the man on his right shoved his arm up his back hard enough to tear at his shoulder. "Just you and me. Let's see how scared you are then."

The man nodded to his friends. But he didn't wait for them to release Colby's arms to sucker punch him in the stomach and, before Colby could get his fists bunched, landed a blow to his nose.

Ignoring the pain and the blood pouring forth, Colby exploded into a fury of fists. He had the man on the floor before the other two grabbed him. They succeeded in dragging him to the door and tossing him out on the street but Colby made them work for their victory.

As he wiped away the blood and scrambled to his feet, several decent folk passed by on the other side bound, no doubt, for some noble event.

"Why, it's Colby Bloxham."

"As rowdy as ever, I see."

A loud sniff and then a pious "Let's pray he leaves again real soon," followed.

Colby grabbed his hat and smacked it hard on his head. He'd give it until morning for Anna to hear that Colby had been brawling. He could explain if she'd give him a chance. 'Course she'd given him many chances in the past and he'd mangled each of them. Not much wonder she wasn't about to throw open the door to welcome him this time.

No point in expecting a chance to explain himself.

He strode away, heading for the camp he'd set up on the edge of town, close enough to the river for ease of water, close enough to the church he could slip over and watch the goings-on, yet not so close as to give anyone cause for concern.

Anna covered the little cakes with clean towels and arranged the fancy teacups on the table. The members of the Ladies Sewing Circle would be arriving any minute. Everything was ready, in precise perfection. She should be calm and serene.

She was not.

Her emotions raged as she filled the kettle. Father had said it was only natural for Colby to want to see how Dorrie was faring. And perhaps he had truly changed. They needed to encourage him in that direction. After all, hadn't they often prayed he would turn to God to meet the needs of his heart?

Anna couldn't meet Father's eyes as he spoke. Some time ago her prayers had shifted from asking for Colby's redemption to asking that he never return. How would she survive having her heart ripped out and left to whimper and bleed again? And now the threat was twofold. She could also lose Dorrie. She'd said so to Father.

"Did he say he wanted to take her?"

"He asked to see her."

"Natural enough, as I said. Let's leave it in God's loving care." He'd taken her hand in his and prayed.

But Anna didn't find the peace and release she'd hoped for. She couldn't stop wondering what Colby really wanted. She couldn't stop worrying how his plans could upset her life.

Her teeth ached from continually fighting this inner battle and she forced her jaw to relax. *Please, God, put Your mighty hand on his back and send him down the road again.*

Such an ache consumed her that she bent over and moaned. *Anna, forget the boy you once knew. Colby is no longer that person. Let him go.*

Forcing herself to concentrate on the task at hand, she filled the cream and sugar then paused to run a hand over her hair, making sure every strand was in place. She'd changed earlier and the white shirtwaist was immaculate as was the black skirt she'd brushed thoroughly. No one could find fault with her appearance.

But if they could see the turmoil of her heart they might have cause to wonder about her suitability to run the pastor's home.

She pulled herself taller. She needed to trust God.

She said the words. She meant them. But she still felt no peace. Would God allow her to experience loss once again? Pain shafted through her, consuming her. Then she pulled her self-control tight as a corset. Whatever lessons God wanted to teach her through her sorrows, she had tried to learn them. She didn't want the lesson repeated.

Lord, I try to be obedient and do what You would want.

That's what she needed to concentrate on—trusting and being obedient.

She hurried into the other room where she had pushed back the wooden armchair and moved the little side table to make room to set up the quilting frame. The top was finished and waiting. The ladies had each contributed to the squares for the quilt. Today they would assemble it with batting and backing and tie it. Anna would finish the edging and then present it to the Anderson family, who had lost everything in the fire.

"It's a mercy no one was killed," Mrs. Klein said later as the ladies worked on the quilt. The fire still filled their thoughts and conversation.

"God be praised," Mrs. Berglund said.

"Now we must do our part to help those who lost their home. Thank God we can make this quilt."

"God be praised," Mrs. Berglund said.

Anna bent over the quilt, hiding a smile. Mrs. Berglund was a dear soul but so predictable, her comments invariably limited to one or two of her favorite phrases.

"I thought Mrs. Anderson might enjoy helping us with the quilt. Did you ask her to attend?" Mrs. Percy directed her question at Anna.

"I did invite her but she is struggling to cope in the

little shack they're living in. I don't think she feels up to visiting just yet." Mrs. Anderson had fluttered her hands and looked about wildly when Anna had gone to visit. Anna couldn't imagine losing everything and trying to live in a building that hadn't been intended for human habitation.

"Some of us gathered for tea last night." Mrs. Percy sat up and looked around at her announcement. She waited until she had everyone's attention before she continued. "Now that everyone is safely sheltered and resuming their lives, it's high time, I say, to get the church fixed up so we can meet there." She sniffed. "I've never cared for taking my children to that room above the saloon."

Anna said nothing as the other women murmured their comments. Certainly it wasn't ideal, but helping the people who lost their homes and belongings took precedence over fixing the church. She waited, knowing Mrs. Percy had more to say on the subject now that all eyes were on her.

"Pastor Caldwell said he'd look after the repairs but I've seen no evidence of it getting done." She cleared her throat and gave Anna a hard look, driving Anna's heart to the bottom of her stomach in alarm.

"Remember we agreed to be part of the town's celebration in honor of Mr. Steves. It's imperative the repairs are done in time. After all, Mr. Steves donated the money for building the church. We need to remember him for that."

Anna felt every pair of eyes turn toward her. Though no one spoke she knew what they were all thinking— the same thing as she. Father's intentions were good but every one jabbing their needles into the quilt knew he tended to get lost in his thoughts and forget such practical things as filling the stove, or closing a window. She couldn't imagine he would keep his mind on the mundane things such as carpentry and painting long enough to see the task completed in time for the big seventy-fifth birthday party planned for the town's founder. Why had he agreed to be in charge?

She sat up straight and met each pair of eyes around the quilt, smiling serenely and reassuringly. "I think you can count on Father to get it done in time." She'd personally see that he did. She'd remind him to arrange the workers needed. Father was a godly man and his concern for others was genuine but he needed help with practical matters. She would provide that help, gently and discreetly, not only because it was her duty as her father's unofficial assistant as running his household turned out to be, but also because it was plain if the repairs weren't done she would be found wanting in the eyes of the women seated in her front room.

The others murmured approval and returned to their sewing.

"Mama, Mama, Mama," Dorrie called.

"Excuse me. I have to get her up from her nap." Anna hurried to the little girl. Having Colby show up stole from her bliss in having a child she considered her own without benefit of marriage nor condemnation of a child born out of wedlock. *Please, God. Send that man on his way. I don't want Dorrie hurt by the things he does.* She knew people would find it easy to blame every naughty thing Dorrie did as evidence she was living up to her heritage. Or rather, down to it. Anna could well imagine Mrs. Percy sniffing and saying, "An apple doesn't fall far from the tree."

Although Dorrie wasn't the only one who could be hurt, she was young and might easily forget Colby wandering into her life and out again.

Anna doubted she would recover as quickly.

She slipped a clean white pinafore over Dorrie's blue dress and put on her shoes. "There you go. All pretty. Remember the ladies are here so I want you to say hello to them all and then play quietly." Anna took from the shelf the Noah's Ark and animals reserved for times when Dorrie had to play quietly at her side.

She returned to the front room and the sewing circle.

Mrs. Percy oohed over Dorrie a minute then turned her sharp gaze toward Anna. "I saw her father last night."

Anna's heart dropped to the soles of her feet. Whatever the woman intended to say had the potential to upset Anna's world.

"In the most shameful state of being tossed from that horrible saloon. I'm not much to pay attention to rumors—"

Anna steeled her expression to remain kind and calm, displaying none of the disbelief she felt at the woman's assurances, nor her fear of what more would follow.

Mrs. Percy continued. "But it seems whenever I hear the name Colby Bloxham it comes in the same sentence as robbery, plunder or other illegal activity." She sniffed and pasted on a pitying expression. "I wouldn't be surprised to see a wanted poster with his likeness on it."

Anna wanted to cry out a protest. But why should she want to defend him? The man had gone from bad to worse. Her only concern was to protect Dorrie from the ugliness of such speculation.

Thankfully, Dorrie was too young for the discussion to affect her. But how long before the unkind words would sear her little heart like a hot branding iron. As it did Anna's. How shocked Mrs. Percy would be to discover the secret, impossible longing of Anna's heart.

"I expect he'll be visiting here soon."

Anna ducked her head rather than face the woman and try and guess what she meant by that statement. Everyone knew she and Colby had been friends at one time. Before he had left her to cope with her sorrow on her own.

Just as everyone knew he was Dorrie's father.

Caution kept her from mentioning Colby's visit.

The quilt was finished. The ladies rolled it and left it for Anna to complete. As they settled in to visit, Anna slipped to the kitchen to prepare the tea.

Her friend Laura followed her. "Baby needs nursing." She sat in a nearby chair and fed her newborn daughter.

"You look tired."

"It will take time for the baby to sleep through the night. In the meantime—" She shrugged.

"How is Adam feeling about Gloria?" She wondered if the three-year-old felt pushed out by the demands of his new sister.

"Carl takes Adam with him as much as he can. Adam loves it." Laura gave Anna a long considering look. "Has he been here?"

Anna knew she meant Colby but she pretended otherwise. "Adam or Carl?"

Laura only laughed. "You know who I mean."

"He was here."

"Drunk?"

He hadn't staggered or slurred his words. Officially

she'd have to say he wasn't drunk. For all that was worth. "Says he's changed." She sounded every bit as weary as she felt.

"Has he?"

"How would I know? Saying so doesn't make it so, does it?"

"What did he want?"

Anna's gaze slid toward the little girl playing on the floor. "To see her."

"Only *see* her?" The concern in Laura's voice matched Anna's worry.

"That's all he said but…"

"What are you going to do?"

Anna relaxed and grinned. "Why, I thought I'd hand her over without a word."

Laura laughed. "And if I believe that you could sell me roosters as laying hens. Is he likely to let it go without a fight? How long do you suppose it will take for him to give up and go away? You know him as well as anyone. What's your guess?"

How well did she know him?

They'd enjoyed so many good times—wandering down by the river sharing secrets and fears. She'd counted on him for support and understanding but when her whole world had fallen apart and she needed him he'd disappeared. She'd waited for him to come. Her heart ached more with each passing day.

The final bit of bottom had fallen out of her world when she discovered he'd left town. She'd had to deal with the accident on her own.

The memory of it lived forever in her mind, in vivid color and sharp sounds. A wagon skidding on one wheel for what seemed a very long time. The scream of horses.

The terrified cries of a woman with a baby clutched to her chest. She'd watched, powerless to stop the accident. Then in scenes so slow, so detailed she knew she would never erase them from her mind, the wagon hit a rock, flipped skyward, tipped over and landed upside-down. The woman flew through the air, landing with a heart-stopping thud. Then only the wheels moved, turning round and round.

She thought they would never quit.

She'd remained frozen to the spot until warm, demanding arms drew her away.

Her beloved stepmother, Rose, had died. As had baby Timmy.

She sucked in air and pushed away the memory, barring it from her thoughts.

At sixteen she had become a mother to Alex, six years her junior, and she had taken over her father's household.

And Colby had left. He didn't come for the funeral. He didn't come to offer comfort. He didn't come to share her fears. He returned eighteen months later with a wife soon to have a baby. Nora had died giving birth to Dorrie and Colby had thrust the newborn into Anna's arms.

She shouldn't have been surprised when Colby left a second time even though she could blame herself. She told him to leave. What she'd meant was for him to change his ways.

She no longer held out hope of him doing so and with decisiveness, shut her heart against caring, against hurting, and answered Laura's question. "He's never been one to stick around when things get difficult."

"Then I expect he'll soon be gone again."

The thought should have been comforting. Instead it sliced through her heart like an out-of-control butcher knife. She turned away lest Laura guess at her turmoil. Why did she still care even after all the pain he'd brought to her life?

Thankfully there wasn't time to discuss the matter further. Nor mull over silent questions. The ladies waited.

As she served tea and cakes, fourteen-year-old Alex came in from school. She went to the kitchen to speak to him.

"Come and say hello."

"Do I have to?" He shuddered, headed for the back door and escape, his face alternating between a flush and pallor.

She knew how he struggled with social occasions but he must learn to do what was proper. "Yes, you do. It's common courtesy." She wished she could inject Alex with some self-confidence but every effort she made only seemed to cause him to pull back more quickly. She rested a hand lightly on his shoulder and steered him to the parlor where the ladies enjoyed tea and visiting. "Just say hello and then you can play with Dorrie."

"'Lo." It was barely audible and more of a mumble than anything.

She ached for the way he shied away from people, preferring to live with his books and toys. She'd done her best for him but she knew nothing about raising a child.

Rose had married Father when Anna was almost five. Rose had brought joy and love into both Father's and Anna's life. After her death, Father had withdrawn into his Bible study.

Not, Anna realized, unlike Alex and his withdrawal from people.

Alex played with Dorrie a few minutes before he sidled up to Anna. "Can I go now?" he whispered.

She nodded.

As he slipped away, Dorrie protested loudly because her favorite playmate had left.

Anna picked up Dorrie to quiet her and realized every eye watched her. They had been talking about her. And decided she needed their helpful, friendly advice. She shifted her gaze to Mrs. Percy, expecting she would be the self-appointed spokeswoman. When Laura reached out and squeezed Anna's hand, Anna understood she wasn't going to like what she was about to hear.

Mrs. Percy adjusted her posture so she looked even more imperious than ever, which had always been enough to strike fear into Anna's heart. "What's to be done about the cross?"

Anna knew she meant the wooden cross that graced the wall behind the pulpit. It had been badly damaged by the fire. She wondered what the women thought should be done about it.

"We obviously need a new one." Mrs. Percy spoke as if it had been firmly decided.

She thought of the burned cross and how important it had been in her life. "When you think of how the cross saves us from the flames..." She meant in a spiritual sense but seeing the confusion on the faces of the women around her, she knew they didn't understand, perhaps thought she meant the cross had somehow stopped the fire from consuming the church.

She didn't finish her thought but if there were any

way possible, she'd salvage the cross. Not because Mr. Steves had been the one to hang it on the wall. Not because it was part of the original decoration, but because of what it meant to her.

But it was not the cross, nor repairs to the church that crowded her mind after the ladies left. It was Mrs. Percy's report of Colby's behavior.

He hadn't changed.

Colby would never be the man she needed and ached for.

She must persuade Father to talk to Colby, make him see the harm his presence was doing and convince him to leave town.

She would talk to Father tonight as soon as Alex and Dorrie were in bed.

Chapter Three

But it was the next morning before she got an opportunity to speak to her father. He surprised her with an announcement.

"Father, you didn't?" She had no right to question Father, but it took all her rigid self-control to keep from revealing the depth of her shock.

"I think it is an excellent idea. It takes care of many problems at the same time." He nodded as if completely satisfied with his decision and settled before the desk in the front room where he opened his Bible and prepared to turn his thoughts to study.

Anna stared at the contents of the room—the wooden armchair now back to its normal place beside the desk, the small table with a lamp and stack of pleasure books, the brown leather sofa that seemed best suited for decoration rather than comfort, the bookshelves holding Father's precious library, the ornately framed daguerreotypes—one of Rose and Father's wedding and the other of her own mother whom she barely remembered. She saw nothing in the contents of the room to calm her fears.

"How does hiring Colby solve any problems?"

"Isn't it obvious, dear daughter? He will get the repairs done to the church on time, leaving me to attend to other things. He'll be close enough to get to know Dorrie.".

Exactly. Close enough to make it impossible to keep him from seeing her. And who knows what he'd want next? How that solved anything, Anna could not begin to understand.

"The young man and I had a good talk. I believe he's sincere in wanting to change. Who better to help him than us? Isn't that what the church is for? To provide help for those who need it?" He sent Anna a gently re-proving look that brought a flood of guilt to war with her anger and fear.

"Of course but…"

Father smiled gently. "Don't give up on him. Nor disregard the Lord's work in his life."

Tears burned the back of Anna's eyes. It wasn't that she didn't have faith in God and what He could do, but believing in Colby had brought her nothing but pain and disappointment. She could not survive another shattering experience with him—trusting him, loving him against her best intentions, only to watch him ride away. Or worse, hear after days of waiting and wondering that he'd left town.

"By the way, he'll be sharing our meals."

Anna gasped.

Father's eyes flashed a challenge. "Are we not to show hospitality?"

"Yes, Father." She knew when to accept the inevitable but how would she cope? "When does he begin?"

"He's over there as we speak. He'll join us for lunch."

Colby hoped Anna would slip over to the church and speak to him. But it was her father who wandered over at lunchtime to invite him to join them. Colby followed across the yard with a mixture of anticipation and dread. No doubt being tossed out of the saloon had been duly reported to her. No one would believe that Colby Bloxham had been defending a helpless old man. They'd think he was drunk and rowdy as he once would have been.

But a stronger, more insistent emotion prevailed. He wanted to sit at the same table as Anna, have a chance to watch her, enjoy the sound of her voice.

He took the place Anna indicated—to the left of Pastor Caldwell and across from Alex, who rushed in from school to join them. Anna sat opposite her father.

He didn't miss the fact his plate had been shoved as far away from Anna as possible but it only served to allow him opportunity to study her without the risk of being caught staring. She wore her hair in a roll at the back of her head. Supposed it was more in keeping with her role as the pastor's homemaker than letting it fall down her back as he remembered—the sun catching in it like gold glinting in a river. He'd already had a chance to see her eyes. Not that he needed any reminder. Light brown. There was a time they would look at him with warmth like a banked fire instead of coal-like coldness he now received.

Anna turned the high chair where Dorrie sat so the baby had her back to him. At Dorrie's protest he understood his daughter didn't like it any more than he did. He wanted to be able to study this little scrap of humanity he'd had a part in creating.

He met Anna's considering look. Saw the challenge in her eyes. Seems every time he tried to be different, something jerked him back to his old ways. But this time he'd run as far as he dared. He'd seen where he could end up.

He pulled his thoughts away from the journey that readied him to return. And away from the despicable deeds he had done. If Anna heard them...well, he could only hope she wouldn't.

Anna had often begged him to stop drinking and take a role in raising his daughter. His response had been to hit the trail with a bottle in his hand.

But that was over and he was back.

He felt Alex eyeing him under the shield of his lashes. The boy had grown considerably since Colby last saw him, though he was still small and puny. And lacking in confidence if the way he kept his head down indicated anything. Colby had learned to never duck his head, always fix a man with a bold, defiant stare, but then he supposed Alex didn't have any of the reasons Colby had for the way he viewed the world.

The strain in Alex's posture and Anna's averted eyes scraped along Colby's nerves, magnified by the way Dorrie fussed because she had to face the stove.

"She ain't invisible," he muttered. "I see her fine. She's got real purty hair."

Dorrie squirmed, trying to turn around. Then she kicked her heels against the chair legs. It sounded like she said, "Mama, wanna see." She threw her head back and shrieked.

No mistaking the determination in her voice, tinged with a pout. *That child needs a cuff alongside her ear.*

The words bellowed through his head in a voice he recalled from his past—his pa's. How often had he heard it and felt the blow that followed.

His insides tightened in a familiar response, ready to duck or run and if that failed, to fight back. He forced himself to relax and something unfamiliar in its insistency edged past the words from his past. He wouldn't run if someone tried to hit that little girl.

He'd left his baby daughter with Anna and her father, knowing they were good, gentle Christian people who, he hoped, would not treat the baby harshly. Yet he knew many good people believed in a strong hand with children. Conquer their spirit. Spare the rod and spoil the child. He understood the need for discipline but he hoped Anna had found a way to do it gently and kindly.

He had no idea how he would handle the situation other than to cuff the child. His nerves remained tense as he watched to see what she would do.

Anna took Dorrie's hands and spoke gently. "Dorrie, sweetie, you must not speak to Mama like that." She held the baby's hands until Dorrie settled down.

The air in Colby's lungs released in a hot blast. Her kind correction of Dorrie caught him somewhere between his rib cage and his gut. He'd forgotten how gentle her stepmother had been, even when she felt it necessary to speak to Colby regarding his behavior. In fact, he only now realized she'd been correcting him. Her words were so soft he'd welcomed them. Only other correction he'd had had come by way of Pa's fists. His insides twisted with remembrance of his pa's anger. He would not be like his old man. He would never hit that little girl. No matter how angry he got.

The hitting ended with him.

He bent over his plate, forcing himself to concentrate on his food as he pushed aside the bad mem-ories.

Anna was a good cook. A man learned to appreciate fluffy homemade bread, rich brown gravy and a variety of vegetables.

"You do all those bad things they say?"

Colby jerked his head up at Alex's question. Had news of his activities reached Steveville? Or was it only gossip and speculation? If they heard the whole truth…

"Alex." Anna kept her voice soft but couldn't disguise her shock.

"It's fine."

Anna's quick glance said plainly it wasn't so far as she was concerned, but Colby figured he might as well deal with the spoken and unspoken questions right up-front.

"I don't know what all folks are saying about me but I did things I shouldn't have. Things I wish now I hadn't done. But that's behind me."

"God is good. He waits for his sons and daughters to return to Him," Pastor Caldwell said.

Colby nodded. He and the preacher had had a good talk. Colby had soaked in the words of love and forgiveness the preacher read from God's word and Colby had chosen to accept God's forgiveness for his sin, but Colby wasn't sure he'd go so far as to call himself a child of God. After all, God must have pretty high standards about who could be part of His family.

Dorrie mumbled something softly. He guessed she pleaded to be turned around. He wanted to add his pleas to hers but clearly Anna didn't care that he ached to see his daughter. Anna's lack of welcome hurt more than a fist to his face. Not that he would let it deter him. He was back. He had changed. He intended to prove it.

"Very well, seeing as you've been so good." She turned the high chair around.

Anna had always responded positively to gentle prodding. Colby remembered that about her. As clearly as he remembered so many other things.

He stared at Dorrie. She had his dark blond hair and

his blue eyes. She had Nora's mouth and nose. And his directness. She stared unblinkingly at him and his heart sank to the pit of his stomach where it turned over twice and spun around leaving him struggling to fill his lungs. This was his child. Flesh of his flesh.

"You gonna take her away?" Alex demanded.

Colby noted Anna didn't correct his curiosity this time.

The pastor leaned forward. "Colby has explained his intentions to me but perhaps—" he faced Colby "—for Alex and Anna's peace of mind, you could tell them, as well."

Colby nodded. "I had to make sure she was okay. And I intend to start over right here."

Anna fixed a look on him. Her expression was composed but, though he guessed she tried, she failed to hide her anger. "Haven't you done this before?"

"Anna," her father warned. "He is a guest in our house. I believe he deserves a chance. After all, what would God want us to do?"

Anna ducked her head but not before Colby could understand she didn't think he deserved another chance.

He had his job cut out proving to her he meant it for real. But now was not the time or place to discuss it. Perhaps if he hung about he might later get a chance to explain things to her.

He turned his attention back to Dorrie. "It's amazing to see bits of myself and Nora in her." Conviction burrowed into his thoughts. He wanted to be part of this child's life. He wanted to watch her grow and change. He wanted to teach her to channel that boldness he saw in her gaze, use it for good and not ill.

Anna put her arm around Dorrie's shoulders as if she could shield the child from his stare.

He ducked his head and tried to concentrate on his food. His throat felt thick as he understood her fear that he would take Dorrie from her. He didn't want to do that. A man alone wasn't the way to raise a proper little girl. But he did want to be part of Dorrie's life and he didn't know how best to do that. Was being in Steveville, proving himself changed, enough? He couldn't say.

"How do you purpose to begin work at the church?" the pastor asked.

It took a great deal of effort for Colby to force his thoughts to the fire-damaged church. "The first thing I need to do is tear out and burn the damaged wall then begin to rebuild."

"Father, everyone is expecting the church to be reopened in time for the birthday celebration." Anna spoke softly, but Colby heard a cautious note in her voice.

Pastor Caldwell explained about the birthday party for the town's founding father.

"When is it to be?"

"June seventeen."

"A month away." Colby considered it a moment, mentally measuring the work to be done. "Shouln't be a problem to finish by then." From his quick study of the damage he figured he could finish in ten days or a little more if he really pushed it. He shot a quick glance at Dorrie, shifted his gaze to Anna. Seemed no reason to hurry.

"You'll burn everything damaged by the fire?" Anna sounded cautious.

He wondered what she wanted but didn't care to ask directly. "Seems the best thing to do. Why?"

"Just curious."

Distracted by the way Dorrie continued to stare at

him, he let it go. Besides, he figured if Anna didn't want to tell him what she wanted, he wouldn't prod it from her. He knew beneath her gentle, patient exterior lay a streak of stubbornness to challenge most mules.

Dorrie lifted one hand toward him. "Da-da."

Her word slammed through his insides, reverberating against his ribs, resounding inside his head.

Anna gave a short laugh as she grabbed Dorrie's hands and pushed them to the tray. "She calls every man that. It's a little embarrassing. Except Father, she calls him poppa. I don't know how many times she's called a perfect stranger da-da. If people didn't know better they might think…" She trailed off as if realizing she'd been running over at the mouth.

Dorrie flashed him a smile and turned to the pastor. "My poppa."

Pastor Caldwell chuckled. "My Dorrie. You're a little minx, aren't you?"

Dorrie babbled something.

Colby wondered if anyone else understood what she said. He didn't but he grinned simply because her pleasure was contagious. He shifted his gaze to Anna, wanting to share the moment, but her eyes challenged him so directly his enjoyment deflated.

Anna rightly wondered how his presence affected her role as Dorrie's mama. She had every reason in the world to wonder if he'd run again at the first sign of trouble.

He was determined he would not. But he would have to prove it.

Chapter Four

Not until the door closed after Colby did Anna's nerves stop twitching. She watched out the window as he strode down the road to the right. Where was he going? Apparently it was too much to hope he'd leave town now rather than later after they all started thinking he might stay.

But at least he was out of her house, out of her sight. Just not out of her thoughts. Try as she had over the months, she could never get him completely out of her thoughts.

"Anna, what if he does want to take Dorrie?" Alex's voice thinned with worry—a worry that scratched the inside of her mind, as well.

Father appeared in the doorway. "He says he doesn't. Do we have any reason to doubt his word?" Carrying his Bible Father left to visit a family whose mother lay sick.

Anna could think of many reasons for mistrusting what Colby said—and even more for not counting on him. Experience had taught her those cruel lessons. But it had not taught her a way to subdue the portion of her heart that longed for the closeness they had shared. It had been a childhood friendship. Nothing more. But she couldn't stop the yearning in her heart that wanted to reignite that friendship. Feel again the closeness, the bond, the instant understanding they once had.

Only her rigid, well-honed self-control enabled her to dismiss such foolishness and turn her attention back to Alex's need. She squeezed his shoulder. "Alex, we can pray and trust God to be in control of the situation."

Alex skittered a sideways look at her. "I'm afraid." He ducked his head so he spoke into his chest. "Sometimes bad things happen."

She pulled him to her side, wanting to assure him he was safe. But how could she? He'd lost more than she when his mother and baby brother had died. "We have to trust God knows best." She had fought a hard battle in her heart to get to the place where she could trust God again. Alex lacked her adult perspective to rationalize events and apply faith. His thin shoulder pressed into her ribs but he remained stiff as a stick.

Knowing she had nothing more to offer than words, she released him and turned to wash Dorrie's face.

Her disobedient thoughts returned to Colby and the way he'd edged his way into Father's good graces. Father believed in extending forgiveness, which was fine in theory. Not so great when it put so many people at risk. Father would be shocked at the words biting the back of Anna's tongue. If she voiced her thoughts he would gently chide her for being uncharitable, for not showing the love of God.

Alex's mouth remained in a tight line. His eyes clouded with troublesome thoughts.

Her heart went out to her younger brother. "Alex, I'm sure there's no reason to worry." She wished it were so. "Now help me with the dishes and then you can start your homework." She lifted Dorrie from her chair. As soon as Dorrie's feet hit the floor she went to Alex and babbled something, her face wreathed in concern as if sensing his uncertainty.

He scooped her into his arms and tickled her, making her giggle.

"Lexie," she protested, but they all knew she loved it as much as Alex.

Anna watched the pair. Not only did she have her heart to protect, she must shield these two children from hurt, as well. She constructed a quick, impenetrable shell around the thoughts that remembered happier times with Colby. She could not let them divert her from her present concerns.

Later, as she helped Alex with his homework, she resolutely kept that shell in place. One effective way to do so was to think of the cross hanging on the fire-scarred wall. So many things raced through her mind— the times she'd knelt before that cross, giving her problems and struggles to the Lord, seeking His help in dealing with the loss of Rose, the challenges of raising her younger brother and running her father's home. How frightened she'd been when Colby had thrust his newborn baby into Anna's arms and begged her to take care of it.

At first, her prayer had been for Colby to stay, stop his foolish behavior and become a true partner in the raising of his daughter. Her cheeks burned as she recalled how she'd imagined him confessing his love and asking her to marry him. She now understood he could not be the man she needed. She'd done her best to accept it and focus her thoughts on being a mother to the two children in her care and running her father's household efficiently. *God, why did You let him come back when I was sure I had put thoughts of him behind me?*

She wanted to slip over to the church as she'd done so often and find help, strength and renewal of her faith at the foot of the cross. It meant more to her than a symbol of Christ's death. It was a visible reminder of God's faithfulness in her life.

Despite Mrs. Percy's edict, Anna couldn't bear the thought of having the cross burned along with the rest of the debris, especially now when she knew her faith and resolve were about to be tested yet again by Colby's return.

She'd always found what she needed in prayer and she turned her thoughts toward God in a burst of faith. *God, my first concern is protecting Dorrie. And I need Your wisdom to do that. But I also need to rest in Your strength as I face Colby each day. Help me be faithful to what You've called me to do.*

Calm returned to her soul for the first time in many hours. God had always been faithful and loving as she struggled with her many doubts and fears. It was as if He patiently held out His arms, welcoming her after each bout of uncertainty.

She wanted to save that cross. It was only a piece of wood but was a monument to her—a sweet reminder of all the times she'd turned to God for help and received more than she asked or dreamed.

Once Dorrie was sleeping she could leave. "Alex, listen for Dorrie while I run over to the church."

Each Sunday she accompanied Father on the piano as he led the song service so she often ran over to practice on the church piano. Only this time her interest wasn't in music.

As she stepped into the dim interior she breathed in the acrid smell of the fire still clinging to the air, but it failed to rob her of the peace and tranquility she felt in this place. She moved slowly up the center aisle pausing to wipe her fingers along the top of one of the wooden pews. She checked her fingertips, saw a trace of dust. She'd tried to keep the place clean after the fire even though it wasn't used for services. Somehow it seemed sacrilegious to let dust accumulate. Besides not only did she pray and play the piano here, Father still came over to study and pray.

She arrived at the front. The pulpit had been taken to the meeting place so nothing obstructed her view of the cross or the blackened wall. Raw wood had been nailed over the bottom where the fire had broken through. She climbed the three steps to the platform, her heels thudding on the wood, and stood in front of the cross. The foot had been burned off completely and much of what remained was blackened by smoke or charred by the fire.

Her vision blurred. She couldn't explain it in words but she felt the cross surviving the flames was a visible lesson of a spiritual truth—that Jesus's death had spared them all from the flames of judgment.

She scrubbed at her eyes. This was a lesson she wanted to share even as much as she wanted to preserve the cross that had such significance in her life.

She slid her fingers along the wood, carefully going with the grain to avoid slivers. It fit tightly to the wall. She wouldn't be able to simply lift it off.

If she could only see how it was secured but the evening light had faded to a gentle dove-gray.

"Figuring to steal it?"

She jerked back and caught her finger against a rough patch as she spun around to see who spoke. A sliver dug into her flesh. "Ouch." She squeezed her finger to stop the pain.

Colby stood before her, a grin splitting his face.

She scowled. "It's you. I should have guessed." It would be too much by far to think he'd wandered down the street and found some place miles away to hang out. She gritted her teeth but not before the barest moan escaped.

He shifted his amused gaze to her hands and sobered. "Are you hurt?" He grabbed her finger and bent over to examine it.

Heat scalded her throat and cheeks at his touch. A thousand dreams and wishes blossomed like flowers after a rain. She knew she should protest and pull away but she stood as immobile as a slab of clay.

He turned her finger gently toward the last bit of light from the west-facing windows. He probed the site with a light touch then yanked out the sliver.

She gasped yet welcomed the sudden pain. The flowers withered and died and saneness returned. There were no dreams, no wishes with this man.

He pressed the site, ending the pain as quickly as it came. Then he squeezed the tip of her finger. "A little blood flow will wash away the dirt." Two drops of blood plopped to the oiled wood of the floor. She'd have to scrub it off later.

He watched her finger a heartbeat longer. "I think I got it all but you best wash it thoroughly when you get home." When he released her hand she couldn't seem to move. She stared at her arm suspended between them, felt the heat from her cheeks spread to her hairline and scald the roots of her hair. She yanked her arm to her waist. Her heart throbbed where the sliver had been.

He leaned back, his head bare.

At least he had the decency to remove his hat in God's house. She realized her thoughts were uncharitable but found perverse strength in them.

"So what were you doing?" he asked.

"Looking."

"Don't get slivers by looking."

"So I touched it." She had no intention of telling this man anything more than that. "What are you doing here?"

He chuckled. "I was enjoying a quiet evening." He sounded vaguely regretful, as if her presence had spoiled his solitude.

"Maybe you could enjoy it somewhere else. Don't you have friends you can stay with or something?"

"You suggesting I go to the saloon?" His quiet words challenged her. "I seem to remember a time when you begged me to stay away from that sort of company."

"That was a long time ago. Things have changed."

"I'm glad you admit it. Because—" he leaned close "—I've changed. Didn't you promise to pray for me? Did you do it? Or decide I was a lost cause?" His nose was only inches from hers. "Perhaps you prayed I would never return."

She refused to step back and let him intimidate her. Instead she drew herself up tall and tipped her chin. "I did pray for you. At first."

He nodded. "Then you decided to give up on me?"

She narrowed her eyes. "Then I prayed you'd never come back and embarrass Dorrie with your sinful ways."

He straightened and stepped back.

Even in the fading light she glimpsed what she could only take for as hurt. She almost regretted her honest words then he grinned and she didn't regret them one bit. The man was far too blasé about life. Just as he was about responsibilities and friendships.

Not even to herself would she admit it was one of the things she had enjoyed about him—his ability to smile through troubles, laugh at adversity and enjoy life.

"Sorry to disappoint you." He shifted to stare past her. "What would the good people of the church say if they knew you tried to steal the cross? Do you suppose your father would be embarrassed?"

"This is ridiculous. It's a burned piece of wood. Aren't you planning to burn it tomorrow?"

"So what were you doing?"

He wasn't about to leave the topic alone. But neither was she prepared to share her emotional attachment to the cross. It would make sense to no one else. They would see only how it was burned, damaged beyond repair. Mrs. Percy was right. It should be destroyed. But a flurry of regrets swamped her at the thought.

"Something hidden behind it maybe? Something you don't want anyone to discover?"

A dull churn of anger ignited at his accusation. She suspected he was purposely trying to annoy her. But how dare he suggest she might be guilty of doing anything wrong. She was a preacher's daughter who carefully lived a circumspect life. And if she ever missed the expectations of her role by so much as a hair there were plenty of people who would point it out to her. "I was only seeing if there was a way to salvage it." She lifted her skirts and descended the steps. "Obviously I am being foolishly sentimental. Might as well burn it and put up a new cross." As she hurried down the aisle, she struggled to control this unfamiliar indignation.

She marched across the yard and into the house. There wasn't time to dwell on her unexpected reaction to Colby. She planned to finish the quilt tonight and deliver it as soon as possible. Thankfully the evenings had been warm enough of late, but if they had a cold, damp spell the Andersons would be hard-pressed to keep warm with the few things they've been given.

Anna paused as she sewed the edging on. She thought of how close she had come to sharing Hazel Anderson's situation. The fire had been within inches... She shuddered. Life was so uncertain.

She jabbed the needle through the layers of the quilt with unusual vigor. Father might feel charitable toward Colby Bloxham. But all she felt was an enormous need to get the man on his way as soon as humanly possible before he upset her life. Again.

She needed divine help and paused to bow her head. *Our Father in heaven, be so kind as to put Your mighty hand on the man's back and move him onward. Before he turns my world upside down and my heart inside out. Again.*

Chapter Five

Anna woke the next morning with a heavy feeling in her limbs. She wanted to believe it was because the night had been unbearably hot. Or because the wind wailed and moaned around the house like a woman in mourning yet did nothing to relieve the heat.

But it was not the warm air or tormented wind that prevented Anna from sleeping.

She had mentally scolded herself far into the night.

Why did she still react to Colby with the same swift pleasure and longing as she had when she was young and foolish?

Why had she let Colby affect her so she said such a foolish thing as burn the cross? Not that the cross mattered except to her.

But his intentions regarding Dorrie did matter. Would he take the child? Could he? She gave a snort of disbelief. Who in their right mind would let him? And she didn't mean just herself. The town would rise up and stop him. Colby Bloxham raising a little girl?

With sluggish inefficiency she prepared breakfast and tended to Dorrie. It was Saturday so she left Alex sleeping. She didn't feel up to coping with his reluctance to do his assigned chores even though she suspected he would open his eyes, turn to his back and read as soon as she stepped from his room. She shrugged. What did it matter if he enjoyed a few relaxing moments?

She turned her thoughts back to the cross. During the night she had made up her mind. The cross might mean nothing special to anyone else but it did to her and she wanted to keep it. As soon as breakfast was over she'd take a hammer and screwdriver and figure out a way to get it off the wall before Colby could follow her rash instructions.

Father returned from his morning prayers, his step light. He'd plainly enjoyed his time with God.

She needed some time alone with her Lord, as well. Time to pull her worries into submission. Time to find her peace.

Knowing Colby might show up any moment to start repairs, the church would no longer be a place of refuge for her.

Another reason to resent the man's reappearance in her life.

She sighed inwardly, her weariness increasing with each moment.

Breakfast was almost ready and she called Alex but didn't wait for him to get dressed before she informed Father the meal was ready and put Dorrie in her chair. Neither of them could bear to wait for their morning meal.

As she helped Dorrie with her glass of milk she suddenly paused and lifted her head. "Do you smell something burning?" Since the fire any hint of smoke sent her scurrying to check the nearby buildings, her heart twisting with fear. The flames had come dangerously close to the house. She'd never been so afraid nor prayed so hard. God had answered that prayer.

God had turned the tragedy into blessing in many ways—people had come back to Him like prodigal sons, cause for much rejoicing in many homes.

She raced to the window without waiting for an answer from Father about the smell of smoke. Flames licked skyward from the churchyard. "Fire," she called.

"It's probably Colby burning garbage." Father sounded so calm she knew he expected it.

"He's at the church already?"

"He was there when I arrived. Already had some boards pulled off the wall. Seems eager to get the work done."

As she stared out the window, Colby sauntered over and tossed some boards into the flames. He'd filled out over the years. Looked like he could handle any physical challenge. She blinked back a hard stinging in her eyes. He could certainly toss an armload of wood but could he handle problems? How long before something sent him riding out of town? Again.

Then she realized what he was doing.

The cross. She thought she'd have lots of time to rescue it. "Father, watch Dorrie. I have something to look after." She didn't wait for him to ask what was so important to take her away in the middle of serving a meal.

She picked up her skirts and ran to the back entrance of the church. She didn't slow until she faced the wall. The raw boards had been peeled away. Much of the damaged area had been knocked down. The cross was gone. She stood in ashes, disappointment burning through her veins.

Colby sauntered in, whistling through his teeth. "Morning." He picked up bits of wood.

"Where is it? Did you burn it?"

"Burn what?" He paused on his way to the door.

"The cross."

He grinned. "Thought you said to."

"I didn't mean it. I wanted to save it." She pressed her lips tight to stop a wail from escaping.

"Hang on a minute while I dump this armload." He disappeared out the door. She heard a clatter and caught a whiff of smoke.

She hadn't moved. Didn't know if she could. Her failure left her stunned and immobile. It was only a piece of wood. She knew it had nothing to do with God's power, His ability to answer prayer, His love or anything of importance. She didn't need the cross to communicate with Him. Or hear Him speak through His holy word. She knew all that. The cross had no significance except as a sentimental reminder of all He'd done.

She heard Colby return but didn't bother looking at him. The shard of annoyance she felt toward him was foolish and out of place. He'd only done what she said. She'd been rash in her words and regretted it from the moment she'd uttered them.

"Come with me. I have something to show you."

She shook her head. She wasn't interested in anything he had.

He grasped her elbow, gently turning her about.

His touch fired up her nerves like flames. She jerked back. She didn't want him touching her. Didn't want him reawakening feelings and awareness she'd fought so fiercely to quell.

But he wasn't about to let her discourage him. He

again took her elbow, a little more firmly, and steered her relentlessly toward the back into the cloakroom. Only so he would leave her alone did she let him drag her along. "Look," he said.

Her eyes widened like Dorrie's would if given a gift. Her heart resurrected from the pit of her stomach and exploded against her ribs. "The cross." The words blasted from her. Fractured, it leaned in an empty corner.

She rushed over and touched it to assure herself she wasn't imagining it. "I thought you burned it."

He shrugged. "You said to. But I figured there was something special about it. Didn't find any money behind it. Not even a long lost letter from some beau—" He chuckled at the pained look she sent his way. "So I figured it was the cross itself you wanted."

She nodded, unable to find words beyond her surprise.

"What do you want me to do with it?"

She knelt to examine it more closely. The fire damage was worse than she thought. "I wanted to save it." She sat back on her heels and swallowed a lump of disappointment. "I guess I thought there must be some way to repair it, restore it. I didn't realize how badly it's damaged." She pushed to her feet. "Leave it here. Maybe I'll figure out something." She couldn't bear the thought of burning it even though it seemed the only thing to do.

Turning, she came face-to-face with him, staring into his blue eyes. Found it impossible to sort out her feelings. He'd understood this piece of burned wood meant something to her and saved it. His insight surprised her, shifted her thoughts so she wasn't able to maintain her anger toward him. "Thank you," she murmured. "It was kind of you to save it."

His eyes blazed with amusement. "I'm really a nice guy."

She couldn't break away from his gaze, knew a jab of regret that what they once shared no longer existed. There was a time she would have told him her doubts and fears. He would have told her his dreams. Just as he'd told her about the harshness he'd suffered at the hands of his father.

She blinked. Seems he could never run far enough to escape that memory. She tried to protect herself with such knowledge yet something soft as warm butter had eased her anger. "You didn't come for breakfast," she murmured.

"I didn't know if I was welcome."

Guilty as accused. For the moment she couldn't remember why she should have made him feel so cautious. "It's not too late."

He nodded, a tangle of hope and caution filling his expression. "I'll be over then."

She stepped away, sucked in smoke-laden air that seemed lacking in oxygen, and hurried to the yard, the smoke out there even heavier. No wonder she couldn't breathe normally. In the house, she placed another plate on the table. She heard Father moving about and went to inform him Colby would be over and suggested he keep him company.

Father sorted through some books, no doubt looking for a commentary or something.

She glanced around the room. "Where's Dorrie?"

He looked up, surprise widening his eyes. "She was just here."

Anna resisted an urge to roll her eyes. Father could become so focused on something the world could fall down around his feet and he'd barely notice.

"Dorrie," she called.

"She's with me." Alex's voice came from his bedroom.

The impact of what she'd just done hit her so hard she groaned.

"Something wrong?" Father asked.

"No." Not in the sense he meant. But she'd extended a welcome to a man who not only could tear out her heart but rip her family apart, as well. She scrambled to think how she could undo her foolish deed.

She hurried to Alex's bedroom. Dorrie's head lay close to his on the pillow and she scrunched up beside him peering at the book he read to her.

"Keep Dorrie here for a bit, would you?"

Alex lowered the book to look at Anna. "How come?"

"Colby is coming for breakfast and—" She sent a warning look in Dorrie's direction.

"Sure. We're going to finish reading this book, aren't we, Dorrie?"

Dorrie babbled something, pointing at one of the pictures and Anna hurried out, grateful for Alex's understanding.

Knowing Dorrie would be safe from Colby for a bit longer, her heart grew lighter and she sang the words to one of Issac Watt's hymns, "Alas! and did my Savior bleed?" as she fried more potatoes and eggs and sliced more bread.

She could protect Dorrie. *Thank you, God.*

The cross had been saved. *Thank God.*

And thank Colby? a fragile voice whispered.

She'd thanked him. Even invited him to breakfast against her better judgment. And she'd thank him good and proper...

When he waved goodbye as he rode from town, leaving them in peace.

Colby tapped on the door then stepped inside and quietly sat at the table. Father poured them coffee. Colby glanced past her as if searching for Dorrie.

She sent him a look intended to inform him he could eat at her table, rescue the cross she attached sentimental value to, maybe even renew bits and pieces of their old friendship, but he needn't expect her to let him see Dorrie if she could help it.

She wouldn't stand by and let him gaze at the child with the longing and sadness she'd seen last night.

"Mama." Dorrie raced into the room, Alex hot on her heels.

"She wouldn't stay." He sent Colby a curious look before he ducked his head, hiding his face.

Anna scooped up Dorrie hoping to whisk her away before she saw Colby. But she was too late.

"Da-da," Dorrie gurgled, adding a whole lot more that no one understood.

Anger—as unfamiliar as palm trees, as powerful as the fire that destroyed the buildings down the street—raged through Anna. Anger directed as much at herself as at Colby. She'd put Dorrie at risk. But he had no right to come back. Not even if God had changed him, something she wasn't yet ready to believe.

Oh, Lord, forgive me. I rejoice that one of Your lambs that was lost has been found. But why, God, did he have to come back here? Couldn't he just as well start over in California or Alaska?

She handed Dorrie to Alex and he carried her back to his room. Rather than sit at the table with Colby and Father, she remained at the cupboard, staring out the window at the flames consuming the old lumber from the church, a cloud of gray smoke billowing upward, blotting out all but a blue edge of the sky. Colby's presence had done the same for her, blotting out all but fragments of her normal peace of mind.

It was Saturday, one of her busiest days. The Sunday clothes had to be brushed and ironed; the shoes polished; and as Father insisted on observing a complete day of rest, every bit of food for Sunday prepared ahead of time. Normally she anticipated the coming day of rest with nothing much to do unless she counted caring for Dorrie and reading, neither of which constituted work in Anna's mind. But today she scurried about almost resenting the extra work Sunday required. She could find no peace in her heart or satisfaction in her chores. She ached for a chance to sit quietly before the cross and take her concerns to God, knowing she would find both comfort and guidance.

Instead, each time she glanced out the window, she caught glimpses of Colby carrying more wood to the fire or standing back considering the building. She wished he would leave.

The idea cut through her. Not like he'd left before—far away and for many months. Just for the afternoon so she could enjoy a peaceful hour in the church.

Suddenly she realized she hadn't seen him for some time. She went to the open window and listened but heard no sound of work from inside the church. Nothing.

"Alex, watch Dorrie. Don't let her out of your sight.

I'm going to run over to the church." She couldn't sit on a pew and meditate in front of the cross, but Father had given her the list of hymns a few days ago. She knew them all. Could play them with her eyes closed, but she'd go over them again. The music spoke to her soul as much as did prayer and Bible reading.

She tiptoed into the sanctuary and listened but didn't see or hear Colby. She sat at the piano and was soon lost in the music as she sang the familiar hymns with real joy. She finished and sat with her eyes closed, rejoicing in the beauty of the words, letting the peace they gave her fill her soul.

The sound of one person clapping jolted her eyes open. Colby sat in the nearest pew. "That was excellent."

"Thank you." She felt no gratitude, only annoyance as she left the piano bench and stood facing him. "Where have you been?" *How long have you been watching me?*

He grinned. "Did you miss me?"

"No and don't be facetious."

"I can't possibly be facetious seeing as I don't even know what it means."

"It means silly."

He tipped his head and smiled.

She wanted to believe it was a teasing, insincere smile but something serious lay behind the blue glitter of his eyes. Something that reached for her heart. Something her heart welcomed. She slammed shut an iron-clad mental door.

"I meant it. I enjoy your playing and singing."

He spoke in the present tense. Just like the days when he came to the church and listened as she practiced. Not until Rose died did she take over playing in the services. By then she knew the hymns by heart.

"I remember some of the church songs from when I used to come here."

Did he remember the way their hearts had seemed to beat a common song, finding so many things they both enjoyed, almost able to read each other's thoughts? Obviously it had meant more to her than him or he wouldn't have found it so easy to leave.

Why had he bothered to come back?

She fully believed he would leave again. He always left. The peace she had achieved drained out the bottom of her soul, leaving her edgy and unsettled.

"You sing them like they mean something real. I enjoyed it. You play even better than I remember."

People seldom commented on her playing unless she made a mistake. To hear words of praise melted a layer of her defensiveness.

"I envy you. Your life has always been filled with God's word, and songs such as these." Regret seemed to fill the crevices of his face.

His words gave her pause. Did he remember she'd told him God didn't care where they came from, only whether or not they were willing to allow His love into their lives? Basically, since his return, she'd been denying her belief in that truth and guilt burned through her. But it couldn't get past the hard shell she'd forged around her emotions. She'd trusted him too often and too easily and she wouldn't be doing it again.

"Yes, I've been blessed. I know that."

She wasn't about to dispute the beauty of the hymns, nor discuss the benefits of her upbringing, something else she could not dispute.

It took a concerted effort to pull her gaze away from his, which seemed so endless, so hungry, so—she jerked her attention to the scarred wall at the back of the platform.

"I'll get out of your way so you can get to work." As she hurried to the house she wondered where he'd been when she first entered the church.

It wasn't until the door closed behind her that she wished she'd confronted him about Dorrie. What were his intentions? Was he about to snatch the child from her? At the idea, she moaned deep inside, beyond sound, beyond reason.

Chapter Six

Colby watched fine people in their fine clothes climb the outside wooden steps to the room above the saloon. He didn't own a suit or anything remotely like it. He wore the best of what he had—a new white shirt he'd purchased at the mercantile and his best pair of black trousers, brushed clean. But it didn't seem quite fitting. He felt more like his father's son than a changed man and fell back into the shadow of the mercantile store as he tried to decide if he would climb the steps or walk away and find something else to do with his time— something more fitting for a Bloxham.

Trouble was—he didn't know what a Bloxham determined to be different would do on a sunny Sunday morning apart from going to church like all decent people did.

Would the decent folk think he should be in their meeting place? Or would they think he fit better in the room below?

He brushed away a persistent fly and continued to watch people arrive.

A family hurried up the sidewalk, a man with a little boy in his arms and a young woman carrying a baby.

His heart bucked once before he tamed it. Family. Like he and Anna had both dreamed of. Would it ever be possible for him?

The man noticed him and headed over, his hand extended. "Carl Klaus." He waited for Colby to give his name and when he did, Carl nodded. "Welcome. Why don't you go up with us?"

His wife came to his side. "I'm Laura, Carl's wife. These are our children, Adam and Gloria. Perhaps you remember me. I'm Anna's friend. Have been since we were children."

Colby nodded a greeting, his hat gripped awkwardly in his fists. He remembered Laura hanging about when he was younger. Never paid her much attention. Guess he never really saw anyone but Anna and her family. They had been his whole world.

He wondered that Laura's friendship with Anna didn't make her a little less welcoming.

Wheezy organ music began.

"We better hurry," Karl said, and Colby allowed himself to be drawn along with the family, up the stairs and into the smoky interior of the room. He should have felt at home in such an atmosphere but his nerves twitched like a gun had been pressed to his spine. He was aware of glances aimed at him, full of doubt or even edged with condemnation. Not that he blamed any of them. He didn't belong here with these righteous folk. But he meant to start over as a man, and as a believer. And that meant attending church services.

His faith was new and untried, uncertain even, but he had prayed the sinner's prayer with Pastor Caldwell and he meant it. Soon enough they'd all see.

Colby Bloxham was done with running.

Colby Bloxham was different. Though he figured God might find him a bigger challenge than most.

Caught up in his thoughts, he'd blindly followed Carl and his family to the front row of seats before he realized where he was.

No way would he sit with nothing between him and the preacher. It left him too exposed. Not that he expected anyone could see what lay behind Colby but he wasn't taking any chances and quickly slid to the chair behind the Klaus family.

Alex already sat in the front row, holding Dorrie's hand, and allowed her to edge close to Laura.

Dorrie turned, spotted Colby and flashed him a welcoming grin. His heart stomped over his doubts and headed straight for determination. He wanted to be part of this child's life. He'd do whatever necessary to gain that position.

He stole a glance about and saw many of the ladies pressed handkerchiefs to their noses. He tested the air, found it full of smoke and fumes from the saloon below—something he wouldn't have noticed if not for the obvious discomfort of the others.

More proof that Colby Bloxham did not fit here. But he settled down hard. He would learn to be comfortable. Might some day even feel he belonged.

Anna sat at the organ, pumping madly and playing songs he recognized from yesterday. He'd allowed himself only one glimpse at her as he entered the room. Now he ducked his head to study her from under cover of his lashes. So selfcontained, so in control. Not at all like the girl he'd known prior to Rose's death. Would she remember how she'd told him she wondered if she would ever be what she should be and confessed a myriad of fears and what she thought were dreadful sins? How he'd laughed when she'd complained of her wicked temper. The worst thing she'd ever done was slam her bedroom door. She'd been shocked when he told her the things his old man did in anger.

She'd be equally shocked, if not more so, if she were ever to learn the things Colby had done.

He hoped she never would.

Pastor Caldwell announced the first hymn, bringing Colby gratefully from remembering things he wanted to forget.

He opened the hymnal and as they began to sing, he recognized the song—"Amazing Grace." Rose sang it often. Said she never got tired of the victory of the words.

Suddenly he missed Rose with an ache that sucked away all his resolve and indifference.

Rose had welcomed him into her home, treating him kindly. She'd touched his shoulder, ruffled his hair. He'd learned not to cringe when she touched him. Even found excuses to invite her gentle gestures. And then she'd died in a stupid senseless accident along with her tiny baby. He'd lost his own mother when she walked away from his old man's fists. He'd failed to stop her. But it hadn't hurt near as much as losing Rose.

Overflowing with sorrow, Colby sought Anna's face. Anna's loss had been even greater and he'd had nothing to offer her.

Afraid she'd discover the truth of how inadequate he was he'd left.

She met his eyes, their gazes locked as they sang together the words of the hymn. Was she remembering, too, hurting, too? He wanted to do something but again, just as when it happened, he failed to find anything to give.

The song ended and she jerked away to listen to her father, and then another number was given and she flipped the pages of the hymnal and focused on the notes.

Colby turned his attention to the words.

But even though he kept his head down, reading from the hymnal, he heard Anna's clear voice. Sweetness swept away bits of debris in his heart.

The song service ended and Anna left the organ bench to sit beside Laura, pulling Dorrie to her lap. Dorrie fussed a moment and kicked her little feet. Only because Colby watched so closely did he see Anna flinch.

He cringed, knowing if he'd done that, even as young as Dorrie, his pa would have smacked him hard. He remembered his ears ringing, his eyes smarting from the pain. He understood Dorrie must stop kicking but the thought of someone hitting her, even with a small hand like Anna's made him want to grab the child from her and run out the door.

Anna simply caught the thrashing feet and held them still until Dorrie settled.

Relief eased away his tension. His shoulders relaxed.

He stilled a jolt of surprise as he realized he had no idea how to be a father without being like his pa and he would sooner ride out into nowhere and camp there until he was old and gray than be that kind of father. He watched Dorrie settle into submission.

He wanted to be what he'd always wanted—a good father—but could he? Or would he fail as he had in the past?

Pastor Caldwell announced his text, "Deuteronomy, Chapter 10, Verse 12, 'What doth the Lord thy God require of thee, but to fear the Lord thy God, to walk in all His ways, and to love Him, and to serve the Lord thy God with all thy heart and with all thy soul.'" The pastor closed his thick Bible. In calm, thoughtful tones, Pastor Caldwell spoke about fearing God.

Colby certainly did that. Sort of thought God watched him to see if he would measure up. Colby figured to do his best to meet God's requirements.

As the pastor closed the meeting, Colby vowed he would do his best to please God and prayed it would be good enough.

And if it wasn't...

The next day he returned to work on the church, still mulling over the words of the sermon and what his response should be.

Last night he'd read the Bible until it grew too dark to see the words. He was going to change who Colby Bloxham was. According to what he read, God had given him a fresh start and God would help him be a better man.

He figured God had His hands full with that job.

But how to learn to be a father? He hadn't found an answer for that.

Nor had he found anything he could offer Anna. Maybe he never would. But he was here to stay. Perhaps in time he would discover something she needed that he could give.

He knew the minute she stepped from the house. Could tell by the way she hesitated and fumbled with the basin in her hands she had something specific in mind that involved him.

He knelt at the ragged foot of a stud he had cut out and waited. Pretending—every bit as good as she—that he wasn't so aware of her presence he couldn't remember if he'd driven in a spike or not.

She stepped closer, pausing. Out of the corner of his eyes he observed how she glanced back at the house and then seemed to push invisible iron rods down her backbone. He recognized that look and knew she intended to do business with him—business he suspected they both might find awkward.

She drew close, saw what he was doing and gasped. "What have you done? You were supposed to repair the hole. Instead you've made it larger."

He sat back on his heels. "The fire did more damage than you might think. I've had to take most of it down. The basic structure needs repair. Even some ceiling rafters."

"No one else thought that. You'll never finish if you keep tearing apart the place."

Her obvious shock at discovering he might be around longer than she'd originally believed left him cold and lonely. Such a contrast to the pleasant thoughts he'd been enjoying—remembering her singing so sweetly at church, remembering details of walks they'd taken and conversations they'd shared when they were but youngsters.

"You couldn't see it until you knocked off the plaster. I showed it to your father and he agreed it needed to be done." He watched her with unblinking patience, waiting for her response, hoping she might regret her initial reaction and voice some word of approval, if not for him then at least for the work he did.

"I thought—I wanted you—"

"You want me gone." His flat voice revealed none of his disappointment that she continued to hearken back to him leaving as if it were a given and couldn't happen soon enough to suit her. "I told you. I'm not going anywhere."

Her eyes practically lit a fire beneath his skin as she glared at him. "I must know what your intentions are regarding Dorrie."

"I want to be a father to her."

"What kind of father?"

He steeled himself to hide his own doubts. "The best I can be." He thought of the way Dorrie's eyes brightened and how she called him da-da. It didn't matter that Anna said she called others the same. She would soon learn that Colby was *her* da-da.

"Do you think it's fair for her to think people can walk in and out of her life? Shouldn't she be able to trust people to be there for her through good times and bad?"

He slowly put his hammer down, crossed his arms over his chest and faced her squarely. "Say what you mean. That I left her when times were bad."

Anna nodded. "You did. You thought of no one but yourself."

It was the farthest thing from the truth but she didn't look to be in a very receptive mood for explanations. "It was the only way I knew to deal with Nora's death. I know you tried to tell me about God's way but I couldn't see it. I couldn't believe it. I guess I wasn't ready. But I've changed. If you don't believe me then maybe you should at least give me a chance to prove it."

She stared at him.

"Anna, I thought you believed everyone deserves a chance. I recall how you used to say God didn't care where we came from, only whether or not we allow His love into our lives." He lowered his voice. "Don't you still believe it?"

"Of course I do. I just don't know if Dorrie should be the one you get to practice on. She needs security and the assurance those she loves will always do what's best for her."

"I'm not going to leave. But you're right about Dorrie. I don't want to upset her. She's obviously happy and well cared for." And disciplined in a way that was foreign to Colby. "I promise you, I won't take her away without your complete approval."

Anna's mouth fell open. She shook her head as if to clear her mind. "How can you make such a promise? You'll grow fond of her and want to take her when you leave. Or you'll marry—"

Her words might as well have been edged with razors they cut so deeply. Didn't she realize he'd only loved one woman in his whole life—her. He hadn't even loved Nora as he should. They'd married because they were both wanting someone who could share their problems.

He stopped her before she could go on. "Anna, I am not leaving again. Count on it."

A dark, haunted look filled her eyes. "I wish I could." She turned and fled before he could respond.

He stared after her for a long time. Truth was he didn't know what to say…or think. Her words gave him a sort of hopeless hope. As if she might care a bit about him but didn't want to.

He finally shook his head and returned to his work.

The pastor said to pray and so he did. *God, I've ruined so many things in my life. The good pastor says You will allow me to start over. I fear it's too late for me and Anna. But if You're like the pastor says and like I read in the scriptures, maybe You can change things. Make me into what I should be. Give me a chance to win Anna's love.*

Chapter Seven

$\sim$

Anna's thoughts went round and round, buzzing cease-lessly. He promised so much. To stay. To leave Dorrie with her.

None of it gave her any peace.

Suppertime approached and there were a hundred different details to attend to but her wayward emotions slowed her actions. She couldn't seem to catch up. And Alex needed reminding to do his work.

She found him playing with Dorrie in the front room. "Alex, run and do your chores now."

"Aww."

She ruffled his hair. "You have to do them so you might as well do them cheerfully."

But he scuffed the toes of his boots on the floor as he carried out the ashes. A few minutes later he rushed inside with the bucket of coal. "My chores are done. Can I go help Colby?"

Wonderful. Now Alex was falling under his spell, as well. He stood to be hurt and disappointed, too. But when had her brother ever been interested in anything to do with work?

She hesitated. It might do him good. As quickly as the thought came, she amended it. She couldn't encourage fondness between them. It wasn't worth the risk. Alex had endured enough losses already. "Maybe you should start your homework."

"I can do it after supper."

"Why don't you go outside and find someone to play with?" Persuading him to join in the play with other children was always a challenge. He preferred to stay in his room and read or play with Dorrie. She knew he needed companionship of others but she knew no way of making him seek it.

He sighed loudly and plunked down at the table. "You don't want me to go be with Colby."

"I guess I don't." At his disappointed expression, she felt she should explain. "Alex, I don't want you getting hurt."

Alex jutted out his chin. "How's helping him gonna hurt me?"

She could think of a hundred different ways, but she didn't want to get into a discussion when she knew Alex would demand explanations and details she didn't want to give him. "You just could, that's all." She turned away to prepare potatoes for supper.

"I guess I'll go outside," he murmured and dragged himself out the door with all the vigor of a man headed to the gallows.

Maybe she shouldn't have quelled his enthusiasm. It would do him good to work with a man for a change.

Her guilt lasted less than half a minute. She knew she'd done the right thing. Colby claimed to be changed but words came easy. She had no reason to trust him. It could be that about the time people began to count on him he'd toss it all over to disappear without a backward look. No, he had certainly given her no reason to trust him in the past nor in the present.

Supper was ready. Father, Alex and Colby would soon come in and sit down for the meal. Despite Colby saying he would leave Dorrie with her, she couldn't still the urge to hide the child. His assurances carried only as much weight as any promise from Colby had.

But Dorrie was hungry and would certainly fuss if confined to her room. Besides it was her duty to serve the meal. She had no choice but to put Dorrie in her high chair as Colby and Father came in.

Partway through the meal, Dorrie threw her food on the floor and wailed. "She's tired," Anna said, glad of a reason to take her from the table. As she prepared Dorrie for bed, the child fussed uncontrollably. "Poor baby." Sundays were always hard on her, upsetting her regular routine and Anna often paid for it on Monday. She wrapped Dorrie in her favorite blanket and rocked her until she fell asleep.

She returned to a kitchen now empty except for the remnants of the meal. Colby had left and Anna let out a heartfelt sigh of relief. Having Dorrie fuss had worked out rather well except for one thing—she was behind in her work. She should have the kitchen cleaned by now and be making sure Alex did his homework. She checked that he worked on his studies before she tackled the kitchen but she didn't disturb him to get his help with the dishes.

Finally she finished her chores. Dorrie was asleep. Alex in his room reading. Father had gone to visit. Anna felt the need for some fresh air and stepped into the yard, letting the warm evening wrap around her. A hauntingly, achingly beautiful tune filled the air. One of the hymns they'd sung on Sunday. She tipped her head toward the sound. Drawn by an invisible, melodic thread she followed it across the yard, past the ashes of the fire and in the back door of the church.

Colby sat on the front pew, his black-clad legs stretched straight out. He cupped his hands to his mouth playing a mouth organ. The sound encircled her. She'd only once before heard one played and that was for bouncy camp tunes. He played hymns, the pace much faster than one would sing, making the words dance through her head in a frenzy of joy.

He saw her and paused. "Am I bothering you?"

"No." She wasn't bothered so much as enticed to hear more. "I never heard you play one of those before."

"Something I picked up on my travels. I'm trying to learn the hymns you played."

"You're welcome to borrow one of the hymnals."

"Can't read music. I only hear it."

"Play some more."

His gaze stayed on her as he lowered his head and played the song that had drawn her over.

Something fragile as morning mist, soft as Dorrie's baby skin, hovered just outside her heart, reminding her of what they had once shared—how their hearts had beat to the same music, how their dreams had merged into one, how—

How he'd left.

She forced away the earlier feelings even though the action left her feeling lonesome.

He stopped before the end of the hymn. "I don't recall the rest." He shifted his gaze toward the piano. "Would you mind playing it for me so I can learn it?"

Glad of something rational to do, she took her place on the bench.

"Play it all so I can be sure I got it right."

She began to play. Before she'd played two bars, he joined. She'd never made music with anyone else. Most times she couldn't even find someone to accompany her when she sang a solo in church. To have someone to share this love flooded her heart with joy and uncovered secret, lonely places she hadn't even known existed.

When he faltered, she played the ending over for him. He got it right immediately and sat back, grinning. "Thank you."

Her smile filled with pleasure. "I enjoyed it."

His gaze searched hers, looking deep into her heart, as if seeing things that had grown and developed since the last time they had been open and honest with each other.

She let her thoughts grow and expand, knew they filled her eyes even as they filled her heart. She was being more honest with him at this moment than she had been since his return.

They had often sat in this very building as she practiced the piano. She'd told him how she loved music and hoped someday to play as well as Rose. Shyly she'd shared how the words and music spoke to her.

"Would you mind singing it as I play so I can hear the words inside my head?"

His voice seemed to come from a long tunnel, taking its time to reach her brain.

She jerked away and turned back to the piano keys. She must guard her heart. And thoughts. Hadn't she learned that lesson already?

So she played. He played. And she sang.

And despite her constant mental warnings, she let the music wash over her, numb her caution. She knew a height of pleasure so new and unfamiliar she didn't even know what to call it.

It was the music. That was all. Nothing more.

He stopped. "Wait. What was that last phrase?" He joined her on the piano bench so he could read the words himself.

She repeated the tune and they sang together. They finished the hymn. She paused, her hands in her lap. He grinned at her, his eyes sparkling with what she could only describe as pure, unfettered joy. Entangled in the music, she let his smile slip right past her reservations straight to her heart where it stirred together enjoyment and bliss into a surprisingly, delightful happiness. All the things that kept them at odds with each other vanished like dew in the morning sun. She allowed it.

Only because of how much she loved the music. Nothing more.

He flipped the pages of the hymnal. "Do you know this one?"

She chuckled. "I know all of them." She played it for him. Again they made music together. Song after song they played on, wrapped together in the melody and words, united in their enjoyment. She paused to turn the page.

"I remember when you said the songs were like God whispering in your heart. Now I know what you meant." His voice reverberated through her as if someone had struck the lowest key on the piano. At that moment, her defensive walls teetered.

Colby turned his attention back to the hymnal. "It's so dark I can hardly see the words anymore."

Anna looked around. The last golden rays of sun slanted through the window, sending bright lines across the pew, filling the rest of the room with shadows.

What was she thinking sitting here into the evening with this man? How could she consider trusting him again? Every time she thought he might be staying, he left. Every time she trusted him, he let her down.

She scooted off the bench. "I had no idea it was so late." No hiding the edginess in her voice.

"We were having too much fun."

She relented slightly at his quick smile. It wasn't his fault she'd let the music make her forget. "I enjoyed playing and singing together."

"I hope we can do it again."

At the invitation in his voice, she hesitated. In the fading light, she studied him. Who was he? Colby of her youth who shared the secrets of her heart? Or Colby of a year ago? Four years ago? Something hard and heavy lodged beneath her rib cage at the memory of being alone after Rose's death. The heaviness increased as her thoughts cleared. Only this moment did she realize she'd waited for his return, hoping and praying, only to have her heart scalded when he'd returned with a wife. He couldn't have made it any clearer that he did not share the feelings she had for him.

"I don't think that's wise. I must go." She scurried out the door, not slowing her steps until she slid into the silent kitchen. She padded into the front room. Father slept in his chair and she shook him awake. "It's time to go to bed."

He stirred. "I was waiting for you to come home."

"I was playing the piano." She often lost track of time as she practiced, but this time she hadn't been alone.

Her cheeks stung with heat. What was she thinking to be with Colby all evening? She could imagine Mrs. Percy's comments if she knew. Thankfully there was no way she could.

She tiptoed in to check on Dorrie. The baby slept with her bottom in the air, a finger inserted in her mouth.

Anna clamped her hand to her lips to keep from crying out. Colby seemed changed—everything she'd always hoped he'd be—everything she knew he could be. She'd enjoyed his company more than she wanted to but the longer he hung about, the worse it would be for all of them. She couldn't see his presence being a cause for anything but disappointment and sorrow for Dorrie, though she guessed Dorrie was young enough to forget Colby when he left.

It was her heart that would be shattered yet again.

She doubted she'd survive the torture.

She hurried to her room and sat on the edge of her bed, her troubled thoughts tumbling around inside her head.

Lord, help me. Guide me to be wise. I don't want to be hurt again. I don't want Dorrie or Alex hurt. Oh, Lord. Help me. Protect me.

She knew God was all she needed but a great loneliness pushed at her insides until she feared it would consume her. Why had Colby come back? Why couldn't she simply forget him?

Chapter Eight

Anna worked at breakneck speed the next day as if she could outrace her troubled thoughts. She swept the floors until not even a hint of dust lingered. The mats had been shaken to within an inch of their lives. Every window ledge gleamed from a thorough washing. Even the stove had been blackened and polished. It was almost a shame to ruin the finish by cooking on it but knowing Mrs. Booker was still ill, she set a pot of soup to cook. Later in the morning, she poured the thick soup into jars and gave it to Father.

"Take it to the Bookers."

"This will be a real blessing to them. It will relieve her worries, too." He paused as if considering his words. "I'm sure you know what it's like when the woman of the house is ill or… Nothing has been the same since Rose died." With a resigned sigh, he left with the jars balanced in a shopping basket.

Her throat closed off so she couldn't bid him goodbye. She understood what he meant, yet it made her feel as if she could never measure up to Rose's standard. Not that she expected to.

Poor Father. He must be so lonely.

With a start, she realized she, too, was lonely. And despite her best efforts to pretend otherwise, her loneliness had a Colby shape to it.

Once they had discussed their dreams of families of their own. Anna always thought it was a shared dream—the two of them creating home and family together. She sighed. This was old business. He obviously didn't share the same hopes she did. She had learned to accept that and move forward.

Except his return had brought the dead dream back to life.

Only she and Dorrie remained at home and she spoke her thoughts aloud. "I'm so confused." The baby babbled away as excitedly as if Anna had promised her a trip to visit Laura. "And it's your father's fault. I don't know what to make of him."

Last night they'd spent two sweet hours playing and singing hymns together. At such times it was easy to forget her caution. To dream about the Colby who had once been her best friend, her confidant and the one she continued to hold close to her heart. But she didn't dare trust him.

She wanted to. She ached to. But she couldn't.

What did Colby really want? Why had he returned? Would he stay or leave again at the first hint of difficulty? And would he want to take Dorrie when he left?

She tried to reassure herself that he couldn't manage a baby girl on his own but it failed to still her doubts.

Anna scrubbed the soup pot with unusual vigor as her thoughts rocked back and forth between a renewed longing and too many uncertainties.

Father returned with news that Mrs. Booker sent her

thanks for the soup. "She says her sister is coming to help while she regains her strength."

"That will be a blessing."

"Indeed." He went to his desk and pulled his Bible close.

Anna pressed her lips together. Father had never said Anna was a blessing for taking over after Rose's death.

She was only doing her duty and shouldn't expect praise for it but a word or two of acknowledgment would assure her she did a good job.

Enough feeling sorry for herself. God had given her a task and she would gladly do it, rejoicing she had the strength and ability.

She hummed as she returned to her work. It didn't pay to let her thoughts stray too far from God's goodness. Yet she wandered so often to the window, hoping for a glimpse of Colby that she began to wonder if she needed a tonic.

When Colby joined them for dinner, Anna could hardly look at him for fear he would see the confusion in her eyes. Why did she have this longing to be around him, to know he was nearby?

She must be overtired. And with well-honed self-discipline, she pushed cold hard steel into her thoughts.

She'd needed him before. Each time he had left. Now her life centered on Dorrie and Alex and running Father's house.

Dorrie went down for her nap and Father settled at his small desk in the front room. Since Colby had started repairs at the church, Father spent more time studying at home.

Anna looked at the pile of clothes to mend. She didn't want to tackle the job. She pulled out a bowl to mix a cake and put it back in the cupboard without measuring one ingredient. She heated some water and filled a basin, grabbed a couple of rags and washed the window behind the table. It gave her an unobstructed view of the church.

There was a time when her thoughts troubled her this way she would slip across and make her way to the front pew to sit and pray, her eyes open and focused on the cross. She always found what she needed—peace, wisdom, strength, courage....

She wished she could go to that place again, find what she needed.

She polished the glass slowly, not checking for streaks.

The cross no longer hung from the back wall. It leaned in the corner of the cloakroom. Perhaps she could slip in the front door without detection and recreate a special place of prayer near the cross. She needed so badly to feel God's assurance and direction right now.

She dropped the rag on the cupboard and hurried to the front room. "Father, I'm going out for a little while. Can you listen for Dorrie while I'm gone?"

Father waved acknowledgment without looking up from his notes.

She left the house through the front door and crossed to the church. Carefully she turned the knob and cracked the door only enough to allow her to duck through. She closed it soundlessly and tiptoed into the cloakroom. The cross leaned into the corner, so scarred and damaged she knew she would have to abandon hope of fixing it. No doubt someone would donate a new one. But for now she found comfort in this place of prayer—at the foot of an old rugged cross.

She sank to the floor facing it and let her thoughts

roam freely until they grew quiet. Only then could she pray and bring her doubts and fears to God. *Lord, I feel like life is spinning out of control. I need Your wisdom.* She paused as more doubts and concerns sputtered to the surface. *I don't understand my feelings toward Colby. Part of me cares about him—has always cared about him. In fact—* Her thoughts stalled. *I have always loved him. But how is it possible when I'm not sure I trust him? Lord, I ask for You to give me a sign of what I should do.*

She heard a sound behind and glanced over her shoulder. Colby stood in the doorway.

"I heard something and thought I should investigate."

"I came here to think and pray."

"I won't interrupt then."

"I'm done." Though she had hoped God would speak in the stillness of her heart and she'd understand her feelings.

Colby crossed the small room in two strides and plunked down cross-legged on the floor beside her. "It means a lot to you, doesn't it?"

She knew he meant the cross. "It does."

Neither of them spoke but the silence was companionable.

Anna's heart filled with unutterable cries. "When Rose died I had to take over running the house and caring for Alex. I learned not to show my own grief in front of anyone. The only place I could acknowledge my sorrow was in the church. I would sit on the front pew, look at the cross and cry. I was so scared." She turned to confront him, doing her best to keep the accusation from her eyes as well as her voice. "I was so alone. I needed someone. Of course, I had God but I wanted more. Colby, where were you? Why did you leave?" She clamped her lips tight to stop the cry clinging to the tail end of her words.

Colby leaned closer. For a moment, she thought he meant to drape an arm across her shoulders, perhaps pull her against his heart where she wondered if she would find the release she longed for. And then he settled back. She told herself she wasn't disappointed but a part of her longed to bury her face against his chest and cry out the years of disappointment.

"Anna, I didn't think you would need me."

"How can you say that? I'd just lost Rose and baby Timmy. Suddenly I had to take Rose's place. How could you not realize how difficult it was for me? I thought we were friends."

"We were. I hope we still are."

"Friends don't abandon each other when things get tough."

Colby flinched. "How could I have helped?"

"By being here."

"You would have been disappointed in me. Besides, Rose's death hit me hard, too. She was like a mother to me."

They'd both been hurt by Rose's death and too young to know how to cope. Still... "I had to find my own way. Alone. I spent hours praying for wis-dom and peace and strength to carry on." Her lips softened with the calm she reclaimed from that experience. "I found all I needed praying before this cross."

"You've managed very nicely."

"No thanks to you." She recalled another time she'd been frightened and uncertain how to face the task handed her. "Then you thrust Dorrie into my arms. I was so scared. I knew nothing about caring for a new-born. I used to come here when she was sleeping and beg God to guide me so I wouldn't kill her."

Colby jerked back. "Why would you think of killing her?"

She snorted at his shock. "I didn't *plan* to, but I feared I might make some colossal mistake. What if I fed her the wrong thing? What if she choked? What if she got sick and I didn't know how to treat her or, worse, didn't notice she was sick? The worries are endless."

He gave her a look of blue-eyed sympathy and something else—maybe regret. "I had no idea."

"Most of my worries were needless. I know that now. But at the time they seemed so real. So pressing. Only by trusting God could I face them."

"I'm here now. I'm not leaving."

At the moment she wasn't sure she wanted him to stay. She had too many unsettling doubts and fears. Too much to lose. And too much to forgive. Things too painful to even mention.

Colby sat there several minutes after Anna left. She'd had a lot to deal with but she'd coped. She'd done well. But she'd wanted him. Maybe even needed him. Why hadn't he stayed? Part of him wanted to. Why did he feel driven to leave whenever things got tough? What made him feel that was the best option for everyone? Not just him but Anna…and Dorrie.

He stared at the cross. Anna had come here often—only then the cross hung on the wall. She said she'd found answers. Would it work for him, too?

God, I feel like there is something bent in my life that pushes me to leave when I really want to stay.

Thoughts filtered through his brain. How much Rose's death had hurt. How he wanted to find comfort with Anna's family and maybe even do something to help them.

He tried to hear God speak but all he heard was his pa's voice. *What good are you, boy?*

Not that he put much pay on what Pa said. The old man wouldn't know a good thing if it reached up and grabbed him around the throat. As soon as Colby got big enough to realize he didn't have to take a whopping from him, as soon as he realized he could inflict as much pain as he took, he'd left, not wanting to start using his fists to equalize things between them.

Was that when it became easier to leave than to stay?

He shook his head. Somehow it didn't seem to fit. Walking away from his pa had been the right thing to do. It didn't have the same feel to it as leaving Steveville.

Nor did anything about Pa pull at him. But no matter how far he went, how fast he ran, and how deep into trouble he got, long invisible reins at the hand of an invisible, persistent, gentle driver pulled him back to Steveville.

And Anna.

"Man, you sure making a mess."

Colby turned from cutting away more damaged areas. "Slink, you old dog. Come on in." Slink had been one of his drinking buddies in the past.

Slink flashed a nervous smile and hung suspended in the doorway. "I ain't never been inside a church before. You think anybody would mind?"

"You're most welcome here. This is the place for sinners and the sick." Not everyone thought it but Pastor

Caldwell said it was so and showed him a verse in the Bible to prove it.

Slink, always lean, had grown downright gaunt. "Looks like you could use a good feed."

"Don't eat much."

Colby guessed Slink likely lived on a liquid diet of cheap liquor. In fact, he clutched the neck of a bottle as he gingerly stepped into the sanctuary.

"That stuff is going to kill you."

"'Spect so." Slink looked at a pew as if he wanted to sit then changed his mind, a tight look around his mouth.

"Come on. Let's chew the fat."

Hesitantly, glancing up as if he expected a voice from heaven to order him to leave, Slink perched on the edge of a pew. His bottle tipped dangerously. "Heard you was back. Heard you wasn't drinking no more."

Colby took the bottle and set it upright on the bench then sat across from the man. "That's right. I've turned around with God's help and forgiveness." He explained how God accepted sinners.

"Yeah, but you ain't never been as bad as me." Slink looked miserable.

Little did the man know. Colby hoped no one would ever find out. He hadn't told the pastor all the details of his past. Pastor Caldwell had insisted he didn't need to know. It was between Colby and God, and the Almighty promised to wipe the slate clean. Colby figured if God said so it had to be true but he knew the shame of his deeds tinged his thoughts black. Expectation in Slink's expression told of his desire to hear more and Colby repeated what the pastor had said. "Nothing's too big nor too hard for God."

Hope laced with desperation on Slink's face.

Trying to recall Pastor Caldwell's words Colby explained the things God had done as best he could.

The back door opened, interrupting their discussion.

Anna strode in, pausing as her gaze lighted on Slink. "I didn't know you had company." Although she spoke softly Colby heard the unspoken criticism in her tone.

She shifted her gaze to the damaged wall. "It's going kind of slow, isn't it?"

Colby chuckled. "It will be done on time."

Slink scrambled to his feet, grabbed his bottle and shuffled toward escape.

"Come back anytime and we'll talk more," Colby called, then turned to Anna. His grin slid across his mouth, full of gladness at seeing her. Something happy bubbled behind his heart. "It's a fine day." Maybe they could sit and talk. It seemed they had almost found again that place of sweet agreement when their hearts had shared unspoken words.

She sniffed—a sound signaling displeasure, and grating up and down his spine.

He tensed, knowing whatever they gained talking before the cross had been taken back.

"I thought you'd be working."

He nodded as he slowly got to his feet. "I was. Took a break to talk to my friend." He didn't know why he felt he had to explain. Knew, too, how useless any excuses were when someone wanted to be mad at you and he knew, despite her quiet demeanor, that she was upset about something. Part of him said to back away, apologize, do whatever necessary to avoid fueling her anger but he'd stopped running from situations either physically or mentally. "Have I done something wrong?"

She blinked as if surprised at his directness. "Of

course not." She stared again at the wall. "I can't help but worry a little. The work must be done in time for the celebration."

He knew there had to be more on her mind. "I know that already and it will be done. You can count on it."

Her nod seemed uncertain.

"Did you want to play the piano? I don't mind if you do. In fact, I'd kind of enjoy—"

"No. No. I wouldn't want to distract you from your work." She glanced over her shoulder. "Really I came to look at the cross again. I'm trying to figure out some way to redeem it." She headed toward the back.

He began to follow but she waved her hand. "I know where it is. Ignore me."

He hesitated. Seemed awfully clear she didn't want his company. And his disappointment was out of proportion. Yet he strained toward the cloakroom, aching to join her, recapture the few inches he thought they'd gained.

A few minutes later, she headed back down the aisle and out the door. "I won't bother you further."

He returned to fixing the wall, pounding in nails with two blows, finding release in the way his muscles burned.

Why had she gone over? What had she expected? Maybe to give him a chance to explain more about why he left and why he'd returned with a wife when she thought he loved her.

Instead she found him commiserating with a guy she'd only seen at a distance and even then the smell of booze almost knocked her off her feet. She'd seen the bottle on the bench. Had he been guzzling from it?

Changed indeed!

She fumed at her foolishness at hoping he had.

She fretted at how Colby could hurt Dorrie.

And she fussed about having to cook for the man.

But by the time Father came in for lunch, accompanied by Colby, she had her emotions firmly in hand. She would not allow her heart to rule her head. She would not allow herself to become a woman who couldn't see a man's falseness for the silly flutterings of her heart.

Colby smiled. "Hello."

Her control slid sideways. How could she feel this way about him if he was a scoundrel? How could he look so honest, meet her eyes with such calmness if he only pretended?

Alex slid in, out of breath from running from school. Father waited for him to settle in his chair then said grace. As he passed the biscuits and gravy, he said, "Mrs. Booker's sister arrived today."

Anna tried to gather her thoughts. "I should welcome her."

"That would be very nice."

There was nothing unusual about his announcing the arrival of visitors, nor of his expectation that she should be the official welcoming committee, yet there was something different about Father. Anna tried to get past her own heart turmoil to assess it but after studying him a moment decided she was mistaken.

As she turned to take the butter, her gaze collided with Colby's. He didn't say a word, didn't do anything more than look at her frankly, openly, but in that look she saw something that filled her with confusion—longing, promise, steadiness? Or was she only letting her own emotions fill her to overbrimming?

The whirlwind of confusion twisted through her as the day progressed, leaving her struggling to deal with the trials of the day. And there seemed to be a generous portion of them.

Dorrie didn't nap soundly and was irritable upon waking. At supper she didn't like the soup Anna served and threw her bowl on the floor. Anna scooped the screeching baby from her chair and carried her to the crib.

"Dorrie, you must stay here until you can stop screaming."

Shrieks followed her back to the kitchen where she cleaned up the mess.

"Anything I can do to help?" Colby asked softly.

His gentle tone almost proved her undoing. She stiffened her spine to keep from wailing and saying, *Yes, you can hold me. You can handle Dorrie's temper tantrum.*

Father answered Colby's question. "Dorrie exhibits a defiant attitude at times. I've found it's best to leave Anna to deal with it."

Out of sight as she scrubbed the floor, Anna rolled her eyes. Since Rose's death Father left the discipline of Alex to Anna. Before that Rose ran the house with order and control. After Dorrie came, it was one more responsibility for Anna, one Father never seemed to notice. Not that she minded. She loved Dorrie like she hadn't thought possible after watching Rose and Timmy die. In fact, she sat back on her heels momentarily as she considered the revelation, loving Dorrie healed some of the hollowness Anna carried inside her heart after the accident robbed her of her stepmother and baby brother.

She finished cleaning the mess and dumped out the dirty water. She returned to the table but her own food had grown cold and held no appeal as she listened to Dorrie crying.

Colby squeezed her shoulder as he left the table. "Do you want me to talk to her? She might listen to me." He lowered his voice to a growl. "I can sound quite menacing if I try."

She suddenly felt better. She'd gladly let someone else tackle Dorrie in her present state. "Go ahead. See what you can do."

As he went to Dorrie's room, Anna strained to catch what he said. She couldn't hear his words but his voice rumbled, not growly and menacing but calming. Dorrie shuddered a sob or two and grew quiet. Colby talked on for a few minutes. Anna caught only a word or two. Not enough to know what transpired.

She stared as Colby returned, a sobered Dorrie in his arms.

"Dorrie has something to say to you." He smiled encouragement at his daughter.

"I sorry, Mama." At the catch in Dorrie's throat, Anna's heart almost melted from her chest. She jerked to her feet and kissed Dorrie's cheek.

"I forgive you, sweetie." She lifted her gaze and realized how close she was to Colby, close enough to see the silvery flecks in his irises, to see the warmth in his gaze and feel the endless connection between them that had never quite been quenched. It promised endless sunshine.

They'd once shared so many things—from the games they enjoyed to their secret thoughts. And recently they'd shared a love of music and an unspoken love of this child. But it wasn't enough.

She turned and gathered dishes from the table. For

the space of a heartbeat she thought of speaking to Father about her worries but he'd only say a person had to accept people at face value. He despised suspicions and mistrust between people. He would not understand Anna's need for caution.

But she must be careful. If Colby broke her heart once again she might never recover. She must be strong, not only for her sake, but for Dorrie's, too. As well as for Alex and Father.

Colby held Dorrie a few minutes longer then set her down. Anna allowed herself a quick glance at him. His smile flooded with love and longing as he watched Dorrie. He looked up, met Anna's eyes. She felt his expectation, his silent pleading but she couldn't give the response he sought. The walls she'd constructed around her heart prevented it. As did her experience.

His eyes filled with dark regret. "I best get to work." He grabbed his hat and rushed outside.

Anna watched long after he'd disappeared from sight, unable to conquer a wish that they could go back in time.

It was impossible to recapture what they'd had. Yet... Her heart swelled with "what-ifs" and "if onlys."

Enough.

She grabbed dishes and plunged them into hot water, scouring them so hard it surprised her she didn't break something. Her efforts did nothing to ease the storm raging within her heart.

Later, after Alex returned from school, Anna mixed up a cake. She checked the oven. It wasn't hot enough. She reached for the coal pail. Empty. Alex's after-school chores included filling it.

"Alex?"

He didn't answer. Where had he gone?

Chapter Nine

Anna checked each room in the house, calling her brother's name but didn't find him. Where was he? He never wandered away without letting her know. Finally she glanced out the window what she saw made her knees buckle. She grabbed the cupboard for support and sucked in a gulp of air that stuck partway to her lungs. Ignoring her shaky limbs, she raced out the door. "Alex, get down from there this very instant." She paused, picturing him coming from the roof in a tumbling fall. "Use the ladder and be careful."

Alex lifted his head but other than that made no move toward obeying. "I'm helping Colby pull off the burned shingles."

"I don't want you on the roof. You might fall."

"He's perfectly safe." Colby's look was steady, re-assuring.

But she was not reassured and sent him a glare meant to scald him. "How dare you put him at risk."

Colby's gaze remained steady, solid. "I wouldn't."

She pressed her palm to her chest, massaging the tightness that refused to let go. "He might get hurt."

"Anna, believe me, I wouldn't let that happen."

She desperately sucked in air, which did nothing to relieve the tension in her chest. "You can't guarantee that. No one can. Accidents happen. It's best not to take chances."

He studied her with unblinking concentration, his gaze going on and on, past the brittleness stinging in her eyes, straight toward the fear surrounding her soul.

She averted her eyes, afraid of exposure, and looked at Alex but couldn't bear the sight of him perched so nonchalantly on the roof. Instead, she glanced at the bare studs of the back wall. A shiver raced across her shoulders. So many things could happen—accidents, fires—

"Are you planning to wrap him in cotton wool and keep him so close he can't breathe just to make sure he doesn't face risks?" Colby had come down from the roof and stood two feet away. He kept his voice low, meant for her ears only.

"What do you know about dealing with bad things? Seems to me you drown your sorrows so you can't feel or else you run. I don't have those sort of options nor would I take them if I did." She gasped at the accusations she had spewed at him. "I'm sorry. I should not have spoken so hastily."

"You spoke the truth. I don't deny it." His voice was harsh as if he wished he could. "But I'm back. To stay." He lowered his voice. "But we were talking about Alex. Anna, you can't protect him from life. You need to let him grow up."

"He's only fourteen." Even as she spoke she knew Alex should be more mature than he was. But she didn't know how she could make him grow up. Didn't it happen in its own good time?

"I was on my own by his age."

"He has nothing to make him run away from home."

"I appreciate that."

She nodded and turned to again order Alex from the roof.

Colby touched her shoulder, causing every nerve in her body to tremble. "Anna, what about your faith? Doesn't it teach you to trust God with the things that come into our lives?"

Red-hot flashes burst across her eyesight. She blinked, fearing another fire but the flames were inside her and posed no threat to anyone but Colby. "How dare you lecture me on faith?"

His eyes turned stormy-blue. "I am not lecturing, merely pointing out that life involves risks and faith should make us able to face them without fear."

The truth of his words drilled through her head. Her faith should be stronger. Her faith was her only defense. If she neglected to honor it, what protection did she have from disaster? "You're right, of course. I must trust God to take care of me and those I love."

He nodded, his eyes still filled with uncertainty as if he expected something different from her.

"Like I told you, He sustained me through the loss of Rose and Timmy. He upheld me when you—" She stopped. She would not confess how her world had crashed when he came back with a wife. Or when he'd left again. He must never know that she still loved him in some forbidden corner of her heart that she had barricaded.

"When I what?"

She avoided meeting his gaze, afraid he would read the truth in her eyes—her pain, her love. "You left me to raise Dorrie."

"It was the best thing I could do at the time. I wasn't ready to be a father."

If he meant that to give her reassurance...

Did he think he was ready to father Dorrie now?

And if so, where did that leave Anna?

But she couldn't deal with the possibility he might take her away, and she forced her thoughts back to Alex.

Colby struggled with his feelings. Was he ready to be a father now? This afternoon he had successfully dealt with Dorrie in a gentle manner even though she kicked and screamed when he approached her. He had not resorted to his father's methods. It felt good. And right. But it was only one time. Could he do it day in and day out?

He didn't know. But he knew one thing. He was through with running. He intended to stay right here and be as involved in Dorrie's life as he could without putting her at risk.

In the meantime, he had a church to repair.

He glanced toward Alex who continued to pull out damaged shingles, oblivious to the drama on the ground below him. The boy—almost man—needed to cut the apron strings both he and his sister clung to. "What about Alex?"

By the way her eyes darkened and narrowed, he knew she struggled with her need to keep Alex safe and her desire to prove she had enough faith.

How much faith was enough? He didn't know. It was a question he'd have to ask Pastor Caldwell.

Fear and caution seemed about to win the battle in her mind. "I don't want him on the roof. It's too dangerous." She called Alex and again told him to get down.

Alex glanced at Colby, seeming to want his approval.

"How about you burn the lot?" Colby said.

"Sure."

Colby felt Anna gasp as Alex scampered down the ladder to grab the wheelbarrow and race it over to the smoldering pile. The flames lick higher as he tossed on bits of wood.

She pressed her palm against her breastbone as she watched the flames. "I will never see a fire without remembering the fear of seeing homes engulfed and waiting, praying, fully expecting to see our home go." She swallowed hard.

Colby ached to comfort her. He thought of pulling her into his arms and holding her until her fears subsided, but she stiffened if he so much as brushed her hand. Yet his need to help her could scarcely be bottled up. "I heard how the good Lord spared the church and your house." He bravely touched her elbow. "Seems God protected you."

She turned her gaze to him, the flames still flickering in her irises. "But why us and not the others?"

He tried to think of an answer but he was no preacher and he was distracted by the warmth of her arm beneath the fabric of her sleeve, and even more than that—the way his blood gathered up the glow where they connected and fired it all the way to his heart to throw fresh fuel on the flame of their past. He wanted to rekindle what they had once had.

Or did he want to take the embers from the past and start something new? The latter, he realized with all his heart. Something new, something fresh and powerful. *Please God, give me another chance.*

But how many chances did God give a person? Colby knew he'd had more than his fair share. Making it back to Steveville without detection or interference might have used up the last of his chances. He pushed his thoughts back to the subject at hand.

"He'll be careful. I'll make sure of it."

She held his gaze. Slowly, her eyes cleared and her fears seemed to subside.

He smiled, relieved she chose to trust him with her little brother. Given time, perhaps he could prove she could trust him with her heart.

A little later, he hurried over for supper, eager to see if anything between them had changed, if the tiny crack he'd seen had widened.

Dorrie babbled a greeting when Colby walked into the kitchen. She waved her hands as she talked and pointed toward the table.

"Sorry, little gal. I don't understand you." Apart from the sweet words of da-da.

Anna picked up Dorrie and settled her in the high chair. "We don't understand most of what she says, either." The smile she gave Dorrie trembled when she glanced at Colby.

He sensed her hesitation, as if she couldn't decide if their feelings should be allowed to progress or not. He smiled. He had all the time in the world to prove she could trust him.

She served the meal then toyed with her very tasty brown beans and corn bread as if they had no more flavor than chalk.

"These are delicious, Anna. You're an excellent cook."

She looked at him then, her eyes wide as if his words surprised her. And he saw something more, a flash of pleasure at his praise. Her eyes brightened. Her mouth curved sweetly. "Thank you." Her gaze lingered no longer than a heartbeat but in that brief encounter he saw something he cherished—an acknowledgment of something warm and sweet between them.

He grinned, happy he'd managed to bring a smile to her lips. Even happier because of what he'd seen— she felt something toward him though she might not be willing to admit it yet.

He enjoyed the rest of the meal even though Anna's gaze darted away from him each time he looked her direction. Her actions only made it plainer that she had feelings for him but they frightened her. He silently promised he'd never again give her reason to fear opening her heart to him.

In the next few days, Alex found excuses to check on Colby and offer help if the work interested him. He sauntered over again as Colby prepared pieces of lumber to fix the roof. "Whatcha' doing?"

Colby explained how he had to repair the structure. "Want to help?"

Alex gave the lengths of lumber a dubious look. "Is it hard?"

"I wouldn't think it would be for a boy your size." He'd already noticed Alex avoided anything challenging. "Besides, hard work builds muscles." He had his sleeves rolled past his elbows. He shoved one higher and flexed his biceps to show Alex. "I've been working hard since I was twelve. And it hasn't done me any harm. Isn't that about your age?"

Alex shoved his hands behind his back as if ashamed of his lack of muscle. "I'm fourteen."

"Only one way to get muscles—build 'em with use."

Alex hesitated about ten seconds. "What do you want me to do?"

"I'm going up the ladder. You hand me these one at a time." It wasn't hard work. A six-year-old could handle most of it. "It will save me a pile of time not having to run up and down."

Alex did as Colby suggested. When the boards were all up top, Alex climbed the ladder and started to join him.

"I don't think Anna wants you up here."

"Yeah, she'll get mad if I get on the roof."

"Anna gets mad?" Did she still struggle with a temper that made her slam doors? "I don't believe it." She always seemed so calm and in control. "What does she do?"

"She tweaks my ear."

Colby choked back a laugh at the injured tone in Alex's voice. Little did he know how innocent a tweak on the ear sounded to Colby and what a mercy that was the worst Alex experienced.

Until he'd found his way to this family he had no idea how gentle life could be. He'd wanted a share of it. Had found it for a time. He'd left for what he figured were pretty good reasons. But no matter how far he went, how bad he was, how hard he drank, how loud he roared, he could never get away from wanting that sort of family, and the belonging he'd experienced nowhere else but here. Even if Anna never let him back into her life, at least Dorrie was in the sort of family he ached for. He consoled himself with that fact. "You can hand me nails as I need them."

He and Alex worked in companionable silence as he nailed the new pieces into place.

A door opened and closed next door.

Alex groaned. "I forgot I'm supposed to be getting Anna coal."

"Run along and do it. And if you've caused her any inconvenience, the manly thing would be to apologize."

"I will." He raced off to the coal shed.

Colby returned his attention to roof repairs. Suddenly he got the feeling someone watched him. He sat back to check the surroundings and stared straight into Anna's face—just inches away at the edge of the roof. His heart burned up his throat and he reached to steady the ladder. "You shouldn't be up here."

"Why not? Didn't you say it was perfectly safe?"

"Yes. No." For a man. Not a woman. Especially not a woman who owned a large portion of his heart.

The past few days there existed a tension between them—a not unpleasant sense of anticipation, as if things were about to change.

He prayed it was so.

"Are you here to help?" He sounded as doubtful as he felt. This was not her work. She had her hands more than full running her father's home. That gave him pause. Would she ever be able to leave? What would happen to Alex if she did? He chomped down hard, not liking the questions he'd raised.

She laughed. "I don't think you need my kind of help. No, I'm here to thank you."

"For what?"

"For what you're doing with Alex."

He shuffled about to sit cross-legged so he could face her and sought for the right words to say. A few days ago, she didn't want Alex helping him, feared he might come to harm. But in that short time, she'd changed her mind. Now she was grateful. It was a bigger beginning than he could have thought possible. "Anna, I don't deny I've given you plenty of reason to doubt me in the past. But I vow by everything I care about that I've changed." It wasn't only his determination that made his words true. It was what God was doing. "You can trust me. You can trust God to help me." His voice grew deeper as he risked speaking his desires. "You and I could be friends again."

Caution darkened her eyes.

His chest tightened as though someone squeezed him hard. He shouldn't have said anything. It was too soon.

She tipped her head, squinting against the brightness and searched his gaze. Some hair had fallen from her usual roll and the breeze tugged it across her cheeks.

Resisting an urge to capture the wayward strands and tuck them behind her ear, Colby held still, let her delve deep into the peaks and valleys and secret places of his soul.

With a deep sigh, she lowered her eyes.

He felt both seared by a hot sun and watered by a gentle rain.

"We'll see." She started down the ladder and paused. "Again, thanks for helping Alex."

Anna's thoughts tangled inside her head.

How could they be friends if she didn't trust him? A portion of her wanted to. Another portion warned her to remember his past. What did she want to believe?

She heard the answer deep inside her and it frightened her. She wanted to believe he was different. She wanted to believe he planned to be part of Dorrie's life. A part of hers. Knowing she could so easily switch back and forth from mistrusting Colby to actually enjoying his company and wanting to be friends, caused Anna to lose an hour or more of sleep.

Pain grabbed her heart in a cruel fist and gave it a vicious twist as she remembered watching Rose and baby Timmy die. In that moment she knew she would never again let herself care about someone who might be snatched from her, or who might leave her like Colby had a habit of doing.

If only she could discuss her problems with Rose. But she hadn't had that privilege in four years. She gave a frustrated sound—half sigh, half moan. How could she be so confused?

Next morning, as soon as she finished cleaning the kitchen, she told Father, "I'm going to visit Laura." She had to talk to someone. Perhaps Laura would have some good advice. After all she was now a married woman with children of her own.

Over tea, she and Laura discussed how baby Gloria had grown. "She slept through the night Saturday."

"Seems only yesterday Dorrie was that small." Her fears and worries rushed from their hiding spot in the back of her mind where she pushed them daily and tried to pretend they didn't exist. "Laura, what will I do if Colby tries to get her back?" It wasn't the subject she really wanted to discuss but she feared talk about her mixed-up feelings for Colby would only make Laura think she was weak and fickle.

"Is that what he wants?"

"He said I was doing a good job of raising her. He *said* he didn't intend to take her away." Unless Anna gave her full approval and she couldn't see that happening. She loved the child as her own.

"You don't believe him?" Laura rocked baby Gloria as they talked.

Anna turned her teacup round and round and tried to find words to express her tangled thoughts. "I want to believe him. But I don't know what to think."

"Anna, what's really bothering you?"

"I… I can't seem to decide what to think of him. Sometimes I want to believe he is as good as he seems." Slowly, hesitantly, her feelings almost too fragile to voice, she told how he worked with Alex and how he'd helped with Dorrie. "We have even enjoyed playing music together but—"

"What worries you?"

"I don't want to start trusting him only to have him walk away again."

Laura paused to lay the baby in her cradle. She refilled their teacups and took her seat again before she answered. "Anna, are you beginning to care for Colby in a special way? Is that what frightens you?"

"I—" She gulped as her mind stung with so many things she didn't want to face—her need for more than what she had, her fears at things changing. She was comfortable with who she was, what she had. She liked her security. She wanted to give the same security to Dorrie. "I don't want anything to change."

Laura smiled. "Anna, things must change. Alex is almost grown. He'll be wanting to do things away from home soon."

Anna thought of how eager her brother seemed to help Colby. Was it only the beginning of Alex leaving?

She didn't want to think about it. If she could she would pull Alex close and keep him there.

"Dorrie will go to school. And before you know it, she'll be wanting to marry and start her own family."

Anna chuckled looking at Dorrie babbling away as she played with a doll Laura gave her. "She can barely walk and her vocabulary is limited to half a dozen words. I hope she isn't thinking marriage already."

Laura laughed, too. "Not yet, of course, and hopefully not for a long time but my point is things are going to change whether you want them to or not."

"I wish they wouldn't."

"But life can't stand still. Anna, my dear friend, I have known you a long time. I've watched you cope with tragedies and challenges that would knock most of us to the ground. But it seems to me that you've wrapped life around you in a tight little ball. Isn't it time you let go and let God bring something new into your life?"

Anna squeezed her hands into fists. The idea of change frightened her. In her experience change hadn't proven to be a good thing. "I don't think I can handle it."

Laura laughed until her eyes watered. "I'm sorry," she finally managed to get out between chuckles. "This from a young woman who has handled more in the past few years than most of us handle in a lifetime, God willing."

"I only did what I had to do." Shaking with uncertainty and doubting her ability every step of the way. "And only with God's help."

"Will God help any less in the future?"

Laura's soft words smoothed Anna's concerns. "It would be different if I knew I could truly trust Colby."

"I wish it weren't so but people can't always be trusted. All I can say is take your time. Be cautious. And trust God to show you the way."

As Anna returned home she thought of Laura's advice. *Take your time. Trust God. Be cautious.*

Did that mean she should avoid Colby? Or explore their relationship? She didn't know but when Father handed her the list of hymns at supper, a thrill of expectation raced through her and she stole a look at Colby. "I'll practice them tonight," she murmured. Neither of them needed to speak to know they would play the hymns together.

As soon as Dorrie was asleep, she slipped over to the church. The room was warm from the afternoon sun. Dust drifted in the air accompanied by the cedar scent of newly sawn lumber. She didn't see Colby and could not deny the way her heart dipped with disappointment.

Chapter Ten

Colby heard her enter as he sat cross-legged in front of the cross where he'd been for some time, thinking and praying. He could understand why Anna felt the cross was so special. He, too, found it easier to direct his thoughts heavenward as he sat there.

"Anna, I'm in here." He waited for her to join him, sensing a calmness in this place that made it easier to speak honestly without fears and doubts getting in the way.

He turned as she slipped into the room and at the eager look on her face, his heart took off like a wild horse. He wondered it didn't leap from his chest. She cared. Lifting a hand he reached for her. "Come and sit beside me."

She hesitated only fractionally before she took his hand and let him draw her to his side. She sat close enough he barely had to shift for their shoulders to brush. When she didn't make any effort to move, his heart settled into a steady gallop.

"I was sitting here praying. And remembering."

"Remembering? What sort of things."

A smile started deep in his heart and slowly spread

to his lips, rounding his cheeks and filling his eyes. "You and me."

She lowered her head and studied her hands curled in her lap.

He felt her uncertainty as forcefully as if she'd pressed her palms to his chest and held him at bay. But there were things that needed to be said, things worth keeping despite all that had come after. "Remember the first time you baked bread?"

Her head came up then, surprise swathing her features. And then she whooped with laughter. "That's your top memory? What a disaster. I had to bury it in the garden."

He chuckled. "Several weeks later the Kleins' dog dug it up and dragged it all over town. No one could figure out what he had."

"Rose knew but she never let on."

"It was a lot of fun."

"More like embarrassing. Do you know how I dreaded that someone would figure out what it was and that I was responsible?"

He reached for her hand. Again, she let him. He examined her long fingers, turned the palms upward to see little scars where she'd nicked herself with a knife and hard little calluses at the base of each finger—evidence of how hard she worked.

The air between them was fragile with hopes and expectations.

Slowly she withdrew her hand. "Colby, what brought you back?"

Her whispered words strummed through his heart. He ached to tell her the whole truth but he couldn't.

If she knew…

If anyone found out…

"I didn't like what I was becoming."

"What?"

"My old man."

Something flared in her eyes. Something he took for compassion, maybe even hope. And she claimed his hand, gently squeezing it.

Her touch raced straight to his heart and grabbed it.

"Is that why you run? Because you think you'll be like your father?"

He rubbed his thumb across her knuckles as he studied their joined hands and considered her question. Why did he leave when Rose died? What was he afraid of? Why did he leave again when Nora died? What filled his heart with such dread that he had jumped on his horse and rode straight into the jaws of trouble in the hopes of cauterizing his thoughts?

Anna waited patiently, insistently. She deserved some sort of answer even if he didn't have one.

"I knew I couldn't be what you needed."

She gave his hand a brisk shake. "What did you think I needed?"

He didn't know. He shrugged.

"So what's different now?"

The question caught him squarely between the eyes and he grunted. Had anything changed? Had he changed? "Maybe nothing. I only know I'm through running."

She studied him for a long moment, looking past his words, past his own doubts and questions, straight to the depths of his heart.

He hardly dared breathe as he faltered between letting her see all his secret inner places and the need to shelter them. Slowly, under her intense study, he opened himself to her, all except for one corner, which he barred behind thick doors.

She must never know.

Finally, she nodded as if satisfied. "God's hand has been on you since the first day you rode into Steveville."

Yes. She accepted he was changed, that he was through running. He wanted to leap up and shout to the heavens his joy. Instead he grinned until his ears wriggled in protest.

She pushed to her feet. "I need to practice the hymns."

"Mind if I join you?"

The look she sent over her shoulder gave him even more joy. "Hoped you would."

Colby smiled as he measured boards to fit the wall. Playing music with Anna last night had been especially happy as they shared a new understanding. He felt as if she had opened her heart and welcomed him. Just a bit. Still tenuous. But progress.

He heard a shuffling in the entryway and went to investigate. He found Slink and Luke, another old buddy. Luke had obviously tried to polish his appearance. His old woolen pants had been brushed until only a few flecks of straw remained. He'd slicked back his hair and tried to shave though from the number of nicks Colby guessed he needed to sharpen his razor. Or steady his hand. He twisted a battered bowler hat in his fingers.

"Slink here said you know something about God."

"I tried to tell him what you said but I got it all mixed up." Slink's face wrinkled in concern.

"So we thought best we come and ask you to tell us."

"Glad to." He led the men inside and explained what he knew.

A blast of sunlight filled the room as the back door opened. Facing the glare he couldn't make out who stood in the doorway.

Then the door clicked closed and Anna stood blinking as her eyes adjusted to the dimmer interior. "Colby?"

His heart did a rat-ta-tat against his ribs at the sound of his name on her lips. "Over here."

She walked toward him, saw his friends and hesitated. "You've got...company."

"My friends Slink and Luke. Miss Caldwell," he said to the men. Slink had already jerked to his feet and backed away but Luke rose and nodded formally.

"Pleased to make your acquaintance, ma'am."

Anna tipped her head in acknowledgment but retreated so fast Colby wondered she didn't trip and fall on her rear.

"Did you want something?" he called after her.

"No. Nothing." She ducked out so quickly he could almost believe she'd never been there.

He stared at the dark wood of the door. What had she wanted? Maybe only to spend time with him. The idea filled him with sweet hope.

Slink wouldn't stay after that.

Colby went to the door with the men. "Feel free to come back anytime."

Anna watched out the window as evening shadows pooled between the house and church. She knew she had turned into a spy, but she couldn't help it. The first time she'd discovered those strange men dropping into the church, she'd been shocked, dismayed even. But when it continued day after day, she grew suspicious. These were the friends she'd seen Colby with after his wife died. Drunk and disorderly for the most part.

Could he be toying with the idea of leaving again?

She hated to be suspicious of him. Especially when every day she found something more she liked about the man.

She liked the way he seemed to know how to play with Dorrie—gentle but not babyish stuff. Even though Dorrie's speech was little more than a babble she understood what was said to her. He talked to the child with real words.

The other day he brought her a little puzzle he'd made from wood scraps. Anna wanted to say Dorrie was far too young for such games but she held her tongue and waited to see how he would handle his child.

"Look, Dorrie. A puzzle."

Dorrie babbled excitedly.

Anna laughed. "A whole paragraph that we don't understand."

Colby grinned. "I know what she said. She said, 'Thanks, Da-da. It's the best puzzle I ever got. Now show me how to make it.'"

Anna shook her head. "Seems you both have a good imagination."

"We understand each other."

A quiver of fear trembled through Anna. She suppressed a desire to grab Dorrie, whisk her into the bedroom and lock the door behind them.

Colby's presence threatened Dorrie's security even more than it threatened Anna's.

She did not want either of them to be hurt.

"That's my girl."

His words pulled Anna from her thoughts. Under his

supervision, Dorrie had pushed together the few puzzle pieces. He seemed as pleased as she was at her success.

Colby's head bent close to Dorrie's. Dorrie's hair was lighter but no doubt would darken to the same color as Colby's. They looked at each other, grinning widely, and Anna could not deny the similarity in their facial features any more than she could deny that Dorrie thrived with Colby's attention.

So did Alex. He seemed to have grown six inches and gained a self-confident stride after helping Colby with the church repairs. She liked the way he had managed to get Alex to hold his head up and speak directly to him.

Take your time. Be cautious.

Anna had turned away, pretending to be busy at the stove. Was it too late to be cautious? She couldn't deny she liked the way he smiled so readily and laughed so often. Seems her heart had gone it's own way.

She liked sharing her love of music with someone— someone whose eyes flashed blue depths when their gazes connected.

How could she feel this way toward him and yet still be full of suspicion? One day she felt close to him as if they had recaptured the earlier days of their relationship. The next moment she knotted up with fear and mistrust. She trusted God. Colby insisted that meant trusting God was working in his life. Could she do both? She didn't know.

On top of that, she worried what his presence meant to her role as Dorrie's mama.

She tightened her lips. Her own security felt a little shaky, too, when she considered her reactions to the man.

Anna had vowed to stay away from the church when he was working but to be completely honest, she'd hoped for another satisfying evening of music with Colby.

Instead, she watched as two pairs of tough-looking men slipped into the church. She glanced over her shoulder, wondering if she should alert Father, then she dismissed the idea completely. Father would say the church was open to the public. Anyone was welcome to go in and pray and meditate.

But were they doing that? Or tempting Colby to his old way of life?

She sighed heavily. Suspicion and selfish longing for a repeat of the kind of connection she'd felt a few nights ago twisted like sheets left too long on the clothesline. How was it possible to feel such conflicting emotions at the same time?

She turned from the window. But almost immediately returned to it. If those men left soon she could still hurry over before Colby departed.

As if her thoughts had prodded them, the men crowded out the front door, paused to speak to Colby again then shuffled down the sidewalk talking together.

She waited until they were out of sight.

Suddenly she didn't care about music. She wanted to find out what was going on with those men. "I'm going to the church," she called to Father and rushed across the yard.

Before she reached the door, she heard the sound of Colby playing the mouth organ and faltered as her heart and mind warred with one another. Pushing aside the way the music filled her with memories of shared pleasures, she cranked her spine into stiff attention and marched into the building.

Colby stopped playing and grinned at her.

She cranked her spine a notch firmer. Not even his

smile of welcome must be allowed to divert her. "Colby, what were those men doing here?"

He slowly lowered his hands to his lap as his smile fled. "You object?"

"Depends on why they're here."

"You think they're up to no good?"

She waggled her hands. "Is it so hard to just tell me?"

He shrugged. "Seems to me you're judging without cause."

"I just want to know."

"When are you going to learn to trust me?"

Trust. *Dear God, how I want to. And yet how afraid I am he's going to leave again.* She narrowed her eyes and stared hard at him, revealing nothing of her errant feelings. "When I can be sure it's safe to."

He nodded slowly and repeatedly. "You mean when you can be sure there are no risks. Well, I can't promise you that. No one can. Did Rose promise she would be here forever? She didn't have a say in it, did she?"

Pain spun through her and erupted in a cry. "How dare you compare yourself with Rose?"

"I'm not. But isn't that where our suspicions and failures started?"

"You left. That's where they began."

"I'm sorry. I had nothing to offer you."

"All I wanted was someone to hold my hand. Be my friend." The ache she'd denied since he'd left consumed her. It swept away reason and caution in its relentless invasion. "I waited for you to come. Then I waited for you to come back. When you did, you brought a wife." It took the last trembling remnants of her self-control to clamp her mouth shut so she wouldn't say more.

He stared past her. "I thought you knew."

"What?"

"I didn't love her."

She gasped. "What a dreadful thing to say."

"She knew it. We didn't marry out of love."

"Then why?"

"Because we found comfort in sharing our circumstances. She was under the guardianship of an uncle who confined her to the back room and worked her like a mule." Slowly he brought his gaze back to her and she read the pain, the confusion, the desperation that almost made her cry out again. "Besides, don't you see? It was the ultimate form of running away."

Pain scorched every breath, every pore of her that he would marry someone he didn't love to what—escape her? "Why?" she whispered. "Why did you have to protect yourself against me?"

"It wasn't you. It was me."

"I don't understand."

"Me, either. But all I can say is I've reached the end of my running. I am back to stay."

His words promised things she wanted but they barely scratched the surface of her defensiveness. He said it was because of him but it was her that had been hurt. She could not comprehend.

"I was afraid of disappointing you. Failing you."

"You keep saying that as if I had somehow put unreal expectations on you. If I did, I'm sorry."

"You didn't. Like I said. It wasn't anything to do with you."

"And what happened to this thing that sent you running? This thing you don't seem able to identify?"

"Maybe I outran it."

"What? What is *it?* And what if it catches up to

you again?" Why couldn't he give a straight answer? Though if he said she was *it,* that might prove more than she could handle.

He took her hands and faced her squarely.

She wanted to pull away but his look held her like a freshly spun spiderweb made with steel threads.

"I don't know why I ran. Maybe I will never understand. But this one thing I do know, forgetting what is behind and reaching for those things that are better. I press toward the mark for the prize of the high calling of God in Christ Jesus. That's from Philippians, Chapter 3. Your father explained it was like running a race. If I look over my shoulder I'm slowed down. I might get off course or even stumble. I'm not looking back. I'm not going back. The only direction I'm running is straight for the prize of the high calling of God."

Her mouth dropped open. She blinked. This was not the Colby she remembered—uncertain of who he was, what he was. "You're different."

He grinned as he squeezed her hands and pulled her so close they were almost nose to nose. "You're finally getting it."

She jerked back, stunned by his words, even more stunned by his assurance.

"Isn't it about time you started to accept me?"

"I—" She couldn't finish. This was what she wanted. This closeness. This assurance. Yet— "Those men?"

He sighed and pulled away. "I can see it's going to take some time. Those men are the ones I used to drink with. They've come to hear about God. You see, I told them I was changed…." He let his words trail off.

But she understood what he didn't say…his former drinking buddies were more ready to believe him than she.

"I'm afraid," she whispered.

"Of me?"

"Of being hurt, disappointed." She tore her gaze from him, but felt more lonely than ever and slowly shifted until she met his eyes again.

He nodded. "Anna, there are no guarantees in life. I can't give you any. No one can. But you can't pull life around you like a blanket and hope that you can somehow prevent anything unpleasant."

Hadn't Laura warned her things would change? She couldn't stop it. Normal change was one thing and not particularly welcome at that.

Walking into a situation that held as much threat as promise was quite another.

His voice grew husky. "Don't you ever want more for yourself than to run your father's home?"

Did she? She allowed a door to creak open so she could see inside where her secret longings and denied dreams resided. What she saw filled her with an ache as wide as the Dakota horizon. She longed for more. She wanted it all—her own home, a husband who loved her, children added to Dorrie's sweet presence. It was impossible. Unattainable.

Frighteningly different.

She closed her eyes and prayed for wisdom and common sense.

Colby's whisper persisted. "Don't you wish you could have your own home? Your own family?"

Eyes still closed, she nodded slowly.

"Then trust me."

Her eyes flashed wide as she realized what stood in the way of doing so. "I need to know what makes you run." Giving him the benefit of doubt, she corrected herself. "Made you run." Until she did, it would be a specter hovering in the corners, able to send him down the road if the conditions gave it more strength.

She rose with as much dignity as her shaking limbs allowed and head held high by dint of her rigid self-control, she returned home.

That should have been the end of it. But how could it be when he joined them for every meal, when she had but to look out the window to glimpse him at work and when her heart continued to ache after him. When he spoke words of encouragement to her and offered so much leadership to Alex.

She couldn't seem to turn around without memories of him.

He'd sat in that chair holding a skein of yarn for Rose and listening to Anna's spelling words.

He'd stood at her side at the cupboard washing dishes as she dried, telling her of the stampede of cattle in a vicious storm when he was but fourteen and on his first cattle drive.

He'd stood in the middle of the front room and stared in awe as she came from her room in her new outfit, one Rose had made 'specially for the Christmas program.

Even the church was full of memories—current ones of singing and playing music together, sharing bits and pieces of the years they'd been apart—intermingled with the past when he had eagerly listened to every word Father spoke as if seeking something to fill a vast hunger.

Why did he run? If she understood perhaps she could trust him not to do so again.

But until then...

Chapter Eleven

Colby stepped into the kitchen as familiar as any home he'd ever known. The aroma of fried chops, apples and cinnamon greeted him. He closed his eyes and inhaled the scents and felt a sensation of peace and blessing. This is what home should be like, not the fear-filled uncertainty of his younger years. "Smells great in here."

"Anna made apple pandowdy," Alex said. "She makes the best in the world."

"Alex," Anna scolded. "How would you know?" She smiled apologetically at Colby.

As their gazes connected he acknowledged that all he'd wanted all his life was right here in this room, in the smile of one woman—Anna. Why he'd left her even once was beyond understanding. Yet he had done so twice, three times if he counted Nora. But now he wanted to be with her, together with Dorrie, part of Anna's life forever. He was trying to trust God to make it possible yet the one thing she wanted he could not give—the reason he had left. He could have said because he feared he would become like his pa. She would have understood that. But it wasn't honesty and he wanted nothing but the truth between them.

What about what you did?

He could never tell her that awful truth. It was part of what he had left behind. Pastor Caldwell assured him that God forgave and forgot the past. Colby intended to do the same.

Yet what if his past found him? It scared him through and through. He hoped no one noticed how stiff his joints seemed as he moved to the table and sank to a chair.

Over the meal, the Caldwells frequently shared how his or her day had gone. He remembered this ritual from when he was younger, remembered how foreign it had seemed at first. He couldn't have imagined sharing around the table with his pa. He learned to keep his mouth shut and his eyes open, ready to duck if necessary.

But the practice had made something deep inside him feel warm and welcome.

It still did.

After initial awkwardness with him sitting at the table, they had resumed the habit.

Alex barely waited for his father to say "Amen" before he bounced to the edge of his chair. "The race is coming up. I'm going to try and win the hundred-yard dash."

Colby kept his opinion to himself. He'd only once or twice seen the boy move faster than a snail's pace. But his enthusiasm was commendable. "I could help you practice." He'd gone to school so seldom but one teacher, Mr. Gates, had taken an interest in making sure Colby could both read and run. Colby grinned. Two skills he found equally useful throughout his life.

"Would you? Great."

Alex's gratitude made him grin. He glanced at Anna and saw her gleaming smile. She mouthed the words *thank you*. His heart swelled up his throat, making it impossible to swallow until he jerked his gaze away. She'd been truly friendly since the day they had talked about the men coming to the church. Friendly but reserved. Waiting for the answer he couldn't give. Anna told how Dorrie had said please so clearly. But her eyes shared so much more with Colby—mutual love of this child, and if he looked deep…hope for more. She turned to her father.

"How was your day, Father?"

Anna's question slid through his mind like fresh cream, sweet and smooth. He understood it wasn't what she said but the sound of her voice that had this effect on him. Slowly he lifted his head to steal a glance at her as she spoke to her father. If only he knew the answer as to why he ran, he would willingly give it. But he'd told her all he knew—he believed he had nothing to offer her.

He remembered the power of prayer. *Father God, help me understand what made me feel I had to leave.*

"The Booker family are all feeling better. I enjoyed a pleasant afternoon in their company."

Colby stared at the pastor, wondering at the way he ducked his head. Totally unlike the directness he expected but no one else seemed to notice and Colby decided he had a suspicious nature.

Three pairs of eyes turned toward Colby. It was his turn. "I finished fixing the roof today."

"Good," Pastor Caldwell said.

Colby checked for Anna's reaction, expecting a smile

of happiness at his progress. Instead, her eyes turned dark and bottomless. She held his gaze and in that moment he was sure he felt a promise and a wish.

Then Alex passed her the potatoes and she looked away.

Had she thought how he would soon be finished? Did she wonder if he would leave? Wanting to put her mind at rest he spoke again. "I see Rawlings is looking for help at the feed mill. How long has he had that sign up?"

"Seems it's always up. Hear he's a hard man to work for, though perhaps only because he expects an honest day's work for an honest day's pay."

Colby kept his attention on the pastor as he spoke. "I could promise that." He stole a glance at Anna and in that unguarded moment, her eyes flared, revealing the depth of her feeling for him. He turned his attention to the meal as joy filled his heart with rich strains of music.

"One of the best meals I've ever eaten," he said a little while later.

"Thank you." She pushed back. "Alex, clear up the table while I put soup bones to cook." She reached for Dorrie.

"I'll get her," he offered.

She nodded and smiled as she hurried to the stove.

He lifted his daughter and stole a moment's hug.

Dorrie patted his chin. "Owie," she said as she felt his whiskers.

He laughed and waggled his chin. "Scratchy, aren't they?"

She giggled then squirmed to be down. He lowered her to the floor but kept hold of her as he reached for the cloth on the cupboard and dipped it in the basin of water. "Let's wash supper off your face."

Dorrie lifted her face to him and let him wipe it clean.

He bent and kissed her plump cheeks then released her with a pat on the bottom. "There you go, little miss."

She pushed a chair to the cupboard. "Me help."

Anna rubbed the back of her hand over her brow. "Sweetie, Mama's got to peel this onion." She shot a glance at Colby. "I want to simmer the bones overnight."

"Me help."

Colby chuckled. "Let's do dishes together." He shifted Dorrie's chair to the cupboard and let her put her hands in the soapy water. As Alex brought him the dishes, Colby leaned over Dorrie, reaching around her to wash.

He would never get tired of the smell of his child, the way her hair tickled his chin as he helped her wash the dishes. He wished the moment could last forever but all too soon the dishes were done.

Wanting—needing—to share his joy in this child, he turned to Anna, hoping to see her eyes soften with understanding. Instead, her eyes narrowed with warning. And though she never spoke a word, he heard her clearly.

Don't think of taking her away. I won't let you.

His joy plunged to the pit of his stomach. He had ruined so many things. Was it possible he could undo any of it?

With God's help perhaps. Time alone would tell if God chose to give him such an undeserved blessing. In the meantime, he wasn't leaving. How long would it take Anna to accept that as fact?

"Did you mean it when you said you'd help me practice for the race?" Alex asked.

"Of course. Tomorrow after school if it's all right with Anna."

"As soon as your chores are done. But you aren't to interfere with Colby's work."

"I won't." He hurried to tackle his homework.

"Thank you, Colby." Anna's voice was sharp with warning but softened with gratitude.

"I've done nothing."

"You've offered to help Alex. That's something."

He held on to hope. Perhaps she would begin to see just how they needed each other.

Colby had looked in vain for some sign of Hugh. The man must have been angry when Colby left after accusing him of such dreadful things. Colby knew he had not done anything shifty with Nora. The man had done nothing but help. Maybe Hugh was still mad enough to stay away. He hoped not. Hugh had been the one person besides Anna and her family who saw him as more than a drunken bum. He really wanted to find him and tell him he was sorry for his stupid words.

He asked the men who had gathered in the church again to hear more about God if they knew where he could find Hugh.

"Hugh's gone," Tobias said, his voice slow with sadness.

"Gone?" Shock numbed his cheeks. "Dead?"

"Nah. Gone to the Black Hills looking for gold."

Colby's breath whooshed out. "Scared me for a minute."

Arty let out an expansive sigh. "Could be dead by now. I hear the camps are pretty rough places."

Slink waved an unsteady hand. "Hugh knows how to take care of himself."

"No one's heard from him?" Colby asked.

"No one's said so."

"I wonder how a person could locate him?" Now it seemed he must find Hugh. Make sure he was alive.

Tobias rubbed his whiskery chin making a raspy sound. "Suppose you could write to the sheriff in one of the towns and ask after him."

"Good idea. Maybe I'll do that. Thanks for your help."

If he could locate Hugh and make things right between them, it would be one less thing from his past to haunt him.

But one thing would forever haunt him.

He waved goodbye to the men before he allowed the worst thing from his past to fill his mind.

There was no way he could undo it. The best he could hope for was to hide from it.

"So we all know what we are to do for the party?" Mrs. Percy checked around the circle. The ladies' sewing group had assembled again in the front room of the manse to plan the lunch the church would serve at the town birthday party. The usual people attended. It was nice to see Mrs. Booker, wan but able to be up and about. She had brought her sister, Grace Weaver, who wore a pretty gray dress. Anna decided Miss Weaver was almost as pretty as Rose had been.

The ladies murmured agreement to Mrs. Percy's question. They had gone over the arrangements a number of times. Anna was certain everyone had memorized the details by now but Mrs. Percy was a stickler for wanting things perfect.

"Now about the booth downtown."

There followed a flurry of suggestions.

Anna tried to concentrate on the business at hand as each one listed the items they would donate to sell at the booth to help fund a library for the town, but her thoughts insisted on drifting over to the church where Colby worked.

With each passing day she found it increasingly hard to keep Colby from invading her mind. Every moment they were apart she ached to be with him. Yet when she was with him, her caution made it impossible to fully enjoy his presence.

She was turning into a fussy old woman.

Mrs. Percy cleared her throat, alerting Anna to pay attention as an important item was to be introduced.

"Mr. Percy says the repairs are coming along well."

Anna nodded, pleased for the faint praise on Colby's behalf.

"I'm concerned, however—"

Anna sat up straight. Mrs. Percy's "howevers" usually meant "oh, no" for Anna.

"Are you all aware of what's going on at the church many evenings?"

Anna's heart bolted for her mouth. Had people seen her going over to spend time with Colby? Had they deemed it inappropriate? Even though it had been perfectly innocent, necessary practice for the Sunday hymns, she should have been more careful.

"Unsavory characters hanging about." She fixed Anna with a stern look. "Are you aware of this?"

Oh, only the men visiting Colby.

It took a full minute for Anna's heart to resume its normal pace. "Of course. Father says the church welcomes sinners."

Mrs. Klein nodded. "That's a fact."

"I just think it's suspicious. Colby Bloxham and his old friends." The word was accompanied with a sniff. "Could be they're drinking."

Anna stilled her features not to smile at the woman's distress over such an idea. Then her amusement faded. She'd been equally suspicious and it was every bit as ludicrous on her behalf. "They've come to learn about God."

Mrs. Percy's mouth flopped open. She seemed to struggle with the idea. "Well." *Huff.*

"Why, isn't that wonderful." It was Miss Weaver. "Exactly the sort of people our Lord would have sought out when He was on earth."

Mrs. Percy's eyebrows headed for her hairline. "Exactly the sort He would have driven from the temple, I say. 'My house is the house of prayer, but ye have made it a den of thieves.'"

Miss Weaver smiled gently. "I must have misunderstood. I thought young Colby has repented and asked for salvation."

Anna watched in awe. She had never seen anyone stand up to Mrs. Percy but despite how Miss Weaver spoke calmly, it was a duel as brisk as any with swords.

Mrs. Klein dared to enter the foray. "I understood the same thing."

"Well, praise God." Miss Weaver said with a gentle smile. "He is no longer the Colby you remember, is he? God's word says 'If any man be in Christ he is a new creature, old things are passed away; behold, all things are become new.'"

Anna's respect for Mrs. Booker's sister grew. Yet the words troubled her. She believed God's word. Heaven forbid otherwise. But was Colby a new creature? Was he changed or was this life convenient for now? After all, hadn't he acted much the same before Rose died? Was this any more real?

Mrs. Percy smiled, a look as full of challenge as anything. "In Galatians, Chapter 6, and also First Corinthians, Chapter 4, Verse 2, if I don't miss my mark—"

Anna knew—as did everyone else—that Mrs. Percy seldom missed her mark.

"We are warned that a man must prove himself."

Exactly. That's what Anna wanted—Colby to prove himself before she could trust her heart to him again.

Miss Weaver nodded. "I perceive you are a true student of the word."

Heads jerked from Mrs. Percy to Miss Weaver, and Anna guessed the rest of the ladies were as keen to see how this exchange would end as she.

"But to whom must he prove himself? Does not the word warn us in Romans, Chapter 14, Verse 4, if I remember correctly but then I fear I am not the expert student you are, that 'to his own master he standeth or falleth.' Is it not the Lord's work to change him? As it says in Philippians, Chapter 2, Verse 13, 'It is God which worketh in you both to will and to do of His good pleasure.' Perhaps we need to trust God to do His work."

A couple of the women nodded. Mrs. Percy knew to say anything more would make her seem unchristian but Anna understood she wasn't convinced.

Neither was Anna. Not that she didn't trust that God

could change people, but she wasn't about to risk everything until she saw undeniable evidence Colby had changed. After all, he couldn't even say what made him leave, so how could he be certain it wouldn't happen again? And if he left once more, would he take more than her heart if she gave it to him?

Would he take Dorrie?

She had to clench her hands together to still the pain accompanying the thought.

Mrs. Percy found another bone to gnaw. "What about the cross? I assume a new one will be ready in time for the celebration."

Anna pulled her thoughts back to the demands of the moment and nodded. "Father is taking care of it." When she asked, Father assured her he and Colby had it in hand. She was not privy to their conversations, so had no idea exactly what was being done. But she trusted that if Father said it would be done, it would.

Chapter Twelve

Supper was over and the pastor had gone to the front room. That left Colby alone in the kitchen with Anna. Now was his chance. He would take care of this business of composing a letter to Hugh. "I want to write to a friend and wondered if I could get a piece of paper from you."

"Of course." She slipped into the front room and returned with a sheet of paper and a pencil. "You're welcome to sit at the table to write."

He accepted her offer and licked the end of the pencil then bent over the page. As always the words refused to form in his mind so he could put them to paper. He should start with "dear sheriff" but was it *der?* No that wasn't right. *Deer, dere?* He sighed. The only thing he knew for certain was it started with *D.* He bent over the paper and laboriously made the first letter. He paused, leaned back, tried to remember how to spell the word. Nothing came. How would he manage *sheriff* when he couldn't spell *dear?*

The pencil snapped between his fingers. Guilt at destroying the precious instrument crashed with frustration. "I'm sorry," he muttered at Anna's surprised glance, meaning the broken pencil.

"It's not a problem."

He bent his head, wishing she would look elsewhere. He didn't want her to see his inability to write a simple letter. He read passably well, had managed to hide the fact from both Rose and Anna that he had trouble writing. How would she react?

His old man had jeered and called him stupid.

Only now did he realize the hurtful words came from a man who signed his name with an *X*.

Somehow the knowing should have made him feel better about being able to do more.

But it didn't.

Anna moved closer.

He felt her stop at his side. Knew she studied the page. She'd have to be blind to not see the crudely made letter and stupid not to realize his difficulty. She was neither.

"Do you need some help?" Her quiet voice seemed to carry no opinion.

"I don't write very good." His throat clenched around the words allowing each to escape as a tight croak.

"I can write for you...unless you don't want me to know what your letter says."

His relief was so palpable he wondered it didn't plop to the table quivering like warm pudding. "Nothing private about it at all." He shoved the paper and sharpened bit of pencil toward her.

She pulled out a chair and sat at his elbow. So close he could smell bits of cinnamon and basil, and the clean fragrance of her soap.

He shifted, rested his arm on the back of her chair, barely an inch from touching her.

She bent over the paper, exposing the pearly white of her slender neck. "You dictate and I'll write."

He struggled to remember what he wanted to say. Her nearness made it impossible to think. He loved her. Plain and simple. He continued to pray she would give him another chance to prove himself worthy of her love.

She turned toward him. "Colby, what did you want me to write?"

Her eyes filled with golden color that came from streaks of light brown alternating with darker brown. Her lips parted in surprise at the way he stared at her and she looked expectant as if she wanted more from him. Like a kiss? How he ached to kiss her, but he dare not until he knew she would welcome him with a heart of trust.

It took every scrap of his mental strength to pull his gaze from hers and stare at the page.

She jerked her attention the same direction.

He removed his arm from the chair back and planted his hands firmly on his knee. "I'm trying to find a friend." He could barely grate the words out. "But I don't know where he is." The tightness in his throat relaxed as he thought about Hugh. "I'm going to write a sheriff on the off chance that might locate him."

She nodded, her head bent over the paper.

"Dear Sheriff," he began. "My name is Colby Bloxham. You might have heard of me in the past. I am no longer that man. I am now a good, God-fearing man." He paused. "Just put 'a God-fearing man.'" He didn't know if anyone would call him good. Not yet. He waited until she erased the word then continued dictating. "I'm looking for my friend Hugh Mackenzie. Is there any chance you have heard of him? If so, could you let him know Colby wants to hear from him? He can contact me at Steveville, Dakota Territory." He spoke slowly as Anna wrote the words, amazed at how quickly the beautiful script appeared at her hands.

"That's about it I guess."

She put the pencil down and leaned back. Her shoulder brushed his.

He steeled himself to keep from wrapping his arms around her and pressing her to his chest where she would surely feel the demanding beat of his heart.

She pushed back. "I'll get an envelope."

It took concentrated effort to force air into his lungs. He held it there waiting for sanity and reality to replace the trembling of his thoughts.

She returned and stood across the table from him. "How shall I address it?"

He'd thought it through and decided on the most likely place. "The Sheriff, Lead, Dakota Territory. He went looking for gold."

She wrote the words on the envelope then handed it to him.

He folded the letter neatly, tucked it inside and sealed the flap. "Thank you. I'll mail it tomorrow."

She smiled, something warm and understanding in her gaze. "Glad to help and I hope you find your friend." She ducked her head and when she looked at him again he saw uncertainty in her eyes.

His blood felt thick as it pushed through his veins. He did not want to hear again how she couldn't get over him leaving in the past, so he headed for the door.

He paused only long enough to thank her again then chased his regrets outside.

Anna stared after him, her mind in a whirl. Since the ladies had left, Miss Weaver's words had haunted her. Was God changing him? Could she trust God? Yes. But Colby...

Not, she knew, without evidence.

And how she longed to see that evidence and be able to recapture the sweet bonds they had once shared.

Lord, help us regain the trust and closeness we once had. Now, if it be Your will, please show me if it's safe to trust him.

The next day was busier than usual. Dorrie got into a hundred things before the day was an hour old and from there she gained steam.

In her haste to catch up, Anna sloshed the dishwater and ended up washing the floor unexpectedly.

Little annoyances built one on another.

She paused as a bout of tears threatened. Why was she letting things bother her?

She knew the answer. Because she cared for Colby. He'd laid claim to a great portion of her heart. She'd only been sixteen when he left and yet he continually filled her hopes and dreams for the future. How she ached for the closeness of the past.

How foolish her thoughts...to want the very thing that could destroy her. With great effort she pushed stubborn resolve into her heart. She could not allow him to hurt her again.

The day sped past. Alex came home from school and slipped out to do his chores.

Out the window, she watched Alex and Colby talking. Alex leaned over as if waiting for a signal to run. Colby leaned over, too, planting splayed fingers on the ground. He must be showing Alex how to start a race.

She smiled and tucked away this little picture of just what a good man Colby was.

As she watched, she mixed up cake batter. She turned to put more coal in the stove to keep the oven at an even temperature. The coal bucket was empty. One of Alex's chores was to fill it. Anna sighed. He might want to run but when it came to chores he was slower than a spring thaw. She grabbed the bucket and headed to the shed.

Colby was right about one thing. She coddled Alex. He needed to grow up and accept the few responsibilities he had. She must speak to him.

Colby and Alex came in for supper a little later, both of them grinning with eagerness.

"Colby says I'm a good runner."

"You've got potential. A little practice and perseverance and you'll do fine." The smile Colby sent Anna's direction melted away a great deal of the day's tension. It was good to have him here. His presence seemed to give each moment a slice of calmness. She wished he could stay longer, share a few more hours but he spent his nights elsewhere. And tonight when she relished every minute, he left early, saying he expected Slink and a few others to stop by.

As soon as he left, she forced herself to deal with Alex. "What about your chores after school?"

A guilty look flitted across his face. "Forgot," he mumbled.

"I shouldn't have to remind you all the time. You're old enough to be responsible. For the next two days, you're confined to your bedroom after school."

"That's not fair," he yelled. "It's just a bucket of coal."

Dorrie's eyes grew big. She looked from Anna to Alex, her little mouth round with concern. Anna patted her hand, silently assuring her.

"It's your job. I have enough to do."

"It's sissy work. I'm too old for it. Besides, Colby is training me to run."

"You can train again after you've spent some time in your room. Hopefully it will help you remember your responsibilities in the future."

He pushed back so hard his chair fell with a clatter. "Stop treating me like a baby." He rushed to his room.

Dorrie whimpered.

"It's okay, sweetie." But it wasn't. Her whole life frayed apart before her eyes. She wanted it back, neat and orderly. She didn't want things to change, especially this way.

Alex should have helped with dishes but she didn't want to deal with his anger, so she did them alone, even though she realized it probably defeated the purpose of confining him to his room in the hopes he'd learn responsibility.

By the time she got Dorrie in bed, Anna wanted nothing more than to lie down and cry. Knowing that served no purpose, she did what she learned to do throughout previous times of trial. She headed to the church to pray, pausing at the door to make sure Colby's friends had departed. Hearing no sound, she crept in through the front door. Colby sat in a pew near the front, his head bent as if reading.

She didn't want to attract his attention, needed to think about him without his presence invading her thoughts so she tiptoed into the cloakroom. She needed to sit in front of the cross and find peace. She stopped in the middle of the tiny room and blinked.

The cross was gone.

The frustrations of the day boiled over, filling her with despair-laced anger. She spun around and stomped into the sanctuary.

Colby, hearing her, turned to face her.

"It's gone. One of your friends must have taken it."

"What are you talking about?"

"The cross. Where is it?" The enormity of her loss sucked the strength from her knees and she sank to the nearest pew. Her anger melted into sorrow. A sob caught in her throat where she trapped it. Her reaction left her feeling foolish and vulnerable.

"It's safe."

"Where is it? Who's taken it?"

"Trust me."

The words mocked her, drove spikes through her thoughts. Trust? The one thing she wanted to do but seemed unable to. She'd even prayed for a chance to test it. Was this an opportunity?

Memories assailed her. She could barely remember her mother except for a fleeting picture of her in a beautiful steel-blue dress and a feathered hat, bending over Anna to kiss her cheek. The whiff of flower-scented toilet water.

But she could never forget the wagon flipping over, the incredible agony of learning to live without Rose, of having to clean out Timmy's belongings. The sob she'd held back escaped in a gentle wail. "It hurts so much to lose the people you love. I think it would be easier to never care about people."

Praying at the cross had held her together through it all. She sucked in air, forcing back sobs she feared would tear her apart if she let them out. "I want the cross back."

"You'll get it. Trust me." His words sounded like a promise. He sat beside her and tucked his arm around her shoulders, pulling her close. "Not everyone leaves. And whatever you face, God will never leave you."

She searched his eyes, found an undeniable strength there. She let his promise, his strength reach deep into her being and filter into the dusty chambers she'd kept locked for years. The doors cracked open and she discovered that his smile had cleansed the room. He reminded her of where she got her strength—God, and he offered what she wanted and needed—his promise, his presence. She had only to take one small step into her fears to get it all.

His eyes filled with soft evening light. "I won't disappoint you."

She considered all he asked, measured it against what she had to lose. If it was only the cross, she could bear it. It was only a symbol of God's love and grace, which flowed freely without need of a damaged piece of wood.

But her heart...that was something else entirely.

She couldn't risk breaking it again. Doubted she would survive another time of loving and losing. Firmly she shoved the doors to the secret, dark places closed.

"I'm sure whatever you and Father decide will suit." She returned to the house, her insides more knotted than when she left, not from external stresses but from her inner turmoil.

Colby's chest muscles didn't release their vicelike tension until Anna slipped out the door and crossed the yard, her steps firm, her shoulders back, her spine rigid. Not until she entered the house did his thoughts spring into action.

She would trust her father, but refused to trust him. Not that he could blame her but his whole heart and soul longed for her love and trust.

Would she ever give it?

Would he ever be worthy of it?

He collapsed on the pew and buried his head in his hands. How could he prove he was different? *Lord God, show me a way.*

A few minutes later he left the church. With God's help he would not disappoint her again.

The next week was extremely busy with the day of the big celebration approaching. He pushed to get the final touches done to the repairs and enlisted the help of several of his friends. He also involved them with his plans for the cross.

A group of people descended on the church two days before the big event. In the cemetery, the men cut grass, pruned scraggly trees and scoured the tombstones. Inside, the women washed windows, scrubbed the floor and polished pews.

Colby cleaned up the materials and equipment from his work. As he stood back to admire the result, several people gathered at his side.

"Good as new." It was an elderly gent who had come inside to borrow a broom.

Mrs. Percy stood at the front of the sanctuary staring at the wall behind the pulpit, which had been returned from the room above the saloon. "Where's the cross? Shouldn't it be in place? Who is in charge of that detail?"

Pastor Caldwell stepped to the woman's side. "I am."

"Well, where is it?"

"We'll have it in place on the seventeenth." Despite the woman's fussing, the pastor refused to say anything more.

Colby met Anna's gaze across the room as she polished the piano. He felt in her look the same questions and doubts Mrs. Percy expressed.

Trust me. You'll see.

Asking her to trust him about the cross would give him a chance to prove himself. If she would only take this one little step perhaps she would see that more was possible.

They looked long and hard at each other until she finally jerked away, her attention claimed by someone wanting to know where to put a lamp.

Colby let out a frustrated sigh. Her expression had not shifted one bit. Would nothing ever change?

The work bee ended. The church was ready.

The next day another crowd descended and long plank tables soon filled the yard. Colby glimpsed Anna hurrying from one task to another.

Determined to speak to her, to urge her to trust him about the cross, he edged around the crowd, planning to catch her as she trotted toward the house for yet another errand.

He fell in beside her.

"Can I help?"

"All the seats need to be wiped off. Can you do that?"

"Of course. I'm willing to do whatever I can to ease

your responsibilities." He meant so much more than preparing for the birthday celebration.

He wanted to share her life.

"Anna, we had so much. Can't—"

She handed him a basin and a rag. "There's hot water in the reservoir."

He wanted to talk. But now was not the time and he filled the basin with water and wiped the benches.

After a community-style lunch with everyone contributing, Colby headed to the little shack where Tobias lived and where they'd been working on the cross.

Every street in town looked as if it had been swept. Every window gleamed. The storefronts had either been repainted or scrubbed, all in preparation for the upcoming birthday celebration. Colby felt pride at the way the town showed its solidarity, and excitement at the little part he'd had in the upcoming party.

Slink, Tobias and eight others crowded the tiny room when Colby arrived.

"It's almost finished," Slink said.

Colby admired the handwork. "It's beautiful." He hoped Anna would see the love that had gone into every detail.

Chapter Thirteen

June 17

The day the town had prepared and planned for the past six months.

Anna checked Dorrie. She looked perfect in her white dress and stockings. And it didn't matter in the least that she would come home at the end of the day dusty and soiled.

She stepped to the street, turned as she heard the church door click. Colby paused on the step.

Thankfully, the past few days had been busy, leaving them little opportunity to talk and even less to be alone, which suited her just fine. She wasn't sure how to deal with the longing to trust him, the feeling that somehow trusting God and trusting Colby were linked.

Because they felt so totally different. She had no trouble trusting God. He loved her. But trusting Colby was another matter entirely. She'd once thought he loved her. As she loved him. But she had misjudged his feelings.

Trusting him again would take time. And proof.

Dorrie saw him. "Da-da," she chirped, and Colby moved to take Dorrie's hand.

Anna's heartbeat picked up pace as she saw he meant to accompany them. Despite her misgivings, she could not pretend her love for him had died. Although she'd done her best to quench it.

They headed toward the heart of town.

The main street had been closed off and turned into a fairground. Booths lined each side of the street—one selling popcorn, another with a fishing game, yet another with a guess-your-weight challenge, and past that, a test-your-strength bell.

Alex came by with a couple of schoolmates as Colby and Anna stood in front of the strength game. "Try it out, Colby."

"We'll both do it." He paid a penny for each of them as a crowd gathered round cheering him on. He wiped his hands then grabbed the hammer and swung it over his head and hit the pad at the bottom. The metal indicator shot upward, stopped three quarters of the way up and dropped down.

The spectators jeered and laughed.

He handed the mallet to Alex.

Alex hesitated. "I can't do that good."

"No one expects you to, but you might be surprised at how well you do." Colby squeezed Alex's upper arm. "Feels to me like you've put on an inch or two here."

"You think so?"

"Give it a try."

Alex widened his stance and swung with all his might, groaning when the indicator went about halfway.

Colby clapped him on the back. "Let's see if your friends can beat that." He paid a penny for each of the boys gathered round. And when only one, a big lad, beat Alex, he grinned as widely as if Alex had handed him a trophy. "What did I tell you? Nothing like hard work to build muscles."

Alex puffed out his chest.

Anna hid a grin. It was nice to see Alex growing up. She sobered instantly. What had Laura said? He'd grow up and leave home. Anna wanted to pull him back and protect him from all that growing up meant.

But her sudden fear couldn't survive amidst all the fun of the day.

Colby grinned at the men crowded round him. "Who can ring the bell?"

Mike, a big farm boy, paid his penny and tried. He beat Colby by one mark.

Colby clapped. "Come on. Who's next?"

Men pushed closer, vying for a turn to pay for the chance to outdo each other.

Colby leaned over and whispered in Anna's ear, "This will end up making a lot of money."

The funds raised throughout the day were to go to providing a library.

Anna laughed as she understood he egged the others on until the bottle beside the machine reached almost to the top and Father came along and emptied it.

Colby certainly would benefit the fundraiser. The town could use a man like this changed Colby.

Watching him laugh and enjoy the crowd filled her heart with admiration, made the whole scene dance with color and enjoyment. She teetered on the edge of giving up her resistance to him.

But as Dorrie tugged at her hand, she was jerked back to reality. Colby could leave as quickly and easily as he returned. What was to stop him? Neither she nor Dorrie had been enough in the past.

What drove him away?

Responsibilities? Her? She must know before she released the locks on her heart.

Dorrie grabbed her father's hand. "Go," she said.

Colby and Anna exchanged glances and laughed. Their gazes clung. Anna's cheeks grew warm at the look in his eyes. And then Dorrie jerked at them.

She blinked back her feelings. How easily she forgot to be cautious.

They moved on to a puppet show. Dorrie screamed with laughter when the puppets tripped over each other and flew through the air.

They moved on to the bake and craft sale being held under shelter of the hotel portico. Anna picked up a pretty pinafore.

"Did you make this, Miss Weaver?"

Miss Weaver chuckled, a merry sound. "Please call me Grace. And, yes, I made that little thing. I seem to have more time on my hands than I know what to do with."

"It's beautiful." It would fit Dorrie and although she needed a new one, Anna could make one for far less. She went to put it down but Colby plucked it from her fingers and held it in front of Dorrie.

"It's the right size, isn't it?"

"Yes, but—"

"I'll take it." He paid Grace.

They walked on. "I planned to make her a new one," Anna whispered. "It wouldn't cost near that much."

"I thought I'd save you the effort. Seems to me you work hard enough as it is."

No one ever worried that she might have too much work to do. No one even offered to help. Knowing Colby noticed made Anna almost stumble on the wooden sidewalk, not because it was rough but because of her surprise.

She pinched her nose to stop the sting of tears.

Thankfully the mayor spared her from embarrassing herself.Using a bullhorn, he announced games and races over at the schoolyard. Much of the crowd drifted that direction.

If only she could give her heart fully to Colby she could enjoy his support and encouragement every day. For a moment, the idea almost capsized her stubbornness. But again, her doubts prevailed.

A race for toddlers was announced first.

Colby squatted in front of Dorrie. "Do you want to run?"

She nodded. "I run." She took off instantly.

Colby grabbed her. "Wait a minute. We'll go to the start line."

Anna laughed as he tried to explain the event to Dorrie who babbled and squirmed, trying to escape.

"I run, Da-da." Her feet churned as Colby lifted her off the ground and carried her to the marked spot.

Anna giggled at mothers and fathers trying to sort out children under the age of three and explain the concept of a race.

"Go to the finish line," Colby said. "I'll head her in your direction."

Anna did as he suggested and soon one parent of each child did the same.

Someone hollered go and the children were released.

"Dorrie, come to Mama," Anna called. A dozen

other parents yelled at their offspring. She wondered how anyone could make out who called whom. The names were indiscernible in the melee.

Dorrie veered toward a little boy with a ball in his hands.

"Dorrie, no. This way."

Dorrie ignored her and tackled the boy. They tumbled to the ground, the boy shrieking for his mother.

Anna shook her head. She found Colby's face in the crowd and laughed at his stunned look.

Then they joined the race to separate the two. Colby got there first and scooped Dorrie off her victim. She clutched the ball triumphantly.

"Ball. Mine."

"'Fraid not, honey. Give it back."

Dorrie held on with all her might. "Mine."

Anna stood a few inches away but didn't intervene. She couldn't wait to see how Colby would deal with this stubborn side of his sweet little daughter.

Meanwhile the little boy continued to scream as his parents tried to console him.

"You have to give it back," Colby insisted. "It belongs to that little boy."

"No." Dorrie stuck out her chin.

Anna knew the look and settled back on her heels. Colby had two choices—wrestle the ball from Dorrie's hands, or divert her so she let it go.

Colby looked at her, silently pleading for help. Grinning, she shrugged. *She's your daughter. You deal with her.*

He apparently got her silent message for he sighed and rolled his eyes, which sent Anna into a fit of giggles.

"Dorrie, my dear sweet child, if you give back the ball I'll buy you a candy stick."

Dorrie looked at the ball, looked at her father as if to measure his sincerity.

"Ball." She handed it to the sobbing boy. "Canny," she said to Colby.

Colby grinned triumphantly as they joined Anna.

"Bribery," she murmured. "I can't believe you'd stoop to bribery."

"I was about ready to do anything to end that scene." He grinned at Anna and they both laughed.

And without her permission her heart claimed the day for its own to enjoy. Even if he left again, she would at least have this one day to cherish.

They found a candy booth and Colby purchased a red-and-white barber-striped candy then they returned to the games in time to hear a race for twelve to fourteen-year-old boys announced.

Alex headed toward the start line then stopped, uncertainty apparent in his expression.

Colby handed Dorrie to Anna and hurried to Alex's side.

She followed, curious about what he intended.

He leaned close to Alex.

Anna strained to hear his soft words. "This is great practice. You can see how all the things I taught you work in a real race. Never mind if you win or lose. Concentrate on your technique."

Alex nodded and strode to the start, his head high.

Anna shot Colby a look of thanks but his gaze remained on Alex. He mouthed words. She realized he repeated instructions he must have taught Alex.

"That's it. Get into a good position."

Ready. Set. Go. They were off. When Alex gained the lead from the first step, Anna cheered so loud Dorrie jumped. "Look, sweetie. Alex is running. He might win."

Dorrie yelled loudly though she likely had no idea why.

Colby shot a glance at his noisy daughter, his gaze brushed Anna and they laughed as if the moment held wonderful significance.

She hoped it did.

Alex led the pack. A bigger lad gained but Alex crossed the finish line first. His grin at winning rivaled the sunshine for brightness.

Alex had always been shy about competing, didn't like to do anything where he might fail. Anna had never known such pride in her brother marred only by the certainty that this was another step away from her.

"Now for all the men."

Colby acted like he didn't hear.

Anna nudged him. "This is your race."

"Nah, I don't think so."

"Of course you'll run."

Alex reached his side. "Come on, Colby. Show them how it's done."

Colby scrubbed the back of his hand over his chin. "I don't know. Don't you think I'm too grown up for this?"

Alex grabbed his hand and dragged him away.

Colby chuckled as they trotted over to the start.

Anna moved down the side where she had an unobstructed view. Colby flashed her a grin that shot through all her defenses and landed somewhere south of her heart. She loved him. Despite uncertainty about the future, despite everything, she loved him.

Today she would simply accept the fact.

Tomorrow she would deal with reality.

She cheered as the race began. He slowed as he drew even with her to flash her another grin and it cost him the race. Not that he seemed to mind. He was in high spirits as he rejoined her.

They watched the horse races. They shared a huge bag of popcorn. Anna realized she would have enjoyed anything in Colby's company, knowing she loved him, all doubts and fears silenced for the day.

Later they bought sandwiches and pie at the food booth, then it was time to go home and prepare for the evening activities.

Anna's face stung from too long in the sun. And Dorrie's cheeks were far too red even though Anna had tried to keep a bonnet on her. She sponged their faces carefully and put on a clean dress. She put the new pinafore over Dorrie's dress and smoothed her hair.

In the other rooms she could hear Father and Alex preparing.

She smiled at Dorrie. "We're ready."

Dorrie nodded. "I wedy."

They hurried to the church. Already the sanctuary was crowded. More people gathered outside. Anna made her way to the front and handed Dorrie to Laura.

She began to play the hymns, her throat tightening when Colby joined in, playing the mouth organ as he stood to the side of the piano. Their gazes connected and she smiled. Something wrenched inside her, a combination of sweetness and fear. She'd always protected her heart. Life had taught the value of doing so. But her love for Colby could not be denied. For whatever time she had, she would enjoy it and pray she would survive if he left.

The music drifted around her and through her. This was one thing they shared without reservation. She let him take the melody and improvised an accompaniment. A hush fell over the crowd. She knew the congregation enjoyed the music as much as she and Colby.

Father went to the pulpit. He welcomed everyone then announced the first hymn.

Anna could enjoy sharing music with Colby for a few more minutes.

She'd prepared a solo, practicing with Colby accompanying her on the mouth organ and went to the pulpit when Father nodded to her. The hymn she'd chosen was an old Charles Wesley one, "O for a thousand tongues to sing my great Redeemer's praise."

It fit perfectly with her feelings and for this occasion of meeting in the church again.

She finished and sat beside Laura, her heart so full of joy and love it forced tears to her eyes. She blinked them away.

Colby slid in beside her.

She daren't look at him even when Dorrie scrambled from Laura's knee across Anna and straight to her father's lap.

Anna felt Laura watching her and composed her face before glancing at her and giving a quick shrug as if to say what did it matter if Dorrie enjoyed her father's attention?

Father preached a brief sermon on God's faithfulness in sparing them from disaster in the fire and in bringing them back to this place of worship.

"And now for the final act of dedication."

Father's words made Anna sit up straight. They had

gone through the program many times and it was to end now.

Colby plunked Dorrie to Anna's lap and hurried down the aisle.

She couldn't imagine where he went in such a hurry, then her attention was diverted by a murmur at the back and she turned to see what caused the disturbance.

Before she could see any cause, uncertain voices began to sing, "Amazing grace, how sweet the sound." The song, sung in deep male voices without instrumental accompaniment, drew her attention to the door.

A parade of men entered, a cross over their shoulders.

Anna recognized the men as those who had been in and out of the church the past month. They still wore shabby clothes but their faces glowed as they marched up the aisle carrying the cross. Colby was the last man in line.

She swallowed hard as they stepped to the platform and lowered the cross. They turned it for all to see and she gasped. The original cross, scarred by the fire, formed the center of a new one, blending seamlessly into the new structure.

Colby cleared his throat. "The cross is scarred. As it should be. I don't think it was a thing of beauty so much as a crude rough instrument of torture on which my Savior died. He died for all of us here. You, me and these men standing with me. Each of us on this stage has found mercy and forgiveness at the foot of an old rugged cross. Not this one. This is only a reminder. But at the cross upon which Jesus died. However, I know some people have found comfort from looking at this reminder of God's love."

He glanced at Anna and flashed a quick smile.

She could barely see him through the sheen of tears.

"My hope and prayer is that many more of you will find comfort, mercy and forgiveness at the cross."

He signaled the men and they hung the cross on the back wall.

"Have you noticed the border?" Colby asked the audience.

Anna scrubbed her eyes so she could see clearly. An intricately carved design formed a beautiful border.

"You can't see it from where you sit but this border is names, dates and verses. These men have come to the Lord and this is their testimony of salvation."

He nodded and one by one the men stepped to the cross and touched a place.

"Slink, May 25. 'For by grace are ye saved.'"

"Tobias, May 26. 'For God so loved the world.'"

"Luke, June 1. 'He gave the right to become children of God.'"

By the time all the men said their names and read their verses, tears trickled down Anna's cheeks. She heard others sniffing and wondered if there could be a dry eye in the place.

Colby went to the cross. "Colby, May 20. 'If any man be in Christ, he is a new creature.'"

Joy flowed with Anna's tears. God had changed Colby. She needed no further proof. She gladly, willingly trusted him.

He met her eyes across the space of the platform and smiled. *For you.* She heard the silent words. He'd done this for her. He'd repaired the cross so she could remember the times she'd found strength. It was a wonderful gift, blessing her and others, as well.

The men paraded back down the aisle. As they passed, many reached out from the pews to shake their hands. Colby followed them out.

Anna had to wait for the others to depart before she could make it outside. She wanted to find Colby but the crowd kept them apart.

Mr. Steves sat in the place of honor. A big slab of birthday cake practically filled the table in front of him. People filed by extending best wishes as they made their way past to secure a place at one of the benches.

She tried to find Colby in the crowd, caught his eyes across the yard before someone stepped into her path. She shifted, searched for him where she'd last seen him but he had moved. She saw him to one side.

He tipped his chin, signaling her to stay there. He headed in her direction, weaving in and out of the people who crowded around for a chance to speak to Mr. Steves.

She stood watching as he closed the distance between them, her joy mounting with every moment. God had graciously answered her prayer.

Colby finally made it to Anna's side.

She had so much to tell him but didn't know where to start. "Thank you," she whispered. "The cross is beautiful." She meant so much more but couldn't form a solid thought.

"I'm glad you like it. I hoped you would."

And then the opportunity passed as the crowd sang "Happy Birthday."

Miss Weaver had taken over organizing the tea and when Anna went to the table to help serve, the woman shooed her away.

"You go look after that sweet baby."

So she returned to Colby's side. They sat down, Dorrie between them as the ladies served cake to each and everyone.

She wanted to say more. Find words to describe what she felt but the crowd hushed as the mayor gave a speech. Other dignitaries spoke and Mr. Steves responded with a gracious thank you but Anna hardly heard as she watched Colby feed Dorrie cake. She was consumed with a love so full, so sweet, so surprisingly powerful she could hardly think as longing rose up within her, a need to belong to him wholly and completely, be with him always, sharing the joys of each day, supporting each other through the hard times.

Her heart seemed to swell with every beat until she felt nothing but the emotion of the moment.

The clapping as Mr. Steves finished his speech startled her. She scrambled to pull her thoughts back to where they belonged—thinking about her responsibilities—as people pressed in around them, some shaking Colby's hand, thanking him for the job on the church or the gift of the cross. Others paused to thank Anna for her song, or ask about washing dishes from the tea.

She directed the cleanup. When she looked up, Colby was gone.

Chapter Fourteen

As Colby followed the men to help set up fireworks he couldn't stop grinning. Anna had been pleased with how he'd fixed the cross. Her eyes glistened when she thanked him. Her gaze seemed to cling to him, following his every move.

He knew she wanted to say more but there was too much commotion. It would have to wait.

Later, his job done, he found Anna sitting on a bench, Dorrie asleep in her arms. The way she smiled up at him, her eyes laced with gladness and welcome, his heart forgot it was supposed to beat regularly. Instead, it hesitated then pulsed blood through his veins with such force he felt it pound against his eardrum. And welcomed the noise.

He sat close to her, stroking Dorrie's damp head. "It's been a big day for her."

"I'm afraid we'll pay for it tomorrow. She doesn't like having her routine changed."

Her breath, soft and alluring, whispered over his cheek. He wanted nothing more than to wrap his arms around this woman who had stolen his heart, and this baby who was flesh of his flesh, to hold them close forever, take care of them, protect them—could he? Or would he fail?

He shoved the doubts away. Tonight was for celebration and joy. He shifted, leaning one elbow on the table as he faced her. "I'll help with her."

The smile in her eyes spoke welcome and home.

Home. What he'd always wanted.

What he dreamed would be possible with sweet Anna and now, as well, his little Dorrie.

They had to talk but not here. Not now when others dashed by or stopped to speak to them. Not with his precious daughter sleeping in Anna's arms.

The light faded.

"Time for the fireworks," he murmured.

The sky lit with flashes. Smoke trailed after the light and a deep-throated thunder followed.

The crowd clapped and cheered.

Dorrie wakened, crying and throwing herself backward.

Colby lifted her from Anna's lap. "Look at the lights. Fireworks."

Another burst filled the sky and Dorrie stopped crying so suddenly she coughed.

The show went on for twenty minutes, then people began to disperse. Someone had lit lanterns along the street to help the crowd find its way to their buggies and wagons.

Dorrie started to fuss.

"Time for bed," Anna said.

"I'll take her in."

Dorrie was inconsolable by the time they made their way to the house.

Anna reached for her. "She won't settle when she's this upset. I'll have to rock her to sleep." She smiled at Colby as she bounced the crying child. "Good night."

He patted Dorrie's head. He didn't want to end the day but Dorrie needed her bed and her mama. "I'll see you tomorrow."

She nodded and left him to find his own way out.

He made his way to the shack he'd been sharing with Tobias. As he opened the door a gangly youth rushed toward him.

"Mr. Bloxham. Mr. Bloxham. I been looking all over for you. Got a telegram. Real important."

Colby rescued the yellow bit of paper the boy waved about and quickly read it. He grunted and scrubbed a hand over his chin.

Tobias watched. "Bad news?"

"I have to go. Take this to Miss Caldwell first thing in the morning."

Anna fell asleep with her lips curved in a smile. Tomorrow she and Colby would find a time and place to talk. All evening she had turned to him, knowing her eyes brimmed with promise and acceptance. His had responded with such joy she found herself overflowing with laughter. Thankfully others seemed to be in a celebratory mood and didn't think her actions inappropriate.

Something jerked her from a sound sleep. Her room was dark. She listened, straining to hear any unusual sound.

The sound came again. A choking cry.

Dorrie! Something about the child's cry sounded terribly wrong.

She raced for the baby's bedroom but even before

she stepped through the door she heard the laborious breathing.

Hurrying, she lit the lamp and bent over the crib. It took only a glance to see Dorrie's glassy eyes and flushed cheeks. "Poor baby. No wonder you were fussy."

The first thing she had to do was tackle the fever. No, perhaps she needed to address the breathing first. She raced to the kitchen, threw coal in the stove and put a kettle to boil.

As she waited for it to sing she rushed back to the bedroom, dragged the rocking chair close to the crib and used a sheet to prepare a steam tent. Dorrie would protest but it had to be done.

She raced back for the steaming kettle and a basin that she put on a little stool in front of the chair then picked up Dorrie, moaning at how the little one strained for each breath. She stripped her down to her diaper. She poured the boiling water into the basin, pulled the sheet over them and held Dorrie over the steam.

Sweat soon poured from every pore in Anna's body but she continued to pour in hot water until the kettle was drained.

As soon as the steam cooled, she returned Dorrie to her bed and hurried to get a basin of tepid water. Frantically she set to sponging the child, praying desperately for the fever to subside, for Dorrie's lungs to open.

Dawn spilled pink light over the horizon and Anna saw no improvement. Her worry gave way to fear as real and cruel as a fist to her stomach. "Please, God. Take the fever from her. Ease her breathing."

Alex stumbled sleepy-eyed to the room. "She sick?"

"Yes. Get Father."

He stared at her still half-asleep.

"Hurry."

He suddenly came to life and ran down the hall. A few minutes later Father rushed in. "I can hear her breathing from my bedroom."

She pressed her lips together and struggled to control the sobs tearing at her throat.

Father crossed the room and took her in his arms. "Father in heaven, our Almighty Savior and the Great Physician, please touch Dorrie's body and free her lungs."

Anna shuddered. "I'm afraid."

Father hugged her. "What do you need me to do?"

"Get Colby. He needs to be here."

"I'll go right away." He squeezed her shoulders. "Have faith." Then he hurried out.

She heard the front door close after him. Colby would soon be here. She had never needed him more or wanted him more desperately.

"Alex, get me a bucket of warm water." All night she had alternately sponged Dorrie to reduce the fever and steamed her to ease her breathing.

Alex hurried to do her bidding. He hovered at Dorrie's bedside, his eyes wide, his fear palpable. "She looks so sick. I'm scared."

"Me, too." But her efforts were focused on conquering the fever.

A few minutes later she heard the door open and close. She turned to face Colby, ready to throw herself into his arms. Ready to accept his help and support in fighting for Dorrie's life.

Father stood there. Alone.

"Where's Colby?" Something must have detained him.

Father's expression filled with regret and sorrow. "He's gone."

"How long will he be?"

"Anna, he's gone. Left. I managed to waken Tobias but he was there alone. He said Colby rode out last night."

Gone. Just like always. And she had trusted him again. Moreover, she and Dorrie needed him. She pressed her fist to her mouth to keep from crying. With great effort she tossed aside her pain and disappointment and turned back to Dorrie. They would manage without him.

She pushed aside the wail that demanded how. How would she survive? Especially if something happened to Dorrie?

She had no one but herself to blame for believing him.

For a moment she fought for control. She'd done this before. She could do it again.

"I'm sorry," Father said.

"What time is it?"

"Five."

"Go wake the doctor and tell him he's needed."

The doctor came, said to keep on with what she was doing, and left again, promising to stop in later in the day.

Anna wondered how much longer Dorrie could survive her struggle. Nothing but fighting for Dorrie's life mattered.

She would not think of the pain of Colby leaving again.

The hours slipped by marked by trips to get fresh water, to try and dribble a few drops into Dorrie's parched mouth, to steam her until Anna felt like a pile of runny mashed potatoes.

She was vaguely aware of others coming and going, bringing her water or towels or a drink for herself and

Dorrie. She knew the doctor stopped in again and then night fell and she was alone.

But she would not think.

Not of Colby leaving nor of the possibility of losing Dorrie.

"You have to get better, sweetie," she urged and redoubled her efforts to fight the fever, get Dorrie's lungs open.

Morning came unnoticed until Alex and Father slipped into the room, their faces revealing a worry that matched her own.

Again the doctor came by. He shook his head. "If she doesn't turn around soon…"

Anna gave him a look of disdain. "She will." She had to.

Father returned some time later. "Miss Weaver is here."

Grace stepped into the room. "I'm here to help. Now you go rest."

"I couldn't. What if…?"

Grace put her arm around Anna. "You must take care of yourself or who will take care of Dorrie when she's better?"

Anna could have hugged her for saying that and allowed herself to be drawn away. "You'll waken me if…"

"Trust me. I will get you at any change."

So weary she could barely take off her shoes, Anna fell to her bed. Colby had said the same words. *Trust me. Oh, Colby, where are you? Why must you leave me every time I need you desperately?*

"Anna, wake up. Hurry." Father shook her.

"Dorrie?" Was it bad news?

She bolted from her bed and almost fell to the floor

as her knees turned to pudding. Clinging to Father's arm she hurried to Dorrie's room.

Dorrie lay on the narrow cot in the corner of the room so still Anna couldn't detect any sign of breathing.

Grace sat on a chair at her side, her look so full of sorrow that Anna cried out a protest. Every organ in her body spasmed with incredible pain.

Then Dorrie sucked in a raspy breath, her chest drawing in cruelly as she fought to get air into her lungs.

Anna fell to her knees beside the cot and cradled her arms around Dorrie's hot little body.

Grace smoothed her hand over Anna's back. "She's fighting very hard."

"She can't die. She can't. I won't let her. God can't take her from me." She stopped the words that poured forth.

Father patted her back. "Anna, don't blame God for our losses."

"Who can I blame?"

"Death is just part of life."

She rolled her head back and forth in denial. "Not untimely death."

Grace pressed a hand to Anna's head. "Nothing can separate us from God's love. In the dark times we learn to trust Him most and find His comfort sweetest."

Father continued to pat her back. "God loves us. We just need to trust Him."

Anna buried her face in the quilt covering the cot and clamped her lips together. Father would be shocked at the words flooding her mind. But what kind of loving God took away those she cared about? He could have stopped Colby from leaving. He could have prevented Rose and Timmy from dying. And He could, if He chose, heal Dorrie. Her fists curled into the fabric at Dorrie's side and she hung on. She would not let this child go. God could not have her. Her teeth clenched so hard it sent a pain straight to the top of her head but she would not let go. Never.

Dorrie shuddered.

Anna's throat clogged with a rush of emotion. She lifted her head. Tears stung the back of her eyes but she would not let them escape.

Dorrie lay quiet and still. Peaceful even. Was she gone? Hot floodwaters of grief swept through her, grabbing at her heart with vicious fingers, sucking at her limbs as she fought the undercurrent threatening to drown her. She wouldn't fight anymore. She'd simply let the waters wash her away.

Dorrie coughed.

Anna jumped, startled by the unexpected sound. Was it the last dying response? She placed her hand on Dorrie's chest. *My baby. My baby. How can I go on without your sweet presence?* She opened her mouth and closed it again and again as if she could pump out her overwhelming sorrow.

The little chest beneath her palm rose and fell.

She stared at her hand. Had she imagined it? No. It rose and fell again. "She's breathing." Her words were barely a whisper. "She's breathing." Anna jumped to her feet, laughing and crying. "She's breathing."

She hugged Father. "She's breathing."

Father's face was wet with tears. "Praise God. Praise God."

Anna turned to Grace. "She's breathing. She's alive."

Grace, her eyes glittering with tears, hugged Anna. "God has blessed your faith."

Her faith? She'd had none. Only doubts and anger. Why had she not trusted God? Shame crackled at the edge of her joy.

The doctor came, proclaimed it a wonder that Dorrie had turned a corner toward getting well.

Dorrie was alive. Her breathing rattled but at last filled her lungs.

She lived. Anna's joy knew no end even though she didn't deserve it. When she should have trusted, she doubted. But thanks to God, He hadn't punished her lack of faith.

Dorrie was weak and listless. Anna had her hands full caring for her in the following days and welcomed Grace's help running the home.

She gratefully cared for Dorrie, finding unlimited patience with her fussiness.

But in the pit of her stomach lay a boulder of guilt. Hadn't she learned to trust God at a young age? Wasn't it trust that bore her through those dark days of sorrow when Rose and Timmy died?

Who was she that she could forget God's faithfulness when she needed it most?

Grace spent a few hours each day helping with meals. She had left for the day with supper in the oven saying she needed to help her sister.

Anna sat at the table holding Dorrie, tenderly spooning warm porridge into her.

The door burst open without so much as a knock and Colby stood with the light behind him.

Anna blinked. "What are you doing here? How long are you around for this time?" She felt no welcome. No gladness. Only a long dark ache. Why did he keep riding in and out of her life? How much more could she take?

"I came as soon as I heard. As soon as I got back."

Anna returned her attention to Dorrie, ignoring Colby. They'd said it all before. Nothing had changed. Nothing had been resolved.

Colby crossed the room in two strides and knelt at her side. "Oh, Dorrie, my poor little girl." His voice thickened as he stroked her face.

"Da-da," Dorrie croaked and gave a crooked smile.

He lifted his head to look at Anna. "Was it very hard?"

She didn't answer, only gave him a disinterested shrug.

"I wish I had been here."

"Seems you have the habit of leaving just when things get tough."

Cradling Dorrie's hands in his, Colby sat back on his heels. "You read the telegram. You know where I went."

She snorted. "I saw no telegram."

"Tobias was supposed to give it to you." He watched her face and saw her obvious denial then sighed. "I should have known better than to expect him to remember. Anna, I didn't leave."

She turned away, resumed feeding Dorrie.

"Listen to me. Remember that letter I wrote to my friend Hugh?"

He waited but she gave no indication whether or not she did. But of course she did.

"I got a telegram from the sheriff telling me Hugh had been injured and I was to come immediately if I wanted to see him before he died."

A little spark of sympathy flickered in the depths of her solitude. "I'm sorry."

Colby grinned. "He didn't die. I made sure of that. Brought him back with me. He's recuperating in one of the hotel rooms right now."

She nodded, continued feeding Dorrie.

"Don't you understand, Anna? I didn't leave. I only went to help a friend."

"I see." But nothing inside her cared. She couldn't take any more leaving or worrying about him leaving.

When he asked, she let him hold Dorrie and feed her. She let him stay to tuck her into bed. She let him kneel at her crib and pray.

But she could not let him into her heart.

Colby knelt in the church and poured out his heart to God. He'd been back several days. He rejoiced to see Dorrie daily growing stronger. But Anna had shut herself up inside solid fort walls and would not let him near. Not that he could blame her. She had every reason to doubt him.

Just as he doubted himself.

He had failed so many times. He'd failed to protect his mother. He'd failed to protect Nora. He'd failed his friends. He'd failed Anna over and over.

Getting to Hugh and helping was the one time he'd managed to make a step toward undoing the damage he'd done.

But would he ever be able to undo the harm he'd done with Anna? Did he have anything to offer her or would he, when push came to shove, fail her in a big way?

Part of him considered leaving now, before she could be more greatly disappointed in him.

But he was through running from his fears and failures. With God's help.

A little later he stepped into the glaring sunlight, mounted his horse and rode toward the hotel to check on Hugh who grew stronger each day. He planned to be back at the Caldwell house when Dorrie woke from her nap so he could feed her and hold her. To think this precious child had almost died. It filled his heart with praise that God had chosen to spare her.

When he arrived at the house, Grace was there. "Now here's Colby," she said to Anna. "Let him take you for a walk." She turned to Colby. "She needs to get outside. Get some fresh air before she gets sick, too."

Here was the chance Colby had prayed for. "Can't have you getting sick. Who would look after everyone?" He reached for her hand, tucked it around his elbow and was out the door before she could protest.

She jerked free. "I don't want to go for a walk."

"Do it for Dorrie." She sure could be stubborn.

"Fine." Anna faced forward and marched down the street as if ordered to the gallows.

Colby kept pace. "Look, Anna. I know you're angry with me. I know you've been through a lot with Dorrie. I can't imagine how scared you must have been but—"

"Please let me enjoy the fresh air."

Colby sighed. She was so distant and unreachable. "Don't you know it hurts me to know I wasn't here when you and Dorrie needed me? I would never have gone after Hugh if I'd known."

She nodded briskly without turning her attention from the path before her. "Good to know."

"I never thought to see you so bitter."

That made her stop and face him, her eyes flaring

with an emotion that he could not identify. "I am not bitter."

"Sure could fool me."

"I'm—" She shook her head. "I'm not bitter."

Maybe if she met Hugh she would understand. Hugh had said he might venture out into the sunshine. He directed their steps toward the hotel and smiled when he saw Hugh tipped back in one of the chairs on the boardwalk in front of the hotel.

"There's my friend. Let's say hello." She made no protest as they crossed the distance between them. He made the introductions.

"Pleased to meet you, ma'am," Hugh said. "Did this here man tell you how he saved my life?"

Chapter Fifteen

Anna nodded. Hugh was clean-shaven, wore clean clothes, had his foot swathed in heavy bandages, and sported bruises and cuts on his face and hands. "Looks like you might have lost a war."

Hugh chuckled. "Got run over by a loaded wagon. Would have died if Colby hadn't shown up and forced me to get better." He shifted his amused glance to Colby. "Maybe forcing that old quack of a doctor to show a little mercy helped, too."

"I owed you."

Hugh and Colby stared at each other, sharing some secret.

"If you ever owed me the debt is paid."

Anna shifted her gaze from one to the other and when neither seemed about to share any details, she decided to press for more. "What's this debt thing?"

Colby shook his head and shot Hugh a look rife with warning but Hugh ignored him. "I saved his hide a time or two. One time especially that he's referring to—"

"Anna, let's get back. I want to feed Dorrie."

Anna shook off his hand. "In a minute." Hugh knew

something and she wanted to find out what. Perhaps it would explain what had sent Colby running again.

"He kind of went downhill after Nora died."

Anna rolled her eyes at the understatement and Hugh chuckled.

"Yeah, you're right. He fell into a hole. A deep hole."

Colby made a dissenting noise and tried to turn Anna toward home.

She shied away. "So what happened?"

"You mean besides the drinking and carousing?"

She nodded, assuming there was more.

"One night he decided it was the doctor's fault Nora died and he headed out to kill the man. I think he would have if I hadn't stopped him."

Anna gasped and stared at Colby. "Is that true?" She couldn't imagine him a murderer. "You would have hung."

"I was drunk. As soon as I sobered up, I left."

That explained a lot.

"Now can we go?" He waved an arm down the street and gave her an expectant look that said it was time.

She fell in beside him, her mind flooded with questions. "Why did you blame the doctor? He did the best he could." She remembered how she felt when Dorrie was so sick. "Never mind. I know how frustrated I was that he could do nothing when Dorrie almost died."

"I didn't really blame him." He sounded weary— soul weary.

Her heart went out to him. He'd lost his wife. He'd been left with an infant daughter to care for. And he had no one. At least she had her father and brother when Rose died. And later, she'd baby Dorrie to tend to. She'd been so busy with the baby she had little time for Colby. Nor patience with his drinking.

Colby went on in low tones. "It was just easier to blame him then blame myself."

"Why would you blame anyone?" Birthing babies was difficult work. Women often died doing it.

"'Cause it was my job to make sure she was safe. And I didn't."

He confused her. "How can you be responsible for things out of your control? I don't understand."

He pushed out a noisy gust of air. "Guess it's a man thing."

She considered the idea. True, men and women had different roles. Women typically cared for the home and children. Men…she'd never considered their role and she did so now. And, yes, perhaps they were expected to provide and protect. So when things went wrong, things out of their control, did they feel they had failed? It was a new thought. "I don't think anyone has the right to blame a man if he encounters things beyond his control. Even things that threaten his family."

"Seems there is always something a person could do."

"Like what?"

"Something."

She understood he felt powerless and hated it. Maybe rather than face his inability to change things, he left. "Colby, why did you leave your home?"

"What home?"

"With your father. I know he beat you but why did you leave?"

"Because I couldn't stop him from hurting Ma." The

words burst forth as if shot from a canon. "It made my ma leave. I couldn't stop it."

She ground to a halt and faced him. His fist clenched into knots. His face creased into sorrowful lines. "You were a kid."

"I wanted to stop him. I couldn't."

"So you left."

"Comes a time a person can't look at himself in the mirror."

She wondered how many times he would see his reflection, not like what he saw and leave. She wasn't about to pin any hopes on his staying.

Colby jerked to a halt and almost stumbled.

She watched the color drain from his face. And then he blinked and pulled his hat lower. She turned to see what caused this reaction. Didn't seem to be anything out of the ordinary except a stranger riding down the street—a big man with an unfriendly turn to his mouth.

He drew closer and pulled his horse toward them to glower at Colby. Then he shifted to study Anna with such intensity her face burned.

The air crackled with tension. Anna held her breath, wondering what this man wanted with them.

He gave a mocking smile. "Colby. You look a mite surprised."

"I thought you were dead."

"I don't die as easy as you hoped."

Anna's tongue stuck to the sides of her mouth. She struggled to focus her thoughts. Colby knew this man?

Colby grabbed her elbow and steered her toward home. She lurched along at his side.

"Be seeing you 'round," the man called after them.

They were almost at the manse when Anna jerked away to face him. "Who was that?"

"Lew. Someone from my past."

"Why did you think he was dead?"

"Never mind." He hurried on, urging her forward.

There was something sinister and wicked about that Lew fella. He knew Colby too well for comfort. Was he one of Colby's associates? What did he want here? Had he come to persuade Colby to ride away with him?

She almost tripped and Colby grabbed her elbow to steady her. She yanked back her arm and confronted him. "Just when I thought I was beginning to understand what makes you tick…" Would she never get past an endless hope that this time, perhaps now, he would stay and be the man she needed? Her heart turned to coal. "Just make sure he stays away from Dorrie." She forced her wooden legs into the house and closed the door to lean against it, praying she wouldn't collapse.

Grace stepped from the kitchen. "You're back." She sprang forward. "What happened? You look like you're going to be ill."

"I guess I'm more worn out than I realized." She straightened, hoping her quivering knees would not fail her. She knew Colby had been involved in unsavory things while he was away. She'd heard plenty of tales about his wild escapades. But she never thought to encounter that sort of man because of him.

She wanted so badly to believe he'd changed that she looked for nothing but proof.

Oh, Lord. Protect us from his friends. Protect my heart.

It was too late for her heart. Had always been too late. She'd loved him since she was fourteen. She knew beneath that rough exterior, beyond his shameful past, lay a Colby full of tenderness and understanding. Unfortunately his past seemed too full to overcome, his exterior too tough. Yet—her faith protested—wasn't God able to do a work in his life? What was the verse Grace had mentioned in her debate with Mrs. Percy? "He who has begun a good work in you will complete it." She'd pray for God to complete His work in Colby's life. Make him able to resist whatever pull this man from his past had on him. Stay and be the kind of father Dorrie needed.

And she'd confine her thoughts to that. No more. She could not, would not, let herself care about him as anything more than Dorrie's father.

She stepped into the kitchen where Dorrie sat picking at some bread and butter. *Oh, Dorrie. How can I keep you safe?* That man, that friend of Colby's, frightened her. She wanted to grab Dorrie and hold her close.

Colby's thoughts went round and round. He'd left Lew and Harv and everything they stood for behind. He hoped Anna would never learn of what he'd been, what he'd done. Now Lew was here. But where was Harv?

He got his horse and rode through town. Rode a mile or two in each direction. But he saw no sign of Lew. Perhaps the man had moved on. But the thought gave him no comfort. Lew had come for a purpose. Likely revenge. After all, a man wasn't expected to like being shot.

No, Lew would be back.

Colby had taken part-time work at the feed store and headed that direction where he spent several hours. Normally he enjoyed the way work made thinking unnecessary, but today he found no such respite from his thoughts.

He knew the depravity of Lew's heart.

And he feared for Anna and Dorrie.

Might be best for them if he rode out this day, but unless he could be certain Lew followed hard on his heels, Colby would not be leaving Anna and Dorrie unprotected.

Suppertime came and Colby shared the meal with Hugh. He told Hugh about Lew. Telling the story only increased his restlessness.

He pushed back from the table. "I have to check on Anna and the baby. Make sure they're okay."

He rode over. Circled the house. Picked his way down the trail by the river but saw no sign of Lew. His absence only made Colby more concerned. Better Lew out in the open then Lew sneaking about where Colby couldn't watch him.

Still uneasy he returned to his quarters. Twice more before dark he rode out to check on things. No Lew. But at least Anna and Dorrie were safe inside the four solid walls of the house.

The next morning, he was up early and out to repeat his rounds. He came on signs of a campfire near where he had stayed by the river. The ashes were still warm. Could be anyone but he was convinced it was Lew.

Much as he wanted to stop in and see Anna and Dorrie, he dare not. The less Lew saw of where he went and who he saw, the better for all concerned.

Poor Mr. Rawlings must have wondered at Colby that day. He excused himself so often to ride down the street and check on Anna the man would be starting to think Colby didn't intend to put in a full day's work. Or even a reasonable portion of a day.

Once he saw Anna crossing between the house and the church. She glanced his direction, saw it was him, paused a moment then hurried into the shelter of the building.

He couldn't blame her for her caution.

For two days he stayed away. And in those two days he saw little clues that suggested Lew was about—a bit of rag tied to the tree across from the manse, another warm campfire, an *X* slashed into the door Colby went in and out as he did his work for Mr. Rawlings.

The third day he informed his boss he wouldn't be in to work. He planned to find Lew and settle whatever score the man felt needed to be settled.

Anna peeked through the window. That man was there. Lew. He flitted in and out of sight throughout the day, always watching the house. She dared not step outside.

"Father, he's there again."

Father joined her at the window. "You say he's a friend of Colby's?"

"I think *friend* might be too generous a word."

Father watched a moment then Lew slid out of sight. "Is there any reason he is watching us?"

"Not that I'm aware."

"It's not the way I expect a man to act. Perhaps you should refrain from going outside unless you have someone with you. Preferably myself or Colby."

But Colby did not come anymore. She'd seen him ride by a few times but he always passed without any indication of stopping. She thought of waving him in or shouting a greeting but something stopped her. She couldn't say if it was caution, fear or anger. Perhaps a bit of all three.

Under the circumstances how could he expect her to trust him? She didn't know what was going on and he didn't choose to tell her.

She turned from the window but glanced out every few minutes. It seemed better to know when Lew was watching them then to wonder if he was.

The next time she glanced out, she saw Colby stop at the side of the road. Lew stood in the shadows and grinned mockingly as Colby dismounted. Then they disappeared into the trees.

Now was her chance to find out what was going on. Dorrie lay sleeping in her crib. Anna could safely steal away and follow the men. She stepped outside. Had to hurry or she might lose them or miss whatever was about to transpire. She picked up her skirts and ran. As soon as she entered the shelter of the trees and the coolness of the shade they provided, she slowed to allow her eyes a chance to adjust to the change in light. Ahead, she heard the murmur of voices and carefully avoided stepping on any twigs as she crept forward, her heart clinging to the back of her throat with a grip of steel.

She saw Colby first, probably because she knew she would not be able to draw in a breath until she knew he was safe.

He stood, thumbs hooked in the front pockets of his trousers. The stance was likely intended to look casual, unconcerned, but Anna saw tension in the way he balanced on the balls of his feet and how his shoulders crunched toward his ears. Colby was alert in every muscle.

She shifted her gaze to Lew. The man wore a cruel, mocking scowl.

"Where is it?" Lew growled.

"Where's Harv? Ask him." Colby spoke with careful patience, which only served to make Anna's muscles knot. Colby didn't trust this man. That was obvious.

"Harv's dead. You might say he met with an unfortunate accident."

"You shot him?"

"Couldn't be helped. The man wasn't about to share his information. But you and him were pretty cozy. I figure he told you."

"He didn't."

Lew growled. "'Fraid I don't believe you. I should shoot you here like you deserve." He edged his hands toward the gun hanging low at his side.

Anna bit her bottom lip to keep from crying out. Was she about to see Colby shot dead? Would she never get a chance to tell him she loved him? Her knees threatened to melt and she swayed against a tree for support.

"With both me and Harv dead you'd never find out."

Lew considered the idea, and then slowly his hands left his gun belt. "Guess maybe you're right."

Anna backed away. She managed to stifle her shock until she reached the shelter of her home. She dashed into her room and threw herself across the bed, her heart racing so fast it tore at her chest, sending pain radiating through her body. It sounded as though Colby meant to ride away with that despicable man. When would this ever stop hurting? How much more could she take?

Colby knew there was no money. Harv had led the men to believe there was in order to make them obey his orders. A treasure. Money. Lots of it. Hidden in a safe place. He'd take them there. But first they had to… whatever scheme Harv dreamed up.

To start with, Colby had gone along with Harv's plans, not realizing Harv had bigger, badder things in mind.

But one day Lew had grown more belligerent and challenging than usual. Said he took exception to the growing closeness between Colby and Harv. Not that there was any friendship. Harv simply liked playing the men off against each other.

Colby's association with them had ended when he shot Lew. Thought he'd killed the man. No loss to society and nobody would dispute it was self-defense, but as Colby stared at the bleeding man, then considered his pistol, he saw what he was becoming and didn't much care for what he saw.

He'd turned around. Headed home. Back to Anna and his baby. Back to where he'd left his heart.

He thought he could escape his past. But his past had caught up with him.

For now he was safe having led Lew to believe he knew the whereabouts of the fake treasure. But not for long. Lew had never been patient.

But it would ensure that Lew followed him out of town and a good long ways from Anna and Dorrie. What would he do when Lew realized there was no stash of money…

Well, he'd deal with that when the time came.

First he must tell Anna he was leaving.

It would be the hardest task he'd ever taken on. Just when he hoped and prayed he'd begun to prove she could trust him not to run off, he had to do it again.

This time there would be no coming back.

But he couldn't let her guess that.

He followed after Lew, waiting for him to ride up to the Lucky Lady and saunter in for a drink. No chance the man would leave until he got what he'd come for—the non-existent money and, after that, revenge for Colby shooting him.

Hard to believe the man had survived. But he was too mean to die easily.

Rather than follow Lew inside, he slowly made his way back to Anna's and the end of his dreams. He would have to be careful when he hugged Dorrie, or Anna would be suspicious. His insides bled worse than Lew had after being shot. He would never see Dorrie grow up but at least she'd be safe and well cared for with Anna.

Anna. He dare not think any further. Just her name in his thoughts was enough to make him weaken.

But he must do what was necessary. He'd failed so many people in the past—his mother, Nora, Hugh, Anna, Dorrie....

He would not, must not, fail this time.

But he didn't go directly to the manse. He rode down a back trail, tied his horse out of sight of the house and slipped into the church. He could not face this alone.

His knees were difficult to bend, stiffened with regret and resolve, but he forced them to obey and knelt before the cross.

When he found sufficient strength, he rose and went next door.

Anna and Dorrie were in the kitchen. He paused at the door to take in each detail—the cupboard where he had helped Dorrie wash dishes, the stove where he didn't even have to close his eyes to picture Anna busy cooking, the table where they had shared so many meals. At last he let his gaze touch the two he loved with his whole heart.

Dorrie's color was almost back to normal after her illness. Her energy increased every day. He smiled at her greeting, *Da-da.* Let his gaze linger on her hair, her blue eyes so much like his.

Last—his heart kicking against his ribs—he let himself look at Anna, the woman he had loved for so long. He wanted to smile, prove to her there was nothing amiss, but at the demanding look in her eyes, he faltered. Had she guessed why he'd come? Already prepared to be angry about it?

"Anna." He paused. How did he convince her without alarming her? "I have to leave."

"You're going with that man aren't you?"

"Lew. Yes. We have some unfinished business."

"Why not leave it unfinished? Is it so important? More important than me? Than Dorrie?"

"No. Never. Nothing is more important than you. But this is for your good." He couldn't tell her the particulars. She would protest. Might even try and stop him. And he must go. It was the only way to protect them and put an end to this.

"What do you have that Lew wants?"

He stilled his face to remain blank but her question caught him off guard. "Unfinished business."

"Who is he? Why does it matter so much what he wants?" If he didn't hear the cry behind her harsh words, he might have thought she was angry.

He took a step forward but she put up her hand to stall him.

"Can't you at least tell me what's going on?"

He wanted to. He wanted to share every detail of his life with her. But would she understand? Would the knowledge somehow increase her risk?

"Colby, I think I deserve to know."

"Very well, but it's not a pretty story." He sat at the table, plopped his hat in front of him and considered where to start.

"You asked why I ran and I told you I was afraid I couldn't be what you needed. That's the truth. I told you I failed my ma. That's the truth. But there's more. Anna, I can never seem to protect the ones I love." Except this time he intended to no matter the cost. A cruel, sharp blade tore through his insides but he gritted his teeth. He would not let her know how much it hurt to do this.

"Lew is one of the men I fell in with when I was away." He told her how Lew and Harv, and others before them, had welcomed him. How he'd done the things they did, rowdy, drunken things. "I didn't like what I was doing but I didn't believe I could change. After all, I am a Bloxham."

"Change is God's business."

He wondered if she truly believed it or simply repeated familiar words. Not that it mattered anymore. "I shot Lew."

She gasped.

"Left him for dead."

Her eyes grew wider. The pain in his heart grew more vicious.

"Self-defense, it was. But that's when I decided I didn't care what it took. I did not like who or what I was becoming."

"That's when you came back here?"

"I came back to you and Dorrie. I came to start over."

She swallowed hard as if trying to get down something hard and bulky. "Then stay. Stay and start over."

He would not blink. He would not groan. Instead he would rejoice that he heard the words he longed for. He would carry them in his heart until his death. "I can't stay. Trust me when I say this is for the best."

He rose, determination warring with a longing that ached through his entire bloodstream and touched every cell of his body. One more day. He'd give anything for one more day. But he dare not tempt Lew to violence.

He stroked Dorrie's hair. Kissed both her cheeks and hugged her. He longed to scoop her out of the chair and hold her forever. But if he showed any unusual degree of emotion, Anna might grow suspicious.

Then he turned to Anna, drinking in every detail. He would hold this picture of her in his mind until the end. "I have to go." He bent and gently kissed her. He planned to make it short and quick but it would be his one and only kiss and he could not force himself away. He gently pulled her close wanting to hold her forever in his arms.

After her initial surprise she leaned into him, wrapped her arms about his waist and returned his kiss.

From somewhere deep inside he found the strength to slowly, reluctantly, ease back. He squeezed her shoulders and stepped away from her embrace. "Take good care of my Dorrie."

He rushed for escape before he weakened.

But before he reached the handle, the door flew back and Lew stood in the opening, his pistol drawn.

Chapter Sixteen

"Well, well. Ain't this sweet?" The man's voice had a sinister leer to it.

Colby positioned himself between Lew and the other two. "I'm ready to go. My horse is outside. I'll take you to the money."

"I do believe you will."

Colby edged forward, cautiouslike, so as not to make Lew consider doing something stupid.

"Hold up there. What's to stop this pretty little gal from running to the sheriff as soon as I leave?"

It's exactly what she should do. "She won't. Will you, Anna?"

"Not if you say I shouldn't."

Good girl. Let's lead him along.

Lew snorted. "You don't expect me to believe that, now do ya?"

Lew could be way too smart sometimes. "You can trust her. After all, she's the preacher's daughter."

"Better she and the baby come along. Provide me a bit of insurance in case you think you can play me for the fool. Lady, pick up that baby and get yourself over here."

He waved the gun.

Colby considered his options. He'd go for the gun but too risky with Dorrie and Anna so close. He'd have to trust God to provide an opportunity before they left town. "Do as he says, Anna."

He hoped she wouldn't decide this was a good time to reveal her stubborn nature. He knew only momentary relief as she clutched Dorrie in her arms and headed for the door.

Lew stepped aside and waved the three of them out.

Colby tried to position himself between Lew and Anna, but Lew would have none of it. "Keep to one side."

"Just keep walking," Colby murmured to Anna.

"That's right, lady. No funny stuff or someone dies."

Colby knew he would not fire his gun in town because it would bring people running to investigate. He prayed for an opening, for Lew to be careless just one second, but the man had unfaltering concentration when he wanted it. And right now with the hope of discovering a fake treasure, he had lots of reason to keep focused.

Three horses were tied at the shed. Lew indicated they should head that way. They reached the mounts. "You first." He shoved Anna forward.

Colby saw at once that she couldn't get in the saddle while holding Dorrie. He stepped forward to help and stopped as Lew's gun bore down on him.

"I'll take the little sweetheart."

"No." Anna jerked back. "I'll not give her to you." Before Colby could shout a warning, Anna turned on her heel and ran for all she was worth toward the church. He understood she hoped to reach shelter before Lew could stop her.

"Fool woman." Lew turned and steadied the gun on Anna.

He intended to shoot her. Maybe Dorrie, too.

"No." Colby launched himself between Lew and Anna and made a few steps before as a shot rang out. The bullet caught him in his back, pushing him forward. But when he fell, he took Anna and Dorrie with him. At least he could protect them with his body.

The pain turned the edges of his vision red but he was alive. For how long, he didn't know. "Are you hurt?"

"No." Her words were muffled by the weight of his body but he wouldn't have moved if he could. He was a shield for them.

"Is Dorrie hurt?"

Dorrie's wail informed them she was at least alive.

"Don't move. Make him either come here or ride away."

Behind them Lew cursed. "Now see what you made me do."

Anna turned her head, tried to see him. "Are you shot?"

"At least I could protect you and Dorrie. Now be quiet and lie still." Every word thundered through his brain, every move she made drove the pain deeper.

Footsteps thundered down the alley. Men called out. "It came from this direction."

Then more gunshots rang out.

"I love you," he managed to squeeze out, and then all went black.

* * *

An explosive sound had made her ears ring. She was certain Lew had shot his gun. Her heart slammed into her ribs so hard she felt her ribs crack. Then Colby's weight had hit her hard. Anna fell facedown to the ground, dirt filling her nose, dry grass scratching her cheeks, Dorrie clutched to her. Instinctively she'd shifted the baby to one side to protect her from Anna's weight.

She spat out dirt and grass. "I smell blood." Metallic and sweet.

Colby moaned, "He shot me."

Colby! Hurt. Panic swirled around her. Would the man shoot her, too? What about Dorrie? The child was pressed solidly to her side, pinned in place by Anna's arm. She struggled to shift her arm, somehow protect Dorrie more but she couldn't move and her aching ribs struggled for air.

Colby's ragged breath blew hot on her neck.

She tried to squirm from under his weight.

"Lie still. This here is the safest place you could be." His words rumbled from his body, reverberated in her own.

She stopped struggling.

"I love you." His words came on a whisper and then the weight of his body became intolerable.

"Colby," she whispered.

He didn't answer. She no longer felt his breath on her neck. Colby. Her fear crawled up her skin and pooled against her protesting ribs. "Don't you dare die."

He loved her. Now was a fine time to say so. Why had he waited so long to speak the words?

Would she have believed them any sooner? How could she be so blind not to see how much he loved

her? He'd give his life for her. Yet she'd stubbornly refused to trust him. Demanded proof when she should
have simply welcomed his return and believed him.

And not just him.

She'd found it so hard to trust God. Always she asked
herself, would God take her loved ones, would He do
what was best for her or was she simply there for the
good of others?

Colby was willing to die for her.

Jesus had done so.

Trust should be easier.

It would be from here on.

Colby? Was her trust too late? Hot tears scalded her
face and muddied the ground until she lay in a puddle.
Please, God, don't let him die. Please. Now was the time
to put her faith into action. *I trust You to do what is best.*

More gunshots rang out. Anna cringed, fearing she
would feel one thud into Colby's inert body. She tried
to pull Dorrie closer but the weight of Colby's body
made it impossible. She struggled to get in enough air
to keep from blacking out.

Then voices spoke above her. "Here, give me a hand."

Slowly, Colby's body was lifted. Someone called,
"Get the doc."

Another set of hands started to take Dorrie.

Anna fought.

"Let me take her." It was Grace.

She released her grip and Dorrie was lifted. She realized Dorrie was sobbing. How long had she been crying and Anna didn't notice? Didn't hear?

She wanted to flip over but her limbs had no strength.
Her lungs fought to get air. Someone gently turned her
and helped her sit. "Father." She buried her head against

his chest and wailed. "I've been so stupid and blind." It hurt her lungs to squeeze out the words.

"Shush. Shush." He patted her back, offering her comfort in a way he had never before. "You've just had a terrible shock."

She jerked from his arms. "Where is that man? Lew?" She glanced around, her eyes burning with dread. Was he still lurking about, waiting for a chance to finish this business between him and Colby?

"He was shot trying to escape. He's dead."

Anna tried to feel sorrow at a senseless death but felt only relief that he wouldn't terrorize them again.

"Colby?" She tried to get to her feet. Again her body would not do as she ordered. "Is he—?" She couldn't say the word.

"They've rushed him over to Doc's place. He'll do what he can."

"He's still alive?" She had to know the truth.

"I heard someone say he was breathing."

She moaned and fell back into Father's arms. "Please pray he doesn't die."

"Of course. I already am. Now let's have a look at you. Are you injured?"

"I'm fine." Only it took Father on one side and Mr. Percy on the other for her to make it to the house. They helped her to her bedroom and left her to Grace's care.

Grace brought in water and tenderly washed Anna's face. Anna lay with her eyes closed, too weak to even protest. At first, she wanted to, she should be looking after herself, then she relaxed. Time to stop trying to take care of everything. Not only did she need to trust God and Colby, she needed to let others help her more.

"Thank God you and Dorrie aren't injured. You have a

few scratches and no doubt you'll have bruises but nothing serious," Grace said as she cleaned Anna's hands.

Anna tried not to flinch. Her palms must be scratched to hurt so. "Dorrie's all right?"

"I think she was more frightened than anything. Alex is home and he's amusing her. I heard her laugh a few minutes ago."

She and Dorrie had gotten off easy. Unlike Colby. Tears washed her eyes and ran down each side of her face.

Grace made a soothing noise and wiped them away. "Come here." She reached for Anna, urging her into her embrace.

Anna sat up and buried her face against the woman's shoulder. Sobs racked her.

"You go right ahead and have a good cry."

Anna cried like she hadn't cried before. She wept for her fear and regrets over Colby. And her tears carried prayers that he would live, so she could tell him how much she loved him. How much she trusted him. With her life. But she cried for other things, too. Never had she been held and comforted since Rose died. She'd taken all her sorrow to the foot of the cross but now she let warm arms hold her and hot tears cleanse her. She cried until she was spent and Grace's dress front soaked.

"I'm sorry," she mumbled, unable to meet Grace's eyes. The woman must think she was a weak-kneed ninny. She almost smiled. She was certainly weak-kneed at the moment.

Grace chuckled. "Woman-to-woman, let me tell you there is nothing like a weeping session to ease one's emotions. Men don't understand but we do."

Anna grinned, realizing just how right Grace was. She hadn't felt so cleansed in a long time. "Thank you."

"Don't thank me. Thank God who gave us tears. Now you lie down and rest. I'll take care of everything else."

She knew she wouldn't sleep. She intended to stay awake and pray for Colby until she heard one way or the other. But she fell into a deep dreamless sleep as soon as her head hit the pillow.

"Mama?"

Tiny fingers brushed at her face. Anna yawned.

"Dorrie, come away and let her sleep," Alex whispered.

"I'm awake." She moaned. And remembered why everything hurt. She bolted to her feet. And swayed. Grace was right. She ached in places she didn't know existed.

"You sure you should be up?" Alex asked.

"I'm fine." But she sat on the edge of the bed and waited for the dizziness to pass. "Colby?"

"Father," Alex called. "She's awake."

Father was to deliver the news? Fear crept into her throat and made it impossible to swallow. Father's job was to deliver bad news.

Dorrie wanted to be picked up, but Anna didn't think she could lift her, so she patted the bed beside her. Dorrie climbed up and buried her face in Anna's lap. Anna rubbed her back, finding comfort in her nearness. If Colby were gone she would have this sweet bit of him. She pressed her lips to hold back a cry. She didn't want to lose Colby. She'd missed too many precious days already.

Father appeared at the doorway. "How are you feeling?"

"Sore but otherwise fine." She clung to his kind gaze. "Tell me the truth. Is Colby—?"

He sat beside Dorrie and took Anna's hand. "He's alive. But just barely. Doc isn't hopeful."

Alive. That's all that mattered. "Then we'll have to ask God to help him."

Father turned her hand over and seemed to study the many scrapes and scratches. "We need to trust God to do what is best."

What was best was for Colby to live so they could enjoy their love. Raise Dorrie together. She fought an intense battle. She had a choice—trust God or wonder about His love. She'd wasted too much time letting God show His love in areas of her choosing, trusting Him when she got her way. She gripped Father's hand and bowed her head. "Not my will but God's," she murmured.

Father squeezed her shoulder and prayed, "Father, we ask that You see fit to heal Colby, bring him back to us, but in this, as we strive to do in all areas, we release him to You and trust Your good mercy and grace."

Anna sat quietly, her eyes still closed. Great peace filled her. Whatever God sent her way, He would also send the grace to deal with it. And if what He sent was Colby, she would never let another day pass without telling him she loved him.

"Where is he?"

"Doc kept him at his office until he can be moved."

"Who is caring for him?"

"There seems no end to his friends wanting to help. Doc had to chase a bunch of them away. Said they were getting underfoot."

"I want to see him."

Father hesitated. "Are you up to it?"

"He saved my life. I owe him. Besides…"

Father smiled. "I understand your feelings."

She ducked her head, afraid he might see far more than gratitude.

"I'll take you to see him."

"Thank you. Is Grace here?"

"Yes. She said she'll be available as long as we need her."

"Give me a minute to tidy up and then I'll be ready."

She was grateful the doctor's office wasn't any farther away. As it was, she welcomed the way Father tucked her hand around his arm and let her lean on him. The closer they got to their destination, the weaker her legs grew. No matter what happened, she would trust God—with her life, her future—but she ached with unshed tears as she tried to prepare herself for bad news.

They reached Doc's door. Father pushed it open.

Anna stopped. She couldn't step into the room. Couldn't face the news.

Father smiled. "No one has brought a message saying otherwise so I assume he is still fighting to live. Let's go see."

She allowed him to draw her forward. They had to cross a small waiting room where two women sat. Anna was scarcely aware of them except that their murmurs of sympathy increased her tension. *God help me. Be my strength and comfort.*

Doc, having heard the door open and close, stepped into the room, saw Anna and her father. "Come along. The young man is in here."

She somehow crossed the room, her feet numb, and clinging desperately to Father's arm.

"He's lost a lot of blood." Doc spoke with determination. "I had to dig deep for the bullet but he's strong."

Then she saw him and stuffed a fist to her mouth

to keep from crying out. He lay on a narrow black bed propped up on one side. A stark white sheet covered the lower half of his body. A huge white dressing wrapped around his right side.

If Father hadn't been holding her arm, she would have collapsed. He led her to a chair and she sank down.

Slink had vacated the chair and hovered nearby. Tobias sat on the opposite side. He pushed to his feet, nodded politely. "We'll be leaving you alone with him." Both men slipped from the room.

Anna reached out to touch the dressing. Thought better of it and instead took his hand as it lay motionless against the white sheet. "Colby, please get better." Just the feel of his hand gave her courage. He was still alive. That was enough for now.

She looked at his face. Younger-looking with all awareness at rest. And pale. Silently, she prayed for his recovery. Prayed she might get a chance to tell him of her love.

As she sat beside him, she held those three little words he'd spoken—*I love you*—close to her heart. She clung to his hand as faithfully as she clung to hope. And in it all, she felt peace like the rock bed of her life. God would surely do what was best and she would trust Him no matter what.

The hours trudged past as slow as a boy headed off to school on a sunny day. Yet each minute was a chance to see him improve.

Several times Doc came in and checked Colby. He had Anna leave the room while he changed the dressing. Anna pressed him for information…hope. "All we can do is wait and pray."

She did both but waiting was the hardest thing she'd ever done.

Slink and Tobias slipped in and out. As did others. Father left and returned. But she remained at Colby's side.

Sometime later, Father touched her shoulder. "Let me take you home."

"I can't leave him." If God granted nothing more than a moment more of his life, if he came to for even a fleeting moment, she intended to be there to tell him of her feelings.

"You should rest."

"I will when he's better. Would you mind putting Dorrie to bed?"

"I'm sure we can manage." He hesitated, sighed and headed for the door then paused.

She knew he hoped she would change her mind. She couldn't. "I'll be fine. Doc is here. His friends come in continually."

Finally he left.

She glanced around, realized there were no others in the room at the moment and rose to move closer to Colby. She touched his cheek, felt it only normally warm. Thank God. Infection was the worst thing to deal with. She curled her finger and ran it along his face, smiling at the way his whiskers rasped beneath her touch. Amazed at her boldness, she trailed a cautious fingertip across his lips, remembering with a mixture of pleasure and embarrassment how she had responded to his good-bye kiss, though she regretted it not a bit. It might end up being their last as well as their first kiss.

"Colby," she whispered. "Don't die on me. Give me another chance."

Chapter Seventeen

His lips tickled, jerking him from a pleasant nothingness. At first he resented it. He'd been floating like a bit of dandelion fuzz—effortless, bodiless. But a voice called his name, pulling him back…to a body that felt as if he'd been pinned to a barn door with a pitchfork.

"Colby." His name whispered past his pain. The voice was familiar, promising things he had never known.

His floating was filled with soft clouds. He struggled to break through to clear sky.

"Colby."

He knew the voice. It made him want to smile. It filled him with determination to fight through to the surface. Anna. He struggled to take the word from his thoughts to his voice. "Anna." It was nothing more than a croak. He tried again. "Anna." A little better.

He forced his eyes open, groaning as the light burned the back of his brain. Anna's face floated above him, smiling. He tried to smile back then darkness closed about him.

He lost count of how many times he flitted back and forth from darkness to the light of Anna's smile.

If he'd been able to count. He tried. Got as far as two before he lost track.

Suddenly a thought blared through the fog of his brain.

Lew. He had to protect Anna and Dorrie from the man. He again fought through the mists. "Lew?"

Anna hovered over him. "He got killed trying to shoot the sheriff."

He sank back into blissful sleep.

The next time he opened his eyes, he knew the fog had departed. He was left with a deep fatigue and a body that hurt like fury. And Anna's sweet smile. "Hi," he croaked.

"Hi, yourself." She held a cup with a spout to his lips and he drank greedily.

"Am I going to live?"

She touched his forehead, pushed back his hair.

He closed his eyes and let his skin drink in the gesture.

"Do you want to?"

Did he want to spend years teaching Anna how much he loved her? Reveling in this contact between them? Enjoying his wonderful child? Before he could expect her to trust him, there were things he must explain. He managed to lift his arm and grasp her hand. "I want to tell you about Lew."

She pressed her fingertips to his mouth. "Later. When you're stronger."

He gladly left it to later as he let the pleasure of her touch fill his heart with hope and joy. He only wanted another chance to prove to her that she could trust her affections to him.

Daily he grew stronger. He was moved to the house Hugh had rented. He wished he could be closer to Anna but she came by every day, bringing him broth, or biscuits, insisting he eat. Once he was stronger, she brought Dorrie to visit.

As soon as Anna put Dorrie on her feet, the little gal raced for Colby, calling, "Da-da, Da-da," as if she thought the lost had been found.

"She missed you."

"I missed her." He reached for her, ignoring the pain in his side.

Anna noticed his grimace. "Take it easy. I'll lift her."

But he already had Dorrie on his lap and listened carefully as she babbled away on some long, involved story. He nodded and murmured, "That's right" and "Yup" at what he hoped were appropriate times.

As Dorrie entertained him, Anna prepared tea. She'd brought cookies and the three of them sat and enjoyed the afternoon.

Eventually Dorrie scrambled down to explore the empty crate Hugh had pushed into the corner.

"To think I might have never been able to enjoy this."

"You might have died." She squeezed his hand. Her eyes glistened with tears.

His heart leaped with hope.

"I'm awfully glad you didn't."

"There is something I have to tell you."

She shook her head. "It's not necessary."

"I don't want any more secrets between us."

She considered him a moment, her expression seeming to offer hope.

It gave him courage to tell her. "Lew thought I knew where stolen money was hidden."

She nodded.

He hardly dared believe that she didn't wonder if

he had a hand in getting the nonexistent stolen funds. "I didn't because there wasn't any." He told of Harv's method of control.

She only nodded. "He was an evil man."

Once started, he couldn't seem to stop. He told why he kept running from bad to worse. "I didn't think I could be what you needed. I didn't know if I could protect you." He still didn't know if he could or if anything he had to offer was about the same value as the dust on his boots. But he intended to stay and see this through.

She smiled gently and folded her hands over his. "You protected me and Dorrie by taking a bullet for us. I hope you never again feel you need to prove your ability to take care of us in such a way. But it isn't your protection I really want. It's you—here forever."

He stared, uncertain he'd heard her correctly. "Me?"

"Is that so surprising? Haven't we belonged together since that first day we met?"

"It's all I've ever wanted. There's a part of my life that is always silent when I'm away from you. I love you."

She tipped her face to him. "I love you, too. And even more, I trust you. Can you ever forgive me for not?"

He chuckled. "You had every reason to doubt me. I wondered about myself many times. But no more. Your love has brought me home and with God's help I will be the kind of man both you and Dorrie need."

"You are exactly what we need. No proof necessary." She leaned closer, her look intent on his mouth.

He could not ignore her silent invitation to a kiss and he captured her lips with all the hunger and love of the years they had been apart.

A little later, after many kisses, he tipped her face upward to smile into her welcome. "Will you marry me?"

She blinked. Her eyes darkened and she shot straight up, putting a chilling distance between them.

He watched worry and confusion flood her face. He ached to erase it with a kiss, but she turned to look out the window.

"What about Alex and Father? Who will take care of them?"

"Anna, come back here."

She hesitated then returned to stare at him with dark, bottomless eyes.

He pulled her close. "Let's trust God to provide an answer." He kissed her forehead, her cheeks and then her lips, trying to drive away the worry that had replaced her joy.

"I have promised to trust God through good and bad." Her words did not sound full of hope.

He prayed she wasn't looking for a way to refuse him.

She loved him. She wanted to marry him. But Alex and Father couldn't manage by themselves. She owed it to Rose to take care of them. As she tended her chores, her mind whirled until she felt like a top on a wild ride across a tabletop heading in a crazy path toward the edge and disaster.

"Father, I'm going over to the church."

Dorrie slept, Alex lay in bed reading.

She crossed the yard and stepped into the interior of the church. The slanting rays of sunlight coming through the west windows drew long shadows across the floor and up the east wall. The place smelled clean.

The scent of new wood was still discernable. Her gaze lingered on the pew where Colby often sat to play his mouth organ. She missed seeing him there, sharing their love of music.

If she married Colby they could enjoy making music together every evening for the rest of their lives. Her heart jumped with joy and anticipation. She pressed her hand to her chest as if she would control the emotion.

If?

Had she already decided marriage wasn't possible?

She sank to the front pew and stared at the cross. Marred by the fire, yet a thing of beauty. Many had expressed delight with how Colby and his friends had salvaged it. Even Mrs. Percy had sidled up to Anna and murmured, "I kind of thought they were doing something special like this." Anna had smiled and nodded. But she recalled the suspicions the woman had voiced.

Was she like Mrs. Percy? Mistrustful unless the evidence was thrust in her face?

Anna lowered her head to her upturned palms. *Oh, God, you know my heart. How I love Colby and want to spend the rest of my life with him. And yet I know I must look after Alex and Father.*

Trust God. The words filled her mind.

She wanted to, but she'd never known trusting to be so hard. For a long time she sat with her head bowed as she fought an inner battle. *Whatever You will. I submit to You, oh, my Father.*

Unless God provided a solution, her duty was to stay with Father and Alex. She didn't expect Colby would understand her decision.

She slowly rose, and with heavy heart and leaden feet, made her way home.

The next day she moved about slowly, her heart weighted with her decision.

Father, bless his heart, never seemed to notice her moods. Except today. He lingered at the table after lunch and was still there when Anna returned from putting Dorrie down for her nap. "Anna, why are you so sad? Colby's on the mend. I thought you'd be overjoyed."

Yes, he was going to live but her joy in the fact had been diminished by knowing she could not share his life. Yet she made herself smile. "I'm so grateful. God is good." Trust was hard but she had set her mind to do so and she would.

"Then why do you look like you've lost all hope?"

She busied herself at the stove. Was she really so transparent? And if she trusted God, shouldn't she be able to find a bit of joy somewhere?

Father waited for her answer.

"I guess it's just reaction to all that's taken place."

She couldn't meet Father's eyes but was aware of his scrutiny.

"Has Colby been less than a gentleman?"

She gasped. "Oh, my, certainly not." Her hot cheeks at remembering their kisses likely gave Father reason to wonder if she was completely honest.

Father cleared his throat. "Anna, I am going to be very direct with you and I want an honest answer."

She stood in the middle of the kitchen, facing him, unable to move. When Father spoke like that, she knew she was about to deal with an unpleasant subject but she couldn't think of anything she should dread. It wasn't as though anyone had seen her and Colby kissing except Dorrie, and she thankfully couldn't report on their behavior. At least, she didn't think anyone had seen. Unless there were busybodies peeping in windows.

"Daughter, has Colby spoken of his intentions?"

Her breath whooshed out. "He's going to work at the feed mill once he's feeling strong enough. After that I don't know. He hasn't said." She hadn't asked. Her interests had been more immediate.

"I mean toward you."

"Me?"

"I'm aware you and Colby have always had a close relationship and I've watched it grow and flourish since his return. Does he intend to marry you?"

She stared. Father was being very fatherly all of a sudden. She wouldn't have expected he even noticed how much time she and Colby spent together. "He— I—"

"I would think a simple yes or no would suffice."

"He has asked me."

"Then why the long face?"

Tears stung her eyes, clogged her nose, filled her throat. She swallowed hard. Tried to push them back. "I can't marry him."

"Why ever not? Don't you love him?"

She nodded, too full of tears to speak.

Father studied her a moment then nodded solemnly. "I see."

She turned away, having no idea of what he saw.

"I've got a visit to tend to. I'll be back in a little while."

"Fine." She welcomed time to pull her emotions under control. *I trust God. He will only do what is best for me.*

Dorrie woke and Anna got her up. She should think

of making some cookies but she couldn't find the energy. Must be because the house was so hot from the summer sun.

Or because her heart was so dull with sorrow she could barely find the energy to pack it around.

The back door opened. Father stepped aside to allow Grace Weaver to enter. Grace took one look at Anna and rushed over to hug her. "You look exhausted. Sit down and let me make tea for you…us."

Anna didn't have the energy to argue and allowed herself to be led to the table where she sank to a chair and managed to resist the urge to lay her head on her arms and have a good hard cry.

As the kettle boiled, Grace put cookies on a tray.

Cookies? Anna had meant to bake some but it hadn't happened. Grace must have brought them.

Father sat across from Anna and in a few minutes the three of them huddled around the table with full teacups before them.

Father cleared his throat.

Anna wondered what announcement he intended to make that required Grace's presence.

"Anna," he began. "You need to follow your heart."

She nodded, unsure what he meant. Part of her heart wanted to stay here and look after Father and Alex. She loved them. She knew Rose would want her to. A much larger portion of her heart belonged forever and always with Colby.

Grace reached for Anna's hands. "I know you feel your duty is to Alex and your father but I don't think you need to worry about either of them. I will take good care of them." There was no mistaking the soft pink color flooding up Grace's cheeks.

Anna stared, and then her mouth fell open as the impact of Grace's suggestion began to make sense. She returned her jaw to a closed position. "You mean you and Father…"

Grace grinned. "We love each other."

Father nodded. "I intend to marry her. With approval from you and Alex."

Approval? He didn't need it from her. "When? How?" She shook her head. "I can't believe it."

"We've been very discreet."

"I'm delighted." Anna laughed.

"You should be. You are now free to follow your own desires." Grace smiled gently.

Father nodded. "It's time for you to start your own life."

She looked from one to the other then giggled. "How long do you think it will take to plan a wedding?"

"Can we make that two? And I don't care about anything fussy." Grace looked terribly pleased.

"Nor I."

They grinned at each other. Father reached for both their hands.

Anna bolted to her feet. "I have something to take care of."

"Run along, dear. We'll watch Dorrie."

Within minutes Anna stood outside Hugh's house. Perhaps Colby had changed his mind. She smiled. He meant it when he said he loved her. And she trusted him.

Just as she trusted God and He had provided a way for her to let go of her current responsibilities. Even when she hadn't had the faith to ask for such a blessing.

Assured this was of God and propelled by her love, she pushed the door open and stepped inside.

Colby was resting in the chair.

"Colby?"

He blinked, his eyes widening with pleasure when he saw her.

"Let me tell you about how faithful our God is." She told him of Grace's assurance that Father and Alex would be well taken care of.

As she talked the sunshine came to Colby's eyes until they glowed.

She finished but he didn't speak. He just looked at her with such a look of joy that she felt tongue-tied. And yet he still didn't say anything.

"Have you changed your mind?"

"About what?" he croaked.

"About me." She couldn't look at him for fear she'd built a false dream.

He jumped to his feet, groaned with a reminder of his recent injuries. Laughing he pulled her to his arms. "I will never change my mind about you. And I'll spend the rest of my life proving how much I love you." He trailed a warm fingertip down her cheek to the center of her chin. "Anna, I love you. Will you marry me and make me the happiest man on earth?"

He waited, his gaze warm and eager.

She laughed, her heart so full she didn't know how to contain it. "I love you, Colby, and I will marry you."

"When?"

Her smile widened at his eagerness. "I think we need to discuss such things and make plans."

"Later." He lifted her chin with his finger, lowered his head slowly as if delighting in the anticipation, and then sweetly covered her lips with his.

"I knew it would take a miracle for you to leave your family. And we got it. Hallelujah. Let's thank God."

She gladly joined him in thanking their heavenly Father for providing a way for them to be together. And then they sat side by side, holding hands and talking.

She remembered his words about wanting a home. "Colby, I will provide you a home where you always feel welcome and cared for."

He hugged her and kissed her. "I know you will. And I promise to be a man you can trust at all times."

The sun slanted through the window and bathed them in golden light.

She bolted to her feet. "I forgot about Dorrie and supper." She leaned over and kissed him. "You have filled my thoughts to the exclusion of all else."

"Can't have that, now can we? Let me go with you."

Gladly she let him accompany her home.

Dorrie sat in her chair playing with a little yarn doll Anna had never seen before. She knew Grace brought it, probably made it herself. Pots boiled on the stove.

Grace grinned at them. "Wondered if you were ever coming back. I don't have to ask if you worked things out satisfactorily. Your faces say it all."

Anna and Colby grinned at each other, their hearts full of love.

Epilogue

One month later

Father and Grace stood together on one side of the pulpit. Colby and Anna on the other.

Dorrie wore a pretty pink dress Grace made for her. She looked like an angel in her father's arms.

Anna's dress was a deep rose fitted at the waist and wrists and falling to the floor in a gored skirt. She'd made the dress with Grace's assistance. It had turned out rather well, more thanks to Grace's patience than Anna's talent as a seamstress.

Colby had watched her work on it but saw her in it the first time a few minutes ago. His eyes had widened with pleasure that brought warmth to Anna's cheeks. How she loved this man. How she relished his expressions of love—his kisses, his compliments, his restrained hugs.

She shifted her gaze from Colby for fear her heart would burst from its moorings with joy.

Grace had chosen to make a tailored suit in dove-gray. "It will serve me well as the preacher's wife."

Her ruffled blouse was of the same fabric as Anna's dress.

Father looked very handsome in his best black suit and white shirt.

Colby also wore a white shirt and black string tie. His grin threatened to split his face. He'd confessed he never stopped smiling. He said he fell asleep with a smile on his lips and woke the same way.

They'd talked almost round the clock as they made plans. Anna opened every corner of her heart to him, sharing her doubts, her misgivings, things long buried, long denied. She'd always had to be strong and in control.

When she told Colby that, he'd laughed. "You can be as strong as you want but never again do you have to carry your load alone. I'm here to share your responsibilities."

They kept the wedding plans simple. Just the four of them in a double ceremony and a few close friends—Grace's sister and family, Laura and Carl and their children, Hugh, and the men Colby had led to the Lord.

A friend of Father's had come to perform the ceremony.

"Dearly beloved, we are gathered here together..."

Anna had heard the words on hundreds of occasions but this time it was for her and Colby.

Father and Grace exchanged vows first and then stood by as Colby and Anna exchanged theirs.

Then the pastor announced the new Mr. and Mrs. Caldwell. Everyone clapped. He then announced Mr. and Mrs. Bloxham. Anna couldn't stop smiling as she accepted congratulations.

Later, as the celebrations came to an end, Father

hugged Anna. "You have been such a help for so long. Now you can use your skills to build a home of your own. I'm so glad you and Colby are together."

Grace hugged her. "I will probably never live up to your reputation."

Anna laughed. Grace had already proven to be very capable and efficient. "I'm certain I won't be favorably compared to the efficient new Mrs. Caldwell. But I don't care." They shared a laugh. "I am so happy for you and Father."

She kissed Alex and warned him to be a good boy.

He grinned. "I have a job for the summer."

"You do? Why is this the first I've heard of it?"

"Father just gave his permission. I'm going to work for Mr. Ziegler." Colby joined them and Alex flexed an arm. "I'm going to build some real muscles working on a farm."

Colby squeezed Alex's shoulders. "You're going to grow into a fine man."

Then it was time to leave. Anna felt a twinge of regret as Colby lifted her into the waiting buggy and handed up Dorrie. She waved to everyone and gave a tremulous smile.

The buggy tipped as he climbed up beside her. "Why the sad look?"

"I'm just saying goodbye to the only life I've ever known." She shifted so she faced Colby squarely. "And I'm anticipating starting a new phase sharing my love with you and Dorrie."

Colby leaned over and kissed her gently. "We will build a home together. I can hardly wait." They drove through town, waving to everyone they saw. A few minutes later, Colby turned the buggy down a dusty trail to the prettiest little house in the whole county. They had decided to stay here for now and had spent many enjoyable hours preparing the house.

They didn't know what the future held. Maybe a move. Hopefully more children. But Anna was certain of their love for each other and God's faithfulness.

Colby set Dorrie on the ground and let her run ahead. He scooped Anna into his arms and held her there as he kissed her.

"You better put me down before you do damage to your injury."

But he carried her across the threshold of the house where he kissed her again. "Home sweet home."

She glanced around at the place they had worked on together to make livable. "It's simple but I like it."

He kissed her again. "I didn't mean the house. I meant our hearts."

She pulled his head closer and, just before their lips touched, murmured, "Our heart will always be at home with each other." From the first day they'd met, their love was meant to be. It had just taken them a very long time to be ready for it. But thanks to God's tender mercies and faithfulness to them they had a lifetime to enjoy it.

* * * * *

PRAIRIE COWBOY

I have loved thee with an everlasting love:
therefore with lovingkindness have I drawn thee.
—*Jeremiah* 31:3

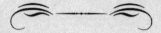

Dedicated to the teachers who have touched my life and the lives of my children in a positive way and especially to godly teachers who both teach and live a Christian example. May you be blessed in your work.

Chapter One

Dakota Territory, 1886

Her dream was about to come true in living, vibrant color.

In a few minutes she would welcome her first class of students. Eighteen-year-old Virnie White stood in the doorway of the brave little white schoolhouse and watched the children arriving in the schoolyard. The brittle yellow grass had been shaved by one of the fathers and the children's feet kicked up soft puffs of dusty mown grass.

A horse entered the gate of the sagging page wire fence. The rider, a man, reached behind him. A child grabbed his arm and dropped to the ground.

The boy wore overalls that looked as if the only iron to touch them had been a hot wind. He wore a floppy hat that did little to hide the mop of wild brown curls. He needed to be introduced to a pair of scissors.

Virnie expected the father to ride away as soon as the boy got to his feet but he hesitated, glancing about until he saw her in the doorway. She felt his demanding look and gathered her skirts in one hand and hurried across the yard. He dismounted at her approach. She held out her hand to the black-haired man. "Miss Virnie White, the new teacher."

He took her hand in his large, work-worn grasp and squeezed. "Conor Russell."

She pulled her hand to her side. "And this is…?" The boy raced over to join the boys in kicking around a lump of sod.

"Ray."

"How old is Ray?"

"Eight."

At the note of longing in the man's voice, Virnie turned. His gaze followed his son, concern evident in the tense lines around his eyes and the way he pressed his lips together. She studied him more closely. A handsome man with thick black hair that needed trimming almost as much as his son's, eyebrows as black as his hair, and dark blue eyes that shifted toward her, giving her a look as full of challenge as the superintendent had given at her interview.

She lifted her chin, clasped her hands together and met the man's look without flinching.

"Ray…well, Ray is…" He shifted his gaze past her to the men in the wheat field bordering the schoolyard.

She'd watched them earlier as they tossed stooks into the wagon and had breathed in the delightful nutty scent of ripe grain.

"What I'm trying to say is Ray's mother is dead."

One thought vibrated through her brain. A widowed father who cared about his child. She wanted to squeeze his hand and tell him how noble and wonderful he was. But the knowledge of his concern picked at a brittle scar and somewhere behind her heart a tear formed. Willing herself to ignore the place that held those hurtful things, she tipped her chin higher. Her lips felt stiff as she spoke. "Mr. Russell, rest assured I shall treat Ray with kindness and fairness." As she intended to treat all the children.

He touched the brim of his hat in a gentlemanly expression that made her feel she had given him the assurance he needed. "I hope so." He swung back into the saddle and kicked his horse forward, urging the animal to a gallop as soon as he left the schoolyard.

She stared across the field to where the men worked. The creak of the wagon as it groaned under the weight of stooks made little impression on her conscious thoughts.

Four little boys, Ray among them, raced past her chasing the steadily shrinking clump of sod. Did the child realize how fortunate he was? But then he was a boy. Obviously not the same thing to deal with as a motherless girl.

Virnie pulled herself back from the ghost of her past and with clipped steps headed for the schoolhouse. She glanced at the empty bell turret. How pleasant it would be to ring a large bell by means of a rope, but the community could not yet afford one so instead she picked up a hand bell from the step where she'd left it.

At its ringing, the children hurried toward her.

"Girls on my right. Boys on my left."

They quickly sorted themselves out except for Karl and Max who didn't appear to understand English.

She went to the pair and pointed them toward the boys' line. She counted the boys—only eight and she knew at last count there were nine boys and eight girls.

She checked the girls' line and immediately saw the problem.

"Ray, the boys are in this line."

Several of the children tittered and Ray shot her a blazing look.

Hilda, twelve and the oldest Morgan girl, leaned over and whispered. "Ray is a girl. Rachael Russell. It's just her pa doesn't know what to do with a little girl."

Shock burned through her veins as hot and furious as the prairie fires she'd read about with a shiver of fear. Her vision alternated between red and black. She feared she would collapse. No. She couldn't do that. Not on her first day of being a better-than-average teacher. She sucked in a breath, amazed the rush of air did nothing to dispel her dizziness. She knew firsthand how it felt to have your father wish you were a boy. Her father had gone so far as to say it. "Too bad you weren't a boy. Would have made life simpler."

How could she have run so forcibly into such a blatant, painful reminder of her past? A past she had vowed to completely forget? And she would forget it.

Miss Price had rescued her, taught her to be a lady, and modeled how to be a good teacher. She was here to emulate Miss Price.

Lord God, give strength to my limbs and forgetfulness to my thoughts.

She straightened her spine and went to the little girl. "Rachael, what a beautiful name. I'm sorry for my mistake."

The child ducked her head, hiding her face beneath the brim of her hat.

Virnie gently removed the hat. Her eyes widened

as a wave of brown curls fell midway down the child's back. "Why, what beautiful hair you have."

Rachael sent her a shy look of appreciation.

Something in the child's eyes went straight to Virnie's heart and pulled the scab completely from her wound. Her past stared at her through the eyes of Rachael Russell. And in that heartbeat of time, Virnie knew she had come to Sterling, North Dakota, for a reason as noble and necessary as teaching pioneer children. She had set her thoughts to becoming a dedicated teacher who found ways to challenge each student to do his or her best. Those who needed the most help would be her special concern. Those who excelled would receive all the encouragement she could provide. She'd make Miss Price proud of her by imitating her noble character as a teacher.

But just as Miss Price had done seven years ago when she saw Virnie's need and reached out to help her, she'd repeat the way Miss Price had helped her by reaching out to Rachael and perhaps repay her by doing so.

Her mind made up, she welcomed the children and had them march inside where she proceeded to get them into grades according to some rudimentary testing. Karl and Max Schmidt were problems. She couldn't test them when the only things they said were, "My name is Karl," or, "My name is Max," and, "Please." But here was her first challenge. Teach these two to communicate in English.

Correction. Her second challenge. Rachael was her first.

During the lunch break, she whispered to Hilda that Rachael's hair would look beautiful brushed. She gave

Hilda ribbons. Hilda smiled and nodded. A bright girl. And before the lunch break ended, she'd fixed Rachael's hair and so no one would realize it was for her benefit, she redid her two little sisters' hair as well.

When the school day ended and Virnie dismissed the children, Rachael hung back waiting for the others to leave before she sidled up to Virnie.

"Teacher, thank you for the ribbons."

Virnie touched Rachael's head. "I don't need them any longer. You enjoy them."

"I will." She raced outdoors.

Virnie followed.

Conor had no call to get Rae. She was perfectly capable of finding her way home. Had for two years now. But he wanted to see the new schoolmarm again. All day her face had filled his thoughts. Was she really as pretty as his memories said? He muttered mocking words. He knew pretty was useless out here. How did it help anyone create a solid home?

It seemed all the other children had left but he waited on horseback for Rae to exit. She ran out, the new school teacher at her heels.

Yup. Just as pretty as he recalled. Her hair was a doe-soft brown and pulled back into a bun. He couldn't say for sure if her eyes were brown, only that they were dark and watchful and this morning he'd decided she had a kind look. Soft, too. He could tell just looking at her. He'd give her a month, two at the most, before she found life a little too much work on the wild prairie and turned tail and ran. Took a special woman to survive frontier life and Miss White didn't have the hardy look at all.

Without even glancing at Rae, he reached down and

pulled her up behind him then touched the brim of his hat by way of greeting to the schoolmarm. As he tugged the reins and left the schoolyard he wondered why she gave him such a disapproving look.

"How was your day?" he asked his daughter.

"Good."

"You like the new teacher?"

"Yeah, Pa."

He didn't say more as he thought of that pretty new teacher. Now if they were back East, living in relative comfort, he might just think about courting the young woman. But he wouldn't be thinking another such foolish thought. Two months, he decided. She wouldn't last a day longer than that. Too many challenges. Like… "How did she manage the Schmidt boys?"

The family had been in the community only a few months. John, the father, could barely make himself understood and he knew Mrs. Schmidt spoke not one word of English.

"Miss White taught them lots already. She said we must all help them. When George said he didn't come to play mama to some foreigner, Miss White said she would tolerate no unkindness."

Conor grunted. He knew George Crome. A big lad. It surprised him George's father hadn't kept him home to help with harvest, but then the Cromes weren't exactly suited to farming. They seemed to think the work would take care of itself. He imagined the way George would lift his nose and sniff at having to help two small boys. "What did George do?"

"At first he growled but Miss White reminded us we are all newcomers. Wouldn't we want people to help us?"

Sounded like a smart woman.

They neared the Faulks' property and a big brute of a dog raced toward them, barking and snarling. "I see Devin is visiting his folks." The dog belonged to the grown Faulk boy who wandered in and out at will. Conor turned the horse to face the dog and shouted, "Stop. Go back."

The dog halted, his hackles raised, his lips rolled back to reveal his vicious teeth. But he didn't advance.

Rae's fist clutched at his shirt as if she thought the horse would rear and she might fall.

"Noble isn't about to let an old dog make him act crazy."

Her fingers uncurled. "Yeah, I know." She sounded a little uncertain.

"You aren't scared of that old dog, are ya?"

"Nah."

"Good, because he's nothing but hot air and bluff."

They resumed their journey and his thoughts slid un-invited and unwelcome back to the schoolmarm. Rae's mind must have made the same journey because she resumed talking about the day.

"Miss White asked George what his best subject was. He's very good at arithmetic. Miss White gave him all sorts of problems to solve and he did them all. Miss White said he needed to cap'lize on his strengths. Pa, what does cap'lize mean?"

He grinned, picturing little Miss White finding a way to make George feel good after a scolding.

"Capitalize means to make the most of something."

"I like Miss White." Rae's voice was soft, filled with awe.

Conor's skin prickled. He knew his little daughter

missed having a mother. But she would only be hurt if she looked for a substitute.

"I hope she stays."

Best to make Rae face the truth. But he wanted to spare her pain. Maybe with a little help she would figure it out herself. "You think she will?"

"She's smart."

"Uh-huh. But is she tough?"

"She's awfully pretty."

He squeezed the reins until they dug into his palm. He'd endured enough pain and disappointment with pretty women. So had Rae. Best she face facts and deal with them. "Now, Rae, how many times have I told you what use is pretty?"

"Yeah, Pa. I know. A person has to be strong to survive."

"Don't you be forgetting it." They turned toward their little house. This was where they belonged. He would fight to keep this place. He'd teach Rae to deal with the hardships. "You go on in while I unsaddle Noble."

A few minutes later he returned to the house, intent on getting a drink of water before he resumed working. Rae stood peering into the cracked mirror over the washstand. She turned as she heard him enter and grinned, waiting for him to admire her hair.

He felt like someone whacked him alongside the head with a big old plank. Oh, how she looked like her mother. "Hair ribbons." Pretty stuff. Useless stuff. The sort of thing that made women pine for a life that wasn't possible here. People—men and women alike and children, too—had to forget the ease of life back East where supplies were around the corner, help and company across the fence and being pretty and stylish mattered. Out here survival mattered and woe to anyone who forgot. Or pined for things to be different. His wife had done the latter. She'd willingly left the comfort of Kansas City to follow his dream of owning land but she'd been unprepared for the challenges. In the end, she'd let them defeat her. She got a cold that turned fatal because she didn't have the will to live. "Where did you get them?" His mouth felt gritty.

"Miss White gave them to me. And Hilda did my hair." Her eyes were awash with hope and longing.

He could allow this tiny bit of joy. But no. He must not allow weakness in himself any more than he could allow it in Rae. "Tomorrow we give them back."

"Pa." Pleading made her drag out the syllable.

"How many times have I told you? Only the strong survive out here. You want to survive or don't you?"

"Yes, Pa."

"You and me are going to make ourselves a home out here. Now aren't we?"

"That's right, Pa."

"Then put the ribbons aside before they get dirty and tend to your chores."

She nodded. In her eyes determination replaced hope. And how that hurt him. But he had to be strong for the both of them. She pulled off the ribbons, rolled them neatly and put them beside her lunch bucket.

"There's hours of daylight left. I've got to get the crop cut and stooked. Uncle Gabe will be coming any day." He and Gabe helped each other. "I won't be back until dark. You know what to do. Think you can handle it?"

She tossed him a scoffing look. "I can handle it. You know it."

He pulled her against his hip for a quick hug. "Proud of you, Rae."

"You'll come in and say good night when you get home? Even if I'm sleeping."

"Always. You can see me from the yard. If you need me all you have to do is bang on the old barrel."

"I know."

He hated to leave her although he'd been doing so longer than he cared to think about. Since Irene had laid down and quit living more than two years ago, leaving him to raise Rae on his own. But he didn't have much choice. The work did not do itself, contrary to the hopes of men such as Mr. Crome.

He turned and headed for the field as Rae went to gather eggs.

It was dark when he returned. He searched the kitchen for something to eat and settled for a jam sandwich. He wiped dried jam from a knife in order to use it. They were about out of dishes fit to eat from. He'd have to see if Rae would wash a few. He'd also have to find time to go see Mrs. Jones who sold him his weekly supply of bread.

Rae had dumped out her lunch bucket in preparation for tomorrow's food. The hair ribbons lay on the lid.

Miss White would no doubt look all distressed when he returned the ribbons and set her straight about what was best for Rae. He could imagine her floundering as she tried to apologize. Best she learn life here was tough.

Maybe she could return to her safe home back wherever she'd come from. Before she had to endure the harshness of a Dakota winter.

Yet he felt no satisfaction at knowing he would be

among those who drove Miss White away. And his regret made him want to kick himself seven ways to Sunday. He knew better than most the folly of subjecting a
pretty woman to the barren pioneer life.

He checked on Rae. She slept in her shirt, her overalls bunched up on the floor beside the bed. Dirty
clothes lay scattered across the floor. He didn't have
time to do laundry until after harvest.

He pulled the covers around Rae and stood watching her for a few minutes. He would never understand
how Irene could give up on life. He thought she shared
his goal. Having grown up in Kansas City with a father
who went from one job to another and took the family
from one poor hovel to the next, he'd vowed to provide
for himself and his family a safe, permanent home even
if he had to wrench it from this reluctant land with his
bare fists. He would let nothing stand in his way. Not
weakness. Certainly not a hankering after silly, useless,
pretty things. Rae's mother should have fought. For Rae
if not other reasons. He renewed his daily vow to make
sure Rae had a safe and permanent home.

Chapter Two

He took Rae to school the next day. "Run and tell Miss White I need to speak to her, then go play with your friends." He didn't want Rae hearing this conversation.

Miss White paused to speak to one of the Schmidt boys as she crossed the yard to where he waited. She smiled at him as she drew closer. Her lips were pressed together. No flash of white teeth like he'd seen as she spoke to the children. Perhaps Rae had said something to warn her of his displeasure.

He held out his hand. "Here's your hair ribbons."

She refused to lift her hand and take them. "I gave them to Rachael. They're hers."

"She has no need of them. This is pioneer country. One has to be strong to survive."

"And how, sir, does a ribbon in one's hair make for weakness. Does it somehow suck life blood out the roots of one's hair?" She faced him squarely, her eyes bold and challenging.

What happened to the apologetic distressed female he'd imagined? "It's what it signifies."

"You mean self-respect?"

She was one argumentative woman. "Useless things. Things for looks."

"Beauty is not a useless thing. It's a refreshing thing. Like a rainbow, a sunset or a blossom."

Conor wondered what use a blossom was. "Do any of those put food on the table or hay in the barn?"

"'Man shall not live by bread alone.'"

"Might surprise you to know that I recognize that as a Bible verse and I'm pretty sure it refers to needing God's word. It has nothing to do with things just for lookee see." He grabbed her hand and pulled it forward. He uncurled her fingers and pushed the ribbons into her fist. "Don't have no need for hair ribbons."

My how her eyes did flash, as full of fire as a winter stove. Faint color brushed her cheeks, making her look like some kind of fine china. But the way she stood, her fists clenched at her side and her jaw jutted out as if about to challenge him to defend himself, he knew she was a little scrapper. He liked that in a person.

His thoughts collided so harshly he reached for his forehead intending to grab it to stop the sudden headache, but then he thought better of it. No way would he let her guess she'd surprised him.

Yeah, she might fight for an ideal while surrounded by safety of the schoolyard, a town within walking distance and a home in one of the finest houses in the virgin settlement. But real life was vastly different. "Pretty little hair ribbons and righteous indignation are about as necessary and helpful as..." His thoughts stalled. "As dandelion fluff."

She sniffed and tossed her head as if his words were meaningless. "Are you going to tell God His creation is useless?" She stomped away—daintily, of course—without a backward look.

Which left him no choice but to call to her back. "Me and Rae are survivors."

Survivors! As if that provided excuse enough for the way he treated Rachael. Forcing her to grow up like a boy. Virnie paused inside the door where no one could see her and struggled to gain control of her emotions.

Miss Price had helped her get past the feelings deposited by her father.

She lifted her head. She would do the same for Rachael. There were things she could do in school and she intended to do them but she'd like to help the girl more.

Lord God, provide me an opportunity.

The next two days Conor brought Rachael to school and returned to wait for her when the day ended. He didn't ride away until Virnie looked at him. And his look warned her not to interfere with the way he raised his daughter.

His silent insistence only increased her determination. She *would* find a way to help Rachael. She continued to pray for some kind of opening.

Friday afternoon, the children raced home, happy for the weekend. Except for Rachael who sat on a swing outside, waiting for her father.

Virnie, having no desire to see Conor again and relive all the emotions that insisted on surfacing each time she saw him, remained at her desk marking papers. Or at least she tried. Finally she put her pencil down, planted her elbows on the ink-stained surface and tipped her head into her palms. It was seven years since she last saw her father. She'd firmly put that part of her life behind her when she left with Miss Price. It was dead and gone as far as she was concerned. So why did it haunt her?

She sighed and returned to marking the papers. She knew Conor was the reason. Conor and Rachael. Their situation too clearly mirrored her early life and brought back unwanted memories.

The swing creaked. Virnie glanced out the window. Rachael still waited. Where was her father? She moved to the window and glanced down the road. No sign of dust indicating a rider. She slipped out to join the girl, sitting on the nearby swing so they could talk.

"Is your Pa coming for you?"

Rachael scuffed her shoes in the dust and studied the tracks she made. "Don't think so."

"How are you to get home?"

"Walk. Done it lots of times."

Virnie waited, wondering why the child hadn't already left but Rachael didn't seem about to offer any answers. "Did you want something?" Perhaps this was the opening she'd prayed for. "Is your father at home?"

"He's cutting the crop."

"I see." Only it didn't answer her question as to whether or not he would be watching for her return. "Do you want to help me clean the chalkboard?"

"Sure." She raced back to the school, Virnie on her heels. As they washed the board and cleaned the brushes, Virnie talked and silently prayed.

"I sure appreciate your help. You're a good worker."

"Pa says a person has to pull their weight in this country."

Virnie supposed it was true about most places. She wanted to know how Rachael felt about being a girl.

"Guess it doesn't matter if you're a boy or a girl, you can do your share."

"Pa says women have to be strong in order to survive out here. Say there's no room for weakness."

He did, did he? Well, strength could be disguised under velvet just as much as it could be revealed in leather. And it was time Conor found that out. Except she didn't plan to be the person to show him. He reminded her too much of her past and she didn't welcome the reminder.

She washed the chalk dust off her hands. "The blackboard and brushes are nice and clean, ready for Monday morning."

Rachael had no reason to linger and yet she did. Tiny bubbles of apprehension skittered along Virnie's nerves and she shivered. Was there a reason Rachael did not want to go home? Was Conor hurting her physically and Rachael wanted to tell Virnie but didn't know how? "Is there something wrong at home that you don't want to go there?"

Rachael shot her a surprised look. "Not at home."

Relief warmed Virnie's veins. Somehow she found it difficult to contemplate an abusive Conor. "Then what's wrong?"

Rachael hung her head and studied her toes.

Virnie caught the girl's chin and forced her to face Virnie. She kept her voice soft even though tension made her feel brittle inside. "Tell me what's wrong."

Rachael scrubbed her lips together as she considered Virnie. Finally, her dark brown eyes wide, she whispered, "I don't want to walk home."

"But why? Haven't you done it lots of times before?"

Rachael shrugged and pulled away. "It's nothing."

"No. Something is bothering you. Tell me what it is and maybe I can help."

"You can't do nothing."

She ignored the poor grammar. "Why don't you let me decide that?"

Rachael shuddered. "It's Faulks' dog." The child's fear beat like something alive.

But Virnie wasn't getting any closer to what bothered Rachael. "Who are the Faulks?"

"They live on my way home."

"Ahh. So you pass their place and you're afraid of the dog?"

Rachael shot her head up and gave Virnie a defiant look. "I'm not scared." But her eyes said she was.

Virnie made up her mind to see if the fear was legitimate or not. But she sensed she would offend Rachael if she made her plan obvious. "Rachael, I'm planning to visit all of my students' homes. This afternoon would be a good time for me to visit you. Would you mind if I walk home with you?"

Tension drained out of the child so quickly she swayed. "That would be nice."

Virnie closed the windows and the door then followed Rachael outside. They walked along the dusty road. The day was warm with a breeze that kept it from being unbearable. The sky was so blue that if Virnie lifted her head she could feel like she walked into a vast flat lake. Birds lifted from the yellow blades of grass as they passed, calling out a warning as they flew away.

Rachael skipped along beside her, chattering about all sorts of things until they had gone a mile and she slowed drastically. A house stood on a rise of land a few hundred feet away.

Virnie made a few quick assumptions. "This must be where the Faulks live."

"Shh. If we're really quiet maybe the dog won't hear us." Rachael tiptoed at the far edge of the road.

Virnie abandoned the middle of the road in favor of the side as well, not sure what she faced but certain of Rachael's fear. Surely, she consoled herself, no one would keep a dog that threatened a child. Surely, Rachael's fears were unfounded.

A snarling black shape bowled toward them.

Virnie's heart clamored up her throat. This was the dog Rachael feared and for good reason. He barreled toward them like a freight train. Virnie backed away, her mouth suddenly as dry as the dust at their feet.

Rachael grabbed Virnie's skirt and pressed close to her back. "It's him. He's going to get us."

Something fierce and hot surged through Virnie. "No, he's not." She faced the attacking dog, now within twenty feet of the road. "Stop," she yelled with all the authority she could muster. "Stop."

The dog didn't slow down one iota.

"Don't move," she told Rachael though she wondered if either of them could force their limbs to run.

She lowered her voice to her deepest tones. "Stop."

A distant voice called, "Tictoc, you get back here right now, hear."

The dog slowed slightly.

Virnie tore her gaze from the approaching menace to the house. A plump woman stood on the step waving a broom.

"Tictoc, don't you make me come after you." The woman banged the broom against the wall.

The dog stopped, still growling, still considering

whether he wanted to continue his attack or obey the cross mistress.

"Tictoc, I'm warning you. Get back here. Now." Another solid whack with the broom.

The dog edged backward, clearly wanting to complete what he had started. But another whack of the broom made him turn and slink away. Virnie stared as he skittered past the house and disappeared under a nearby fence.

The danger was over but she couldn't move. Couldn't speak. Her lungs seemed to have forgotten their job was to provide oxygen to her body. Her brain remained in shocked numbness.

"He's gone," Rachael whispered. "Let's go."

Virnie's breath escaped in a loud whoosh and she leaned forward as she sucked in air. She must not let Rachael know how frightened she'd been. Sudden anger pushed her fear into distant corners. "Does that dog threaten you every time you walk by?"

"If he's here. He belongs to Devin Faulk. He's their son. He has a farm south of here and takes the dog with him. I like it when he's not here."

Virnie started to giggle. She knew it was a mixture of relief and anger. "Tictoc? What sort of name is that for a dog?" She tried to control her giggles but couldn't.

Rachael stared at her and blinked, then her eyes sparkled. "Tictoc like a clock." For some reason the little rhyme amused them both immensely and they giggled like mad.

They continued toward the Russell home.

"That's my house," Rachael said with obvious pride, pausing to let Virnie have a good look.

Virnie saw a low house of moderate size and felt an

instant sense of relief. At least Rachael didn't live in one of those tarpaper shacks some of the settlers had for a dwelling, nor in a sod shanty. The wood had not been painted but it looked a substantial enough place. To one side were pens for the animals and a sod-roofed building she took for the barn. A small pen housed chickens and another fenced area indicated what might have been a garden. Some buckets lay scattered along the garden fence. Rags were caught along another fence. Apart from the general air of untidiness, it seemed to promise a solid future. Virnie stood several minutes taking it all in, trying to confine her feelings to how this affected Rachael but she couldn't stop a trickle of memories. She enjoyed hours with her brother, Miles, at a farm. One bigger and more developed than this one, but seeing the pens and the barn brought things to mind she'd purposely pushed away. Following Miles around, trying to imitate him, trying to earn his approval, hoping if she did, her father would voice his...what? She didn't know what she'd expected then any more than she did now. Perhaps a word of praise, a sign that he didn't regret having a daughter? She turned from studying the Russell farm. "Are you going to show me your house?"

Rachael grabbed her hand and ran. Virnie had no choice but to trot after her.

They ducked into the house. Virnie remembered her manners in time to stifle a gasp at the mess before her. They stood in a nice-sized room that served as living quarters for the residents—combining sitting area, dining area and kitchen. The room had potential to be bright and cheerful but it did not live up to its possibilities. Dirty dishes covered the table. The stove held an array of blackened pots and pans. Clothing of every description from a

Rachael-sized shirt to a heavy winter coat lay scattered across every surface. Virnie had to wonder where they sat, how they managed to prepare a meal, how they kept clean. She deliberately shifted her gaze to the two doors opening into the room. Both stood open to reveal beds buried beneath clothing and assorted objects. How did they find room to sleep in those beds? And how did Rachael manage to find clean clothes to wear to school?

Mentally, Virnie began to roll up her sleeves. She could tackle the worst of this mess while she was here, perhaps show Rachael a few coping skills. She wondered how long she had until Conor returned because she didn't have to be a genius to sense he would object to her interference.

"Rae." The faint call came from outside, some distance away.

Rachael grabbed Virnie's hand. "Don't tell Pa about the dog."

The child's request drove all else from Virnie's mind. She assumed it would be the first thing Rachael said. Such an encounter should be reported and dealt with. Why was Rachael afraid to tell Conor? "You need to let him know so he can do something."

"No. Pa needs me to be strong."

"Rachael, you need to be protected."

Rachael swallowed so hard she grimaced. "I can take care of myself."

Virnie knew she couldn't. What if Mrs. Faulk hadn't been there to call the dog off? Virnie shuddered to think of the child facing that dog alone. "You need to tell him."

Rachael shook her head. "Promise you won't tell."

Virnie considered her responsibility to report the incident against the child's obvious reluctance. "I won't tell him but I want you to promise you will. He needs to know."

"Okay, I will." Her reluctance was obvious.

Conor burst into the house and Virnie could not pursue the subject. She had given her word. Now she must trust Rachael to keep hers.

"Where have you been? Why are you so late?" Conor demanded of Rachael and then he shifted his gaze to Virnie. "Why did you bring her home?"

"Pa, she is visiting all the families and I got to be first."

Conor narrowed his eyes, still studying Virnie. "Is that a fact?"

Virnie's struggle to deal with her reluctant promise about the dog ended suddenly at the challenge in his voice.

"Do you have any objections?" She meant both visiting in general and making Rachael her first visit.

He blinked before her directness. "Why is Rae so late?"

"She helped me clean the chalkboard and brushes so we could walk home together." She darted a glance at Rachael, hoping to convey that now would be a good time to tell her father about the dog. But Rachael refused to meet her eyes.

"Do you expect me to serve you tea?"

She almost laughed but managed to confine her amusement to a grin. "I'm not sure that would be a good idea." She let her gaze circle the room and knew a sense of victory when he looked uncomfortable.

"It's harvest time. Don't have time to spend cleaning up the house. It can wait. The crops can't."

She didn't say it looked like the house had waited a very long time but knew her eyes must have flashed her disbelief when he scowled.

The sound of an approaching rider reached them.

"It's Uncle Gabe," Conor said.

Rachael screamed and raced outside calling, "Uncle Gabe. Uncle Gabe."

Conor did not release Virnie from his look, rife with warning, but beneath that she read more—his latent worry about Rachael being late. Realizing his unspoken concern, something sharp and hot drove through her thoughts. This man cared about his daughter even though he treated her like a boy. Perhaps she could appeal to him on that basis, somehow make him see the harm he inadvertently inflicted on his child. She could explain—but pain twisted through her at the mere thought of telling someone how it felt.

The look in his blue, bottomless eyes shifted, seeking a response that had nothing to do with Rachael.

A noise outside made him jerk toward the door, freeing her from his stare and allowing her to think clearly. She didn't intend to get involved with this man. Yes, he might care in a flawed way about his daughter but Virnie did not have any desire to relive her own experience in order to help him. She would pray for some other way to help Rachael.

"I've been expecting him," Conor said.

"Your brother?" Virnie asked.

"No, just a good friend."

"I'll be on my way." But before Virnie could make her way through the door, Rachael returned, pulling a man by his hand.

His eyes widened when he saw her and he whipped off his hat. "Didn't know Conor had a lady friend visiting." He grinned widely at Conor then shifted his attention back to Virnie. He didn't say anything but the way his grin deepened, Virnie knew he thought she was worth a second look.

She took the liberty of giving him a good look, too. A man with fine features, blond hair, blue eyes and unrepentant amusement.

"'Bout time old Conor acknowledged there's more to life than work."

Conor grunted. "Miss White is the new schoolteacher." He nodded toward Virnie. "You probably figured out this is my friend, Gabe. Gabe Winston."

"Pleased to meet you, ma'am. And might you have a Christian name?"

"Virnie." She looked at Conor as she spoke, wondering if he would ever take the liberty of using her name. But he scowled like he had a pain somewhere. She pulled herself straighter. She knew that look. Had seen it often from her pa. And she understood she was the source of the pain. For Conor as well as her pa. "I'll be on my way. Good day."

Gabe made a protesting noise but stepped aside as she steamed out.

She hurried away with long, furious strides. Why did she let Conor's attitude pull unwanted memories to her mind?

She stomped hard on the dusty surface of the road, raising dust to her knees. She'd have to polish her shoes and brush her skirt when she got home. The extra emphasis to each step did nothing to stop her from remembering.

Too bad you're a girl.

After all this time, the words still twisted her heart into an agonized knot.

Lord God, the past is past. You provided Miss Price to give me a different life. Help me forget those days of pain and uncertainty.

Her thoughts slipped to Rachael. How similar their

situations. If Miss Price were here she'd surely find a way to help. What would she do?

Virnie stopped at the school to get some papers and texts so she could prepare lessons then returned to Maxwell house where she boarded. She liked living with them. Their formal parlor and old-fashioned furniture reminded her of living with Miss Price. She found comfort in their routine and stiff mannerisms that also reminded her of Miss Price. She paused to greet Mrs. Maxwell then retired to her bedroom to pen a letter to Miss Price. In great detail she told about her first week, asking advice on how to teach the Schmidt boys English and how to challenge young George to apply as much interest to literature and penmanship as he did to arithmetic.

She closed with, "There is a child who reminds me of myself. She is motherless. Her father dresses her like a boy. He expects her to be tough. I would like to help her but find myself dealing with memories of my own past that I prefer to ignore. I must in all honesty say this child's father doesn't seem to be unkind toward her."

Thinking of Conor filled her with confusion. Her first glimpse of him convinced her he cared about Rachael. Today she knew she'd seen worry in his eyes over Rachael's tardiness in returning from school. She'd seen something in him that made her lonesome inside. But when had she become so maudlin? She had only to consider Rachael's fear about the Faulks' dog to know there was something wrong.

She turned back to her letter. "Please pray that I might have wisdom in this situation." What if God wanted her to do more like Miss Price had done? "And the courage to do what needs to be done."

Chapter Three

Gabe stared after Miss White and as soon as she was out of earshot, let out a low whistle. "You sure know how to pick 'em."

Conor snorted. "She's Rae's teacher. I had nothing to do with her being hired." His insides had gradually grown tenser as he watched for Rae to return from school and when he'd seen Miss White escorting her, all he could think was Rae had been hurt. He'd crossed the field in great leaps. To discover Miss White only wanted to check on him had only twisted his insides further because of the strange mix of unwanted emotions—embarrassment at the state of his house, defensiveness at her silent accusation and—he didn't want to acknowledge it but he couldn't deny it—*loneliness*. He'd had a sudden flash of what life could be like with a woman to share the load.

Even now he kicked himself mentally at his nonsense. He'd learned the pain of expecting a beautiful, gentle woman to accept frontier life. He dreamed that dream and reaped the disappointment and grief. A lesson he didn't intend to repeat. He'd ask for and expect help from neither God nor man—or perhaps he meant it was only from women he couldn't expect help.

Not that he'd lost his belief in God. Just his trust.

"Being a teacher don't make her less pretty." Gabe poked him in the ribs to emphasize his point.

Rae hung from Gabe's arm. "I told Pa she was pretty, too."

Conor shot them both a look burning with fury. "Tell me what good pretty is." He strode out the door. Of course it was too much to expect Gabe would take the hint and shut up on the matter.

"Pretty is mighty nice to see when a man returns home tired and hungry."

Conor put up mental barriers at Gabe's reminder of what he missed. "I suppose you count yourself an expert? Don't see you inviting young Diana to join you." Gabe had left his intended back in Philadelphia when he came West promising to send for her when he was settled. That was two years ago.

"Figure it's about time. Soon as I get the barn up and the harvest in."

Conor scoffed. "Heard that last year."

"My barn's still not up."

"We'll do that this fall." He figured mentioning that fact would give Gabe something to think about. Seems he came up with more excuses than necessary for not sending for Diana. Conor kind of figured Gabe wasn't quite ready to commit to marriage. He guessed the delay wasn't a bad idea and wanted to warn Gabe that Diana might have unreal expectations about what pioneering meant but didn't want to turn the conversation back to the one topic he wished to avoid—the risk of expecting a woman to labor at his side. Gabe's side, he corrected.

"So what was Virnie doing out here? Seems a long way from the schoolhouse."

"Miss White—" he emphasized the proper title "—seems to think she should visit each of her students' homes."

He felt Gabe's amused grin directed at him but ignored it and tromped toward the field where the last of the sheaves waited to be stoked. "Rae, you look after your chores."

"Yes, Pa." She dropped back, disappointed at missing out on the conversation.

Gabe waved to her. "See you later, little gal." He closed the distance between himself and Conor. "So how many other homes has Virnie visited, do you suppose?"

"I'd guess none."

"Mighty interesting that she chooses this place first."

Conor stopped and faced his friend. "I know what you're doing. But I am not interested in Miss White. You saw her. Does she look the type to embrace frontier life?"

Gabe shrugged. "She came of her own free will, one would assume."

"And I expect she will leave of her own free will before Christmas."

"Conor, not every woman is like Irene. Some are even stronger than their men. Why, you only have to look down the road to the Faulks. It's the old lady who does most of the work while the mister supervises and her son wanders about looking for who knows what. Sure, he says he has a farm somewhere but I have my doubts."

His example supported Conor's argument. "When

was the last time you had a good look at Mrs. Faulk? She's built like a small ox. Nothing pretty or soft about her."

Gabe laughed loudly. "I bet all that padding's plenty soft."

"You know what I mean."

Gabe stopped and faced him, forcing Conor to stop, too, or reveal his dislike of this conversation by ducking around him. He chose to face the man squarely.

"I know what you mean better than you do." Gabe seemed intent on speaking his mind.

"Humph."

"Yup, you're scared you might get hurt again. I've said it before and I'll say it again. Not all women are like Irene."

Conor refrained from voicing a warning that Gabe might soon enough discover for himself the true facts of the situation. "Look, are we going to stand around jawing all day or get this crop harvested? Could be you're delaying so you don't have to send for Diana."

"I guess I'll have to prove you wrong." He bent his back and worked like this was the last day available.

The next two days Rae teased Gabe into giving her a ride to school and picking her up afterward. It interrupted their workday and made Conor uneasy. Sure, Rae liked Gabe's attention but was this something else? He began to suspect Miss White had said or done something to make Rae think she must be escorted to school. On the third morning, he decided to test his theory.

"Rae, Gabe's too busy to take you to school. You'll have to walk. Same after school."

"Okay, Pa." She skipped off down the road.

Conor stared after her. There went that suspicion and

with it the argument he'd used to deflect the memory of Miss White standing in this very room.

Gabe, as always honing in on his secret thoughts, punched him on the shoulder. "If you didn't want me seeing Virnie every morning you only had to say so or take Rae yourself."

Conor grabbed his hat. "Come on, let's get to work."

Several days later they worked on the last of Conor's crop. He enjoyed the hard work. It kept him from thinking too deeply about anything but the grain, the cows and his plans for the fall. Like Virnie White. It seemed everything he said or did made him think of her.

"I warned Diana how cold Dakota winters can be and she says she will bring lots of warm clothes and make some extra warm quilts."

If Gabe brought Diana out right after harvest, the two of them would share the cold winter months. Conor straightened and let his gaze rest on the house across the field. His house. His lonely house. When he'd moved West he had envisioned a home full of warmth and welcome. A flash of Virnie's pretty smiling face flitted across his mind. He blinked and dismissed it. He wasn't lonely enough for the kind of pain brought by sharing his life with a pretty woman.

Gabe watched him. "Virnie seems like a fine woman. I saw how she handles the kids. A fine woman, indeed. Perhaps you should get to know her better."

Conor didn't answer but he tossed bundles to Gabe fast enough to make him pant.

That night they scrounged a meal by opening several cans. They gave three plates a quick wipe and found a place to set them by pushing things off the table.

Conor saw the knowing look in Gabe's eyes and silently dared him to mention the state of the house and suggest it needed the touch of a woman. "Now my crop is done I'll make arrangements for Rae then we'll go to your place."

After they'd finished their simple meal, he rode over to the Joneses' where he normally left Rae if he planned to be gone overnight. They lived close enough Rae could run back and forth to look after the cows and the chickens. But Mrs. Jones was down with something and said she couldn't manage.

He returned home with the awkward news. "Can't take her with us. She needs to tend to the chores."

Rae edged forward. "You could get someone to stay here."

Something about the look on her face warned Conor her suggestion wouldn't be to his liking. "Maybe. But most everyone has chores at home."

"I know someone who doesn't have chores. Miss White."

"No." The word exploded from him.

Gabe chuckled. "You sound mighty scared and you won't even be here."

Conor did not want to picture her in his house, touching his belongings, filling his kettle, sweeping his floor. "No."

Gabe laughed hard. "Man, what's gotten into you? You're jumpy as a spring colt. Virnie must really have gotten under your collar."

"You can't begin to understand. And her name is Miss White."

"Ain't what she told me."

Conor knew an incredible urge to physically remove that teasing grin from Gabe's face.

Gabe leaned closer, making it even more tempting. "Seems to me you're overreacting, unless…" He dragged his sentence out as he sat back waving a finger. "You're more interested in her than you're willing to admit."

"You're plumb loco."

"Then ask her."

"Please, Pa, please."

Conor sighed loudly, letting the pair know just how annoying they were. "Fine. I'll ask. But don't expect she'll say yes."

Virnie had been grateful to Conor's friend for bringing Rachael to and from school. But it only lasted a few days. When Virnie got a chance to speak to Rachael privately, she learned the Faulk boy or man, whichever he was, had left again and taken the dog with him.

"Did you tell your pa about the dog?"

"Didn't need to. He's gone."

"What about when he comes back?"

Rachael gave an unconcerned shrug. "Maybe he won't." And Virnie had to be content with that. So why did she stare down the road every morning until Rachael arrived and check every afternoon, sighing in disappointment when Rachael marched down the road, swinging her lunch pail and kicking up little clouds of dust? It wasn't because she hoped Conor would ride up for his daughter. It couldn't be. Because she wouldn't allow herself such silly thoughts. His behavior was too much like her father's. And forget the worry and concern she'd seen in his face over Rachael. It didn't count.

And forget the way his probing look had stirred such an unfamiliar response deep inside in places she had never known existed. Now those places refused to be ignored despite her firmest efforts. The ignited feeling both frightened and thrilled her. With a decided shake of her head, she pulled her thoughts into submission and focused on the letter from Miss Price.

She skimmed over the suggestions on ways to help the Schmidt boys learn English more quickly and nodded as she hurried through the problems Miss Price had sent that would require George to do extra reading before he could solve the challenging arithmetic problems. She found what she really wanted at the end.

> As to your questions about your little student, bear in mind that not all parents are willing to let their children benefit from personal involvement with a teacher. In my experience, there has only been you and Belle.

Belle had been a student before Virnie. She came from a large family and when her parents decided to move farther west they made the choice to let Belle continue her education. Boarding with Miss Price had been a perfect solution for Belle. Her parents had left her reluctantly.

Unlike Virnie. In her case, she had learned to accept that her father was glad to be rid of her.

She turned back to the letter.

"That is not to say there aren't other ways of helping this child both inside and outside the classroom." Miss Price went on to list several scenarios such as involving Rachael in extra reading, or performing in a drama or being involved in some community endeavor. "I will pray for such opportunities."

Virnie folded the letter and put it in the drawer with the previous letters from Miss Price. She owed it to her mentor to do something for Rachael even if it meant having to deal with Conor and her errant feelings around him.

But what?

God would have to provide the answer.

The next day, Conor surprised her by bringing Rachael to school. Rachael ran to Virnie. "Pa wants to talk to you."

She wondered at the excitement in Rachael's voice. But her main concern when she crossed the yard to where Conor waited was controlling the sudden roll of her heart that left her breathless.

"You wanted to speak to me?" She kept her voice admirably calm despite the way her insides vibrated at speaking to this man who had inadvertently opened up an unwelcome door in her heart. She didn't know what lay past that open door and didn't intend to find out. She had her life plans laid out firmly. She would be a dedicated teacher such as Miss Price had trained her to be. And because it was what she wanted.

Conor seemed very interested in the reins draped across his palm. "Umm. I have to go to Gabe's farm and help him with his harvest."

She nodded. "Does that mean yours is done?"

"Yes, and a fair harvest, too."

"Good. I'm glad for you." Though she wondered what it had to do with her and why he continued to twist the reins.

"Rae can't go with me."

"Of course not. She has to attend school."

"And do the chores at home."

She nodded. "You'll miss her, I suppose." She had to see his response, assure herself he did care, that Rachael being a girl wasn't reason enough to resent her.

Conor's gaze rested on Rachael standing near the school watching them. Then he turned to look hard at Virnie.

She saw his stark feelings about his daughter. He loved her so much it seemed to almost hurt him.

"I will miss her." His voice was low, edged with roughness. "But out here we do what has to be done without complaining."

She nodded, not understanding the warning note in his voice.

He sucked in air and jerked his gaze away as if aware of the tension lacing the air between them. "She needs someone to stay with her."

"Certainly she does."

He shifted back to look at her. "Would you?"

His gaze was so intent, so demanding, she found it difficult to think. "Would I what?"

"Would you stay with her?"

Her mouth fell open. She forced it shut and swallowed hard. Was this God's answer for a way to spend more time with Rachael? He'd certainly found a unique way of doing it.

Conor took her hesitation for regret. "I wouldn't be there. Be gone for a week or two."

"Why I'd love to stay with her. On one con-dition."

His eyes narrowed. "Tell me before I agree."

"You allow me to teach her a few skills around the house."

Darkness filled his eyes. "Don't need fancy stuff."

"Seems to me from the little I saw that you would

benefit from someone knowing a few basics like washing dishes and tidying up."

They did silent battle with their eyes and then he nodded. "So long as you don't teach her to be a silly, weak female."

She laughed, despite feeling like her past had slapped her full-on. "Female doesn't necessarily equate weak and silly." She'd tried to prove it to her father. Unfortunately, she had failed so miserably he had sent her away and never again contacted her. She pushed the hurt of her former life back into the shadows. This was not about her. It was about Rachael.

Conor only quirked his eyebrows at her quick defense. "I have to leave immediately. Take good care of her." He waved Rachael over.

Rachael raced to his side, darting cautious glances at Virnie. "She's going to do it?"

Conor nodded.

Virnie thought he looked like he regretted it already. She left them to say goodbye. But as she walked away she overhead him say, "Don't expect her to stay when things get hard."

Virnie grinned. If he thought she'd turn tail and run at the first challenge she encountered, he didn't know the things she'd faced in the past.

Chapter Four

Virnie found lots of work to do in the house and enlisted Rachael's help, hoping to teach her a few coping skills. Her first task was to wash dishes. It was a standard kind of job that occurred in every house across the nation every day. Only this was Conor's kitchen and as she scraped the dirty dishes she got glimpses of what he ate, the meager sort of meals he endured and wondered how either he or Rachael survived. She felt his presence in every corner of the room. She wondered how he spent his evenings. Did he read? She saw little evidence of it though she didn't venture into his room. She tried not to think of him sitting over a cup of tea, wanting to share his day with someone.

She pushed aside an increasingly familiar awareness of the empty areas of her life. It would be nice to share stories of her day with someone. She scoffed at her silliness. If she wanted to share she had only to sit down and pen a letter to Miss Price. But it wasn't the same.

When Rachael complained they didn't need to wash all the dishes, only what they needed, Virnie chuckled. "Sounds like something your pa says."

"Yup." Then thinking Virnie might expect better English from her, corrected herself. "Yes. 'No need to waste time on needless chores,' he says."

Virnie tried to think of a way to show Rachael that house chores were as necessary as farm chores. "Why does your pa insist the pens are cleaned every day?"

"Easier to move a little manure than a lot."

"Same with dishes. It's easier to wash what you use every day than face the dirty stack when you run out."

Rachael looked startled.

"So we'll wash all these dishes and put them away and then every day you wash the ones you use. That way you don't have to try and find something clean when you're hungry."

They finished the stack. Virnie scrubbed the cupboard and put everything away. "Doesn't that look nice?" The tabletop was clean and scrubbed, the stove shiny black.

Rachael giggled. "Pa wouldn't know it was the same place."

They tackled the rest of the room. Virnie discovered beautiful wood floors that gleamed once she'd scrubbed and polished them. She saw Conor's handwork in the hand-hewn window ledges and his craftsmanship in every detail of the house. The house revealed a pride that belied its current condition. There must have been a time he valued a nice home.

As Virnie polished a window, she wondered what had caused Conor to change his mind. Certainly the death of his wife formed a large part of it. Aching for his loss, she pressed her lips together to stop their trembling.

Friday afternoon, she followed Rachael into the

cleaned house and stopped as a wave of sensations poured over her again, making her feel teary. She struggled to identify the cause of her reaction. The place felt like home. She felt she had a part in making it welcome. It wasn't her home and never would be but a longing for such a home and welcome grabbed at her insides until she struggled to catch her breath.

She closed her eyes momentarily to stop the sensation.

This was not what she wanted. No. She had set her heart on being a teacher like Miss Price—helping many children, devoting herself to a worthy cause.

She gathered her thoughts and hung her hat on the nearby hook. Next to Conor's coat. His scent filled her senses—masculine, and hinting of his work with animals, reminiscent of her days helping Miles. She rested her head against the wall and fought for control. This was Conor and Rachael's home. Her home was a tiny room in the home of Mr. and Mrs. Maxwell. Miss Price had taught her to enjoy the privacy of her own room and to realize the rest of the house belonged to others. It was the way things were for teachers. Virnie knew it well and not only accepted it, she enjoyed it.

So why this sudden, overwhelming reaction to a house she had cleaned and polished, this blur of tears at the bouquet of scents from Conor's coat—reminding her both of Miles and Conor?

Rachael ran out to gather eggs then returned for the milk pail.

"Pa says I'm the best little milker. I can milk the cow faster than he can. I think it's 'cause she likes me."

She was gone again, leaving Virnie struggling with her war of emotions. She touched Conor's coat, fingering the woolen texture, freeing another waft of scents. Why did he treat Virnie like she couldn't be counted on? Why did he try and make Rachael so tough? What had happened to his wife?

She jerked her fingers from the fabric and pushed herself from the wall, away from her silly meanderings. It was the weekend and she intended to tackle Rachael's room today. Tomorrow she would wash clothes.

As soon as Rachael returned and the milk was tended to, Virnie led the way to the bedroom. "Rachael, remember what I say in school? A neat desk is an efficient desk. Same with your bedroom. Keep it clean and you'll waste far less time looking for things."

Before they could put anything away, it was necessary to clean out the drawers of the chiffonier. In the bottom one, under a collection of rocks and feathers and other little treasures, Virnie found a picture.

"This must be your mother. You look very much like her." A beautiful woman with lovely hair.

Rachael grabbed the picture from Virnie's hands. "Don't tell Pa I got this. I'm supposed to forget her."

Virnie struggled to hide her shock. It hurt to forget one's mother. "Why is that?"

"Because she was weak. She was supposed to help him but Pa says she just lay down and quit living all because she missed the easy life of the city. Pa says we have to work hard to have a home no one can take from us."

That explained so much. His insistence that Rachael be tough, his neglect of the house—no doubt the poor man had lost his dreams along with his wife. Or did men *have* dreams?

Rachael put the picture back in the drawer and covered it with an old shirt. "I don't want to disobey Pa but I want to have a ma, too, even if it's only her picture."

"I understand. I won't tell your pa."

They worked together sorting out the room, but Virnie's thoughts tended to stray. She identified with Rachael's need for a mother. In Virnie's case, Miss Price had proved an adequate substitute. But a person needed a pa, too. Hers hadn't wanted her so she'd struggled to forget that need. But in spite of her sincerest attempts, she could not shake the desire for recognition from her father. Somehow, she had to make Rachael realize how fortunate she was to have that even if it carried a requirement to be tough.

"At least you have your pa and you know he cares about you."

Rachael giggled. "He loves me but says it might make me soft if he tells me. So he saves it for special occasions."

Virnie couldn't help wondering what occasions constituted as special enough for the words so she asked.

"Christmas morning, the first thing he says is, 'I love you, Rae.' And my birthday." Rachael giggled again. "He makes up special occasions, too—the first robin of spring, the first snowfall. Stuff like that."

Virnie's throat tightened and her teeth felt brittle. Tears threatened. As Miss Price often said, her eyes had a tendency to leak. But thinking of Conor's tenderness hidden under the cloak of his toughness touched her in secret places that ached for something she didn't dare identify. It so filled her with longing and wanting that she struggled to contain her emotions. If only she could have the same tenderness extended to her. Her imagination raced out of control. She saw herself standing in the living area she had recently cleaned, a savory meal simmering on the stove as she awaited Conor's return and a taste of that tenderness.

Chastising herself for her inability to rein in her thoughts, she grabbed an armload of dirty clothes off the bed. "Tomorrow you can help me do the laundry." Hooks on one wall burgeoned with more clothes. "Let's sort these out." She quickly determined many of the items were too small or needed serious repair. The last item on one hook was a pretty blue calico dress. Virnie held it out. "This looks new."

"It is. My grandma from Philadelphia sent it."

"Why don't you wear it?"

"I'd only get it dirty."

"It will wash."

"Overalls make more sense."

Virnie didn't pursue the topic knowing Rachael quoted her father but she had an idea.

Sunday morning, she approached her plan. "I attend church Sunday. I'd like you to come with me."

Rachael brightened at the idea. "Can I?"

"Of course. Let's get prettied up." She'd worn a simple cotton dress in demure gray with a lace-trimmed collar. She'd fashioned her hair into a loose chignon. "Why don't you wear that dress?"

Rachael shook her head. "Pa says I don't need to dress up to impress God. Says God's seen me before I was born and every day since and lots of times naked."

Virnie laughed. "That's true but I think putting on our best clothes for church shows God we respect Him. After all, we wouldn't go visit the president in anything but our best, would we?"

"I guess not."

"Then run and put on your dress."

Rachael headed toward her room with obvious reluctance. She emerged a few minutes later in the dress. The blue brought out her natural coloring.

"You look very nice." Virnie had one more challenge. "I have some pretty hair ribbons that match that dress perfectly."

"Pa said we got no need for useless pretty things."

"I only thought they might keep your hair in place. Keep you tidy. But if you don't want to…" Virnie made as if to put the ribbons away.

Rachael's eyes followed Virnie's hands with obvious regret. "I guess it wouldn't hurt to be tidy. Seeing we're going to church."

Virnie hesitated. "You're sure?"

Rachael nodded. "I think Pa would agree they serve a useful purpose."

"Of course they do. Now sit on a chair while I tend to your hair." The child had thick wavy hair that required patience to brush. But Virnie didn't mind. She loved caring for this child, doing for her all the things Virnie had never had done. As she brushed Rachael's hair she wondered why she couldn't recall her mother. Virnie had been five when she died but she seemed to have disappeared from memory. In fact, until she met Rachael she had forgotten her father and Miles, too, except for brief, unwelcome flashes. Of course, Miss Price's counsel to put her past life behind her had caused Virnie to do her best to forget it. But she wished she had a picture of her mother like Rachael did. Somehow it would be comforting to have some reminder.

"There. You're done. Have a look."

Rachael went to the small mirror over the washstand and turned back and forth examining her reflection.

"What do you think?"

"It looks nice."

Virnie hugged her. "You look very pretty." Rachael stiffened a bit and Virnie guessed she thought of her father's words about pretty being useless for a pioneer. But he was wrong. A person—a woman—could be pretty, or at least pleasant-looking, and still face the challenges of this new land.

Monday after classes ended, Rachael hopped about as she waited for Virnie to close up the school. "Pa should be back tomorrow."

"How can you know?"

"'Cause the weather's been good. He said it would take seven days of good weather. He'll be back. He never stays away longer than he has to."

Rachael had such confidence in her father's affection. "Shall we make it a special occasion?"

"How can we do that?"

"Well, you could help me make a special meal." She'd been able to fashion simple meals from the eggs, milk and a decent supply of canned goods. On Saturday, as she draped the wet clothes on the fence surrounding the garden patch, she'd found evidence of potatoes and carrots.

Rachael had explained, "Pa plants a garden every spring."

Virnie shook her head. Weeding the garden might actually allow them to reap some produce. But upon closer examination she unearthed useable potatoes and carrots. "Where does your pa get meat?"

"Goes to the store. I can go and Mr. Brown will sell

me something and put it on Pa's bill. I've done that before. Are we going to make a real meal?"

A real meal. For a real family. In a real home. The
words danced through Virnie's mind like the taunt of
teasing children. Or the echo of her own heart. "We'll
get some meat on our way home tomorrow." She
squeezed Rachael. "We'll cook a real meal." And then
her sojourn into pretend would end and she'd return to
her lifetime goal.

There was no reason she should dread the idea. None
whatsoever.

Conor rode into the yard. Through the window, he
glimpsed Rae and Virnie. He wanted to see Rae and
assure himself she was fine, put to rest his loneliness,
but he hesitated. Virnie was there, too. He didn't know
if he liked the idea or not. Or perhaps he knew the answer and shied away from it.

He rode Noble to the corrals, unsaddled him and took
his time about rubbing him down all the while telling
himself his only reason for not rushing to the house as
he normally would after being away was because of his
concern for his horse.

But soon he had no more excuses.

He must face what lay beyond the door across the
yard. And what lay within his heart. Things he'd been
trying to escape all week. Of course, Gabe's constant
yatter about the pretty schoolmarm made it impossible.
But even on the ride home, alone with his thoughts, he
hadn't been able to escape thinking of Virnie.

Stupid. Stupid. He knew she would be anxious for
him to return but only so she could go back to her safe
little room at the Maxwells'. No doubt she'd had more

than enough of pioneer life by now. He tried to convince himself he didn't care nor expect anything different.

But still he found reason to pause at the corral gate and adjust the bar. He discovered a great need to check the corner post to make sure it was sound. He found an undeniable urge to give a good look around to make sure his fields were still there. He snorted. Like someone could walk away with ten acres. Finally he forced himself to the house, stopping outside the door to gather up his strength to face—what? Disappointment? He had only invited her to stay with Rae. Nothing more. Of course she'd leave as soon as he returned. So what did he need to face then? He sighed and reluctantly acknowledged this house signified a dream that had died with Irene. A dream of home and security and belonging and warmth and—

The dream was dead. Long live reality.

He shoved the door open and staggered back as Rae launched herself into his arms.

"Welcome home, Pa. It's a special occasion. I love you."

He squeezed her tight, and recognizing the game they had played for years, he said, "I guess if it's a special occasion, I love you, too."

She giggled. "You love me anytime."

He buried his face in her hair. It smelled sweet and clean. Slowly he raised his gaze and his heart punched a hole clear through his reason as Virnie stood before him smiling a welcome. He glanced about the room. It positively shone. The hole in his reason widened. This was how he imagined the house looking when he had lovingly built it. He jerked his gaze to the stove where pots stood waiting. The scent of roast beef and potatoes caused a flood of hunger. He missed good meals. He tried to stop himself from looking back at Virnie but couldn't. His willpower had turned all mushy.

She continued to smile. "Welcome home. We've made supper for you."

He let Rae slip to the floor. She continued to press to his side. He squeezed her shoulder, needing something solid to anchor himself to.

He wanted someone to share his life, his home, his daughter. He wanted someone to welcome him home. Someone who would share responsibility in every way, from preparing tasty meals to cleaning the house to— reality kicked in with a vengeance that froze every other emotion.

What he wanted and needed included a woman able to tackle whatever challenges this fledgling country sent. And Miss Virnie White was not that sort of woman. Too soft and pretty to be truly practical.

He pushed his dreams back into the grave and turned to hang his hat and coat on a hook. Right next to a pretty cape and wide-brimmed hat that surely belonged to Virnie. He inadvertently brushed the cape, lifting the scent of sunshine and flowers to his nostrils. For a moment he couldn't move as his insides responded to the scent. For a heartbeat he let it lift his thoughts from reality. His dreams weren't about to rest in peace nor to allow him peace.

Rae grabbed his hand and tugged him toward the table. "We made a nice meal. A real meal."

"We?" He cocked an eyebrow at Rae but his eyes found their way to Virnie who stood demurely to one side, her hands clasped ladylike at her waist and her smile gentle and cautious, almost impatient. Had she been keeping the meal warm for some time?

"Rachael is a wonderful help," Virnie said.

He turned his attention back to his daughter. "Rae can do most anything she sets her mind to."

Rae rewarded him with a blinding smile. "I'm tough."

"That you are," he agreed.

"The meal is ready." Virnie's voice remained low with no hint of disapproval but Conor would not look her way to see how she'd reacted to Rae's pride in being tough. He didn't want to deal with it. Not tonight. Not with the house clean and a meal on the table. For today, he would accept the gifts without worrying about what the giver thought of him.

He washed up and sat at one end of the table. Virnie sat at the other end and Rae on the side between them. He trailed a finger over the wood, remembering how he had planed and polished it to smooth perfection. Then, realizing what he was doing, he pulled his hands to his lap. The table didn't matter any longer. Any more than the rest of his dreams. Dead. Gone.

"Would you like to say grace?"

Virnie's question pulled him from his mental meanderings. He nodded. Been a long time since he'd felt the need to thank God for anything. He wasn't sure he should be grateful now. No, he was wrong. For the food ready to eat, he was thankful. As to the other stuff—his resurrected dreams, the gentle woman at the end of the table who was responsible for their revival—perhaps that was his own fault. He should have never asked her to stay with Rae.

But he appreciated a good meal and he bowed his

head. "Our Father in heaven, hallowed be Your name." He stumbled. He hadn't intended to say the Lord's Prayer. "We're grateful for food and home and blessings. Amen."

"Amen," Virnie whispered. She met his gaze briefly then shied away as she reached for the bowl of little potatoes. "Rachael told me what you liked to eat and we've done our best with what we could find."

His jaw tensed. Did he hear a barely hidden criticism of how little she'd found? "Found your way to the store for meat?"

Virnie blinked, either surprised or defensive. He wasn't sure which. "Rae said it was all right but perhaps I shouldn't have—"

"No. Rae's right. Mr. Brown knows to let her buy supplies if she needs to."

"Good, because she really wanted to make a real meal. Her words."

Conor relaxed and grinned at Rae. "Getting tired of my cooking?"

Rae giggled. "Pa, you don't cook. You open a can."

Conor felt defensive color creeping up his neck and gave Rae a playful cuff to cover his embarrassment. "Never heard you complain before."

"'Cause I was hungry."

He filled his plate with slices of beef, a stack of potatoes, some carrots and drowned it all in rich, brown gravy.

"Rachael prepared the potatoes and carrots," Virnie said.

"Sure are scrawny carrots. Where did you get them?"

Rae answered even though Conor sent a quick glance

at Virnie. "We found them and the 'tatoes in the garden."

Conor blinked and stared at Rae. "I plumb forgot about it." He tasted a carrot then bit into one potato. "Good."

Rae and Virnie exchanged glances. Rae giggled and Virnie ducked her head but not before he caught a look of amusement.

"What's so funny?"

Rae pressed her hand to her mouth to hide her giggles.

Conor silently demanded an answer from Virnie.

She wiped the smile from her lips. "We decided you expect garden plants to be tough, too. No coddling them by pulling weeds." Her eyes danced with amusement.

He had the feeling he was being teased, his tough-routine being gently mocked. But he had no idea how to respond and turned his attention to the food. "Excellent meal," he said when he'd scraped the plate thoroughly. He eyed Rae, wondering when she would be old enough to prepare such meals.

As if reading his thoughts, Virnie spoke. "There are things Rachael could learn to prepare even though she's young. Simple meals that would be more satisfying than eating out of cans. I'd be willing to teach her if you like."

Conor's insides knotted with warring emotions. He had to let his dreams remain buried and in the hour he'd been back home, he knew having Virnie in the house made that impossible. Seeing her hand in every item in his house, seeing her smiling across the table, feeling her quiet spirit blessing his home were dangerous things to acknowledge to liking but admit them, he did. He should refuse her offer.

On the other hand, he'd like to eat better. Rae needed to eat better, too. And she needed help learning to cook. Help he couldn't provide.

"Would you like that, Rae?"

If she showed the least resistance it might give him the ability to say no to Virnie.

But Rae almost bounced off her chair. "I'd love it, Pa." She looked at Virnie, her eyes shining.

Conor understood it wasn't the idea of learning to cook she liked so much as the thought of Virnie's attention. He had second thoughts. Third thoughts. But none of them quelled the arguing idea of how good this would be for Rae. Not even in the deepest, darkest corners of his heart would he admit it was not for Rae but for himself. "Perhaps we could work something out."

Chapter Five

They agreed on three afternoons a week. Virnie assured herself that would enable her plenty of time to deal with her teaching responsibilities. She would not allow herself to neglect any of the other children and their needs.

The only stipulation Conor had made was, "So long as you don't interfere with my teaching Rae to be tough."

Virnie figured there were ways to show him a woman could handle pioneer life without acting like and dressing like a man and being so tough.

That was her sole reason for going—to teach Conor to accept Rachael as a girl and help prepare the child to cope without a mother.

It had nothing to do with the way her heart skidded sideways whenever Conor walked into the house and glanced at her with a mixture of resistance and—

And what? He had offered her nothing more than tolerance and she wanted nothing more.

She wondered how she could silence the argumentative voice itemizing the reasons to the contrary—his obvious love for Rachael, which he tried unsuccessfully to mask, the beauty of his home that surely revealed deep longings in the man.

Longings dead and buried along with his wife.

But she was helping Rachael as Miss Price had helped her. That's what mattered.

So she concentrated on showing Rachael how to make a pot of vegetable soup.

But Conor did not show up at the usual time.

"He must have found something important to do," Rachael reassured her.

"This happen often?" She had scary visions of Rachael alone after dark. Yes, she understood Rachael must face the realities of her life. And certainly other children stayed alone for short periods of time out of necessity, but this child was not yet nine.

Rachael shrugged. "Sometimes he gets busy."

Virnie wished she could be as unconcerned as Rachael who picked at a slice of bread. But her stomach coiled and recoiled. Conor could take care of himself. He surely didn't need to rush home to see that Rachael was safe. He knew Virnie was with her. But the sense of dread would not leave her.

She stared out the window into the late afternoon sun. It wouldn't set for a couple of hours yet. And Rachael would not be alone. Virnie would stay until Conor returned.

She tried to stop her thoughts from skipping backward to a time she was about Rachael's age. No, younger because…

She was alone in the dark. Mama was gone. Papa was gone. Miles was gone. She didn't know where they were or when they'd be back. Or were they coming back? Hadn't Papa said, "No. She's not coming back. Never." Or was that Mama?

Mama was gone. She remembered now. And not coming back. Papa kept saying it until he got angry at her.

But where was Papa? Gone, too? And Miles? He'd been the one who held her as she cried because Mama wasn't coming back. He'd promised to look after her. But he was gone, too.

She shivered as she huddled in the corner. Everyone was gone but Virnie.

She couldn't remember how long she'd remained there, crying, certain she'd been abandoned. It had seemed like forever. When the outside door opened, her terror had increased a thousand-fold. They were coming to take her away, too.

A golden glow signaled someone lighting a lamp.

"Virnie, are you here? Where are you?"

It was Miles. He'd come back.

Miles had found her sobbing in the corner, pulled her to his lap and wiped her eyes. "Did you forget I went to work at Mr. Zingle's farm? I told you I would be back after dark."

Papa had come in then. "Too bad she ain't a boy. You could take her with you."

She remembered Miles putting her down and pushing to his feet. "Boy or girl, I'm taking her when she isn't in school."

Papa shrugged. "Might be for the best. I ain't got time to babysit her."

Virnie shuddered at the vivid picture, then pushed it back, back, back into the room of forbidden memories. She needed something to keep her hands and mind busy. "Let's make a bouquet for the table."

"A bouquet?"

"Yes, something pretty—" Remembering the normal Russell objection to pretty, she found a different explanation. "Something to remind us of God's gifts of the season—the harvest, the cooler weather, His provision of things to see us through the winter."

"All right."

Virnie found a pair of shears and a basket to carry their findings. Staying close to the house, watching for Conor's return as she worked, they sought out stalks of grain, a branch with some burnt orange leaves and two bluebells. Virnie's thoughts were unsettled by the flash from her past. But perhaps God had sent it to make her realize how Rachael might have similar fears. She prayed for a way to discover how the child felt but knew she'd been taught to hide her fears.

They carried their find back to the house and arranged it in a blue granite jug, which they put in the center of the table. Virnie decided it was too tall and distracting. She wouldn't be able to see Conor without tilting to one side or the other. "Let's put it on the sideboard."

Rachael chose the spot. As they stood back to admire their work, they heard a horse riding into the yard.

Rachael raced to the window. "It's Pa. He's back. He always comes back." There seemed to be nothing but confidence and acceptance in her voice.

Perhaps Conor was right. Perhaps teaching Rachael to be strong made it possible to face being alone without fear.

Darkness had fallen by the time the meal was finished. The first time Virnie helped Rachael she had planned to slip back to the Maxwells' before the meal was served but Conor would not allow it.

"Inhospitable." He'd practically growled the word.

Rather than argue, Virnie agreed to share the meals she helped prepare. And it certainly caused her no hardship to do so. She would allow herself to admit she enjoyed playing house in this home. Temporarily, of course.

She insisted on helping with the dishes then reached for her hat and cape. "I best be getting back." She still had some papers to grade and lessons to prepare for the next day.

"We'll walk you back." Conor reached for his hat.

"That's not necessary. It's three miles and then you'll have to turn around and walk back."

Conor handed Rachael a sweater. "It's dark. We'll see you get home safely."

Virnie wanted to argue. This went beyond helping Rachael. It slipped past barriers, her rationalizations and headed straight for a tender spot in her heart where someone actually cared about her safety and security. It was a dangerous place to visit and certainly not a need she wanted to set free. "Conor, really, I don't need an escort. I'm used to being on my own."

He stepped outside and waited. "It's my fault for being late."

Rachael, set to dash down the road, paused to announce, "Virnie was worried about you."

Conor blinked in astonishment. "Miss White," he corrected Rachael but she had already run along the path, waving her arms and singing. He turned to stare at Virnie. "You were worried?"

"It's just that I remember what it was like to be alone after dark." She marched after Rachael.

Conor didn't move. "Rae isn't afraid of the dark. Are you?"

She couldn't explain how it felt to be alone and uncertain if anyone cared. "Not of the dark."

He caught up to her. She felt his measured study and was grateful for the dusk to hide her expression. He saw only her weakness. Not unlike her father who found her weak and useless. Only she wasn't. Not anymore.

"Rae loves the dark. Look at her." Conor sounded pleased by the way Rachael ran ahead, almost disappearing into the gloom. "She can face almost any challenge."

"You have every right to be proud of her." She half expected him to deny it.

"I guess I do. She's proving to be a good pioneer girl. Together we'll build us a solid future."

He was not like her father, she again discovered. He adored his daughter and sought only to prepare her to deal with the life he had chosen for them. She might not agree with all his methods but she couldn't deny his affection.

Ahead of them, Rachael stopped and tiptoed toward the edge of the field alongside the road. She squatted down.

"She's found something." Conor picked up his pace. "What is it?"

"Pa, it's a baby kitten."

Virnie and Conor reached Rachael at the same time. She held a tiny mite of a cat, too young to be on its own and squalling frantically.

"It's crying for its mama. Poor little kitty." Rachael

cuddled it against her neck and giggled when the kitten nuzzled about searching about for something to eat. "She's hungry."

"It's too small to be of any use. Give it to me and I'll take care of it." But when Conor reached for the kitten, Rachael backed away.

"I want to keep it."

"Rae, it's just a useless little kitten. I doubt it will even survive."

"No. I'll feed it and take care of it. It will live. You'll see. It will be a good cat."

Conor sighed. "What good is a scrawny little thing like that?"

Until now Virnie had been content to stand back and watch, but hearing the harsh condemnation in Conor's voice seared her insides. Just because something was small and defenseless didn't make it valueless.

Rachael appealed to her. "Miss White, don't you think I should keep this kitten?"

She stilled her arguments. This wasn't about her. It was only about a helpless kitten. "A cat is good for keeping the mice down."

"This scrawny thing?" Conor's voice rang with scorn.

She faced him and smiled. Even in the dusk she could see him hesitate, caught between his need to always be practical and the longing in Rachael's voice. "You might be surprised what this scrawny cat will grow into."

He stared into her eyes but it was thankfully too dark for her to be able to guess what he thought of her remark. She could only hope he didn't read anything more than a vote to give the kitten a chance. She didn't

want him wondering if her remark held far more personal information.

He nodded. "Very well. You can see if you can keep
the thing alive. But no moaning and crying when it
dies."

"It won't," Rachael protested hotly. "And I wouldn't
cry. You know I wouldn't."

"We'll see."

"You want to hold her, Miss White?" Rachael held
out the kitten for Virnie to take.

She cupped it in her palms. "It's soft. And such a
pretty color. All gray." She examined it more closely.
"With little white tips on all four paws."

"I'm going to call it Tippy."

Conor groaned. "You name it and it will only hurt
more when it dies."

"Tippy isn't going to die." Rachael took the kitten
back and held it close as if protecting it from Conor's
dire prediction. She hurried ahead.

Conor groaned again.

Virnie stifled a giggle at his frustration.

He heard her. "Don't laugh." They continued their
journey toward Sterling. "But I suppose she might as
well learn the cycle of life and death in this country."

"I expect she's plenty familiar with it. After all, her
mother died." She couldn't keep the memory of her own
loss from edging her words.

Conor didn't speak for a moment. "I guess you have
a point though I don't know how much she remembers.
Or if she thinks about it ever."

"She does."

They walked on in silence for a few steps.

"She's said things to you?"

Virnie couldn't reveal Rachael's secret but Conor ought to know that Rachael hadn't forgotten. "Just enough for me to know she remembers her mother but is afraid of forgetting her."

He stopped, forcing her to stop, too, or walk away from him. She was too curious about his reaction to walk away. "I want her to forget. She can't hold on to the past."

"Conor, she can't forget. And if she does it will cause her more pain and distress than remembering."

"How can you say that? Is it a theory they teach all fledgling teachers?" His voice rasped and she guessed his concern for his daughter caused it. Or perhaps he was dealing with his own pain and distress at remembering.

"They don't tell teachers that. I speak from personal experience. My mother died when I was five. I can't remember anything about her. Not what she looked like. Not the sound of her voice. Not her scent. I can't even remember her holding me." She realized her voice grew thin as if her the tension of her innards held her throat captive.

Conor lightly clasped her elbow. "I'm sorry." He pulled his hand away.

The touch was brief, quick, as if he thought better of his action as soon as he made it, but brief as it was, it touched far more than her skin. It melted her tension and filled her with a strange mixture of regret and longing, of loneliness and hope. She scrubbed her lips together as she fought for a solid core of purpose as she had taught herself to do. But she couldn't find it and jerked around, making her feet move down the road, trailing after Rachael.

Conor easily kept pace with her. "I always thought it was best to erase any memory of Irene. That's Rae's mother."

She noticed he said Rae's mother and not his wife, and wondered if he tried to erase Irene's memory from his own thoughts. She wanted to explain the futility of insisting on forgetfulness. "I've tried to forget things in my past but it seems I remember the things I don't want to remember and forget the ones I wish I could remember."

"What do you try and forget?"

Her heart cried out to tell him, perhaps receive another gentle touch of sympathy, but for too long she'd pushed those things into hiding and she feared bringing them out. "Just stuff. I expect we all have things we don't want to remember."

He sighed. "You're right there."

She ached to ask him about the things he wanted to forget, perhaps offer a bit of sympathy in return but her emotions frightened her. The intensity of her longing for something beyond being a teacher, her desire to reach out to Conor—they were all too unfamiliar and taking her away from the safe boundaries she had created for her life. And so they walked on in silence, hearing only Rachael's murmuring to her new pet and the soft sounds of the evening—a night bird cooing, the grass rustling in the breeze and, as they neared town, the warning bark of someone's dog.

Sunday morning, Rae turned to Conor. "Pa, I'd sure like to go to church."

Conor laughed. "Last time I checked Christmas was months away." He made a habit of attending regularly—

Christmas and Easter. Saw no need of more. Attending every Sunday sure hadn't helped Irene cope with life.

"I know but I went with Virnie and liked it. Besides, I could see Alice Morgan. She's my best friend."

Conor shrugged. He didn't suppose going more often would turn either of them into sissies. "Sure. I got nothing better to do."

Rae ran to her bedroom. She emerged a few minutes later in a dress. A dress! "Where'd you get that?"

"Grandma Russell sent for Christmas, 'member?"

He surely didn't. Then he noticed how she'd attempted to braid her hair and tie it with ribbons matching her dress. He wouldn't ask if Grandma had sent those, too. He didn't want to know.

He knew two days ago when he saw the jug on the sideboard full of flowery stuff that he'd made a mistake.

He was certain of it when Virnie convinced him to let Rae keep the kitten who had refused to die.

His certainty grew when he felt an incredible urge to comfort her when she made her painful confession about not being able to remember her mother.

But seeing Rae in a dress, her hair fussed with, proved it beyond a shadow.

He had to put a stop to Virnie hanging about.

"Why did you get all dolled up?"

Rae shot him a look faintly reminiscent of Virnie's disbelieving looks. "You'd put on your best clothes for the president, wouldn't you?"

"That sounds like something Virnie would say."

"It's true, isn't it?"

He couldn't argue with her self-assured logic. "Just don't think it will get you out of your chores."

"I ever miss a day yet?"

"Come on, let's go. You sure you can ride in a skirt?"

"I 'spect I can if I want."

Shaking his head, he swung to Noble's back and pulled Rae up beside him. Yup. She managed just fine in a skirt. And why that should annoy him half to death made no sense.

When they arrived at the church, he dropped her to her feet. She waited as he hitched Noble then took his hand as they walked inside. He glanced upward but the rafters didn't threaten to collapse at his unscheduled visit.

He followed Rae into a pew, realizing too late that she chose to sit next to Virnie. So much for putting her from his mind.

She smiled at him then turned her attention to Rae.

He stared at the top of Virnie's head. Or rather the top of her bonnet. A very pretty bonnet but of absolutely no use whatsoever. She wore a nice dress, gray as a soft evening with little frills around the collar. Practical enough for a teacher but a pioneer? Why he could just imagine how she would fuss if she had to get it dirty. No, sir. She wasn't made for pioneering. He resisted an urge to slap his forehead. Who was asking her to be a pioneer? Certainly not him.

At that point she lifted her head and met his look. Her brown eyes filled with what he could only take as appreciation. For what? Bringing Rae to church? But her soft brown gaze wrung out all his firm reasons and hung them to dry. No, she wasn't hardy enough for pioneering but he wished she were. He wished he could dream of sharing his life with her, having her help him build a future together.

The pastor called them to worship and Conor gladly turned his attention to the front.

He would tell her right after church that they had no more need for her to come to the farm.

But the sermon had been about God's sufficiency and had filled Conor with a queer mix of doubt and hope. He wanted to think God could meet all his needs but he feared opening his hands and releasing self-control. He was so muddled by his thoughts that he plumb forgot his intention to tell Virnie not to come anymore. It didn't escape his attention that he found the excuse very convenient.

And Monday when Virnie came to the farm and made a very nice meal of fried chicken and biscuits, making sure to report how Rae had helped, well, it seemed downright unnecessary to forgo the good meals and the cooking lessons for Rae.

She came twice more that week and twice more there were downright good reasons not to ask her to stop coming. Real good solid reasons that had absolutely nothing to do with the fact he counted the hours until she showed up, practically writhing with disappointment the days she didn't come. No, sir. It had nothing to do with that.

Since the Sunday when Conor had dropped to the pew beside her, since their gazes had connected and she'd felt a deep sense of welcome—which she knew made no sense—Virnie had to restrain herself from going to the farm every day. So far, she had excused her visits as helping Rachael and answered the few questions from the townspeople about her trips as helping Rachael learn to cope on her own.

Only she didn't believe it anymore.

She continued to go because the days she didn't felt empty in a way she'd never experienced before. She found herself storing up little stories to tell Conor about the games the children had played at school or the way she'd been able to help the Schmidt boys or how Hilda Morgan had written such a lovely poem.

And she loved hearing about his day. The work he'd done, his plans for the winter and for next year's crop and the little things he'd thought noteworthy.

She knew something had shifted between them but she couldn't say how or why it mattered. Perhaps it was only a truce—a silent agreement to overlook their differences and enjoy the present without regard to the future or past. The past she had no trouble dismissing but the future was a different matter. One she didn't want to deal with. She had her future clearly mapped out— imitate Miss Price in being a teacher who dedicated her entire life to helping children.

The fact that the idea no longer filled her with intense longing and pride didn't matter. It was what she wanted to do.

Today was bright and sunny. Too nice to be indoors enduring the heat of the cook stove.

She turned to Rachael. "Let's go to the garden and see how many carrots and potatoes we can find. They need to be dug before the frost comes."

Rachael didn't have to be asked twice. She threw down the dusting rag and abandoned the task Virnie had assigned her of dusting all the furniture.

Virnie had found it necessary to whack great huge weeds out of her way for the few potatoes she'd already uncovered. She whacked more out of the way now and swung the spade to clear a path down what she guessed to be the row of potatoes. A great cloud of dust and weed seeds billowed up and she coughed and turned away. Her shift in direction allowed her to stare across the field to where Conor plowed down the stubble. For the most part he walked in dust from his task. The ground needed a rain. Or snow. But Conor wanted to finish the plowing first. She knew he worked from dawn to dusk trying to accomplish the task.

He reached the end of the field and turned the horse for the return trip. He paused to wipe his face with a big blue hanky. He stared her direction. It was too far to know if he saw her but then he waved. Just a quick little salute as if he'd acknowledged her unintentionally.

She lifted her hand in response. As she lowered her hand, she curled her fingers as if she could grasp and hold forever the way her heart rejoiced at his wave. It was nothing. He would have waved to any passing neighbor. Only she wasn't a neighbor. He didn't have to look her direction. He didn't have to acknowledge her at all.

But he had.

Smiling, she turned back to the garden calling Rachael from playing with the kitten to help as she dug potatoes. "You put them in the gunnysack."

Several times, she took a break from searching for the root vegetables and straightened. But each time she managed to catch Conor with his back to them. Not that she expected him to wave again. That was plumb silly. Yet a vast emptiness sucked at her lungs each time. It felt suspiciously like disappointment but she denied it hotly.

The sun began its descent toward the western hori-

zon by the time Rachael and Virnie stood at the edge
of the garden, now a tangled mess of bent weeds and
freshly dug soil.

"Three bags of vegetables," Rachael announced.

"Not bad for a neglected garden."

She glanced toward the field. Conor was on the last
furrow. He would soon be in for supper. The thought
brought such a pleasant taste of honey to her thoughts
that she lifted her face to the sun and smiled.

Rachael chased her kitten through the weeds, laughing as they played a game of hide-and-seek.

The harnesses jingled and Conor called to the horse
as he walked the plough across the yard and unhitched
the horse.

Virnie knew he would rub the animal down and see
it had water and feed before he tended to his own needs,
which, she grinned as she saw his dirty face, included
a good wash. He had rolled his sleeves to the elbows,
revealing muscular arms darkened by the sun. Broad
shoulders filled out his faded blue shirt. His dark trousers were liberally coated with dust. A battered hat protected his head but the exposed hair had turned from
black to brown from the good earth that settled there
after he'd stirred it up.

He met her eyes over the yard and smiled, his teeth
flashing white in his dust-covered face.

She nodded and smiled. There was something very
appealing about a working man.

She jerked her thoughts back to reality. For a moment she watched Rachael play. How she enjoyed being
part of all this. Helping Rachael, making meals, keeping the house clean and tidy and waiting for Conor to
come home for supper, even rescuing the meager gar-

den produce. This was only temporary, a pretend life that couldn't be hers. She and Conor—

Enough silly mental games. She took off the gloves she had borrowed from the house and tossed them on top of the shovel. She shook the dust from her skirt and wiped her face with a hanky.

"Do you have someplace to store them?"

Rachael returned carrying little Tippy. "We have a root cellar. Sometimes I like to play there when it's hot outside. It's always nice and cool in there."

"Of course." She'd seen the hump behind the hill and the three steps descending to a narrow door. "I suppose these vegetables will keep better there. Help me drag them over." The bags weighed more than she could carry. But with Rachael pushing and her pulling, they managed to get them to the steps to the root cellar. Getting them down the steps would be no problem. If she had the door open, perhaps the momentum would allow her to get them inside.

"Wait here while I open the door then we'll push the bags down."

Rachael sat on the top step, more interested in Tippy than the potatoes and carrots. Virnie knew in the middle of winter the Russells would be grateful for her foresight in making sure they had them.

The door stuck at one corner. She pushed at it with her shoulder. It slowly creaked back. She didn't move—not one muscle as she stared at cobwebs hanging from the corner of the doorway and clinging to the top of the door, waving and quivering.

Her skin crawled like it was alive with spiders. She shuddered. Her teeth chattered. Her heart grabbed her throat and squeezed off her air. One long, dusty mat of webs swung free of the door toward her.

She screamed as terror erased every thought but escape. She dashed up the steps, panting as if she had run all the way from town. Frantically, she brushed her hair, her arms and shook her skirts. "Ugh," she groaned.

"The pretty little teacher is afraid of getting dirty." Conor stood beside the bags, his fists balled on his hips. He laughed. A very unpleasant mocking sound that scraped along Virnie's nerves. However, it failed to erase the crawly feeling of spiders.

She shuddered. "I hate spiders." The look she gave him dared him to laugh at that.

He didn't laugh but his wide grin was just as bad.

She felt an incredible urge to stomp on something. Like every spider within a hundred-mile radius. Or even better, a smiling, mocking man who would no doubt take her fear of spiders and turn it into a full-length serial about the weakness of women in general and school-teachers in particular. "Put your own stupid vegetables in the root cellar. Or leave them to freeze. I don't care." She spun on her heel and marched for the house.

"Pa, I think you made her mad."

Conor chuckled. "'Pears maybe I did."

Virnie didn't slow down until she was safe inside the house. The man would do well to choose more wisely his times to be amused at her expense.

Chapter Six

Conor didn't know what possessed him to say what he did to Virnie. He'd enjoyed watching her dig in the garden. Resented the time it took to go north the length of the field knowing she was within sight but he had to keep his back to her. And the south length seemed to go far too quickly as he watched her in the garden.

She'd whacked at the weeds, jabbed the spade into the soil and crouched on the ground, digging for the hidden little nuggets of vegetables.

He'd been too far away to be able to see her face clearly but he saw the dust rising from her work and suspected she would be getting down and out dirty. And he grinned. Virnie White grubbing in the soil, getting soiled. The idea warmed the bottom of his heart. Melted away resistance.

It wasn't until he put away the harness and tended the horse that he realized how foolish his thoughts had grown.

Virnie didn't belong on a farm. He knew only a tough, hard, strong woman could survive this sort of life. Digging in the garden was child's play compared to some of the tasks she would face. Raging storms, wild animals, sickness with no medical help available. This was not a life for a pretty little thing like Virnie.

By the time he left the barn, his resentment at her had reached unreasonable proportions.

And his insides felt as if he'd walked through snowstorm breathing in sharp, razor-like frozen pellets.

Seeing Virnie run screaming from the root cellar had solidified his rationale. She did not belong on the farm. His laugh had been as much at himself as at her. Not that she knew it. Nor would he tell her. But he had let himself veer far from the reality of his life.

This was a good reminder to pull his thoughts back where they belonged—on survival.

He took his time putting the sacks in the cellar, grunting under their weight. "How did Miss White get these bags here?"

"I helped her." Rae obviously thought that enough explanation.

He closed the door tightly and stared at the house wondering if he should stay away until Virnie left. "Do you suppose supper is ready?"

"It's stew so it's ready."

Stew. His mouth flooded with anticipation. He loved stew. He'd worked hard all day and he was hungry. Still he hesitated.

Rae squinted up at him. "You scared because Miss White is mad at you?"

"Scared? Nah. Not me." But he was nervous. Would she find a way to punish him? Or—

Would she refuse to come again?

He scowled into the bright sky. Good thing if she did. It was what he wanted. Wasn't it? So why did his mind suddenly scramble for ways to apologize and convince her it was only harmless amusement?

Rae pulled at his hand. "Come on, Pa. I'm hungry."

He allowed her to tug him toward the house, his insides warring unmercifully over his conflicting reactions. He'd been trying to find a way to tell her not to come. But not like this. Not with unresolved anger between them.

He let out a whoosh of air as relief stilled his confused emotions. That's all it was. Concern about the anger. He'd do his best to resolve that. *Then* he'd figure out a nice way of telling her not to come again. "Wait." He glanced around, then saw several stalks of golden wheat at the edge of the field. He jogged over and cut them clean.

"What's that for?" Rae demanded.

"Thought Virnie might like them for the jug of flowery things she keeps on the sideboard."

Rae stared. "Thought you said they were useless pretty things."

"I might have."

Rae slowly grinned. "You want Miss White to like you." She started to giggle

He snorted. "I just don't want her to be mad at me."

Rae giggled the rest of the way to the house.

Conor put his hands on her shoulders at the doorway. "Now you be quiet. I don't want her wondering if I'm still laughing at her or if you are. That's what made her angry in the first place."

Rae sobered. "I wouldn't laugh at her."

"Fine." He pushed the door open.

Virnie stood at the stove, her back to him, the stiffening of her shoulder the only sign she heard him step into the room.

He stood with a handful of wheat stalks, feeling about as foolish and awkward as a seventeen-year-old meeting his future father-in-law. "Brought you something."

She took her time about setting a spoon down and turning. "Yes?"

He held out the wheat. "Thought this might look nice in the jug." He tipped his chin toward the sideboard.

Confusion and surprise chased across her face as she took the stalks. "Thank you." Then she faced him squarely, her eyes fierce with some kind of challenge. "It's just a useless bunch of pretty things."

He nodded. "Guess it ain't hurting anything." He wasn't sure what he meant. Perhaps that there was a time and place for pretty. Just as there was a time and place for tough and hard. Trouble was the latter belonged on a frontier farm. And pretty belonged in a house, sheltered and protected. A long aching loneliness, a sad wish it could be different, made his chest feel like a giant weight had settled there.

"Thank you." She placed the stalks in the jug, rearranging them to her liking. She turned to see he had remained rooted to the spot watching, wanting and fully aware how useless such feelings were.

"I didn't mean to laugh at you."

She grinned. "I expect it was funny to see me run screaming from such harmless things." Her smile flattened and her eyes grew wide, stark. "I hate spiders. Ugh."

"Uh-huh." Now if he could eliminate spiders from

the world… Well, it was as impossible as thinking she might fit into his life.

"Supper is ready." She waved toward the table.

"Let me wash up."

The next day Virnie paused from dusting the furniture to study the jug with the stalks of wheat. It meant nothing. Just some unharvested wheat he'd given her by way of apology.

Only it meant so much more. He'd allowed there was a place for pretty things that served no purpose except to make the house more pleasant.

But it meant even more to her foolish, errant heart. It meant he cared that it mattered to her. She ducked her head and closed her eyes. Why were her thoughts being so disobedient?

She turned away and went to the table where she was showing Rachael how to make a meatloaf. She didn't expect Rachael would remember all her cooking lessons. In fact, she didn't care if she did. For now it was enough to work with the child and see her learning how to cope. And if Conor smiled his appreciation and thanked her after each meal, well, that was nice, too.

Conor dashed into the house. "Rae, I need some help. The bull has a bad cut on his leg that needs doctoring but I can't get him in by myself."

Virnie could hear the bull raging with pain and frustration outside. She glanced out the window as Rachael ran after her father. The pair of them struggled to get the bull headed for the barn. Virnie gasped as the bull lowered his head and charged toward Rachael. She'd be hurt. She dropped the tea towel she held and ran to help them. They had managed to get the bull in the barn and she hurried to the interior.

Conor danced back and forth, waving his arms and trying to direct the bull toward a pen. Rachael stood at the rails with a long pole ready to slide it in behind the bull and stop him from backing out once he was persuaded to step into the pen.

Conor prodded the bull into place. "Rae, the pole."

She pushed it across but the bull backed up, caught the pole partway and tossed Rachael to the ground. Conor rescued the pole and jammed it into place, trapping the bull. The animal couldn't back up but he could paw at the boards in front of him and toss his head.

Virnie saw what the bull needed. She grabbed a rope. "Let me help."

Conor snickered. "You going to lecture him or sweet-talk him?"

She sent him a look fit to make him repentant. "You might be surprised by the effectiveness of a little sweet talk." And to prove her point she murmured softly to the bull as she gathered her skirts and climbed the bars of the fence, reaching toward the bull's head.

"Hang on, you'll get hurt," Conor warned. "Step back."

She ignored his order. "I know what I'm doing." She waited for the bull to lower his head, snagged the rope around his ears and in quick movements fashioned a neat halter and snubbed the rope to the fence. The bull jerked back but he was effectively restrained. She climbed down, shook out her skirts and patted her hands. "There you go. Do your thing on that wound."

Conor's hands hung at his sides as he stared open-mouthed.

Rachael climbed out from the adjoining pen and stared as well.

Virnie grinned. She took great delight in surprising them both. "Shows you what a little schoolmarm is capable of."

Conor seemed too stunned to move.

"Don't you have something you need to do?" She waved toward the animal.

He gathered up his vet supplies, all the while darting wide-eyed glances her direction.

"Do you need me to stay and help?" She managed to sound innocent though she suspected her eyes gave her away. She could feel them dancing with amusement.

"Uh. No. I can manage." He went to the side of the pen and reached through the boards to tend to the wound.

"Well. Then I'll leave you to it." She managed to contain herself until she reached the house where she leaned against the door and laughed loud and hard.

She hummed as she finished meal preparations. Rachael had remained with Conor but she didn't mind. She enjoyed the time to herself, allowing a chuckle now and then in private without anyone to ask what was so funny.

The two of them returned.

"Did you get him fixed up?" Her question was reasonable enough even if the way her words rounded with amusement made Conor shoot her a bewildered look.

"Pa cleaned the cut good and said the old boy would be like new in a few days."

"That's good."

They sat around the table. Conor said grace. They passed the food. Nothing new. They'd done it numerous times. But something had changed. She felt it in the air between them, in the look he gave her and in the bubbling excitement in her heart.

Conor ducked outside as soon as he finished eating. She smiled at his departing figure. She had set him back on his heels and she understood he didn't like it.

She and Rachael cleaned the kitchen. Still Conor did not return. She wondered if she should leave until he did. "You better start your homework," she told Rachael. She wandered over to stare out the window. "I'm going to see if your pa is in the barn."

Rachael had the kitten on her lap and spent more time letting it chase a string she draped over the table edge than she did doing homework. She barely noticed Virnie's announcement.

Virnie slipped out and crossed to the low sod-roofed barn and stepped into the gloom. "Conor, are you here?"

"Right beside you."

She jumped as his low voice came from her right. He stood to the side of a small square window. He would have been able to watch her cross the yard. She quickly ran a hand over her hair. Was everything in place?

"Where did you learn to do that?"

"What? Tidy my hair?"

"No. Halter a bull. Not many women can do that. Lots of men can't, in fact."

She chuckled. "Surprised you, didn't I?"

He laughed, too. "You could say that."

"I have to admit it feels good to surprise Conor Russell."

"Why is that?" He moved closer. In the light from the open door she saw his eyes were dark and watchful.

She met his look without revealing any sign of how

her nerves jittered at having him so close. "Because you have it all figured out. Women are weak and useless. There is no place for them on the farm or in your life. And pretty things have no value."

He didn't speak or indicate how her statement affected him.

"Maybe I proved you wrong."

He jerked away. "I don't think you proved anything. I've seen the folly of putting pretty ahead of reality. Of expecting any but the strongest and sturdiest of women to live out here."

Disappointment seared through her. She had hoped he'd admit he was wrong. "You're talking about your wife, aren't you? Hardly seems fair to judge every woman you see by what she did."

He faced her, his face wracked with fury and pain. "What do you know about her? What she did?"

She backed away a step. "All I know is what I see. How you treat Rachael. And what she says about not allowing weakness."

"She's right. There is no room out here for weakness."

"Nice things, pretty things don't signify weakness." She thought of the bouquet on the sideboard and his contribution.

"Yeah, what purpose do they serve?"

"To brighten the days. Seems to me a person can face most anything if their heart is happy. Pretty things do a lot toward that."

His expression hardened. His eyes darkened. "Where did you learn to snub an animal?"

She didn't want to tell him about that part of her life. Not because Miss Price had told her she was now a lady and she should forget her former life but because she didn't want to confront the pain her past carried.

But Conor moved closer. He touched her shoulder. "What are you hiding?"

The weight of his hand on her shoulder, the soft tone of his voice made her want to tell him everything. Not just how she'd learned to fashion a quick rope halter, but how abandoned she'd felt, how alone and afraid.

She lowered her eyes as she spoke. "I used to follow my brother, Miles, around when he worked on a farm. He said I might as well learn to be useful as be underfoot. He was the one who taught me."

Conor caught her chin and tipped her face up. "What else did he teach you?"

She couldn't move. Couldn't think. Couldn't speak. His gentle touch erased all reason from her mind. She couldn't shift her thoughts from the way his finger ignited such intense longings in her. She had ached most of her life for touches that conveyed such caring and kindness.

"Who taught you to be a prim and proper schoolmarm? Not your brother, I think."

She jerked back and pulled herself to reason. "That would be Miss Price. She raised me from the time I was ten."

"What happened to your brother? I know your mother died but where was your father?"

His question roared through her dragging in its wake all her unwanted memories, scouring her insides with them. She didn't dare let even one of them find words. If she did, how would she ever stop the flow? "It doesn't matter." With limbs as wooden as the door beside her, she jerked around. "I must go now."

* * *

She wouldn't go back. Her errant emotions made it too risky. So she set her heart to being the best teacher ever. She made flash cards to spur the Schmidt boys into learning more English words. She searched her texts for problems to challenge George. She began to plan a Christmas program that would involve each child and showcase their strengths. And she wrote a long letter to Miss Price carefully avoiding mention of her tangled emotions regarding Conor. She settled for reporting the progress Rachael had made in learning basic skills.

She managed to stay away from the farm for four days. It was Rachael's hurt expression when she gave excuses that changed her mind.

"I'll go home with you today, Rachael, and see how you have been managing without me." She smiled to prove to herself it was the main reason.

"I washed all the dirty dishes. And put my stuff away."

"Good girl. Help me tidy the schoolroom and then we can go."

Rachael grabbed the broom and did a reasonable job of sweeping. Virnie would give the room another once over before school opened in the morning.

Rachael ran ahead on the way home, leaving Virnie plenty of time to think.

But she knew she returned to the farm for more than Rachael's sake. It was because of Conor. Though she realized how foolish it was to dream he'd see her in a new light—see that she wasn't weak, helpless, useless. She knew why it mattered so much what he thought. Somehow, gaining his approval convinced her she could erase the hurt of her past.

Rachael paused to watch a bug scurry across the road then fell in beside Virnie. "I thought you might be too mad at Pa to come again."

Virnie prayed for wisdom to say the right thing. "I'm sorry you thought that because it isn't true. Your pa and I aren't angry at each other."

"Good. I don't what you to stop coming."

Virnie felt a familiar ache from her childhood. The feeling of abandonment. She couldn't think of any kind way to respond to Rachael's statement. Yet at some point they would both have to face facts. There would be no reason to continue her visits. They would move on in different directions.

She pretended a great interest in the puffy clouds along the horizon as she struggled with a fresh wave of pain that had nothing to do with her past. She loved Rachael more than a teacher should love one particular student. She wished she could be part of the child's life for more than a few months.

"Pa's been working on the barn."

Thankful for the change in conversation, Virnie asked, "What's he doing?"

"Says it's time to put a proper roof on. Says the sod was only temporary. He's going to put up big—" She put her fingers together in a V to indicate.

"Rafters?"

"Yes. Going to make room for a loft."

"Sounds like an ambitious plan."

"Virnie, what's a loft?"

Rachael had slipped into the habit of using Virnie's given name when they were alone. Virnie enjoyed the sense of closeness it gave her so she never corrected the child. "A loft?" She explained the large attic area for storing hay. "It's fun to play in a loft. When the hay is gone, you can skate on the floor. My brother showed me how."

"You have a brother?"

"Yes, Miles." For a time he had been both mother and father to her. How could she still miss him after all these years?

"Where is he?"

"I'm not sure. I haven't seen him in a very long time."

"I wish I had a brother or sister." She slowed as they neared the Faulk place, watching for any sign of the dog.

"I thought you told me Devin Faulk was gone along with his dog."

"Shh." She held her finger to her lips. "You never know." Her whisper was barely audible.

Just then a snarling black ball of fur erupted from under the porch and barreled toward them.

Virnie's heart landed in her mouth with a shuddering thud. She faced the animal, afraid to take her eyes off the menace.

Rachael whimpered and took one running step before Virnie grabbed her and shoved her behind her back. "Don't run. He'll only chase you." She edged down the road. Where was Mrs. Faulk with her broom? She should have brought her own broom from the school. She glanced to the right and left but apart from some dried blades of grass there was nothing that would serve as a weapon. "Stop," she ordered.

That had about as much effect as a waving a hanky.

"Stop," she shouted. "Tictoc, stop right now."

The animal didn't even slow down.

A door banged. Mrs. Faulk stepped to the porch with her broom.

Thank You, God.

"Tictoc, get back here." Whack.

The dog's snarl ended on a whine.

"Now." A series of whacks. "Don't make me come after you." More whacks.

Tictoc stopped. He turned, made three steps, then spun back to Virnie and Rachael, growling and snarling.

"Tictoc. Now."

Virnie didn't wait to see if the dog would obey. She sidled along the road as fast as she could without running, Rachael clinging to her back.

Not until they were safely away from the threat did Virnie stop and bend over her knees to suck in air. "I see Devin is back."

Rachael scowled in the direction of the Faulk house. "I wish he would go away forever."

Virnie straightened. "Did you ever tell your pa about the dog?"

"I can't."

The danger of this child dealing with the dog on her own made Virnie's knees go weak. "You must. What if Mrs. Faulk isn't there some day? I need you to promise me you'll tell him today."

"He'll think I'm weak. He says the dog is all bluff."

"I don't want to see if that's true or not." She squatted to meet Rachael's eyes full-on. She grabbed the child's shoulders. "This is something you *should* be afraid of. I'm sure your pa will agree."

Rachael didn't look convinced.

Virnie couldn't contemplate what the dog could do to Rachael. "I don't want to see you hurt. Promise me you'll tell your pa. I'll help you if you want."

She could tell Rachael struggled between her fear

and her desire to please her father. Virnie waited. Finally Rachael nodded. "You'll stay with me when I tell him?"

"Of course." She hugged the child, relieved this danger would be dealt with.

At the farm she found the floor needed mopping and the stove polishing but Rachael had indeed washed the dishes and the table had been cleared. Virnie stared at the jug on the sideboard. She had expected Conor would have tossed out the pretty things. Instead, she saw several of the old branches of colored leaves had been removed and fresh ones inserted.

Her smile tugged the corners of her heart. Conor had changed. She could almost hope—

She closed her eyes and prayed for strength to be what she knew she must be and ignore the tremors on her heart that made it difficult to think.

Rachael helped her prepare a simple meal of fried eggs and potatoes.

When Conor stepped into the house, Virnie's heart tremors escalated to earthquake proportions. She grabbed her emotions and forced them to submission before she turned to face him.

Sweat soaked his shirt. Dust hid in each fold and wrinkle. He took off his hat to reveal a dusty rim of hair that had been exposed. "Hello."

The uncertain, husky quality of his voice echoed in her head.

She managed a squeaky, "Hello." She tried to tear her gaze from his but her eyes would not obey. The scent of masculine sweat and dust made her think of hot summer days. Made her wish and want for things she knew did not fit into her well-laid plans.

"Smells good in here." He turned to hang his hat, freeing her from her tangled thoughts.

A mat of cobweb hung from his hair, draping down his back. She shuddered and pointed.

Rachael giggled. "Pa, you're wearing a cobweb."

Conor twisted to look over his back, making the web move like it was alive.

Virnie clamped her fist to her mouth to stop a moan.

"Brush it off," Conor said to Rachael.

Virnie managed to squeeze out one word. "Outside."

Conor glanced at Rachael and they both laughed at her fear but thankfully stepped out the door to brush his back.

"The spiders really like the space under the sods," Conor said as he washed. He made a great pretense of brushing his hair as if seeking for lost spiders. He grinned wickedly at Virnie when she shuddered.

"It's not funny," she muttered.

Conor wisely ducked his head but she knew he found it amusing. But it provided her the perfect opportunity.

"Some fears are good. They prepare us to face danger." She nodded toward Rachael who looked about as eager to talk to Conor as she would be to face Tictoc.

"Rachael, tell him."

Conor's head came up and he alternately studied the two of them. "What's up?"

Rachael ducked her head.

"She has something she needs to tell you," Virnie prompted.

"Rae?"

Slowly, Rachael faced Conor. "Pa, it's Faulks' dog."

"That noisy beast. What about him?"

Rachael sought support from Virnie. She smiled and nodded. "Pa, I'm scared of him."

Conor stared at his daughter then jerked his gaze toward Virnie. "Is this your idea?"

Anger roared up her throat and scalded her tongue. "Rachael, why don't you take some food out to Tippy and play with her for a few minutes."

Rachael looked about to argue but with both Conor and Virnie looking ready to fight, she sighed and dragged herself out the door, pausing once. "I told you I didn't want to tell him."

Virnie waited until the door closed but before she could speak, Conor leaned forward, his forearms on the table, his fists bunched. "I don't want her taught to be afraid of things."

"No one taught her to fear that dog coming after her. If Mrs. Faulk didn't call it off…"

"The dog is all bluff. The worst thing she can do is show fear."

They glowered at each other. What had given her the stupid idea he might have softened? She'd gladly let it go and leave for home, perhaps to never return. She denied the aching protest the idea brought. But for Rachael's safety she must pursue the subject.

"Everyone is afraid of something. Sometimes little and unreasonable things like my fear of spiders. Other things are real and valid. Like Rachael being afraid of that dog. Even you have fears though you'd never admit it."

His scowl deepened. "What am I afraid of?"

"Weakness. You're afraid to allow any weakness will destroy you. You're afraid any softness makes a person vulnerable and useless." She breathed hard. The feeling of being little and useless billowed up inside her with a bitter bile taste. Her father had treated her that way and now Conor had effectively made her feel the same.

She pushed to her feet. "I have to go. I'm sure you can figure out how to clean the kitchen on your own. Or does doing so indicate weakness?"

Not waiting for his answer, she stomped out. She calmed her anger enough to tiptoe past the Faulk place. Thankfully the dog did not come out though she thought she heard him bark from inside the barn. They ought to be made to keep that animal locked in the barn all the time.

By the time she reached the Maxwells' she'd pushed her anger to the back burner. She was not a weak, useless creature anymore. She was a teacher with the futures of seventeen children to shape and guide. It was what she wanted. All she wanted. She had to remember that.

Chapter Seven

Conor stared at the dirty dishes on the table. He didn't need a fancy schoolteacher telling him how to run his life. He should have told Virnie to stop coming long ago. Instead, he'd let his silly notions of—he slammed a mental door closed. He had no idea of anything beyond surviving this harsh land. But his reluctance to say a final goodbye to Virnie had undone all his hard work in teaching Rae to be fearless.

Rae tiptoed in and hovered at the door. "Pa, is Miss White mad?"

Mad as a woman alone on the prairie. Mad as a bull eating locoweed. "Rae, you can't let fear run your life. You have to face it and conquer it."

"Yes, Pa."

"Never let that dog see you're afraid."

"Yes, Pa."

"Now do the dishes while I get something."

"Yes, Pa."

He fled the house. He'd equip Rae to handle the dog. He found a length of wood and smoothed it into a thick bat. She had nothing to fear except her own thoughts.

This bat would give her the idea she was strong. That's all it took. Believing in your own ability.

He returned to the house and gave it to her. "You carry this with you. When that useless dog comes running out, you wave this and yell. He'll leave you alone soon as he sees you aren't scared."

She took the length of wood and waved it.

"Think you can handle it?"

"Yes, Pa."

He sat and watched her swinging the bat back and forth, testing its use. "Rae, you know what it takes to survive out here, don't you?"

Her arms fell to her side. She looked at him and nodded. "Being strong."

"That's right. And what happens if you're weak?"

"The country kills you."

"So what are you going to be?"

She grinned. "I'm tough as can be. You'll see."

He pulled her to his lap. "Good girl." He tickled her. She screamed with laughter and tried to wriggle away.

"Not too tough to be ticklish I see." He stopped tormenting her and they grinned at each other. She understood the necessity of survival. "You're a good kid."

"I know." She scooted away and retrieved the bat. Again she swung it back and forth. She seemed pretty intent on trying different stances and checking her swing from both the left and the right.

"Whatcha' doing?"

"Practicing so I'll be ready."

"Good girl."

Virnie watched for Rachael the next day, wondering if Conor would have said something to end their friendship. She waited as long as she could before she rang the bell. Surely, Conor wouldn't refuse to let her attend school.

As the children lined up in twin rows, Rachael scurried down the road then slipped into place.

"Good morning, Rachael. I was afraid you might be late."

"Morning, Miss White," she murmured.

But though Virnie waited, Rachael refused to look directly at her, staring instead at the ground in front of her.

Virnie felt a great wave of disappointment but perhaps Rachael was only uncomfortable about being late. As the children had filed in, she wondered if it was more. Rachael scurried past Virnie without glancing up. Her shoulders were halfway to her ears and she twisted sideways as if she felt she had to protect herself from the teacher.

Virnie sighed quietly. Whatever Conor had said it had effectively created a barrier between herself and Rachael. It shouldn't matter so much. She'd done what she could to help Rachael and that should be enough. But it wasn't. She felt as alone as she had when she was a child. She forced her thoughts back to instructing the children before her.

At recess, Hilda hung back until all the others had left. "Miss White, I think you should look at Rae's leg." She hurried out before Virnie could question her.

Tiny little skitters of worry skipped along her nerves as she went outside to supervise the children. As she stepped out, Rachael fled to the far corner and displayed a devout interest in the grass.

Virnie circled the yard innocently as if interested

only in what the children did. As she neared the corner, Rachael skipped away, headed for the outhouse. Virnie followed more slowly and waited nearby. But recess time was over and Rachael did not come out.

Virnie signaled to Hilda. She met her a few feet from the outhouse and whispered, "Ring the bell and get the children into their seats. Tell them to work quietly."

Hilda nodded and soon after the bell sounded. The children marched inside.

Virnie waited. Rachael would have to come out soon.

Sure enough. She heard the hook clatter. The door cracked open as Rachael peeked out. Virnie stayed out of sight until Rachael stepped to the dusty ground and reached down to fiddle with the bottom of her pants. Virnie could see she was trying to fold the edge to hide a bloodied tear.

Virnie clenched her teeth together. Why did Rachael hide an injury from her? Did she think it would make her weak to take care of it? She reached the child before Rachael noticed her. "I'd like to have a look at that."

Rachael jerked away. "It's nothing."

"Then I don't suppose there's any reason I shouldn't see it." She caught Rachael's arm gently, making it impossible for her to run away, and bent to lift the pant leg. A flap of skin gaped with ragged edges. Blood oozed into her sock.

Virnie bit her lip. Tears stung her eyes. Rachael must be in pain. And the wound needed attention. "Come to the cloakroom and I'll clean this up."

Rachael whimpered.

They paused at the schoolroom door. Virnie bent over to be eye level with the child. "Rachael, what happened?"

She shook her head.

"You must tell me."

"I can't. It's my fault."

"Come on. I'll see what I can do." She led the child into the cloakroom and left her on the narrow bench while she went to her desk and found a clean hanky. "Children, I am leaving Hilda in charge while I take care of something. George, you can borrow my grade nine text and see how many of the arithmetic problems you can do." She filled her cup with water from the pail at the back of the room and returned to Rachael. "Honey, this is a serious wound. I don't think you caught it on a fence or nail." There was another possibility. One that filled her stomach with such heaviness she felt ill. Tic-toc, the ugly dog. She waited, hoping Rachael would choose to reveal the truth.

She washed the wound as well as she could but it needed to be disinfected and bandaged and she didn't have the supplies. She made a mental note to buy some things and keep them on hand. She tried to be gentle but Rachael quivered. Her eyes pooled with tears. White pinched the corners of her mouth. In fact, she looked like she might faint or throw up.

Virnie grabbed a sweater left on one of the hooks, scrunched it on the bench. "Put your head down here until you feel better."

The fact that Rachael did so without arguing about how strong she was and how she didn't need help indicated how much she hurt.

Virnie sat on the floor stroking Rachael's forehead, waiting for the pain and weakness to pass before she pressed Rachael for more information. When the child's color improved she cupped Rachael's chin. "It was that dog, wasn't it?"

Rachael shook like hit by a strong wind and she choked back a sob.

Virnie sat on the bench and pulled Rachael to her lap. She pressed the child's head to her shoulder and held her tight. "It's all right. It's all right. You're safe now. I won't let him hurt you again. I promise." This was Conor's fault and his responsibility to make it better.

Rachael sobbed quietly for several minutes and clung to Virnie.

Virnie continued to soothe her. Poor little girl. Trying to be tough in a situation too big for her to deal with.

Rachael quieted. She tipped her tear-stained face back to look at Virnie. "You mustn't tell Pa."

"I can't promise that."

"I told him I'd be strong. He'll think I'm not fit to survive on the farm." She shuddered. "Maybe he'll send me away."

Virnie's insides swept empty at the words. She'd been sent away. Yes, it was for the best and she had no regrets. But it still hurt. She pressed Rachael's head back to her shoulder so she wouldn't guess at the pain that washed over and over Virnie. She forced herself to take slow, deep breaths.

Forget the past. You're a lady now and someday you'll be a fine teacher.

Slowly, with a struggle that shredded secret, forbidden parts of her heart, she pulled herself under control. "I'm sure he won't send you away." But he must face a few hard truths as well. And Miss Virnie White was just the person to dish them out. She had nothing to lose. It wasn't like he was the answer to her maidenly dreams or anything. Not that she had such dreams, although she had gotten lost at his house, for a little while, in the fantasy of family and home. But no more. She intended to imitate Miss Price and be a dedicated teacher the rest of her life, helping hundreds of children. She ignored the ache edging those thoughts.

Certainly, if she had any lingering hopes of something besides being a spinster teacher they wouldn't include the likes of Conor Russell with his harsh outlook.

"You stay here and rest while I look after the rest of the children."

When Rachael curled up without protest, Virnie studied her with concern. It wasn't like Rachael to admit even a hint of being needy. Perhaps it was only the shock of the attack and her pain, but Virnie would be keeping a close eye on her until school ended and she could escort her home.

She'd arranged for someone from town to take them to the Russell farm in a wagon. Rachael's leg had swollen during the afternoon and she could barely walk. As soon as she got the child home, Virnie intended to start hot compresses.

She had the driver carry Rachael to her bed. She settled the child, elevating the injured leg on a pillow before she hurried to heat water. She'd seen Epsom salts in a cupboard when she cleaned and she dug them out and found an old towel that would do for making the pad.

She was stirring the salts into the water when Conor stomped in. "What's going on?"

"Sit down. We need to talk."

He shot her a startled look then obeyed.

She sniffed. Even a grown man didn't argue with Miss

White, the teacher, at her finest. "I warned you about that dog. Rachael told you how afraid she was. What did you do? Give her a stick and tell her to be brave?" Rachael had told her everything on the ride home. The driver of the wagon had used his whip to repel the dog.

"Should be shot," he muttered.

Virnie couldn't help but agree. She was tempted to do it herself but there was something equally important to do here—convince Conor it wasn't weakness to need help or protection.

"The dog is all bluff," Conor said. "Rachael can handle him."

"That dog bit her. Badly."

He jolted to his feet. "How badly?"

"Tore her leg but she's fortunate it wasn't her face. Or her stomach."

"Where is she?"

"I'm not finished."

He scowled at her. "I don't need—"

"Maybe you do. No child should have to prove herself to her father."

"Maybe I was wrong about the dog. But it doesn't mean I think Rachael has to prove anything."

He breathed as hard as she. "She's small and defenseless. But it doesn't mean she's not of any value."

He stared at her for a moment, as though realizing she'd let something slip.

"I didn't say it did. Now where is she?" He headed for Rachael's bedroom.

Virnie sucked in air and prayed for strength. She'd failed to make her point clear. Her past got all tangled up with Rachael's situation. Then she followed him to the bedroom.

"Pa, I'm sorry. I tried my best."

"I didn't think he'd bite." He examined the gash then straightened and turned away, his face twisted with sorrow. "I'll take care of that dog." He strode from the room.

Virnie followed.

He paused to face her, bleakness drawing the skin tight across his face. "Will you tend to her while I'm gone?"

"Of course."

"That dog will not threaten her ever again."

Conor did not need the accusation in Virnie's eyes. He had enough from his own thoughts. What was wrong with him? He'd failed as a father to protect his child. He'd been so busy teaching her to be strong that he neglected to take into account the limitations of her size. Being small shouldn't be a cause for neglect. And that's exactly what he'd done. He'd given Rae no protection and certainly no tenderness. And he knew why. He'd given both to Irene and it hadn't been enough to make her survive the harsh winter. So he'd swung the other way. Indirectly, he was making Rae pay for her mother's weakness. Well, no more.

He rode into the Faulks' yard. The ugly, old mutt raced out and tried to bite Noble's heels. Conor was ready with a whip and caught the dog on the nose. It backed away whimpering and crouched behind a fence snarling.

Mrs. Faulk came out wielding a broom. When she saw the dog already skulking away from Conor and his horse, she put the broom down. "How can I help you?"

"Devin around?"

"Out at the barn, I 'spect."

"Thank you." He remembered his manners and touched the brim of his hat. "Ma'am."

He found Devin sitting in the shade of the barn, his hat pulled over his eyes. The man jerked up with a snort when he heard Conor approach. Conor didn't bother with any niceties. "Your dog bit my little girl. He threatens her every day as she goes to and from school."

Devin began to sputter a protest.

Conor cut him off before he could form a word. "You get him out of here immediately. If I ever see him again, I'll shoot him. On sight." He yanked the reins away and loped toward home and his hurting daughter.

Back home, he grabbed the saddle off Noble and hung it over the fence. He'd put it away later. And he'd brush Noble extra well later to make up for turning him loose with no more than a pat on the rump.

He threw back the door to the house and strode to the bedroom where Virnie sat on the side of the bed, tending a poultice on Rae's leg. "How is she?"

She nodded toward the door and followed him into the other room. "I'm concerned about the swelling. And she's restless. I expect she's in pain but too brave to let us know. Did you take care of the dog?"

"I refrained from shooting it on sight, if that's what you mean. But I warned Devin if I ever see the dog again I will. I should have done it long ago. Just like I should have listened to Rae when she said she was afraid."

"It's all right to be afraid sometimes. In fact, it might be the smartest thing we can do in certain situations."

He shrugged. He didn't know about that but he had

been wrong about making Rae so tough. "I have to talk to her."

Not caring that Virnie heard every word, or maybe glad she did so she would know he'd changed, he sat on the edge of Rae's bed. "I am so sorry I didn't listen to you when you told me about that animal. If I had this would never have happened."

"I'm sorry, Pa. I tried to be strong and brave like you said."

"You were very brave. But you shouldn't have had to be. It's my job to protect you from things that are too big for you. I will try not to fail you again. You have my word on it. But I need your word on something, too." He ignored Virnie's barely audible gasp. He didn't blame her for thinking he was about to make some impossible demand on Rae. He'd given both of them plenty of cause to think he didn't know how to be understanding.

"I'll try, Pa. Whatever you want me to do."

"Good. Because you'll face more scary things in the future, but I want you to promise me you will come to me when something is too hard for you. That way I can help you."

Her smile flashed and her eyes shone with love. "Pa, I promise."

He hugged her. She was so precious to him. How could he have put her at such risk because of his need to eliminate weakness from his life?

Virnie squeezed his shoulder.

Suddenly, his world felt whole and good—apart from Rae's injured leg.

He set Rae back on the pillow and stroked her head until she fell asleep. Both he and Virnie tiptoed from the room.

She turned to face him, her eyes glowing. "That was wonderful. You made her feel so special."

"I never meant to make her feel any other way."

"I understand that but sometimes a person's expectations of another can make them feel a failure."

He studied her, saw something dark in her eyes, something that went beyond his mistakes with Rae. He wondered if she'd had personal experience. "Do you know about this firsthand?"

Her expression switched to bleak and then to the mask of a professional teacher so quickly he blinked.

"This is about you and Rachael."

It might be but he wanted to know more about her. "Someday maybe you'll choose to tell me what makes Virnie White tick?"

She jerked around and seemed suddenly very interested in checking the pot she'd prepared for the poultices, moving jerkily as if controlled by an unseen puppeteer.

Sensing if he pushed too hard she would leave, he let the subject drop. "Would you mind staying around to help with her this evening?"

Her hands paused from their restless activity. She seemed to consider the idea then she slowly lifted her head and faced him, her eyes revealing nothing but calmness. "I'd be glad to help and make sure she's going to be all right. Would you like me to make supper?"

He held her gaze a moment without speaking, searching for the secrets she kept locked inside. But she allowed him no access. "I won't say no to such an offer."

Later, they sat beside Rae as she slept restlessly, moaning often and rolling her head back and forth.

"What's wrong?" he whispered to Virnie.

"I suppose she's reliving the fear and of course, her leg is painful."

He groaned. "I wish I could trade places with her."

She nodded. "None of us can change the facts, can we?"

There didn't seem to be a need to answer the question.

"Conor, can I ask you something?"

"Certainly."

"Have you ever regretted that Rachael is a girl?"

"Huh? What do you mean?" It was hard for him to guess what she felt as they whispered back and forth and when he turned to study her, she ducked her head.

"Have you wished she was a boy?" They hadn't lit a lamp, not wanting to waken Rae and even though Virnie watched him, he couldn't make out anything in her dark eyes.

"I have never regretted one thing about Rae. Not from the time she was born. She made her appearance in the middle of the night on a blustery October day threatening an early storm. I loved her so much it frightened me at first." He thought about that. "Maybe that's why I tried to make her strong. You know, so I wouldn't be tempted to coddle her. I learned my lesson with Irene on that matter."

"Not everyone is like Irene."

He nodded. "I think I'm learning that." He wished he could say more—something that would erase the tension in Virnie's expression—a tension that might be partly about Rae but he knew it went beyond Rae to something deep inside.

He could only hope she would tell him about it at some point. Because, he admitted, he cared how she felt.

Somehow, learning to admit that Rae had needs allowed him to think of caring about a woman who had weaknesses.

He turned away as confusion raced through him. Taking care of a child who was small and sometimes powerless in no way meant it was safe to trust a weak woman. And he would do well to remember it before he invited pain and disaster into his life again. Except it wasn't that simple. Virnie had done things that proved she had strengths. The way she handled the sick bull left him floundering to maintain his excuse that women were too weak for his kind of life. His insides bounced back and forth between protecting himself and Rachael from the hurt of depending on a weak woman and the evidence that said Virnie was different.

In the end, he could only allow himself to admit she was complicated. Didn't fit into any picture he had of a woman. Acknowledging it only increased his confusion.

Chapter Eight

Virnie wanted to stay and make sure Rachael was going to be all right. But she needed to get back before dark, before people could question her honorable intentions, so she made sure Conor understood how important it was to keep warm compresses on the wound. She prayed the swelling would subside and there would be no infection—the worst thing they could deal with.

She continued to pray as she walked to town, for Rachael and Conor and herself. She needed divine help sorting out her confusion.

Fear dried her mouth as she neared the Faulk place but no dog threatened her. At least she had accomplished something if she'd helped eradicate that danger.

She paused long enough to greet the Maxwells. She'd asked the wagon driver to let them know she would not be back for supper and now she explained about Rachael's injury then she retreated to her room and a chance to think.

Conor loved Rachael and had since the day she was born.

Had Virnie's father ever loved her? Maybe before her mother died? She didn't know.

Conor didn't care that Rachael was a girl.

Her father had clearly stated he wished otherwise for Virnie.

She jerked her thoughts to a halt. Why was she comparing Conor and her father? Her feelings toward Conor had nothing to do with her father.

Or did they? She studied the thought. She yearned for her father's love and acceptance. What did that have to do with Conor?

She faced the truth. She was angry at how he pushed Rachael to be strong but the feeling alternated with a lonesome yearning to share his love—like the obvious way he showed it to Rachael.

When he'd hugged the little girl, she'd instinctively clasped his shoulder, wanting something that could never be hers from either Conor or her father—acceptance, belonging, loving.

Yet briefly, as father and daughter hugged, she could not deny herself a taste of it.

Sharing their love, feeling it was temporary and she'd eventually go back to being Miss White, an admirable and devoted teacher.

But not until Rachael was better.

Rachael was not in school the next day nor did Virnie expect her. It would take a few days for her leg to heal. *Please, God, let it heal without infection,* she prayed.

She'd promised Conor she would check on Rachael as soon as school let out. Never before had a day seemed so long. She thought dismissal time would never come. As soon as the last child scampered off, she closed the school without bothering to sweep the floor or clean the chalkboard. She'd arrive early tomorrow and do it. For now, she couldn't wait to see how Rachael was.

She alternately walked and ran the three miles to the farm, not caring that anyone seeing her would think it unsuitable behavior for a schoolmarm.

As she approached the yard, she noticed the stillness. No childish chatter, no sound of Conor working on the barn. Even the animals were quiet.

Her heart in her throat, fearing the worst, she tiptoed into the house and crossed to Rachael's room. The child lay on her back stroking Tippy. Relief flooded her to see Rachael looking pale but clear-eyed. "Where's your pa?"

"I don't know."

Anger chewed up her relief. Had he left the child alone? She turned and left the room. Her gaze swept across the space. She glanced into Conor's room. He lay sprawled facedown across the bed, his boots still on, looking like he had collapsed of sheer exhaustion. She returned quietly to Rachael's bedside. "He's sleeping. Did he stay up all night with you?"

"I don't know. I can't remember."

"How do you feel?"

"My leg hurts."

"Can I have a look?"

Rachael shrugged.

Virnie folded back the compress. The swelling had gone done a little but it still didn't look good. The edges of the wound showed a slight redness. "We need to keep hot compresses on this." She headed for the kitchen to prepare more salt solution.

As she placed the fresh compress on Rachael's leg the bed in the other room creaked and Conor moaned.

Virnie's heart stalled. She wasn't ready to face him. All her self-talk last night had done nothing to erase a long lonesomeness. She'd tried to blame it on wanting something from her father he'd never given. But it had not served to convince her. It wasn't her father she ached for. She wanted to be part of what she saw in this home—love and belonging. Even telling herself Conor's expectations were unreasonable didn't end her longing.

Because no matter what she told herself, a part of her refused to believe it.

When Conor didn't appear, she relaxed. The longer he slept the better for him. And the better for her. Surely, with time, she could end this foolish mental weakness.

She grinned. Now who was despising weakness? She glanced at Rachael to see if she noticed her teacher grinning at nothing. Rachael slept again, the cat curled at her side, purring.

"What's so funny?" Conor stood in the doorway, his hair mussed, his eyes still full of sleepy confusion.

She giggled. "You. You look a little rough around the edges."

"I feel it, too."

"Come on. I'll make you coffee." She drew him from the room.

"Rae?"

"Sleeping. Her leg looks a little improved."

He sank to the nearest chair.

"Tough night?"

"She had a lot of pain. It was hard to deal with. And I could do nothing."

"You kept the compresses on so you did something." She waited for the coffee to boil then poured him a cup.

He grabbed her hand.

His touch gave new life to all the arguments she had worked so hard to put to rest. She should pull away but she couldn't. Not when she saw the desperate look on his face.

"If anything happened to her—" He choked out the words. "How could I ever forgive myself?"

Feeling his fear and guilt, she sank to the nearby chair and wrapped both her hands around his. "Conor, you have made mistakes. Don't we all? But you have given her the best thing any parent can give a child. You have given her your love."

His gaze clung to her. She let him search her eyes, let him find her comfort and appreciation. After a moment, he said, "How could I not love my own flesh and blood?"

"Not everyone feels that way. Not all fathers love their children." She wanted him to see how special his love was.

Still he held her gaze and still she let him.

"Your father didn't love you?" His whispered words blew through her mind with the vengeance of a tornado.

She jerked her hands free and bolted to her feet, turning her back to him as she stared at the cupboard, trying to force her thoughts to what she could prepare for supper. She could be frozen in a block of ice for all the ideas she managed to come up with.

His chair scraped on the floor. His boots thudded toward her.

She couldn't move. She couldn't think past the words that had never been voiced. They had circled her mind, filled her thoughts, directed her reactions but they had never been given sound. Sound had given them a power she didn't believe possible. They cut through her defenses. They mocked her high and noble ambitions. They cut away all her progress. She stood alone and afraid in the middle of the floor feeling as frightened as the day she'd huddled in the corner of her childhood home wondering why she was alone.

Conor touched her shoulder. "I didn't mean to hurt you."

She wagged her head back and forth, unable to speak.

He made a frustrated sound. "Seems I manage to hurt people without even trying. First Rae and now you."

The pressure on her shoulder increased and he slowly turned her to him. Not speaking a word, he pulled her into his arms and held her. "I'm sorry. So sorry. I wish I could change things."

She didn't know if he meant what he'd said or the lack of love from her father. It didn't matter. He couldn't change anything. No one could. She simply had to accept the facts of her life. Put her past behind her. She remembered how often Miss Price had told her that. Miss Price would be disappointed to see she'd let the past affect her like this. And Conor must despise her for her weakness.

She let herself rest against his chest one more heartbeat. Two. Three. And then with supreme effort, gathered together her rigid strength, wrapped it around her like armor and stepped back. "Sorry about that."

"Really?"

"I shouldn't let such things upset me."

"I'm not sorry." He headed for the bedroom. "It felt

good to offer comfort to someone." He ducked out of sight.

She stared at the open doorway. It almost sounded like he'd found her weakness a welcome chance to show his concern. She snorted. All she was doing was adding things she wanted to a kindly remark.

Rae slept. He was pretty certain that was a good thing. No reason for him to stand there watching her except he knew he'd shaken Virnie with his stupid comment about her father. But it was so obvious from what she said, though if he'd guessed her reaction he would have kept his big mouth shut. He didn't want to upset her.

Though—he grinned—if it meant she would let him hold her it wasn't all bad. He'd been demanding toughness of Rae and himself so long he'd forgotten how good it felt to enjoy a little weakness. It made people come together for mutual support and comfort.

Hmm. Maybe he'd been heading in the wrong direction all this time. Two together was a good thing. If one fell down, the other could help him up. If one got discouraged, the other could point out reasons to keep on.

Rae jerked awake and cried out. "Pa, it hurts."

Conor knelt at the side of the bed and cradled her. "It's a nasty bite from a nasty dog." It about killed him to think this was his fault.

Virnie rushed into the room. "What's wrong?"

"Her leg hurts."

Virnie lifted the compress. "I'll get a fresh one." She kept her face and voice expressionless but she shot him a look that said so much. She worried about Rae as much as he did.

It felt good and right to have someone to share his concern. He held Rae close as Virnie tended the wound. There was so little they could do and he felt a vast helplessness. Maybe it was wrong to expect Rae to face the challenges of pioneer life. But when he thought of the uncertainty of life back East and how he had so often faced homelessness he knew going back wouldn't make things any better. He could do nothing but pray. And he did. For the first time in two years. He prayed for his daughter's healing as he held her and comforted her.

Virnie stood at his side and whispered, "I made some soup. It's ready in the kitchen. Go and eat while I hold her."

He didn't realize he'd been kneeling at the bedside so long. He shook his head.

She touched his shoulder, the warmth of her hand and her concern brushing the cold edges of his heart. "You need to keep up your strength. Besides, she'll be safe with me."

He nodded and stood. She was very close. Close enough he had only to raise his hand to grasp her elbow. "I'm not worried about her safety. I just don't want to leave her."

"I know." She edged him toward the door. "Go eat."

They were far enough away Rae couldn't hear them. Conor grabbed Virnie by both elbows and held on. "I'm afraid."

Her expression softened and she wrapped her arms around him and hugged. "I know."

He held her a moment, taking from her the same comfort he'd tried to offer her a short time ago. And then feeling foolish at his weakness, he broke away and went to the table to eat the delicious creamy vegetable soup.

She stayed until almost dark. "I must go."

He nodded. "Yes, you must."

"I wish I could stay."

"Me, too."

They studied each other, knowing something had shifted between them. For a second, he wondered what it meant and where it would lead. Then he dismissed the questions. Right now all that mattered was they offered comfort to each other. And until Rae was better, he needed it and craved it.

"I'll be back after school tomorrow." She shifted her gaze and pink flushed her neck. "If you want me."

"I'll be counting the hours. It's worse when I'm alone."

She brushed her hand over his arm and then slipped away before he could think what he wanted to do.

Virnie knew Conor turned to her for comfort only because of Rachael. As soon as the child was better, he'd realize he didn't need her and they would slip back into their roles—he the strong one who needed nothing, no one; she the weak female who somehow, despite her perceived weakness, managed on her own.

But until Rachael was better, Virnie would spare no energy on such thoughts. For three days the child's leg remained swollen. Then slowly the swelling began to subside. The wound began to heal though she would have a very ugly scar.

Virnie spent Saturday at the farm, doing the homemaker things that gave her so much satisfaction. She did the laundry, scrubbed the floors and made a chocolate cake hoping to tempt Rachael's appetite.

Rachael was allowed up for lunch though both Virnie and Conor deemed it best she allow her father to carry her to a chair and ordered her to keep her leg elevated.

Virnie tried not to be nervous around Conor. But remembering how they had held each other made it difficult especially when he seemed to watch her. And every time she caught him looking at her he held her gaze for a moment then shifted away slowly. She guessed he was as confused about what happened as she.

"Pa," Rachael said. "Can we go to church tomorrow?"

"No." Conor blurted out the word in explosive surprise. "You won't be going anywhere until your leg is completely better."

"Aww." She shifted her gaze to Virnie. "Are you going?"

"I expect so." Though she hated to be away from Rachael any more than she had to be. Her gaze shifted toward Conor. Yes. She wanted to share her time with him, too, even though she knew it was only until Rachael was better. "Why?"

"I want to see Alice."

"Can I take her a message? Or better yet, why don't you make a card and write a letter?"

Rachael brightened up at that.

Conor squeezed Virnie's hand. His silent approval filled her with a warm glow.

He went out to work and Virnie set up paper and a pencil for Rachael who drew a picture of Tippy and wrote a note before she agreed to go back to bed.

While Rachael slept, Virnie continued to work. The

sound of pounding came from the barn and she paused often to stare that direction. Occasionally she glimpsed Conor swinging a mallet or carrying a piece of lumber.

She jerked her gaze back to the basket of dry laundry. Admitting her attraction to Conor scared her. Especially given how he viewed weakness. Why would letting herself care about Conor be any different than caring for her father—she was bound to disappoint him, and she knew too well the pain of rejection.

As she ironed clothes, her back to the door, Conor stomped in. "Where's Rae?"

"Sleeping." She concentrated on removing the wrinkles from a shirt Rachael wore to school often.

"She is on the mend, isn't she?" His voice sounded almost directly behind her, sending shivers of warning up and down her spine.

"I would say so." She folded the shirt neatly and turned to pick up another item to iron.

His hand caught hers. She jerked to look at him as alarm sent her heart into a frenzy.

"I have never said a proper thank-you."

"It's not necessary." Her words practically stuck to her dry tongue.

"I think it is." He continued to hold her hand, slowly tugging her closer.

She pulled her hand away, pressing it to her waist and backed up until she encountered the ironing board. Her eyes felt several times too wide for her face.

He sighed and scrubbed his hair. "Virnie, why are you so afraid?"

"I'm not afraid of anything."

"I don't know what happened between you and your

pa, but I am not your pa." He closed the distance between them as he spoke.

Anger boiled up inside Virnie. Was she so transparent that he saw her pain, her need? She wouldn't let it be so. Nor did she thank him for rekindling feelings she had put to rest years ago. "I am not comparing you to my pa." The guilt of her lie brought heat to her cheeks. "Why would I?"

He stood only a few inches from her, so close she could see the variation of blue-green in his irises and the white fan lines by his eyes from squinting in the sunshine. "You don't have to be afraid of me."

She shook her head, glancing past him in the hopes of finding escape. He blocked her so there was none. She grabbed the only safe subject she could find. "I'm glad for Rachael that you are willing to change how you treat her. She deserves to have her fears and weaknesses acknowledged."

"I know that. Maybe we all do. I know I'm changing how I view life."

"Good." She pushed past him and headed for the door with no idea of what she intended to do except escape.

But the man wouldn't take a hint. "Virnie, why are you running?"

She spun around to face him. "You misunderstand me. I am only concerned with Rachael."

His eyes darkened. His jaw clenched. "Of course. Like I said, I appreciate it."

He grabbed his hat and slipped past her to cross the yard and disappear into the barn.

She closed her eyes. She'd succeeded in deflecting his questions about her papa, and she'd managed to indicate her interest in being here was solely because of Rachael. It should feel good and right.

Instead it filled her with confusion and a disappointment that sucked at her insides.

It was three more days before Conor decided Rachael could attend school but only because he would personally give her a ride to and from. Every day, he waited until Virnie met his eyes before he nodded and rode away. He seemed disappointed with the way she remained distant and aloof. But she expected disappointment sooner or later so there seemed no reason to feel its sting so sharply.

Once Rachael was well enough to attend classes, Virnie told herself she would no longer go to the farm, but seeing Rachael's exhaustion at the end of the day, she knew the child could not cope with any more responsibilities. She managed to stay away until Saturday, then at Rachael's pleading promised to visit again. She fully intended to do more than visit. She would clean the house and do all the things Rachael couldn't possibly do.

And if she weren't such a coward she would explain her past to Conor. Then he would perhaps understand why she couldn't let herself trust a man to understand her needs.

Chapter Nine

Rae's injury had caused Conor to lose a lot of time rebuilding his barn. Not that he resented it. He was only happy her leg had healed and she seemed as good as new.

As he and Virnie worked together caring for Rae, he allowed himself to think of sharing his concerns and worries. He'd even thought the two of them would be stronger together. But she made it clear she wasn't interested.

He kicked himself all the way across the yard. He'd wasted far too much time thinking about the schoolmarm.

He stared at the remaining rafter he wanted to remove in the sod barn so he could build a nice frame structure. The sod one had served well but it was time for something better.

In the six years he'd been here, he'd done reasonably well. The good years balanced out the bad ones. He'd avoided going into debt and that had paid off. Life was good.

He grabbed the overhead rafter and tested it. Seemed

loose already and he hadn't even removed any spikes. Probably had started to rot. He checked one end and found it solid.

Yes, it was a good life. He had everything he wanted. Everything. He clenched his fists. He had Rae, a solid house and he'd soon have a solid barn. He didn't need anything else. He certainly didn't need anyone to share his life, his concerns. Nor anyone to offer comfort.

He gritted his back teeth as an unwanted memory of Virnie holding him flashed across his mind. He forced the memory away, pushed aside the feeling of restfulness it had given him and marched to the end of the rafter. He shook it. Dirt sifted from the sod roof. This end was definitely loose. He'd have to brace it before it collapsed. He turned, intent on finding something sturdy enough for the task. A clump of dirt hit him in the shoulder. He glanced upward just in time to see the rafter give way and the roof fall. He lifted his arms to protect his head as the roof fell on him, pushing him to the ground.

Dirt stung his eyes, filled his lungs but he was alive. He coughed and sputtered and tried to move. He couldn't. The weight of the roof pushed him to the ground. The rafter pinned him. He could barely breathe as sod and dirt covered him. His neck felt as if something crawled across it. Spiders. He wriggled his fingers but couldn't move an arm to brush them off. He shuddered. No wonder Virnie hated and feared them.

He shifted his shoulders, squeezed his arm muscles, filled his lungs as much as he could in the filthy air and pushed. More dust sifted across his face. He held his breath to keep from inhaling it, but apart from the dust, nothing moved. His lungs hurt. He struggled to fill them but the rafter pressed against his chest. He grunted, sucked in air that tickled his lungs and made him cough. "Help." But who would hear him? He was alone apart from Rae who was still asleep when he left the house.

Sweat soaked his armpits, beaded on his forehead, pooled in his ears and tickled his neck. He shuddered, hoping the tickle came from sweat and not from creepy crawlies.

He struggled a few more minutes but it left him weak. He couldn't get in enough air. He lay still and tried to think what to do. His options proved mighty slim.

No one knew he was here.

No one would even miss him. Rae was used to him being away.

No one knew where he was.

No one would worry that he was missing.

Panic laced through him, making his lungs work even harder.

He forced himself to calm down. One person knew he was here. An all-seeing, all-knowing, all-loving God. A God he had neglected since Irene died. He'd blamed God for failing to keep Irene alive even as he had blamed Irene for her weakness.

Somehow it seemed wrong, weak even, to want God to help now when he hadn't given God more than a passing thought except for the time he prayed over Rae. But he could ask no one else for help. And no one could help him better. He knew that. There was a time he'd sought God more often. He'd trusted God to lead him to this homestead. He'd trusted God during his first Dakota winter when the cold and snow proved such a challenge.

God, forgive me for turning from You. I know I shouldn't have waited for a time such as this to turn

back to You but better late than never. Help me. Send
someone to rescue me. Like Gabe. He hasn't been here
for a long time. About time he paid me a visit. Maybe
Virnie might visit but she wouldn't be much use. A weak
little thing. And scared of spiders.

He coughed as dirt tickled his throat.

Help me, God.

The blackness of his world blanketed his mind.

Virnie waited until after lunch to go to the Russell
farm. She'd used the time to do her personal laundry,
write a letter to Miss Price and grade some papers.
Mostly she was forcing herself to exercise self-control.
She would resist the urge to run to the farm simply to
prove she could.

She walked along the road enjoying the late autumn.
There had been several frosts and the morning air held
a decided chill. Mr. Maxwell warned there would soon
be snow.

But today was pleasant.

She found Rachael playing with Tippy apparently
alone in the house except for the kitten. She refused to
look about for Conor.

"How are you feeling?"

"Good. I'm hungry."

"Haven't you had lunch?"

Rachael shrugged. "I was waiting for Pa."

"You should know better than that. I'll make you a
sandwich then you can help me make something for
supper."

"Stew?"

"I think that would be good." There was some left-over roast that should be used up and Rachael could help peel vegetables.

Virnie tidied the house, then she and Rachael made a big pot of stew. By then the sun had almost slipped away. Virnie wanted to be home before dark but she didn't want to leave Rachael alone. "How long has your pa been gone?"

"He was gone when I got up this morning."

"Was he planning to go someplace?"

"Didn't say so."

"What's he been working on?" She'd managed to stay away for a few days and didn't know.

"The barn."

Alarm skidded across Virnie's shoulders and halted in her throat, making it difficult to swallow. What if he'd been hurt? She'd seen the size of the timbers he moved.

She forced her fear into submission and spoke calmly. "You stay here while I go look around."

Rachael nodded, distracted enough with the kitten to miss the worry in Virnie's voice.

Virnie stepped outside and called, "Conor?"

No answer but the sigh of the wind around the corner of the house. She studied the yard and surrounding area, hoping, praying, to see him headed for the house but saw nothing but shadows that suddenly seemed to vibrate with warning.

"Conor?" she called again as she crossed to the barn and stepped inside. But even the barn was filled with stillness. Where could he be? And why was she so worried? It wasn't unlike him to be away for long periods although he'd stayed close to home since Rachael's accident. Rachael was better now. No need to coddle her. Virnie knew that.

Her inner arguments did nothing to ease her concern. *Lord, is something wrong? Guide me.*

She studied the inside of the barn. The roof was down at the far end where he'd been dismantling it to construct the new one. She considered the mess on the ground. Sods held together by yellowed roots lay scattered on the floor and heaped on the twisted remnants of rafters that had once been on the roof. The air was dank with the disturbance of old soil. She edged closer to examine the debris. Strange that he'd left it this way. She'd seen how careful he was about cleaning up after himself. Something important must have called him away.

She stepped over a pile of sod as she retreated. About all she could do was wait for him to return. Until he did, she would stay with Rachael. She couldn't leave the child alone even though she knew Rachael didn't seem to mind. She admitted it was as much for her sake as Rachael's that she decided to stay. Her insides knotted with concern. Perhaps it was only her imagination that made her fear something was dreadfully wrong.

She paused, called, "Conor?" even though she knew he wasn't here.

A sound came from a great distance. "Conor?" She raced outside to scan the surrounding landscape, saw no sign of him. Strange.

Something scratched at the back of her brain. Something she'd seen in the barn but not noticed. She retraced her steps. Noble stood in a pen watching her.

Noble. Conor's horse. Would he have gone to help a neighbor without riding his horse? Unless the neigh-

bor had come in a wagon and Conor had ridden along.
It was possible.

She stared at the horse and tried to sort out her confusion. Again she thought she heard Conor call from
a great distance.

He had to be outside somewhere. She raced back
into the dusk. "Conor?" she yelled. "Where are you?"

Again, no sign of a man striding toward her. She circled
the barn, checking the shadows in case he had hurt himself and couldn't get up. Nothing. Nothing but emptiness.

*Lord, are You trying to tell me something. Trying
to guide me?*

She stood stock still at the edge of the debris that
had been the roof. She prayed for ears to hear the sound
again, and a mind to know where it came from.

She strained to hear his voice. Her heart thudded
loudly in her ears and she realized she'd held her breath
so long her heart protested. She sucked in air and held it
as she again listened with all her might. She heard the
distant sound. This time she did not move. "Conor?"
she called and waited for the sound to repeat.

It came again. Almost at her feet. Could it be? She
shuddered from head to toe. Goose bumps skittered
along her arms. No! Not under there. She backed away.
Had she stood on him? Perhaps done him damage? No.
She couldn't think he was buried beneath that debris.
But the sound came again. She was certain from under
the pile of dirt.

She skirted the edges. How was she to get him out?
She could inadvertently do more harm than good.

Her mind sprang to action on one front while a second front stared in shock.

Light. She needed to see to do this right. She glanced

about and saw the lantern he'd hung on a nail by the door. She raced for it, lit it and held it out to pile of dirt. From the far end there protruded a square rafter. She set the lantern on the floor and lay down beside it to look under the rafter. She could see nothing but more sod and eased out piece after piece, exposing more of the beam. Dirt fell into her face and she sputtered. She reached farther beneath the rafter, felt something different. Fabric. She peered into the hole. Definitely fabric but she couldn't pull it free. Could it be part of Conor's clothing? "Conor?"

"Here," came a harsh whisper.

Her heart exploded against her chest and she gasped. "Thank God. Can you move?"

"Pinned by wood." He sounded in pain, befuddled.

"I'll get you out." She sat back on her heels to collect her thoughts and come up with a plan. She couldn't move the beam. It was too heavy by itself but now covered in sod…impossible for her to manage on her own and there were no sturdy men around to help. She knelt to speak into the hole. "I'll have to move the dirt off you first and then lift the beam."

"Spiders."

She shuddered. "I'll deal with them later." They didn't matter as long as Conor lay buried. She lifted clumps of sod, careful as to where she stepped aware she could increase the pressure on Conor, perhaps suffocate him. She cleaned away inches at a time, trying to make a path parallel to the beam. Slowly she exposed it. Inch by inch she revealed his face, black with dirt, his eyes like white discs.

"Water," he croaked.

She dashed for the well and pumped a dipper full and

carried it back. She edged as close as she could and held the dipper to his mouth. Much of the water ran down his neck leaving muddy tracks but he sucked in enough to ease his discomfort.

"Can you slip out now?"

"I'm pinned at my knees. I can't feel them. Maybe my legs are cut off."

She managed to stifle her gasp and hide her alarm. "I need to check before I move anything else." If his legs had been severed and she released the pressure of the beam he stood a good chance of bleeding to death.

She moved more clods of dirt. She freed one arm. "Your arm is free and whole."

"I can't feel it."

Might be a good thing. She couldn't begin to guess how damaged it was and how it would pain when feeling returned. "Don't move." She had cleared enough space for her to crawl in close to his shoulders and she carefully edged closer. She wanted to wipe the dirt from his face, smooth away his concern, but that would have to wait until he was safely out of this mess.

Lord, I don't know what I face. Guide my hands and give me wisdom.

"I'm going to reach down and see if I can determine what's going on with your legs." She slid her hand cautiously along the rough timber, found where it crossed his legs and then she could move no further. "I'll have to move more dirt. I know you're anxious to be out of here but I must move slowly and carefully."

"Spiders."

"I don't care."

"In your hair. Now."

She brushed her hands over her hair, hoping she'd

dislodged any unwelcome visitors. She couldn't restrain an audible shudder.

"Sorry," he murmured.

"We'll discuss it later." Right now she had a task to do. Slowly, she eased the clumps of dirt off the beam, holding her breath each time, wondering if the beam would lift and he'd bleed to death before she could get to him.

Every few minutes, she felt along the wood to see if she could locate the rest of his legs. Inch by inch his body was exposed. Every time she saw more she sucked in relief when there was no massive amount of blood. She reached the area where the beam crossed his legs and hesitated. What she did next could mean life or death for Conor. She would not move until she had taken every precaution. She gathered together a length of rope in case she needed to secure the beam and some lengths of leather belting in case she needed to stop bleeding.

"I'm going to see what's under this pile."

He nodded, his eyes bleak, preparing himself for the worst.

Inch by dreadful inch, she moved the dirt until she could finally see his legs. They were intact. "Your legs are okay. All that's wrong is the beam is on them." How was she to get it off? If she rolled it, she would do more damage. She couldn't sling a rope over a rafter and lift it because there was no roof over their head. She stood and considered her options. What she needed was a way to raise it. One end protruded past Conor's head to solid ground. The other lay across his feet. If she could lift the end at his feet…

She'd done something like this when she helped Miles with a wagon that needed to be lifted so he could replace a broken axle. "I'll be right back." She found a solid length of wood and some short chunks used to block the wheels of a wagon. She staggered back to the barn with them and fixed a lever. "I'm going to lift the beam off you. If you can drag yourself out that would be good." Otherwise she would have to find a way to secure it so she could drag him to safety.

"It's heavy."

"I can do it. I know how." But she didn't know how long she could hold it. Or if it would roll as she lifted it. "Be ready to move." She braced herself and raised herself over the length of wood. She wanted to lift the beam slowly. "On the count of three. One, two, three—" She threw her weight to the lever and the beam lifted.

Please, God, don't let it roll back on him. Please, God, give me strength.

Conor groaned but managed to drag himself far enough away that she could drop the beam. She hurried to him, running her hands along his leg. *Let there be no blood. Spurting blood.* His trousers were torn. There were plenty of cuts and scrapes but her worst fears were set to rest. "How do you feel?"

"I don't know. Grateful to be free." He struggled to sit, his arms seeming unable to push him upright.

She helped him up. "Take your time."

"Aggh. My legs are coming back to life. Aggh."

She knew he wouldn't be able to walk but she needed to get him to the house. With his help, she managed to drag him across the yard. At the door, she hesitated. "I think I'll tell Rae to go to her room."

"She's tough." He grunted. "But I don't want her to see me like this."

"I'll be right back." She made sure he was steadied against the wall then slipped inside.

Rachael bounced from the chair where she'd been playing with Tippy. "Pa?"

"I found him. He'll be here in a minute." She tried to think of a way to persuade Rachael to go to her room without alerting her to Conor's condition. "Why don't you surprise him by brushing your hair and putting in those pretty hair ribbons?"

"Aww. He doesn't care about that sort of thing."

She was right on that score. "Then do it for me. I like to see your hair pretty."

"Okay."

Virnie waited until Rachael ran to her room, then quietly closed the bedroom door behind her hoping she would be too busy brushing her hair and playing with the cat to give it a thought.

She returned to Conor and helped him scoot across the floor. She aided him to his bed before Rachael rushed out of her room. "Pa?"

Virnie slipped out, closing the door behind her. "Rachael, your pa's had an accident. He's all right, just a little dirty but I think he'll need us to be quiet tonight."

Rachael headed for the bedroom door. "Pa?"

"Come in," Conor called.

Virnie followed the girl into the room.

Rachael skidded to a halt. "What happened to you?"

Virnie answered for Conor who looked about ready to pass out. "He was working on the barn and the roof fell on him." She still couldn't believe he was safe, that his legs hadn't been severed. Though it was too early to tell if they had been damaged.

She let Rachael check him out for a few minutes as she prepared a basin of warm soapy water. The first thing he needed would seem to be a good scrubbing. And water to drink.

She helped him lift his head and held a cup to his lips. He eagerly sucked back the water, panting with exhaustion when he finished. She held her hand behind his head a second longer than necessary, wanting to wrap her arms around him and hold him close. She couldn't believe he had escaped in one piece.

"I'm going to wash off some of the dirt now."

He made a noise she took for agreement but didn't open his eyes.

She dipped her cloth into the warm water but hesitated. She knew performing this little task would cross a boundary in her mind. It would allow her to touch him at his weakest. It would make her feel as if she gave him strength. And that, she understood, would bind her forever to him in her thoughts.

But she had no choice. She couldn't leave him untended. And she couldn't deny the ache in her heart to wash the dirt from his face and see the man—

She wouldn't finish it. She wouldn't admit she had grown to love him. Her heart felt like it ripped down the center—one half wanting to love him, the other full of warning.

She washed his face, unable to stifle the tender feelings as she saw the bruises. She wiped blood from scratches and saw the tension around his mouth. "Are you in much pain?"

His eyes snapped open for a second. She gasped at the darkness in them. "How much is much?" His voice grated.

"I'm sorry. I wish I could do something."

"You did."

Shock hit her with the suddenness of falling down an endless flight of stairs. He could have died. It was a miracle he didn't. "How long were you there?" she whispered.

"What time is it?"

"Almost nine. At night."

"I went out right after breakfast. Wasn't long after."

"You must have been there almost twelve hours. It's a miracle you didn't suffocate."

"It's a miracle my legs aren't cut off." He caught her gaze and held it. "I prayed someone would rescue me. Didn't figure it would be you."

"Why's that?"

"It was a big job. And spiders." He shuddered. "They crawled all over me and I couldn't do a thing."

"Uggh. I would have gone crazy." She finished washing his face and hands. He needed to be checked for injuries. Her face heated like she'd bent over an open flame. She couldn't do it. After all she was the very proper Miss White—schoolteacher and example to the young ones. But who would perform this task? There were neighbors, of course, but how could she contact them?

She had no way to do so.

Lord, send help. Though she couldn't imagine how He would.

She returned to the kitchen and cleaned up the dirty water.

Rachael hung at her heels. "Pa's going to be all right, isn't he?"

"I believe so." She'd feel more confident if someone could examine his legs. For all she knew one or both could be broken. Her only consolation was the lack of serious amounts of blood.

Rachael grabbed the milk pail. "I forgot to milk the cow."

Virnie laughed. "You were waiting, hoping your pa would do it." He'd milked the cow since Rachael's accident. "I think you're getting a little spoiled." She never thought she'd see that day.

Rachael managed to look both embarrassed and annoyed. "I 'spect I have to do Pa's chores, too, now."

"For tonight, certainly. He won't be going anywhere."

Rachael ducked out the door and Virnie returned to Conor's bedside. She had to watch him carefully for shock or signs of undisclosed injuries.

He opened his eyes and stared at her.

"Any change in how you feel?"

"Actually, I'm feeling a tiny bit better. Not quite so shaky." He coughed and his face twisted with pain.

She found him a hanky, not surprised to see he coughed up dirt. She helped him drink more water.

"Sit beside me."

She did so, uncertain if she should. But she couldn't pretend she didn't care deeply. Until she knew he would be fine…

"You surprised me."

She snorted.

"I didn't know you could be so tough…so resourceful."

"I learned to be as a child."

He reached for her hand.

His touch combined with her fear widened the securely barred door of her memories. She shivered as things from her past escaped, demanding acknowledgment. "I told you my mama died when I was young. I don't remember her." Sadness filled her at the vastness of her loss. She swallowed hard and gripped Conor's hand. "My brother was six years older. My pa—" She swallowed hard and forced back tears. "He didn't have use for a little girl. Told me I should have been a boy. He shifted me off to Miles. I followed him around and learned to do everything he did."

"If he's the one who taught you to be so resourceful, I'm awfully glad you did." He smiled, his gaze steady despite the underlying pain. "I'm awfully glad," he whispered.

"My pa gave me to Miss Price to raise when I was ten. I haven't seen him since. Nor Miles." An ache as wide as the endless sky sucked at her insides and tugged forbidden tears to the surface.

He reached upward with a hand and wiped a tear from the corner of each eye. "No wonder you didn't like how I was raising Rae. You thought it was a repeat of your father."

She nodded.

"It's not. I love Rae. I wouldn't trade her for a dozen sons."

"I know."

A spider crawled across the back of her hand and she jerked to her feet, screaming as she shook it off.

Conor laughed.

She scowled at him. "Nothing funny about the creepy things."

"Don't I know it?" He caught her hand and urged her back to his side. "Yet you paid no attention when you dug me out." His eyes revealed something beyond gratitude, something that held her heart in a gentle, reassuring grasp.

She couldn't pull away any more than she could hide her emotions. "There was something far more important to tend to." She managed to duck her head and hide her face lest he read all that was in her heart. She didn't want to face it any more than she wanted him to guess it.

Rachael returned to the house. "I'll go help her with the milk."

She made her anxious escape. As she helped Rachael she prayed for someone to come and help her and at the same time, fretted about how she'd manage if no one came.

Hoping for someone to come, she thought she heard the rattle of a wagon. She shook her head. Getting fanciful.

But Rachael raced to the door and peaked out. "It's Uncle Gabe and he's got a lady with him." She ran out the door yelling, "Uncle Gabe, Uncle Gabe."

Relief raced through Virnie. *Thank You, God.* She couldn't have asked for a better answer to her prayer. Gabe was Conor's friend.

She waited at the table for Gabe to enter, a young woman on his arm.

"What's this I hear about Conor?"

Virnie guessed Rachael had filled him in. "He's had an accident."

"He's in there?" Gabe tipped his head toward the bedroom and Virnie nodded.

"Gabe?" The young woman spoke softly.

"Oh, I'm sorry. Miss White, meet the new Mrs. Winston. I took Conor's advice and quit putting off our marriage until everything was in tiptop shape. Besides, my new wife assures me she'll help."

Virnie laughed at how Gabe rattled on. "He sounds a little excited," she said to his wife.

"Call me Diana and yes he's been talking nonstop for the past four hours. I keep thinking he'll run down but he shows no sign of it."

Gabe rolled his eyes. "I have not been talking that much."

Diana giggled. "If you say so."

Virnie liked the woman right away. Her pale brown hair was scooped up into a stylish roll. Her bright gray eyes were direct and dancing with humor.

"Gabe?" Conor's weak voice came from the bedroom. "That you?"

Gabe didn't move. "How is he?"

Virnie lowered her voice. "I haven't checked his legs. I'll let you do that." She ignored Gabe's chuckle as her cheeks warmed. "He's lucky to be alive and very fortunate to have both legs." She explained how she'd found him and dug him out. Gabe squeezed her shoulder and Diana took her hand.

"It sounds awful," Gabe said.

"You were very brave," Diana whispered.

"I only did what had to be done."

Gabe stepped toward the bedroom. "I'll have a look at him."

Virnie nodded gratefully, praying he would find Conor's legs intact. Suddenly her knees melted and she grabbed for a chair.

Diana patted her back. "We're here now. You'll be okay."

Virnie knew she'd be okay. But she'd never be the same.

Chapter Ten

Virnie waited with Rachael and Diana as Gabe stepped into the bedroom, closing the door behind him.

Virnie shuddered as she heard Conor groan. *Please, God. Let him be all right.*

Gabe came from the room. "I need soap and water."

He didn't say anything more as she handed him what he required. He just shook his head when she raised her eyebrows in silent inquiry. But his face set in hard lines as if he didn't like what he saw. He ducked back inside without easing her concern.

"I'll make tea." She needed something to occupy her hands as well as her mind.

The kettle boiled. She poured the water over the tea-leaves and still Gabe did not return. She could hear the murmur of voices and wondered what transpired.

She sat across from Diana and tried to find something to talk about, something to divert her from worrying about Conor. She couldn't stop thinking he might have injuries she hadn't discovered. "When were you married?"

"Gabe came home a week ago. We married right away and packed up my things and here we are."

Virnie nodded. "Congratulations."

"How long have you been in the Dakotas?"

Virnie pulled her thoughts into some semblance of order. After all, she was the teacher and should be able to carry on a decent conversation. "I came out in September. I'm the schoolteacher."

Gabe stepped from the room again. He handed Virnie the basin and rolled down his sleeves.

She stood holding the basin, waiting for him to tell her. "Is he…?"

"There doesn't appear to be anything broken though he's badly bruised. Lots of cuts and scrapes but I don't think anything serious." He squeezed Diana's shoulders. His wife rested her cheek against one hand and covered the other with her palm, the tender gesture driving a deep ache to Virnie's heart.

Gabe shook his head. "I'm concerned there might be damage to his legs from being under such pressure for so long." He ground about on his heel. "What was he thinking to be out there without telling anyone? Does he think he's invincible? Well, he proved he's not." He paced to the door and back. "When I think…" He cast an eye at Rachael and didn't finish.

Rachael jumped to Conor's defense. "Pa's tough. He doesn't need anyone to take care of him."

Gabe squatted to face her. "Rae, we all need someone at some time. And what's this I hear about you?" He nodded toward her leg.

"A big bad dog bit me. I tried to beat him off with a stick like Pa said but this dog was really big and really bad." She lifted her pant leg to reveal the angry red scar.

Gabe examined it carefully. "Nasty bite."

"Wasn't nothing," Rachael said, eliciting a chuckle

from everyone. When she glanced at Virnie she lost her braveness. "It hurt some but Virnie took care of me."

Gabe sank to one of the chairs. "I don't know about you Russells. It seems it's not safe to leave you alone. You need someone to keep an eye on you both." His gaze settled on Virnie.

"Don't look at me. I'm only the schoolteacher."

Gabe grinned. "And I would say you've taught them some valuable lessons about taking care of themselves and others."

His acknowledgment touched a tender spot close to Virnie's heart.

"Virnie." Conor's low voice came from the bedroom.

Virnie jumped to her feet and instantly regretted her hurry when Gabe laughed.

"Seems he's taught you to jump to his command."

She hesitated, twisting her hands, trying to find an excuse for her behavior.

Diana smiled. "Pay him no mind. He's only teasing."

Virnie still hesitated, flustered by Gabe's comment and alarmed at her own response. She ached to see Conor and to assure herself he was indeed alive and well.

"Go on." Diana waved toward the door. "You don't want him getting agitated."

She hurried across the room, well aware of the amused glances Diana and Gabe exchanged.

She stepped into the bedroom, leaving the door ajar. Conor wore a clean nightshirt and lay beneath the covers. She was pleased to note Gabe had made sure to tent the covers over Conor's toes to prevent pressure. It was too early to tell if normal feeling would return to his legs and feet.

"How are you?" What a stupid thing to ask but suddenly she couldn't get a clear thought into her head.

His forehead and right eye were even more swollen than she remembered. And so many cuts and bruises. One cut on his cheek oozed blood and she bent over to swab at it with a clean handkerchief.

He caught her hand and pulled it to his chest. Fearing he would see how she felt, she averted her gaze.

"Virnie," he whispered.

She couldn't stop herself from looking into his eyes. Dark blue and bottomless, pulling her deeper and deeper into his emotions. She saw past his strength, beyond his need to be independent, to the soft core of his heart where he longed for the same things as she—acceptance, belonging and understanding of secret weaknesses.

His gaze searched her deepest thoughts. Did he see the same things in her she saw in him? She realized with a start that she wanted him to. Wanted him to understand her weaknesses didn't make her unacceptable. They only made her need someone who understood, accepted them as a counterbalance to her strength.

He cupped her head and pulled her closer.

Aware of her deep longing and unable to exert caution, she responded to his urging until her face was inches from his. This close she could see dirt embedded in the lines of his face. She thought she had washed him better than that.

"Virnie, you saved my life. I will forever be grateful." He pulled her closer still.

She knew he meant to kiss her. Understood she had only to pull away to make it impossible. Instead, she closed her eyes and let him catch her lips in a gentle kiss.

He groaned and she jerked back.

"I think the inside of my mouth is cut." He ran his tongue around the inside of his lips then reached for her shoulder and pulled her to his chest.

She laid her head against his warmth, listening to the beat of his heart. "I'm so glad you're safe," she murmured.

"Umm." He stroked her hair.

For a moment she let herself bask in his attention. But her rigid self-control exerted itself. She could not allow her feelings to follow her heart without restraint. She sat up, remaining on the edge of his bed. "God has answered so many prayers today. I don't think I would have found you without His help and I prayed for someone to come and help us and Gabe shows up."

"I can't believe he up and married. He's talked about it for two years."

Virnie jerked to her feet. "You haven't met Diana yet."

He caught her hand. "I wanted a few minutes alone with you."

Her cheeks warmed and she knew they would signal her embarrassment. Only it was more pleasure than embarrassment.

"You aren't offended, are you?"

She snorted. "You remember me struggling to resist you?"

"No."

"Then I guess you have your answer."

He grinned—slightly off center because of the swelling in his face but the nicest sight she'd seen in some time. Well, since she'd found him safe and sound under the pile of dirt.

"I'll let Gabe introduce you to his wife." She returned to the kitchen. "He'd like to meet Diana," she said to Gabe.

Gabe pulled his wife to her feet. "Now don't you be feeling too sorry for him because of his injuries."

Diana's eyes sparkled with adoration of her husband. "I can feel sorry for him but don't think I'll ever see anyone else but you with any sort of specialness."

Rachael giggled as they went into Conor's bedroom. "They're silly."

"They're in love." Virnie cleaned up the basin and washed the tea things.

"Oh, you shouldn't have done that. I intended to," Diana protested as they returned to the kitchen.

Gabe yawned. "I expected Conor to invite us to stay the night. Guess I'll just have to invite myself." He glanced about. "We'll just bed down next to the stove." He nodded toward the corner stove in the sitting area of the room.

Rachael yawned.

Virnie realized how late it had grown. "Good thing there isn't school tomorrow. I should have sent you to bed long ago."

"Are you staying, too?" Rachael asked.

Virnie would love to just so she could know for certain Conor was fine. But the house was already crowded and the Maxwells would be wondering what happened to her. "I better get back home."

"I'll give you a ride," Gabe said.

She was so bone tired she couldn't refuse.

The next day was Sunday and she hurried to church, eager to pour out her gratitude to God over Conor's safety.

Rachael raced up to her as she reached the church steps. Diana followed at a more sedate pace.

"How is Conor today?" Virnie asked the other woman.

"Cranky. Gabe figures his legs are hurting. But he says feeling and movement are coming back." Gabe had stayed back at the farm with Conor.

Relief washed through Virnie followed by a wish she could be there to comfort Conor.

Diana smiled and leaned close. "He made me promise to bring you back with me."

Virnie nodded and looked away as if greatly interested in something at the far side of the yard. The way her pulse quickened and warmth flooded her eyes revealed far more than she wanted Diana to see. It was only because she was concerned with Conor's well-being, she firmly informed herself.

But she found it difficult to sit calmly through the service and after it ended, had to remind herself to introduce Diana to the others.

"I'm hungry," Rachael said.

Virnie welcomed the excuse to escape. She tried to still her anxious feet as they walked to the farm.

Diana laughed as Virnie's pace increased. "It's hard to be apart, isn't it?"

Virnie slowed her steps. "I'm not sure what you mean."

Diana chuckled. "I suppose it's possible you haven't yet figured it out."

Virnie knew what she meant but didn't want to deal with her emotions and certainly did not want to discuss them.

Conor sat on the chair with his right leg propped on a stool. Gabe, suddenly bossy and nurturing now that he was married, warned him he'd have to take care of his leg until it was back to normal.

"You're lucky you didn't lose it."

Conor sighed. "You think I don't know that?"

"I don't know what you know. You sure aren't as smart as I thought you were to get yourself trapped in the first place. You might have let someone know where you'd be."

"I didn't expect the roof to cave in."

"Good thing for you Virnie had the guts to dig you out."

Conor grinned. "Surprised me some. I wouldn't have thought she could get that beam off me."

Gabe tapped Conor's shoulder. "If you let that woman get away I will know for certain you are crazy."

Conor snorted. He didn't want to let her "get away" as Gabe so elegantly said. But what did Virnie want? He didn't know. Perhaps he could convince her she wanted to share his life. He looked forward to the challenge.

Gabe went out to check on the livestock, leaving Conor alone in the kitchen.

He watched the door. Rae and Diana should return from church soon. Diana had promised to do her best to bring Virnie with her.

He heard their steps and Rae laughing as they approached the house. His lungs stiffened with anticipation bringing on a bout of coughing. He held his breath, stifling the coughs so he could focus on the door.

Rae raced in. "Hi, Pa." She found Tippy sleeping near the kitchen stove and scooped up the growing kitten.

Diana entered next and glanced around. "Where's Gabe?"

"Went out to look after the horses."

She nodded and turned back to find her husband.

Conor waited. Was that all? And then Virnie stepped into the room and ground to a halt at seeing him sitting up. Her gaze darted to his leg as if to assure herself it was still there and then her dark eyes sought his and clung. He read her concern and let it pour into the resistant corners of his heart until he felt warm and full and satisfied.

Well, almost satisfied.

"You're up," she whispered.

"Gabe helped me."

"Your legs?"

"The right one is still a little unsteady but they both feel almost normal."

Air whooshed from her lungs and her eyes glistened. "I'm glad."

As if aware of how much she'd revealed, she turned toward the stove. "I'll make lunch."

He watched her bustle around the kitchen. More and more he realized how much he needed her. How his need made him stronger rather than weaker. How the two of them formed such a strong team. She was so skittery around him he figured he better move slowly.

The others returned and sat down to a simple meal. Gabe rattled on about the mess he'd found at the barn.

Finally, Conor could take no more. "Look, I wasn't being careless. As soon as I realized the rafter was loose I prepared to brace it. It just came down before I could."

Gabe opened his mouth to argue.

Diana caught his hand. "Leave him alone, dear. I think you've made your point."

Gabe grinned at his wife. "You're right. How did I ever manage without you?" He turned to nod at Conor. "Married less than a week and I can already see how much I am going to benefit."

Diana rolled her eyes dramatically, causing Rae to break into giggles. "You only think being married means good meals and clean laundry."

Gabe choked. "I never said that."

Diana chuckled. "Then what did you mean?" Her eyes twinkled and Conor sat back and grinned, happy to see Gabe had found himself a woman would who keep him guessing.

Gabe realized she was teasing and sighed. "Woman, I can tell you will never give me any peace unless I confess it's a whole lot more than food and clean clothes." He bent close and caught Diana's chin. "You make me more whole than I've ever been."

Rae giggled more then sobered. "Uncle Gabe, how could you be more whole?"

"I don't know. I just know I am. It's like Diana here has taken things I didn't know were missing in my life and filled in the blanks."

Conor stared at his friend. "I would have never guessed you to be so…so…"

"Poetic," Diana said. "That was very sweet, Gabe. Thank you."

Virnie rose suddenly and busied herself with tea.

Conor watched. What was she thinking? He saw the tension across her shoulders. Did she find it hard to believe a man valued a woman like Gabe valued Diana? Her father had given her reason to doubt it. Guilt and regret dried his mouth. He'd not given her any reason to trust a man's opinion of a woman, either. Unintentionally he had equated her role as a teacher with weakness.

He sensed he had his job cut out for him in proving he didn't believe it any longer. She had more than adequately proven her strength.

And he wanted to share it with her. Maybe, like Gabe, her strength would fill in the blanks in Conor's heart.

Lord, You rescued me through Virnie when I was trapped. Now I seem trapped by my own reactions to Irene's death. Help me escape from them as well. And show Virnie that I value her in every way.

He hoped for a chance to talk to her privately but with so many people wandering around the house, practically tripping over each other, the afternoon passed without providing him an opportunity.

And then Diana and Virnie worked together to make supper. As soon as the dishes were washed, Virnie announced she had to get back home.

"I need to prepare some lessons and write some letters." Her eyes seemed to beg for something from Conor as she met his gaze across the table.

"If Gabe took you home, you could stay a little longer," he said.

"Yes, please do," Diana added. "Gabe won't mind taking you back to town, will you, dear?"

Gabe nodded, distracted by the game he and Rae played with the kitten, rolling a marble back and forth between them for Tippy to chase.

Virnie nodded. "Very well." She avoided looking at Conor.

He wished he knew what she wanted.

A little later, he yawned.

"You've had a long day," Virnie murmured.

Weariness suddenly made it difficult to think. "I think I'll call it a night."

Gabe jumped to his feet to assist him.

For a moment, Conor thought of refusing to drape his arm over Gabe's shoulders. He preferred to manage on his own. But he'd learned *alone* didn't make him strong. It only made him lonely. He grabbed Gabe's shoulders and hobbled to the bedroom. Gabe helped him to the bed.

"Thanks."

"How are your legs?"

"Sore."

"That's probably a good sign, wouldn't you say?"

"It's better than feeling nothing." They both knew the damage of his injuries could have cost him his legs.

Gabe stared down at him. "Do you need help getting into bed?"

"Do I look like an invalid?" He couldn't keep the edge of frustration from his voice.

"Nope. But you sound like one."

"Sorry. I'm tired."

Gabe backed away. "If there's nothing more you need…"

He needed to see Virnie and talk to her but he could hardly ask her to visit him in his bedroom. Yesterday following his rescue had been an extenuating circumstance.

Today was different.

Chapter Eleven

Virnie closed the school and headed down the road with Rachael. She'd gone to the farm every day this week. With Gabe and Diana there no one could complain it was inappropriate. But only because they couldn't see her thoughts. She ached for the minutes she spent at the farm. If only she and Conor could spend more time alone.

But what would that accomplish? She certainly wouldn't be blurting out that she just might love him a tiny, tiny bit. Besides, the idea churned around inside her like tumbleweed caught in a dusty twister. Loving a man, wanting his returning love was a dangerous thing. She shied away from the idea, afraid of being hurt. Yet she couldn't quite succeed at pulling her thoughts into denial.

The only way she kept up with preparation of her lessons was to rise early and do them before the children arrived. She'd written a letter to Miss Price the first of the week and reported on Conor's accident. At that point she'd paused as she sought for a way to explain how she'd felt at being able to rescue him. Finally she wrote, "It made me feel useful." She wished she could also say how it made her value the hard lessons she'd had before she went to live with Miss Price. But Miss Price had always insisted she must forget the past. In the end she chose to say nothing on the matter.

It was Friday and Virnie felt as if she had been given a long overdue holiday. It was about all she could do not to skip along the road as Rachael did.

"Aunt Diana is going to teach me to bake oatmeal cookies tomorrow," Rachael announced.

"That's nice." Virnie didn't know why she continued to go to the farm. It wasn't as if they needed her anymore. Diana made delicious meals and spent a great deal of time teaching Rachael how to manage.

Gabe looked after the chores.

Even Conor didn't need her. He hobbled about insisting his leg felt better with each passing day.

They approached the farm and Rachael ran ahead calling, "Pa. Pa." Conor sat in the sunshine beside the open door to the house.

Virnie's pace picked up without conscious decision on her part. Then she saw Gabe on the ground next to him and slowed. Maybe if they ever got a chance to talk…

But what did she expect from him? That he'd do more than express gratitude for her help which is what he'd done several times since the night of the accident. His kiss meant no more than that.

She almost stopped walking as she admitted the longing that had tugged at the edges of her mind for the past several days. She wanted so much more than gratitude.

She wanted acceptance, love and acknowledgment.

Things she'd wanted all her life and never had. She ought to know better than to wish for them at her age. Shouldn't she have outgrown those childish wishes?

Conor called, "Hello."

"How are you today?" She asked the same thing every time she saw him as if there was nothing more to say between them.

"Better every day." He, too, said the same thing every time.

She let her gaze search his face for signs of pain and when she saw none sighed. "Good. Good."

He grinned and held her gaze for another heartbeat. "Glad you approve."

Gabe grunted and pushed to his feet. "Won't get the job finished sitting in the sun." Gabe had been cleaning up the debris from the roof falling.

But before Gabe could return to the barn, Diana stepped out. "I just made tea and cookies if anyone is interested."

"I am!" Rachael yelled.

"Then you can help me carry the things outdoors. It's far too nice to be cooped up inside with winter blowing in just about any day."

At the reminder of winter both men looked at the barn.

Virnie understood they were concerned about the fact that one end stood open to the elements.

"I'll be back as soon as we get settled," Gabe said. "Don't you dare touch it until I'm here to help."

"Huh," Conor said and Virnie wondered if he objected to feeling dependent. She knew how he despised any kind of weakness.

It served to warn her how foolish her longings were

and she pushed them to the darkest corners of her thoughts. She would never be anything but what she was—a female, sometimes weak, sometimes surprisingly strong, but never quite good enough.

As soon as they finished tea, she got to her feet. "I'll say goodbye." She'd planned to spend the whole afternoon and evening here but knew it was time to stop pretending.

"Aww, why don't you stay?" Rachael said.

"Yes, please do," Diana added.

Gabe nodded. "I know it's not my home but I see no reason for you to rush away."

"You're welcome to stay," Conor said.

But his invitation felt like nothing more than an echo of what the others said. "I need to get back to town and tend to other things." She darted a quick glance at Conor, wondering if she saw regret in his eyes or was it only resignation—acceptance of her responsibilities as a teacher?

"You'll come tomorrow?" His words smoothed away the dark edges of her thoughts, renewing her hope.

"If you'd like."

"Yah!" Rachael cheered, eliminating the need for anyone else to answer but Virnie was certain she caught a flash of pleasure in Conor's eyes.

Somehow, even though she suspected how this would end—with Conor disappointed with her and her heart filled with failure—she couldn't put her hopes and longings to rest. Not yet.

Saturday morning, she forced herself to do her laundry and leave it on a line in her bedroom to dry. She corrected the children's papers and began another letter to

Miss Price. But by lunch she couldn't make herself wait another minute and left the letter to finish another day.

"I'm off to check on Rachael at the farm," she called to Mrs. Maxwell, still using that excuse to convince herself her visit was strictly professional. She wondered if anyone still believed it.

At the farm, she discovered Rachael had already baked cookies. "They smell delicious. My mouth has been watering for the last mile from the delicious smell."

Rachael beamed. "You can have one if you want."

"Thank you." She made a show about choosing the nicest-looking one and bit into it. "Umm. As good as it looks." She chewed two more bites. "Where's your pa?"

Diana answered. "He and Gabe are looking at the barn and making plans."

Just then the men stomped in. Conor still limped badly.

"We could smell those cookies." Gabe tickled Rachael and made her laugh. "Enough to make a man forget his work." He took a handful and stepped back to let Conor do the same.

Conor smiled at Virnie. She ducked, feeling as if he sent silent messages that she didn't want the others to see. "Good cookies, Rae. I hope you wrote the recipe down so you can do this again."

"I did, Pa."

"See ya later." Gabe wandered outside.

Conor sat at the table and ate his cookies, a thoughtful look on his face.

Aware of his meditative silence, Virnie kept a guarded eye on him as she helped Diana clean the kitchen and begin supper preparations.

An hour later Gabe returned to the house. "Well, that's done."

Diana chuckled. "And what would that be?"

"I've finished cleaning up the mess Conor made bringing down the roof. I tacked a piece of canvas over the end of the barn. It will serve to keep out any nasty weather. Tomorrow, you and I, Mrs. Winston, are going home." He grabbed her and danced her around the room, making her laugh.

"I can hardly wait to see my house," Diana said when he finally released her.

"You've wasted enough time here." Conor sounded weary.

Gabe punched him lightly on the shoulder. "Don't recall wasting a minute of it."

"No, you've worked hard. I owe you."

"And I'm expecting repayment in two ways."

Conor studied his friend with narrowed eyes. "Yeah?"

"Yup. When I'm ready to put my new barn up you can come and help."

"And the second?"

Gabe's grin flattened and he gave Conor a hard look. "I want you to promise you won't try to rebuild your barn until I return to help you."

The men studied each other. Virnie held her breath. She knew if Conor promised he would keep his promise and they could all stop worrying he'd be hurt again. But she knew how hard it was for him to accept limitations. He saw them as weaknesses and something he could not tolerate in either himself or others.

She knew, like she'd known since she was a child, that she could not live up to such a standard.

Suddenly Conor laughed, a great barking laugh that made them all jump. "I have no intention of getting myself pinned under a beam again. You can count on that."

"Shake?" Gabe held out his hand.

Conor grabbed it and they shook firmly.

Virnie was grateful for the nearby cupboard as relief left her knees shaking. She leaned against it and waited for the feeling to pass.

Gabe grabbed Diana about the waist. "How about you and I go for a walk? I haven't even had time to show you all the beauties of this farm."

From the way they looked at each other, Virnie guessed they wouldn't look farther than the person beside them.

Rachael chased Tippy outside.

Virnie and Conor were alone in the house. Alone for the first time since his accident. Suddenly Virnie felt as uncomfortable as if he were a stranger.

"I'd ask you to go for a walk, too, but I think the best I can do is invite you to sit on the bench outside the door and enjoy the sunshine with me."

He rose and held out his hand.

Her nerves so jumpy she could barely walk, she took his hand and followed him outside where she pulled away and folded her palms together in a ladylike fashion.

They sat side by side looking at the barn and corrals. If she shifted to the right, she could see down the road. If she shifted her gaze to the left—

She'd see Conor so she stared straight ahead.

"The sun feels good," he said.

She didn't want to talk about the sun, the weather or the farm. She wanted to talk about them but didn't know how to start. "You and Rachael have been through so much. She seems to be healed up. I guess it will take some time for your leg to be well again."

"Yet I feel stronger than I ever have."

Virnie jolted with surprise. "How can that be?"

"Because I've discovered…" He paused.

Slowly she brought her gaze to his, saw something warm and reassuring.

"I discovered needing help isn't a weakness."

"Weakness. You could never accept that, could you?" It made her feel unvalued and unacceptable. "Like my pa."

"Your father was wrong in making you feel inadequate. You've proved you aren't." His look went on and on, searching her heart.

She shook her head. "Like Miss Price said, 'Better to dwell on your strengths.'"

"Strange." He captured her hand. "I would have agreed not so long ago."

His touch filled her with confusion. His words seemed to hint at something she could trust. "And now?"

"Now it seems to me that admitting my weaknesses or my need doesn't make me helpless but victorious."

She swallowed hard, her thoughts a tangled mess of wanting, fear and—she didn't know what. "I don't understand."

He traced little circles on the back on her hand. "Weakness and need is not the same as fear or giving up."

She tried to imagine what he meant. "I have weaknesses."

"And strengths."

"Like shaping young minds." It was the one thing she'd been taught she was good at.

"And not-so-young minds."

She couldn't look away from his forceful gaze. Did he

mean what she wanted him to mean? Or was he only re-vealing gratitude again? He'd mentioned fear. And fear gripped her heart, squeezing it dry of every other emotion. Once she'd wanted approval so much she hated herself for not getting it. It had taken a long time to get over that.

She would never go back to that dark, lonesome, lonely place.

He must have read her withdrawal even though she didn't move a muscle. "Virnie, you are a very strong woman. Not just a good teacher but so much more."

She stood and walked away two steps before she turned to face him. "You only see me as what you want me to be." Before he could reply, she ducked into the house, in-tent on finding a task but Diana had left her nothing to do.

Conor lounged in the doorway. "You don't have to run from me. You don't have to be afraid of me. I am not your father."

She flung around to face him. "What's that sup-posed to mean."

He shrugged one shoulder. "He said and did things to hurt you. I can't say why but my guess is he was a hurting man. Perhaps afraid of his own weaknesses just like I was until recently."

"No doubt you were scared as you lay pinned under that pile of dirt." She couldn't stop a shudder from rip-pling across her shoulders. Didn't care that he saw her reaction and his eyes narrowed, as if reading more into it than he had a right. "Once your leg is all better you'll forget this big change in your thoughts. You'll be back to despising any weaknesses. And I've already admit-ted I have weaknesses." Right now her insides felt like liquid butter. So weak she could barely breathe.

"I don't care. I have weaknesses, too. Together we balance each other. Together we are strong."

She wanted to believe he had changed. She wanted to believe he could accept her weaknesses but she couldn't. She didn't dare. "Someday you would grow to hate my weaknesses."

"No, Virnie, I promise I wouldn't." He took a step toward her.

His blue eyes blazed, signaling his intention.

She loved him. Wanted him to love her but it frightened her to her very core with its expectations. She held out a hand and backed away.

He stopped. The flame in his eyes died.

She hated to see his hurt but she couldn't help it. She couldn't get past her fear even though she wanted to.

Lord, God, help me forget my past and be able to face whatever the future might hold.

She shivered with anticipation at the idea of a future shared with a loving man. But her fear reared its head and her shivers turned to a shudder.

Conor turned and hobbled outside. He stood in the middle of the yard feeling more helpless than at any time in his life. Why couldn't he persuade Virnie to trust him?

Trust wasn't easy. He knew that from experience. Look at how he'd struggled against trusting God when it was the very thing he needed.

He limped to the corral fence and leaned over the top rail. *God, she's been hurt far more than she realizes. But You reached me with Your healing and I know You can reach her, too. Please do so. I love her and I want to share my life with her.*

He thought of returning to the house and declaring his love in loud, clear terms but somehow he understood she wasn't ready to hear the words. Until she was, he would be patient and try not to push her.

Rae raced up to him. "Virnie's leaving. Tell her to stay."

He turned.

Virnie faced him across the yard. "I think it best if I go back to town."

"There isn't any point in arguing, is there?"

She shook her head.

"Hadn't you better wait for Gabe and Diana to return so you can say goodbye to them?"

She glanced along the path the pair had taken. They were almost back.

He sighed. If he'd hoped that would provide a reason for her to stay… he'd have to find another even though he knew she would have to find the reason in her own heart.

Rae ran to meet Gabe and Diana.

Conor closed the distance between him and Virnie. "I don't want you to leave like this." He couldn't stop himself from stroking her cheek, reveling in the silky softness of her skin. He glowed inwardly when she didn't jerk away. "You could stay for supper. After all, it's Gabe and Diana's last day here."

She ducked her eyes then slowly lifted them to his. "I wish I could feel differently. Maybe in time…"

He laughed. "Virnie White, in case you didn't notice there's nothing much but time out here on the prairie. I'll be here waiting until you're ready."

She nodded. "No promises."

"Except mine to wait."

It was all he could do not to drape his arm across her shoulder as they joined Gabe and Diana at the house.

Sunday morning, Gabe and Diana left shortly after daybreak. "Got to get home before dark," Gabe said.

"Thank you for everything. And in case I didn't say it, congratulations to you both on your marriage."

Rae hugged them both then ran after her kitten.

Gabe leaned over and whispered loudly. "I hope you corral Virnie before someone else does."

"I'm doing my best."

Gabe laughed uproariously at that.

They drove away, looking back often to wave goodbye.

Conor waited until they were out of sight to return to the house. Suddenly it felt very empty. He was more alone than he had ever been. He'd promised to give Virnie all the time she needed. He hoped that wouldn't be long. He was not a patient man.

"Rae, are you ready for church?"

She dashed in. "Just let me change."

He waited for her to put on her dress. Funny how he'd thought wearing a dress would make her weak. She could put on a dress for church and just as easily put on overalls when she got home. She still milked the cow faster than any man. And she managed the household chores much better thanks to both Virnie and Diana.

When they rode to church, they found Virnie waiting at the steps for them. His heart leaped with joy. At least she wasn't pushing him out of her life. They entered the church together and sat side by side in a pew, Rae at Virnie's other side. This was the way he wanted his life to be. Sharing daily events, sharing faith, sharing work and dreams. It was all he could do not to reach for Virnie's hand as they sat together especially when she flashed him a smile so full of warmth and promise that his lungs forgot to work.

He forced himself to concentrate on the sermon and was glad he didn't miss a word of the pastor's encouragement to trust God through both the good and bad things of life.

When the service ended, he didn't want to move. It felt so good and right to sit here with Virnie. He silently prayed the sermon had encouraged her as much as it had him. If she could put her past away and embrace the future…a future shared with him.

"Did Gabe and Diana get away all right?"

He sighed. Her thoughts were obviously not going the direction he hoped. "Left at first light."

"Diana must be anxious to see her new home." Virnie got to her feet and waited for Conor to stand. "Are your legs sore after sitting so long?"

Let her think his hesitation came from pain in his legs not reluctance in his heart. But he didn't want to cause her undue worry. "No worse than any other time." He pushed to his feet, stood a moment without moving as his tender feet adjusted to his weight.

Several people stopped them as they headed down the aisle. "Heard about your accident. Glad to see you in one piece." "Good to see you walking about." "Be sure and let us know if you need help. Anytime."

They reached the door. Conor wanted to stop time right there before they had to part ways. He thought of inviting her out for the afternoon. Not appropriate. Maybe he could spend the day in town.

Mrs. Brown, whose husband ran the general store, stepped aside as they passed and turned to the woman next to her. "I hear our little schoolteacher spends a great deal of time out at the Russell farm."

Conor gave the woman a hard look. He knew her words had been intended for everyone to hear. The woman returned him hard look for hard look, clearly informing him as well as all those watching what she thought about the situation.

Rae, wanting to defend her beloved teacher, announced loudly, "Miss White comes out all the time. She's teaching me to cook and clean. Isn't that right, Pa?"

Conor groaned. He'd taught Rae to be fearless. But he hadn't counted on having it backfire. He stole a look at Virnie. The color had drained from her face. Her eyes were wide with shock.

He heard several tsks from various directions.

Mr. Nelson, a school board member, marched over to face Virnie. "What's this I hear? Is it true? Are you spending time at a farm without adequate chaperoning?" His voice condemned both Conor and Virnie.

Conor stepped forward. "Now wait a minute. What you suggest is totally unfounded. Miss White has been teaching Rae—" He struggled for a word. "Domestic science. Very commendable that she would go beyond classroom expectations."

"Humph." Mrs. Brown's disapproval was evident.

"And my friend Gabe Winston and his wife, Diana, have been there. They only left this morning."

Mr. Nelson shook his finger at Virnie. "Miss White, you have a responsibility to maintain a flawless reputation and to devote yourself to all the children, not just one."

Conor wanted to grab the offending member of the man's hand and shove it down his throat.

Virnie nodded. "You are correct. Now if you'll all excuse me…" She swept down the road toward the Maxwell house.

Conor wondered how she managed to keep her head so high and her stride so unhurried. His heart ached for her. It seemed everyone had high expectations of her, from her father to the school board—though he knew she had reason to watch her conduct before the board. *Lord, help us live wisely.*

He vowed he would find a way to prove to her he accepted her just as she was. More than that, he loved the way she was right now—her fear of spiders, her determination, her noble ideals, her past pain that gave her a vulnerable core he wished he could love to wholeness. *God, am I wanting to do something only You can do? If so, I trust You to do Your work.*

"Come on, Rae. Let's go home."

Rae waited until they rode toward home to ask, "Is Miss White in trouble?"

"I don't think so. After all she hasn't done anything wrong."

"Those people weren't very nice to her."

"Perhaps they didn't mean to be unkind." He couldn't speak for anyone's motivation but wanted no reason for Rae to be upset.

If only he could visit Virnie and reassure her. If only he could tell her he loved her. But he must respect her reservations and give her time to work through their changing feelings for each other.

Chapter Twelve

Virnie kept her head high and her steps measured until she reached the sanctuary of the Maxwell house, then she sped to her bedroom and closed the door. She paced to the window and looked out. What had she done? Nothing. Her conscience was clear. But had she given people cause to wonder otherwise?

She couldn't honestly answer the question. She felt as if she rode a giant rocking horse, tossed from one side to the other by her emotions. First, hope that Conor accepted her, perhaps cared for her deeply, then fear of needing his acceptance. Back to hope for a shared life and a home of her own, then condemnation of her faltering ways.

Lord, show me what You want. Guide me.

She went to school Monday resolved to step back from her feelings toward Conor and not let them control her. Yet she couldn't keep from watching down the road. When Rachael ran to the school on her own, Virnie smiled and pretended she wasn't disappointed Conor hadn't accompanied her.

"Pa said to tell you he had a cow to tend to."

Virnie nodded. "Of course."

She worked hard all day making sure she showed each child the care and attention they needed. She would give no one cause to criticize her.

But part of her heart yearned for things outside the classroom. She loved Conor. And loving made her feel unsettled. As if she'd lost her center of balance. In the past, love had left her needy and unsatisfied. Only devotion to a task, a duty, had made her feel she walked on solid footing. But was it enough? Enough to satisfy for the rest of her life?

She didn't have the answers and didn't know where to find them. *God, You alone have the answers. Show me what is right.*

School ended and she returned to her room. Mrs. Maxwell had left Virnie's mail on the hall table outside her door. Virnie picked up the letter from Miss Price and retreated to her room to read it.

She skimmed the usual greeting and Miss Price's report on the progress of her students. She had another child living with her—Donna—and Miss Price reported the girl showed great promise and dedication.

Virnie gasped at the next paragraph.

You consider that helping a man free himself from his own folly makes you useful? What are you thinking? I would suggest you'd be far more useful if you were to attend to the needs of all your students. Devoting your time and energy to one child and her father is to neglect your duties as a teacher. It is to fail in what I've striven hard to teach you. It is to nullify your calling. It is a waste.

Virnie let the pages fall to her lap and stared out the window. She'd disappointed Miss Price. Let her down. After all Miss Price had done for her.

She picked up the pages and reread the stern warning. Here then was her answer. She had set her heart and mind on being a teacher since the first day Miss Price had taken her in. She would keep her course steadily in that direction. She folded the letter, returned it to the envelope and dropped it in the drawer along with the other letters from Miss Price.

She pulled out the lesson plans for the next day and concentrated on them. This was who she was. A teacher.

Again the next day, Rachael walked to school on her own. Virnie was glad. She didn't think she was up to seeing Conor. Her determination wavered even at the thought.

Wednesday morning, Conor brought Rachael on horseback. When she saw them approaching, Virnie hurried into the school. She could not speak to him and successfully quench the yearnings of her heart.

She struggled through the rest of the day, knowing she must focus on her job of teaching yet feeling as if something dear and precious that she hadn't even known existed had been ripped from her.

She bid the children goodbye at the end of the day and remained at her desk. She'd plan the lessons for the next day and start to prepare recitations for the Christmas concert in a month's time.

Suddenly, the door was flung back and Conor stomped to the front of the room, still limping on his right leg.

"Why are you avoiding me?"

She blinked before his fury. "I've been attending to my duties."

"You did so before but that didn't prevent you from sparing me a 'Hello, how are you?'"

She pursed her lips. He was making this far more difficult than it had to be. "Hello. How are you? See you're walking better."

He planted his hands on the edge of the desk and leaned forward. "You can't shut me out. I promised to be patient but I don't plan to walk away."

It hurt her neck to tip her head to meet his gaze, and the intensity in those blue eye sent shards of confusion through her thoughts, messing up her neat and orderly plans. She ducked her head and stared at his big, work-worn hands. Hands that could be gentle and comforting. "I can't be what everyone wants me to be. I can't be a good teacher unless I devote myself to it fully."

"Like Miss Price?"

She jerked her head up in surprise at his words. "Yes, like Miss Price. I owe her so much."

"Who else are you trying to please?"

"What do you mean?"

"You said you couldn't be what everyone wants. Who else do you mean? Your father?"

"I could never be what he wants. He wanted a son."

"Who else?" he demanded in low, insistent tones.

She straightened the papers on her desk and adjusted the ink well.

"Virnie, who else are you trying to please?"

His prodding pushed her to speak without thinking. "I can't be what you want, either. I'm not strong. I'm not pioneer stock."

He leaned back and laughed. When he sobered he

crossed his arms over his chest and grinned at her. "Virnie, you hide behind your pretty little ways but both you and I know you can be as tough as you want to be or need to be when the occasion arises."

His look, full of admiration, burned away all her arguments.

She had to explain. Make him see what she must do. "I had a letter from Miss Price reminding me of my decision to be a teacher the rest of my life."

Conor sobered. "Your decision or hers?"

"I don't know what you mean."

He sat on the top of the nearest desk so he could face her. She tried to break their look but his gaze demanded her attention.

"Virnie, perhaps it's time to be who you are. Not what your father appears to have wanted—a boy and seeing as he was stuck with a girl, a girl who passed as a boy. Not what Miss Price wants, someone to be just like her. I don't think either of those is the real you."

Confusion washed through her, leaving her weepy and uncertain. "Then who am I?"

His smile was gentle as morning dew. "I think you know but are afraid to admit it."

She ducked her head and sniffed. "You aren't making any sense."

He slipped from the desk and moved close. He caught her chin and tipped her face toward him.

The look of love in his eyes filled her with such sweet befuddlement. She knew it was a precarious state of mind. For a moment she didn't care then her fear at being needy turned the sweet feeling bitter. She lowered her eyes even though he still held her chin and settled her gaze on his chest.

"Virnie, it's time you made peace with your past."

She jerked her startled gaze to his. Peace with her past? "It's not possible. How can I accept how I was treated as a child?"

He stroked her chin, his eyes full of longing. "I think you have to accept it. But you've lost contact with both your father and your brother. Doesn't that make you the least bit sad?"

Her heart clenched like someone bound it in cruel ropes. Tears welled up and overspilled. She clenched her teeth to stop from sobbing.

"Ahh. I see it does." He wiped each cheek, capturing the tears with his fingertips. "Have you ever tried to get hold of them?"

She shook her head. "Miss Price—" She couldn't finish.

"Miss Price forbade it?"

"Said it wasn't wise."

His look probed deep into her soul, exposing unhealed wounds, hungry longings, regrets she couldn't confess. "Virnie, what do you want?"

"I want to see Miles again. He was a good brother to me. He took me with him everywhere he went and tended me like a mother. In fact, he was both mother and father to me." The enormity of her loss choked her words.

Conor stroked her hair. "Seems to me you are mourning him when he's likely still alive and well. Why not see if you can find him?"

She struggled with her longing. So many years she'd denied it. Pretended nothing mattered except being like Miss Price. Pleasing her. Yet she couldn't forget Miles. "I remember crying for him after I went to live with

Miss Price until she finally said I must forget him and everything about my past."

"I think you almost succeeded but perhaps there has always been an ache that wouldn't go away."

She stared at him through her tears. "How do you know all this?"

He chuckled. "Wasn't too many days ago I was trying so hard to forget my own past or maybe push it into a different shape, one that didn't fit." He smiled softly, making her feel trembly inside. "I discovered I can't push the past away but I must learn from it and build on it."

Her ache to see Miles slowly filled her to the point she couldn't imagine why she hadn't tried to find him long ago. "What if he doesn't want to see me?"

"I'll pray he does. And even if he doesn't, at least you will have done what you can."

She bolted to her feet. "I'm going to send a letter to-night." Before her well-developed denial process sprang back into control. She hesitated as she came face-to-face with him. "I hope I'm not setting myself up for major heartache."

"Are you getting ready to blame me?"

She shook her head, then changed her mind and nod-ded. Then she stopped altogether. "I'll let you know when I hear back—if I hear back. Who knows if I'll even be able to contact him?"

He squeezed her shoulder. "I'll pray."

"Thank you." His touch settled her and she turned back to gather her lessons.

He walked her to the door. Rachael waited by the horse. "I'll say goodbye here rather than give Mrs. Brown any reason for more gossip."

She said goodbye to both Conor and Rachael and hurried home. But when she sat down to pen the letter, she couldn't think what to say. Remembering how Conor promised to pray, she bowed her head and asked for wisdom, then picked up the pen and wrote a simple letter saying she had never forgotten him and would like to see him if he was agreeable.

She addressed the envelope to the town nearest the Zingle farm where she had spent many hours helping Miles. She had no idea if he still lived in the same area but if not she hoped the postmaster would know where to forward the letter.

She took the letter to the post office immediately before she could change her mind.

That night she lay in bed, unable to sleep. She would love to see Miles again. But for what purpose? By morning she regretted her impulsive decision. If she could she would retrieve the letter but it was already on its way.

This was Conor's fault. He was all fired up because he'd made some wonderful discoveries while praying for rescue. Virnie didn't think she needed to risk death to know what she was or what she needed. She did not need approval of her father, her brother or Conor. Seeking it in the past had left her with nothing but aching wounds that Conor's probing had uncovered, renewing the pain and uncertainty they carried.

When he rode to the school with Rachael, Virnie had a fine level of annoyance built and spared him a long, accusing look before she turned away.

After school, she waited at the gate, her arms full of papers and books when Conor arrived. As soon as he was close enough that she could safely leave Rachael, she headed for home without so much as a backward look. At least she didn't need to worry about Rachael. She had no lingering doubts that Conor loved his daughter. And Virnie herself had taught the child enough skills to ensure they would eat some decent meals and eat off clean dishes.

She had been perfectly content with her life until he poked his nose into her business.

Nevertheless, she hurried to the hall table to check for mail. There was none.

Every day for the next week, she checked for a letter from Miles.

There was none and she grew more despondent and blamed Conor. She would have never written that letter, awakened that hope, without his prodding.

She had tried to avoid him at church. No need to give the good ladies of the area any reason to criticize her. But two weeks later, he waited after church until she had no choice but to head for home. He fell into step beside her, leading Noble, with Rachael racing ahead.

Virnie tried to convince herself she didn't care that it obviously still hurt him to walk.

"I take it you haven't heard from Miles."

She sniffed. "I should have never listened to you."

"I never made you do anything. I thought it was what you wanted to do."

The fact that his words rang with truth didn't make them any easier to swallow. "Strange, don't you think, that in the past seven years I've never considered writing him? Not until now."

"Now that you mention it, yes." Only his tone was a lot more accusing than regretful.

She flung him a glance full of fury. "Sometimes a

person learns to accept things and not wish they could be different."

He slowed so he could look into her face as he talked. "What things do you wish you could change, Virnie?"

"Nothing. That's just the point. I've accepted my life the way it is."

"Accepted?"

"Don't scoff."

"Accepted sounds like trying to scrape up the dregs and convince yourself it's better than the best. Why would you settle for that?"

His words drove through her heart, pinpointing what she tried so hard to hide. "Because it hurts too much to wish for things that can't be." She stomped away, as angry at herself for confessing her fear as at him for pushing her past her endurance.

"Maybe they can be."

"What?" The man talked in more riddles than a clown.

"Maybe the things you want can happen."

She stormed on without speaking.

He kept pace even though his feet must be hurting something awful by now. Or, maybe they didn't. Maybe they were better. She didn't know, having avoided talking to him for two weeks.

He caught her elbow.

She didn't slow down.

"Virnie, what is it you want? Love, belonging, acceptance? I can give you those if you let me. I love—"

She couldn't bear to hear it. "No one can give me what I want." The enormity of the words she'd uttered made her stumble.

Conor caught her. "Careful there."

No one could give her what she wanted because… the truth hit her like a blast of hot wind straight off the prairie…because she wouldn't let them.

Thankfully they had reached the Maxwell home. "Good day." She rushed inside, her thoughts driving her straight to her room where she closed the door and leaned against it, panting as if she had run a thousand yards.

She wouldn't let them.

The words circled around her like vultures.

Why wouldn't she let them?

It didn't make sense. She fell to her knees at the side of the bed. *Lord, God, help me. I am lost and can't find my way. Be Thou my guide.*

The days passed. Christmas slowly approached. It should be a time of joy and anticipation. For Virnie it was not.

Miles had not written. She'd given up hope he would.

She refused to see Conor other than to nod curtly when they met in church or when he gave Rachael a ride to and from school. Her only excuse was to blame him for triggering her hope that things could be different.

She tried to balance the attention she gave Rachael with what the others needed. Yet her heart called her back to Rachael time after time. The child watched her with brown-eyed sadness.

"You don't like me anymore, do you?" Rachael's question tore raw strips from Virnie's heart.

"Oh, sweetie, I love you." She knew she should not say the words to a student, but she also understood Rachael did not need to carry any idea of rejection with her.

"Then why don't you come visit anymore?"

"It's something grown-ups have to work out, but it's not because of you. Never think that."

Rachael ducked her head but not before Virnie saw the pain and retreat. She regressed into being a tough little tomboy.

Virnie wished she could push her thoughts and emotions back to where they had been when she first came to Sterling but, no thanks to Conor, they proved impossible to control.

One question dogged her every waking hour and filled her nights with restless torment.

Why wouldn't she let people give her what she wanted? She could say what she wanted, had known it since she was very young. She wanted acceptance, approval, love—probably all part of the same thing.

Conor had offered them to her.

She couldn't accept.

And she couldn't explain why it was so.

As was expected of her, she prepared Christmas surprises for the children, filling each little sack with a handful of candies and an orange.

The night of the concert was cold and clear. Snow from a few days ago covered the brown-and-yellow landscape of fall with fresh white.

The men had arrived after class to push the desks together and set up benches along the edges. Mr. Nelson had hung up bedsheets earlier in the week to serve as a curtain for the stage. Everything was ready. Each of the children had a speaking part and they had rehearsed several songs.

"Come on, children." They had gathered behind the curtain and she clapped for their attention. "You all look very nice." The boys wore their best white shirts.

All the girls had on their best dresses. Rachael wore a brand-new dress.

"Pa bought it for me," she whispered to Virnie.

"It's lovely," she whispered back and gave the girl a quick hug before she turned her attention to the rest of the students. "Now remember what I said. Smile. And do your best."

The children nodded, anxious to please her and do a good job. She let satisfaction smooth away her silly notions about belonging and accepting love. This was where she belonged. With children. Teaching them, shaping them, molding them and preparing them to be the best they could be.

It felt much safer than dealing with her inner turmoil.

Enough of such nonsense. She pushed her confusion to the back recesses of her mind, stepped to the center of the stage, parted the curtain and faced the audience. The room was crowded with parents and neighbors. Conor sat dead front. She carefully avoided looking at him.

He could offer her what she wanted.

She wouldn't let him give it to her.

Why?

She again forced her thoughts into submission and welcomed everyone.

The children did a good job. The two Schmidt boys spoke flawless English as they recited a poem she had written especially for them.

Hilda and her little sisters, Gracie and Alice, sang a Christmas song.

George recited the entire second chapter of Luke.

She hugged each and every one of them when the concert was finished. "You did a wonderful job." Yes, this was where she belonged. She felt safe with children. Besides, good teachers were needed. Always would be.

The candy bags were handed to the children and the adults rose to visit with friends and neighbors. Conor moved to the back as if he didn't want to endure Virnie's continued avoidance of him. She barely noticed as each parent made a point of speaking to her, thanking her for the good job she had done and wishing her a blessed Christmas. School would be closed now for two weeks that stretched before her as endless as winter.

She stole a forbidden glance in Conor's direction. He spoke to a man who stood with his back to Virnie. If only Conor's back was to her so she couldn't see that face, those eyes.

Slowly, as if reluctant to end the evening, people drifted away. Conor hung about. She wondered if he wanted to speak to her and busied herself with putting away decorations. She couldn't face him, more correctly couldn't face the quagmire of her inner turmoil.

"Virnie."

She turned. A man faced her. Not someone from the community. Her heart stalled. Her thoughts froze. "Miles?"

The man nodded. "It's me."

Out of the corner of her eye, she saw Conor take Rachael's hand and slip away.

"Miles." Her voice choked off. She couldn't move. Couldn't breathe. Couldn't think.

Chapter Thirteen

"Who was that, Pa?" Rae asked as he tucked her into the buggy he'd recently pulled from the corner of the barn and cleaned up. It had sat unused long enough… since Irene's death.

"That was Miss White's brother."

"The one she hasn't seen in a long time?"

"Yup."

"I hope it makes her happy again."

"Me, too." He'd tried to explain to Rae that Virnie's retreat from them was because she was unhappy. "I think he'll help her find what she needs." He prayed it would.

He'd had a chance to speak to Miles. He liked the man. Straightforward and outgoing. He seemed eager to see Virnie. Conor smiled. That might have been his reason for liking Miles. Anyone who revealed that much affection for Virnie earned approval in Conor's eyes.

The last few weeks had been difficult. Loving Virnie yet being forced to stand back and wait for her to come to terms with who she was. It stretched his rediscovered faith. But one thing he knew—he wasn't about to give up. She'd find in him the strength and staying power she needed.

He prayed God would provide whatever else she needed.

"I invited her brother to join us for Christmas," he told Rae.

"And bring Virnie, too?"

"That was the idea."

Rae giggled. "Won't she be surprised when she sees how big Tippy is and opens the present we bought her?"

"I 'spect so." He'd forced himself to buy her only a small present though he wanted to buy every nice trinket in the store.

Rae squirmed in excitement. "With Uncle Gabe and Auntie Diana coming, too, it will make six of us. It's going to be the best Christmas ever."

Conor hoped she wasn't getting her hopes up for nothing. "We don't know for sure Virnie and her brother will come."

In the moonlight glistening off the snow he watched Rae lift her face to the sky, her eyes squeezed tight.

"What are you doing?"

"Praying they come." She blinked and turned wide-eyed to him. "That's all right, isn't it?"

"I should think so, though we have to be prepared God might not choose to force her. We want her to come because she wants to."

Virnie took a faltering step toward Miles and halted.

He held out his arms. "Virnie, my baby sister."

She ran into his arms, clutching his lapels as tears streamed down her face. "I didn't think you would come," she managed to say.

"I came as soon as I got your letter." He hugged her tight.

If she wasn't mistaken he sounded as choked as she.

"The letter caught up with me west of here. I've been thinking of starting a ranch."

She leaned back and studied his face. He was heavier than she remembered, fuller in the face. Yet his eyes were the same soft brown she recalled. He wore better clothes than they had as children. A rough woolen coat with a white shirt beneath. She remembered him once holding her close as she cried, the reason now forgotten but the feel of his arms about her felt the same. Solid. Comforting. Even though her chin now rested on his shoulder rather than his chest. "You're older."

He chuckled, a familiar sound that made her smile. "You are, too. But my, you look like Mama."

She scrubbed her lips together a minute before she could talk. "I don't remember Mama at all."

"Don't you remember how she used to pull you to her lap and tell you to always be strong? I think she knew she wouldn't live to raise you."

Virnie shook her head. "I don't remember."

Miles laughed again. "You would always pop down to stand in front of her and flex your arm like you'd seen me do. 'I very strong,' you'd say and we'd all laugh."

Brother and sister stared at each other.

Miles pulled her close again. "My little sister, how I've missed you."

She sobbed against his shoulder as she thought of all the years they had lost. He held her, patting her back as she cried out her sorrow. Tears were supposed to heal or so she'd heard, but she didn't find they did. Her insides felt raw, oozing pain she couldn't control. All she could do was push it back into the cages she had built for it.

She sniffed away the last of her tears and straightened, wiping at Miles's coat where she'd soaked it. "Sorry. I didn't expect to be so emotional."

He chuckled, the sound rattling the bars of her cages. "Me neither."

She laughed to see his face tear-streaked, too.

He pulled out a big hanky and wiped her face and then dried his own.

"Do you have a place to spend the night?"

"I'm staying in a room behind the general store."

Virnie knew of the place the Browns let to travelers. "It's adequate."

"I've slept in far worse."

Together they circled the schoolroom, turning out the lamps and making sure everything was secure.

"How long are you staying?" she asked.

"Anxious to get rid of me already?"

She recognized the teasing in his voice and remembered how he had teased her as a child and made her laugh. She laughed now. "I'm afraid you'll go and leave me alone again."

He grabbed her shoulders. "Virnie, now that I've found you I don't intend to let you out of my sight for a long time. In fact, I thought I might hang around here until spring."

Virnie couldn't stop smiling. "I'm glad." She'd been dreading the holidays without school to occupy her but now she couldn't wait to spend every day learning about Miles and what happened to him since they last saw each other. She had to know one more thing before they stepped out into the cold. "Papa?"

"I'm sorry. He died about a year ago."

She cried out with pain.

He held her.

"I didn't expect it to matter." But how would she ever resolve the need to prove herself to him? "Let's go." She pulled the door closed behind them.

They said good-night outside the Maxwell house and arranged to meet right after breakfast the next morning.

As Virnie prepared for bed, she laughed softly with joy that Miles had come. But her joy dissolved into hot tears. How could she ever let Conor give her what she wanted when it was now impossible to get it from her father? She wept into her pillow. She couldn't even say what she cried over—loss of a father who had sent her away, the death of hope for a chance to share her life with Conor?

The next two days spent with Miles were sweet delight to her starving soul—something she had been unaware of until she started to feed it with memories and shared affection of her brother.

"Conor invited us to spend Christmas Day with him," Miles said.

Virnie had told him about the days spent helping Rachael and how she'd rescued Conor.

Miles had laughed long and hard at that. "Just like you were at Mama's knees. 'I strong.'"

She hadn't confessed her love for Conor. She'd avoided spending time with him afraid of her own needy longing. But she wanted him to get to know Miles. "I'd like that."

"Then I need to buy some gifts."

"Me, too." She had already bought a nice fur muff for Rachael but had avoided thinking of a gift for Conor.

With Miles at her side, she enjoyed shopping. In the end they selected gifts for all who'd be at the farm, including Gabe and Diana.

Her anticipation of spending the day in Conor's company seemed to grow with every gift they bought, every story she and Miles shared and every heartbeat that marked the time until they went to the farm. She loved him. Knew he loved her. She yearned to be able to embrace that love. But a fearful lump tailed after her anticipation.

It wasn't until she was alone in her room that her fear made its full fury known. She sat on the edge of her bed shivering. What was she so afraid of that she couldn't accept love?

Lord, there is something dreadfully wrong with me. I don't know what it is or how to correct it. Surely You do. A verse sprang to mind. *"My substance was not hid from Thee, when I was made in secret." Lord, You made me. You know how to fix me. Please do Your work.*

Christmas day dawned cold and clear.

Rachael had been up long before the sun, staring at the gifts under the tree. Conor wondered what he'd do for a Christmas tree but Gabe brought one with him.

"Pa, how long do we have to wait?"

"Until I do the chores and we eat breakfast." He hoped if he delayed long enough, Virnie and her brother would show up.

"Aww."

Diana was busy at the stove. Gabe drank coffee. Conor grabbed the milk bucket. He took care of that task now that it was cold. No need for Rae to do it when he had to go to the barn anyway. "I'll do chores and then return to eat."

He prayed as he milked the cow then forked up feed for the animals. *Lord, it's hard to be patient when I want so badly to share my love and my life with Virnie. But I will trust You. I will allow You to heal her and set her free to love.*

He vowed he would do his best to make the day one to remember even if Virnie didn't choose to join them.

He returned to the house, pausing to look down the road. He saw nothing. Told himself he didn't expect to. Inside, he took care of the milk then sat down at the table. He had just finished blessing the food when he heard the thud of horse hooves and the rattle and creak of a conveyance.

It was all he could do not to bolt for the window like Rae did.

"It's Virnie and her brother," she announced.

The room brightened like the sun had suddenly come from behind a cloud.

"I'll set two more places," Diana said.

Conor grabbed his coat and went out to help put the horse in the barn. He reached the side of the buggy almost before Miles drew to a halt and reached up to assist Virnie. "Glad you could make it," he murmured, shaking hands with Miles and then helping her to alight, holding her several moments more than necessary.

She met his gaze and smiled. He saw in her look a sweetness, an assurance perhaps even a happiness he had not seen before.

"It's been good for you to see your brother."

She tipped her head and pretended to grow serious. "Indeed. And how would you know that?"

He chuckled. "See it in your eyes."

She ducked away and reached back to gather a handful of packages. "I think you see far too much. Here, take these."

He helped her with the parcels. "I think I see far too little."

She stilled and slowly faced him, all teasing gone from her expression. "I'm rediscovering my love for my brother."

Her words effectively informed him it was nothing more. "It's a start." And as such gave him renewed hope for more. He led them indoors.

Rae rushed forward to greet them, hesitated. Virnie held out her arms, inviting Rae into a hug, then she turned toward Miles. "Rachael, this my brother, Miles."

Miles shook hands. "Pleased to meet you. Virnie speaks of you in glowing terms."

Rae beamed.

Conor introduced the others and together they moved toward the table and sat down.

At Rae's urging they hurried through breakfast so they could gather around the tree. There seemed an overabundance of gifts. Conor realized he had neglected this holiday in the past, deprived Rae of so much pleasure and silently, he thanked these dear friends for showing him the need for change.

He handed Virnie the gift he and Rae had chosen together.

She gave him a warm smile that seemed full of promise before she folded back the paper to reveal the stack of pretty writing paper with matching envelopes, all tied with a bright pink ribbon. "It's lovely. Thank you." She hugged Rae as she glanced at Conor.

He hoped the warmth in her eyes signaled a change in her heart about trusting love.

She had given him a very handsome tie. And laughed at his surprise. "I thought you might like to wear it on Sundays."

He couldn't help wondering and wishing that perhaps, just for a moment, she had imagined him wearing it at their wedding because that was his first thought when he saw it. It was a wonderful gift. One he would cherish always. "Thank you. It means more to me than you can imagine."

Rae got a fur muff from Virnie, a little doll from Diana and Gabe, and from Miles, a storybook. Conor waited until the end of the gift exchange to bring out his gift for Rae—a child-sized saddle.

"Pa?" He knew her unspoken question. What was she to do with a saddle?

"I think it might be just a perfect fit for the pony in the barn."

Rae bound to her feet and raced for the door, slowing to get her coat only because Conor called after her.

"I've got to see this," Gabe followed.

Conor grabbed the saddle and the rest crowded after like a gaggle of excited children.

In the barn, Rae walked around the black-and-white pony, patting his rump and running her fingers through his mane. "He's perfect."

She darted to Conor and jumped into his arms to hug and kiss him. "Thank you, Pa."

"What are you going to call him?"

She thought for a moment. "Prince. His name is Prince."

"Fine name for a fine horse," Conor said. The others nodded approval.

"Can I ride him?"

"He's yours. I guess you better try him out." He supervised putting on the saddle, pleased to see she could handle it well. He handed her the bridle and made sure she got it in place. When he reached out to help her mount she shook her head.

"I want to do it all by myself."

"Very well." Best if she did. That way she would be safe riding to school and back and wherever she wanted.

It took several attempts before she figured out how to reach the stirrup and pull herself up. But she did it.

And he couldn't have been prouder.

He watched Rae ride up and down the alleyway and then he opened the door and let her ride down the road.

Virnie stood at his side. "You've made her very happy."

"It's practical to have her able to get around on her own."

Virnie laughed. "Yes. I'm sure that was uppermost in your thoughts when you bought her the pony." She nudged him, tipping his heart far more than she tipped his body. "You don't fool any of us. You knew how much she'd enjoy being able to ride."

The others chuckled, too.

"She's got you figured out, old man," Gabe chortled.

He suddenly wished the rest of them would disappear and leave him alone with Virnie so he could tell her what would give him even more pleasure than seeing Rae so happy—her acceptance of his love.

But none of them made a move to go elsewhere.

He let Rae ride around a bit longer than called her

back. He made sure she put away the tack and brushed her horse.

"Can I stay with him for a while?"

"Sure."

Gabe pulled Diana close. "We're going for a walk."

"The turkey is in the oven. There's nothing to do for a little while," Diana called over her shoulder as they departed.

"We might as well go inside." Conor hoped the two of them would share something that would give him reason to believe Miles's visit would work a miracle in Virnie's heart.

"Anyone care for tea?" Virnie asked, setting about to prepare it without waiting for an answer.

"How do you like Sterling?" Conor asked Miles.

"Nice little town. Mostly farming around here though, isn't it?"

"Miles is interested in ranching," Virnie said, beaming at her brother.

Conor wanted to grab her gaze and make her look at him the same way. He wanted to hear all about her reunion with her brother.

But by the time she finished fussing with tea, Gabe and Diana returned. "It's cold out there." Diana shivered.

And of course, Virnie had to make more tea and put out more cups and fuss about Diana getting too cold.

Then Rae returned. "I'm hungry."

Diana opened a box of cookies to go with the tea.

All the time, Conor could think of nothing but the questions burning at the back of his mind. How was her visit with Miles going? Had it made a difference for her?

Perhaps the others were as curious for different reasons because Diana turned to Miles. "I understand it's been a while since you last saw Virnie."

"Over seven years." He appeared choked up for a moment. "I wondered if I would ever see her again."

"She was just a child when you last saw her then. You must notice quite a change."

Miles grinned at Virnie. "You wouldn't believe what an adventuresome child she was. She'd tackle anything from a rank cow to trying to lift fork loads of hay as big as I did."

Conor snorted. "She caught my bull in a headlock. Said you taught her how to do it."

Miles laughed and slapped his knee. "I can just see it."

All eyes turned to Virnie. Although her cheeks stained a very pretty pink she shook her head. "I had to be tough."

Miles snorted. "You seemed to think you did." He turned to the others. "I figured the only way I could keep her from being hurt on the farm was to teach her as much as I could. She was scared of nothing."

"She's scared of spiders," Rae piped up.

Conor laughed. "Not always." Of course he had to then explain how Virnie had rescued him even though the place crawled with spiders.

Diana turned back to Miles. "But why was Virnie with you? You couldn't have been more than a boy. Didn't you have parents?"

"Our mother died," Miles explained.

"And Papa left me alone," Virnie added.

Miles nodded. "She wasn't yet school-age but the summer was upon us and I had a job at a nearby farm so I took her with me. I didn't like thinking of her alone all day."

Virnie shuddered. "I hated it. I didn't know if everyone would go away for good like Mama had. There were so many things I couldn't do. I couldn't even brush a spider off my hair." She shuddered and gasped. "That's when I developed my fear of them. I remember one crawling into my hair and I couldn't get it out." She shuddered again.

"Yuck," Rae said.

Conor sat next to Virnie and squeezed her hands. "I learned how awful it is to have them crawl around on you and not be able to brush them off."

She sent him a grateful look.

Diana jumped to her feet. "Here I am forgetting about the meal. Christmas dinner. Tsk."

Virnie jolted to her feet to help.

Miles leaned back. "Do you intend to rebuild the barn?"

"Have materials for a wooden one. A real barn."

"That's why I'm here," Gabe said. "I'm going to help him."

"Could you use another set of hands?"

"Of course," Gabe and Conor chorused as one.

"I'd like to help. I want to stay around for the winter and spend time with Virnie."

"Great." But Conor wasn't sure what he thought. An extra man to help with the barn was good. But so long as Miles hung around he guessed he would get little chance to talk to Virnie. On the other hand, maybe it was what Virnie needed to realize she was worthy of love.

Christmas dinner was a true celebration. Diana had baked pies at home and brought them. The turkey, raised by Mrs. Jones, was tender and tasty. Conor wasn't sure where all the different vegetables and pickles had come from but guessed a great deal of it had been provided by Diana.

The meal over, they drew their chairs to the living area around the warm stove.

"This has been the best Christmas ever," Rae said.

Diana clapped her hands. "That gives me an idea. Why don't we each tell about the best Christmas we can remember?" She glanced eagerly around the group and when no one dissented she took it for agreement. "I'll start."

She sat back. "My best Christmas—apart from today—was the year my grandparents were all with us. It was the first time I remember all four of them being present. I just thought it was so special to have all that attention even if much of it went to my little brother who was just learning to walk. It was the year I got my favorite doll. She had a porcelain face and real hair and little black shoes. I still have her. In fact…" She darted a quick look at Gabe before she continued. "I brought her with me. Someday I hope to have a daughter to give it to."

Gabe laughed heartily, sending a flood of color to Diana's cheeks and Conor grinned at Rae. "Yup, a daughter is a pretty special gift."

Rae climbed to his lap and hugged him.

Virnie ducked her head and fiddled with her fingers.

Conor wanted to still her hands and assure her she was special even if her father hadn't believed it.

"Your turn, Gabe," Diana said.

He continued to smile at his wife. "It's easy for me to choose. The first Christmas I spent with you and your family after you agreed to be my wife."

"That was my worst," Diana whispered.

"Why?"

"Because you were leaving in a short time. Going West and I didn't know when I would see you again."

Gabe took her hands. "I had to find us our own place."

"I know. Go on and tell us why it was so special."

"Because of you. That's all."

Conor envied them their love. He forced himself to keep his gaze on them although he wanted nothing more than to look at Virnie and let her see the longing that made his eyes feel stark.

Gabe turned to Miles. "Care to share?"

Miles nodded. "The best Christmas I remember was when both our parents were alive and Virnie was about three. She was just learning to talk really well. Mother had made me socks and a new shirt. She'd made Virnie a rag doll. I remember like it was yesterday how she cuddled that doll. I'm sure she was convinced it was real. She put it down to sleep wrapped in a blanket and turned to inform us all, 'Baby Sue is sleeping. You must be quiet.' Papa said he didn't think she'd mind us talking." He chuckled. "Virnie planted her hands on her hips and stood between us and her baby. 'She's my baby and I know what's best for her.' My how we did laugh."

The others chuckled to think of a tiny version of Virnie defending her doll.

Virnie stared at Miles. "I remember that doll." Her voice was barely a whisper. Her eyes widened and she gasped. "I remember Mama giving it to me." Her voice broke.

No one moved, sensing how special this moment was for Virnie. Conor's eyes stung. She'd wanted so badly to remember her mother, needed it to feel whole and loved.

This could be the answer to his prayer on her behalf. He closed his eyes. His prayer was as much for him as for her. He understood she couldn't let herself love him until she found what her heart lacked.

"Do you have a favorite Christmas memory?" Diana asked her softly after a moment of silence. "If you don't want to say anything, we understand."

"No. I do. I remember that Christmas. I remember Papa and Mama laughing. I remember Mama hugging me when she gave me my baby." She turned to Miles. "It was real, you know. You'll never convince me otherwise."

Conor chuckled as did the others. Virnie had been a spunky child even as she was a strong woman. He knew with an assurance as strong as steel that she would find what she needed to heal her past.

Virnie turned to Conor. "And your best Christmas memory?"

He'd known this moment was coming. Yet every Christmas except this seemed tainted with disappointment or pain. So often growing up, survival had mattered more than gifts or celebration. Then after he married, his hopes for a loving home had been dashed by Irene's unhappiness. Only one thing had brightened those years—Rae. Suddenly he found a memory he cherished. He shifted Rae to one side of his lap so he could look into her eyes as he talked.

"Rae was about a year old. Just learning to walk really good. My parents had sent us gifts. And we'd bought her something. I think a ball but I'm not sure. In fact, I don't remember much about the gifts because all Rae cared about was the wrappings. She rattled them. She folded and unfolded them. She laughed as they made a crinkling noise. She wouldn't let us take them away even to go to bed." He smiled deeply at Rae. "You played with those pieces of paper until they were soft as cotton. You still had fragments of them when spring came."

"What happened to them, Pa?"

"You left them outside one night and it rained. In the morning they were nothing but mush."

"Aww."

He hugged her close. "You cried for an hour until finally your ma scooped up the remains and put them on a plate. They dried into an odd-shaped ball and you carried that until it completely disintegrated. In fact, I'm not totally sure there are specks of it still in the bottom of your drawer."

"Oh, Pa."

"What a nice story," Diana said.

Conor caught Virnie watching him and smiled.

She smiled back though he detected a tremor in her lips.

I love you. He hoped she would read the silent message of his heart.

She lowered her eyes then stole a quick glance. Her gaze was cautious but not resistant.

It was a good sign.

Chapter Fourteen

The men began work on the barn the next day. Miles insisted Virnie accompany him to the farm. Not that it took much convincing. She didn't want to miss a moment with Miles.

And this allowed her a perfectly acceptable way to spend time with Conor. And Rachael. Gabe and Diana, too, of course, she added hastily.

Having Miles visit, remembering Mama, feeling that she might have been loved by her parents had started to scrape back the shell she had built around her heart. She wasn't sure yet what lay beneath, whether it was something she would welcome or something dark and fearful. And that kept her from responding to the love she saw in Conor's eyes each time he looked at her. Not until she faced the depths of her heart could she accept love.

Little by little, with Miles's help, she was rediscovering pieces of her childhood. He'd described the house they lived in. He told her of aunts and uncles she'd forgotten. He reminded her of Papa's job working in the livery barn.

"He loved horses," Miles said as he and Conor took a

break from work. Gabe and Diana had gone to town, taking Rachael with them, to get some needed supplies. "He especially loved the big work horses. Virnie, do you remember him taking us to the barn to show us the horses?"

She shook her head. There was only one thing she clearly remembered about her father. "Why did Papa send me away?"

"Miss Price convinced him he wasn't being fair to you. Said he was allowing you to grow up a little hooligan." He said the word like it was poisonous on his tongue. "Papa found the word so offensive he could hardly talk. Even so, at first he resisted. But Miss Price was persuasive so he eventually agreed. He didn't want to."

Virnie found it hard to believe he had cared. "He said I should have been a boy."

Miles stared at her. "I can't imagine it but if he did I suppose it was because it would have been easier to leave you with me if you were."

Virnie ducked her head, pretending to have something on her fingernail. Her heart pounded with unshed tears and a bolt of fear that she could not deny. Her father had sent her away. Ripped her from her family all because he regretted she wasn't a boy. How could she trust someone to give her the love and acceptance she ached for when her own father couldn't? But was it because he didn't love her? The question roared through her head. It echoed in the silent absence of an answer. Without looking at Miles or Conor, she slipped from the table and pulled out pots and pans to make supper. Though she had no idea why she needed every pot in the cupboard.

The barn was almost finished. Tomorrow Gabe and Diana would return home. Miles announced he had found a job helping a farmer to the west who had broken his leg.

Virnie knew her time of being able to come to the farm would end when Miles left. She could hardly bear the thought. Although she couldn't trust herself to Conor's love, neither could she imagine not seeing him every day, not being aware of his watchfulness nor catching glimpses of his love.

If only she could figure out a way to fix what was wrong with her heart.

At first, when Miles triggered so many memories, she thought she had. But the time of feeling better had been short and transitory. Yes, she appreciated being able to remember her mother. She would always cherish that. But it wasn't enough.

And she didn't know what was.

The next day they went to the farm early to bid Gabe and Diana goodbye.

They stood admiring the raw new barn. "Thanks for all your help," Conor said, including both Miles and Gabe. "Looks good standing there strong and solid."

Strong and solid, Virnie thought. Just as he expected people to be.

Gabe glanced at the sky. "I hope we get home before this nice spell breaks."

They all looked skyward knowing how quickly a deadly winter storm could blow in.

"It looks good for the day. That should see you home," Conor said. "Godspeed. We'll see you in the spring."

Diana hugged Virnie. "We'll see you, too?"

"I'll be here until the end of the school term for certain." She caught Conor's gaze and saw stark disappointment because she hadn't promised so much more.

She held his gaze a moment. She wanted him to know she regretted how she felt. Suddenly she turned away. Seems like all her life she'd been trying to apologize for failing to be something she wasn't. Only in the classroom did she feel differently. Only there was she accepted as a competent human being. It was a good thing school was to resume in three days.

Gabe and Diana climbed into their wagon and drove away. Rachael ran after them until Gabe waved her back.

Miles, Conor and Virnie stared until they were out of sight.

It would be lonely around here without them.

Miles stretched. "Come on, Conor, I'll help you move the rest of the things into place. I told Mr. Andrews I would be at his place tomorrow in time to do the chores. His wife has been trying to manage but with a baby and all it's too much."

"Let's get it done." Conor spun away.

Her heart heavy with regret, Virnie returned to the house. She couldn't give Conor what he needed but she'd make up for her failure by making an especially nice supper. She ached clear through at the thought that once Miles left she wouldn't be free to visit here.

Conor came while she was cooking.

Virnie glanced up. "Where's Miles?"

"Showing Rae something about teaching her pony tricks. I wanted a chance to speak to you alone."

She sent him a warning look.

"Virnie, I promised I would give you all the time you needed. And I mean to keep that promise. But can you offer me any hope?" He rushed on without giving her a chance to speak. "I thought seeing Miles would make you feel better. It's obvious he loves you and he talks about how much your parents loved you. Isn't that enough?"

She shook her head.

He held out his hands in a pleading gesture. "What do you need?"

"I don't know." She pushed the words past the pain tightening her throat and squeezing her lungs. Suddenly the words flowed like water from a broken dam. "All my life I've felt like I didn't measure up. I could never be what anyone wanted. My papa didn't think I was good enough. I guess I wonder if I will ever be good enough."

Miles stepped into sight.

She hadn't heard him enter the house and grew silent. She knew her inability to believe their father had loved her hurt him.

He shed his coat and snow-covered boots before he stepped to her side. "Virnie, you have to understand how hard Papa tried but you pushed him away."

"I don't remember that." She skidded her gaze back to Conor. Would he condemn her for Mile's announcement? But all she saw was sympathy.

"It's like you blamed him." Miles drew her attention back to him.

"For what?"

"Mama being gone."

"Why would I do that?"

"You were only five. How could you understand why your mama had left you? And then you got left alone or sent with me. It really upset your world."

She couldn't swallow as she remembered the fear of being alone in the corner of the room. Mama gone. Papa gone. Miles gone. And then Papa came back. Sudden hot uncontrollable anger surged up her throat. Anger that Papa had left her alone. She spun around so neither Conor nor Miles could see the anger she knew would surely be drawing her face into harsh lines. Then she remembered another time of anger. She flung around to spill the words at Miles.

"He said he wished I was a boy. He sent me away. He never wrote or let you write."

Miles reached for her but she backed away.

He dropped his hand. "He wanted to. But Miss Price had insisted if he let her take you we must never contact you. He wrote one letter anyway but Miss Price returned it with 'Don't do this again' scrawled across the envelope."

Virnie didn't believe him. She glowered at Miles and sent Conor a look full of skepticism. "Why would she do that?"

"She said it was best if you forgot your past."

Virnie couldn't deny the truth of those words. She'd heard them many times from Miss Price. She could only rock her head back and forth, trying to sort out her feelings.

Conor pulled her to his side, one arm across her shoulders. The weight and warmth of his arm settled her churning emotions.

"Papa always said it was for the best but it about killed him to send you away."

"I don't believe you."

"On his dying bed Papa said if I ever see you I was to tell you these words. Say, 'I regret sending her away. She would have turned out fine without Miss Price. She already had the makings of a good strong, resourceful woman. I was proud of her and her mama would have been, too.'"

Virnie turned her face into Conor's chest and clung

to his shirtfront. Tears did not come. They couldn't escape the cages of her heart. Why had Miss Price insisted she never see her father again? Why did she think it was for the best? Had he sent her away because she shut him out? Was it all her fault?

She straightened, brushed her hair off her face and stepped away from Conor's hold. "You're only saying that to make me feel better, aren't you?"

"Oh, Virnie, I'm not. He loved you. Mama loved you. I loved you."

"So it was all my fault because I shut out Papa?"

Miles lifted his hands in a resigned gesture.

Conor again reached for Virnie but she shrugged away from being held. He met her eyes and searched hard and deep. She closed her heart and thoughts to him.

Conor sighed. "Virnie, must someone be made to blame? Can you not accept that your father did what he thought was best? Miss Price, too? I don't think anybody in your life meant to make you feel unaccepted, or unimportant. Maybe it's time to take the good that every one of them gave you and turn it into what you want it to be. I know it's time you saw yourself as you really are—a strong, capable woman who can be loved and admired solely because of who she is."

She searched his eyes for truth. Found love and acceptance. Found it in him but not in herself. She stepped back. "It's easy to say. Hard to do."

"Can you at least think about it? Consider it possible?"

She couldn't turn from the longing and trust and certainty in his gaze. "I'll try."

"Virnie?"

She turned to face her brother.

"Conor is right. No one meant to hurt you. Everyone

thought they were doing what was best for you. Forgive Papa. Forgive me. I should have stood up to Papa. I didn't want you to go."

She went to him and hugged him. "One thing I have never doubted was that you liked me."

He squeezed her hard. "Silly goose. I love you. What's more, I am proud of you and always have been. You've been a fighter since day one. Remember that as you sort through all this."

She straightened, swiped at her eyes. Felt Conor's hand on her shoulder. It seemed natural to go to his arms for a hug from him, too. She knew he silently reiterated Miles's words.

She allowed herself to believe in his love. For the space of two heartbeats.

Then she pulled away. She longed to accept what Conor offered, to believe how Miles explained the past, but her heart simply would not allow it.

She and Miles left directly after supper. Thankfully Miles didn't try to continue the conversation about Papa.

The next morning, he rode by the Maxwells' to say goodbye. "I hate to leave you especially when—" He shrugged.

"I'll be all right. I just need to sort things out in my head."

"Conor is a good man."

"I know that."

"Don't shut him out."

He didn't say it but she heard the words inside her head. *Like you did Papa.*

"Remember what he said."

"You've both given me much to think about."

"I'll be back on Sunday, weather permitting. We'll

talk more then." He hugged her one last time before he rode away.

She trod back to her bedroom and closed the door for privacy. She needed to sort out her thoughts. She wanted to. Instead rejection, hope, disappointment, blame all twisted inside her like a prairie tornado. She could no more separate one from the other than she could turn a tornado around.

School started again Monday and she welcomed the rhythm of the days. She had only one regret. Now that Rachael had her own pony, Conor no longer gave her a ride to school. Perhaps it was for the best. It would give her a chance to sort out her feelings.

Only by Saturday she was no closer to understanding why she couldn't put the past behind her and allow herself a new future, one full of love and belonging.

She kept busy Saturday with chores, hoping she could chase away her confusion. Several times she realized she paused to look out the window in the direction of the Russell farm. If Miles came perhaps they could go there for a visit. She hadn't seen Conor in eight days. She missed him more than made sense considering she continued to hold him off.

Late Saturday afternoon the weather reminded them they were in the midst of a Dakota winter. A storm blew in that obliterated the view out the window. The wind howled endlessly. Snow beat against the side of the house and plastered the outside of the window.

Mr. and Mrs. Maxwell huddled close to the stove in the little living room. "You're welcome to join us, dear," Mrs. Maxwell said.

Her room was frigid so Virnie gathered together her lesson materials and pulled close to the fire.

Sunday, the storm still raged. When she considered venturing out to church, Mr. Maxwell stopped her. "Ye'd be lost before you got there. Best stay home and enjoy a quiet day."

Reluctantly, she agreed. She didn't want a quiet day. At least not here. However, she knew Miles wouldn't venture out. Nor would Conor and Rachael. She tried not to picture them snuggled together close to their little stove. No doubt Rachael would play with Tippy and the doll Diana had given her. What did Conor do on such afternoons? She imagined sitting with them and talking softly of dreams and wishes.

She slammed shut the book she was reading.

Both Mr. and Mrs. Maxwell jumped.

"My dear, what's the matter?" Mrs. Maxwell asked.

"Sorry. It slipped." She returned to a story that made no sense. She had dreams and wishes. They included sharing home and family with Conor. So why couldn't she just accept what he offered?

But by the time she slipped away to go to bed she was no closer to sorting out her feelings.

The storm continued Monday. Mr. Nelson came by and said she didn't need to go to the school. He would go by just in case some foolhardy parent had sent their child.

Virnie wondered how she would keep herself busy through another stormbound day. She wrote Miss Price a letter, finding it hard to communicate with the woman who had been the cause of Virnie never being able to see her father again. She sighed. Miss Price only did what she thought best. How was she to know the hurt it inflicted on Virnie's heart? She must try to explain how it had affected her. Perhaps in doing so she could help Miss Price to change. Certainly continue to give girls a chance for a better life but not at the expense of making them feel abandoned by their family.

"Perhaps you'd like to unravel this old pair of socks," Mrs. Maxwell said after Virnie had sighed loudly several times. "Most of the yarn is still fine."

"Certainly." She was more than grateful to have something to do.

She almost cheered when she wakened Tuesday morning to a clear blue sky and sun so bright off the new snow that it hurt her eyes.

"Better bundle up," Mr. Maxwell advised as she prepared to leave for school. "It's cold enough to freeze you." He wrapped several scarves around his neck and face as he got ready to head for work in the little government office where he filled out land titles and other documents.

Virnie added a scarf and a pair of mittens to her wardrobe. She gasped when she stepped outside. The cold penetrated her layers long before she dashed into the schoolroom.

Mr. Nelson was there, the fire already warming the room. "I'll shovel a path to the barn and outhouses. Don't expect too many children today."

He was right. Only three showed up. None who had to walk or ride any distance.

By the end of the week, she ached for the sight of Conor. The weather had moderated slightly but she didn't know if Miles would be able to come to town. Or if she'd get a chance to see Conor.

When Miles came to the door Sunday morning in time to escort her to church, she hugged him fiercely.

"Missed me, did you?"

"You might say so."

She took his arm as they stepped out to head for church. As they neared the building, she glanced about hoping to see Conor and Rachael.

"I think I'm not the only one you missed."

"What do you mean?" She tried to sound disinterested but Conor and Rachael turned into the yard just then and she feared she'd let a bit of excitement edge her voice.

Miles chuckled. "I'm taking it that you've sorted out your feelings for him."

"My feelings for him were never a problem."

He stopped to stare at her. "I don't understand. If you love him and he loves you, what is the problem?"

She slid her gaze past his shoulder and tried to sort out an answer. Here she was a teacher, supposedly of reasonable intelligence, and she could find no words to explain her feelings.

Miles caught her shoulders and shook her gently. "Virnie, what's wrong?"

"The only problem is me. I'm afraid to trust anyone to keep loving me." Her voice dropped to a whisper. "I'm afraid I'll disappoint them."

"Oh, Virnie, how could you think such a thing? I love you just as you are. I'm sure Conor does, too. Just accept it."

She nodded. He couldn't begin to understand how much she wished it were possible. Just accept it. She was grateful they had arrived at the doorway to the church.

Conor waited, Rachael at his side. He smiled, his eyes sought and found hers and his smile went from his mouth to her heart. He leaned close. "I've missed you."

"Me, too," she whispered, then straightened and let Miles escort her down the aisle to a pew. She hadn't forgotten the disapproval she'd earned by being careless about how she acted.

Conor seemed to understand and let Rachael in to sit next to Virnie then slipped in beside his daughter.

Virnie was very conscious of his presence. Something shifted in her as if her heart had developed a will of its own, demanding she listen to it but she knew she must sort out her warring emotions before she gave in to the urging of her heart.

Conor turned slightly, saw how she glanced at him and his expression filled with promise and love.

This was what she wanted.

What she'd wanted all her life.

But...

The preacher rose to announce the first hymn.

Virnie focused her attention on the front, her eyes lingering on the cross carved in the front of the pulpit. God must surely know what she needed. And what better place to seek and find it than right here?

"Let us pray," the preacher said.

Virnie didn't hear his prayer as she silently voiced her own. *God, show me what it is I need in order to be free to accept Conor's love.*

Chapter Fifteen

"You'll come to the farm?" Conor asked Miles, but his eyes reached for Virnie.

"Certainly. Expected we would. Mr. Brown said I might borrow his buggy."

Virnie turned to accompany her brother down the aisle.

Conor waited to whisper in her ear as she passed, "You and I need to talk."

She slipped past. She'd hoped for some wonderful insight as she listened intently to the sermon. But the preacher seemed to be stuck on one verse: "We are fearfully and wonderfully made." The words mocked her. She felt like God had made a mistake in creating her. She could never measure up to what others expected of her.

How could she ever trust love with Conor as long as she felt this way? She should refuse to go to the farm but she could no more deny herself an afternoon with Conor than she could erase her troubled thoughts. Although she tried. How she tried.

Conor and Rachael reached the farm before Miles

and Virnie and as Virnie stepped into the house, she saw the table set and a pot of soup on the stove.

"I made the soup," Rachael announced.

Virnie dismissed her troubled thoughts in the pleasure of sharing this day and in her joy in seeing how far Rachael had come. She hugged Rachael. "Good for you."

Rachael ducked her head and giggled. "Pa helped some."

Virnie met Conor's eyes over Rachael's head and something at once demanding and promising filled his gaze. She slowly straightened, never breaking eye contact, wondering what his look meant, knowing she didn't want to disappoint him but fearing she would.

After lunch, Rachael begged them to come see the tricks she'd taught Prince so they trouped out to the barn. She'd taught her pony to bow and tap his hoof three times when she asked him how much was one plus two.

Virnie clapped, as did Miles and Conor.

"What other things can I teach him?" Rachael asked Miles.

Miles circled Rachael and her pony. "Hmm. Let's see."

Rachael shot her father a shy look. "Pa, I want it to be a surprise."

"Are you trying to get rid of me?"

"No. Well, maybe just for a little while."

Conor laughed. "Well, fine. Virnie and I will go for a walk." He took her hand and pulled it through his arm. "You'll be warm enough?"

"I think so." If he held her close to his side like this

the warmth from his arm would drive away cold both from the outside and the inside of her body.

They meandered around the yard, Conor pointing out improvements he intended to make. They paused at the garden spot. "Next year I am going to take care of the garden." He shook his head. "Can't imagine why I neglected it in the past. I never want Rae to wonder where the next meal will come from."

He'd told her how his family had struggled to survive when he was growing up.

"I figure if a person works hard and is diligent, he can carve out a solid home on the prairies."

She was glad he chose to talk about the farm and his plans. They left the garden area and walked toward the first field, as far as the snow allowed them. "Land. Lots of land." He swept his arm to indicate the endless prairie.

He lowered his arm, pressed his hand to hers, covering it against his forearm. Filling her with warmth and love. If she could capture the assurance she felt standing next to him, listening to his dreams and plans, and pour it into her heart and cork it there…

She sighed. They didn't make corks for hearts.

Conor shifted to face her fully. He trailed his finger across her jawline. He gazed into her eyes with such warmth and longing she lowered her eyes and studied his chin. He'd shaved recently, probably before church, leaving only a dark shadow on his face. His face had strong line. When he smiled, deep crevasses gouged his cheeks. He didn't smile now. She lifted her gaze to his eyes, saw the warmth and hunger in them. She swallowed hard.

"Virnie, you must know I love you."

She nodded. "I know," she whispered. With love came expectations. That's what filled her with trembling fear.

"How do you feel about me?" The agony in his voice filled her with sorrow.

She didn't want to hurt him. Now or ever. "Conor, I love you."

He took her shoulders and held her inches from his embrace. "Then marry me. Share my life and my dreams."

She pressed her lips together. She could think of nothing in this world she wanted more. "I can't."

"Why?" He shook her gently, his voice almost a moan.

"How do I know I can be what you want me to be? How do you?"

He tucked his chin in and blinked at her. "I only want you to be you. Nothing else."

She rocked her head back and forth. "It's never been enough. Papa wanted me to be a boy. Miss Price wants me to be a teacher and a lady. You…" She sucked back air. "You want me to be strong. You expect it of everyone you care about, even yourself."

He pulled her to his chest and groaned. "Virnie, I confess that's all I wanted a few months ago. You taught me that it isn't enough. And when I waited for rescue, I realized two together are stronger than one alone. We balance each other. I thought I'd made that clear then. I did tell you, didn't I?"

"Yes." Her voice was muffled against his coat.

"You don't believe me?"

She edged back, steeling herself to leave the comfort

of his chest, forcing herself to face the disappointment in his face. "I believe you."

"But...?"

"You would learn to despise my weaknesses." She clutched his lapels, afraid he would turn away in disgust.

He smiled. Trailed his gaze over her face as if memorizing every detail. He smiled. "I think I would only find them endearing."

She shook her head, knowing at some point he would realize she wasn't what he expected.

"Virnie, my sweet, sweet girl, you only have to be what you are. Nothing more. Nothing less. Just be what God created you to be."

"That's too simplistic."

His eyes brimmed with disappointment.

She ducked her head. She couldn't bear to see it starting already. "I'm trying to change. Perhaps in time..."

"How long must I wait?"

"I can't say."

"How will I know when you're ready?"

"I'll tell you."

He sighed. "I hate waiting, loving you but not being able to share my life with you." He pulled her against his chest again and held her like he never wanted to let her go.

She hated hurting him but feared she would hurt him worse if she agreed to marry him. How could she live up to his expectations?

They returned to the house and played a game of dominoes with Rachael and Miles. She did her best to disguise her inner turmoil and sensed Conor did the same. Several times she felt his gaze on her but she refused to look at him.

As they prepared to leave, Conor pulled her aside. "I will be patient but please don't make me wait too long." The way his voice cracked filled her with agony. "Virnie, I will pray for you to find the truth you need to discover about yourself."

She hesitated. Did he know what that truth was? She dismissed the thought. Even if he did, having him say it wouldn't convince her. She must discover what she needed on her own.

Miles left as soon as they returned to town.

Virnie retreated to her bedroom. She tried to think. She prayed for God to show her what her problem was.

But three days later she was no closer to feeling like she had settled her problem.

Wednesday night she excused herself early from the living room and the company of Mr. and Mrs. Maxwell. Tonight she intended to wrestle her inner turmoil into submission with God's help.

She opened her Bible and spread it on her bed and fell on her knees. *Lord, show me what I need to know.*

What did everyone expect of her? Why couldn't she please them?

Surely God had something to say about that.

She searched the pages of the Bible where it lay before her. It had fallen open to Psalms. In fact, to the very chapter the pastor had preached on the past Sunday.

I will praise Thee; for I am fearfully and wonderfully made. It was the end of the column and she paused.

Doubts flooded her mind. But not wanting to face

them, she shifted her gaze to the top of the next column and continued to read.

Marvelous are Thy works; and that my soul knoweth right well.

Only her soul did not know and believe that His creation of her was marvelous. She shifted back to the beginning of the verse.

I will praise Thee.

How could she praise God when she didn't believe her creation wasn't a mistake? She'd tried so hard to please people.

Try pleasing God, being what He created you to be.

Who had He created her to be? A girl who should have been a boy? A young woman trying to forget her tough upbringing? Yet without it she wouldn't have been able to rescue Conor.

She froze.

Something bright and inviting hovered at the edges of her thoughts. Had God used everything in her life to make her into a unique individual with strengths that served her well—a teacher, a lady and yet with a core of strength that came from following Miles around? Or perhaps had been hers since birth?

Had she been trying to please the wrong people?

Happiness begins and ends with God. She'd heard the words or read them somewhere, the source long forgotten. And at the time she thought only about how nice the statement sounded but now it drove deep into her brain.

I have loved you with an everlasting love.

A sob caught at the roof of her mouth. *God, I thank You and praise You for making me. For creating me with individual strengths and weaknesses. I never re-*

alized before how all these things have prepared me to be a wife, a helpmate for Conor and a pioneer in this new, challenging land. She buried her face against the rough chenille coverlet and let waves of joy and acceptance wash over her.

She lost track of time, until her knees started to remind her of the hard floor and she realized how cold she'd grown. She plucked a quilt from the foot of the bed and wrapped it around her as she curled up on the bed. She read the passage in the Psalms over and over. Each time she had to dash away fresh tears. Tears of joy and gratitude.

She was ready to share Conor's love and life.

Conor sat in the easy chair beside the stove, trying to force his attention to the farming publication before him. He'd struggled long and hard to be patient about Virnie. He knew he must trust God but found it easier to say than to do.

He abandoned all pretense at reading and tossed the paper to the side table. Rae had gone to bed. He was completely alone. Even Tippy insisted on sleeping with Rae. Shows how lonely a man was when he wished for a cat to keep him company.

He was tired of being alone. There was a time he was sure he could manage on his own. But he no longer wanted to. He wanted to share his life with Virnie.

If only he could do something to convince her she was all he wanted and needed. Just as she was. But he understood she carried some unreasonable fears she needed to deal with. He'd help her if he could or if she'd let him. But until she asked him to... well, all he could do was pray.

Sunday came and when Conor showed no indication of getting ready to attend the service, Rae stood in front on him. "Aren't we going to church?"

"Not today. It's too cold."

"It's not—" Seeing the warning in his face, she didn't finish. She stomped to her room where he heard her discussing it with Tippy. "It's not a bit cold. He just doesn't want to go."

No. He didn't. He couldn't face Virnie and know he must wait for her to change. Or did he mean, wait for God to work in her life? Whichever it was he decided he preferred to hole up at his farm until it happened.

The next Sunday he again told Rae he thought it was too cold to attend church. She retreated to the barn to spend time with her pony. At least she had the company of her pets.

He made a sugar and cinnamon sandwich for himself at lunch time. Rae hadn't come in. He guessed she'd come when she got hungry enough.

He stood at the stove wondering if it was worth the effort to make tea when he heard the sound of an approaching buggy. He peeked out the frosty window.

Miles and Virnie. Was she intent on tormenting him?

He watched Miles help Virnie down. She said something to him and he nodded and led the horse to the barn.

Conor steeled himself to face her. He must find things to converse about when he wanted to discuss only one thing—their love.

She knocked.

When had it come to this? She used to walk in like it was her home.

He called, "Come in."

Slowly the door opened. She stepped in and faced him across the space of the living area. Her eyes flooded with a joy that she seemed barely able to restrain. "I'm ready."

He blinked. What was that supposed to mean?

She grinned. "I told you I'd let you know when I was ready. I'm telling you now."

He remembered. He'd asked how he would know when she was ready to accept love. She said she'd tell him. "You mean…?" Dare he hope?

She nodded, her eyes shining like they'd captured the brilliant winter sun and carried it indoors.

He took one step, uncertain if it was real. She nodded and he knew it was. He closed the distance between them in two long strides, caught her to his chest and hugged her to his heart—where love had unlocked all his secret longings.

After a couple of minutes, he led her to the easy chair and sat down. He pulled her to his lap. "Are you ready to be happy?"

She rubbed her cheek against him. "I am happy."

He caught her chin and turned her to face him. "Are you ready to let me be part of your happiness?"

She nodded. "More than ready."

He kissed her. He'd wanted to do this for a very long time. He let his lips linger a moment. He'd have the rest of his life to enjoy kissing her. He shifted her to his shoulder so he could talk. "When can we get married?"

She sat up to face him, her expression serious. "I want to finish out my school year."

"But why? You don't have to prove anything to anyone, especially Miss Price."

"I'm not trying to be live up to her plans but still I

do owe her for what she did for me. Because of her I am who I am."

He nodded, knowing she had finally found peace with the events of her past.

"Besides. I need time to learn to be whole—following the life God has planned for me instead of trying to be who I thought would please Papa or Miss Price." She seemed distracted by trailing her finger along his chin—a touch that made it impossible for Conor to think.

She removed her finger, curled her hands together in her lap. "'I am fearfully and wonderfully made.' I realize God used everything in my life to uniquely prepare me to be a pioneer wife."

"I love you, Virnie. I'm tired of being alone but I can wait if that's what you want."

"First, I have to talk to Mr. Nelson and the rest of the board. I'll tell them exactly what my intentions are—to finish the school year and then marry you. If they find that unacceptable, well, I refuse to pretend I don't love you."

He hugged her close then claimed her lips. His love for her filled him until he had to break away from their kiss to shout, "I love you, Virnie White. Now and always."

He pulled her to her feet and danced her around the room. Paused at the door. "What happened to Miles?"

"I asked him to wait in the barn."

He swung her off her feet then put her down and kissed her soundly. "How long until the school year ends?"

Chapter Sixteen

June finally arrived. The intervening months had been both a delight and agony. Agony as Virnie and Conor waited to unite their lives. Rachael knew of the upcoming plans but at the request of the school board, they had told no one except their families. The delight had been in getting to know each other better. Conor had opened up every corner of his heart to her.

More than once he'd laughed as he shared something new. "I never told anyone else this."

She hugged the delight to herself. And she grew more and more confident in accepting who she was, who God had created her to be and in trusting Conor's love for her.

Much of her wedding preparations had been done in secret in order to fulfill the requirements of the school board. Not until a few weeks ago had she informed Miss Price, dreading the disappointment she knew she must cause.

After a long delay, the reply came back.

It is with a heavy heart that I read your news and yet I am not surprised. Although you could be an excellent, dedicated teacher I think I always sensed you wanted something else. If this is what you want and what makes you happy, then by all means pursue your dream. I do hope you will see fit to send me an invite to your wedding.

Virnie had been only too happy to do so. Miss Price had arrived in town yesterday in plenty of time for Virnie to show her the schoolhouse and discuss the successes of her year as a teacher. Then she had taken her to the farm and introduced Conor and Rachael.

Conor was cool at first. Virnie understood that he feared seeing Miss Price would cause Virnie's old fears to surface. She shared some of his trepidation. But she felt only pride and love as she showed Miss Price around.

"You are far more suited to this life than I could have guessed," Miss Price said later.

Today was her wedding day and she knew nothing but joy and anticipation.

Rachael waited with her in the little cloakroom of the church, pirouetting to make the bright yellow of her skirts whirl around. "I'm like a buttercup," she said.

"You're beautiful. Your pa will be so proud."

Rachael stopped spinning and stared at Virnie. "You're beautiful. Pa won't see anyone but you."

Virnie giggled and hugged Rachael. "I'll be sure and tell him to take note of you."

Rachael giggled, too. "It doesn't matter. Getting you for a ma is the best thing of all."

Virnie kissed the child. "I love you."

"I love you, too, Mama. It is all right if I call you that now?"

"Perfect."

Miles knocked and entered the room. "Ready?"

"Ready and waiting." She took his arm and they followed Rachael down the aisle.

Conor stood at the front so handsome it made her heart hurt. He wore the gray tie she'd given him at Christmas. It made his blue eyes brighter, stronger. And the smile he gave her made her knees go suddenly weak. Miles covered her hand as it rested on his forearm and gave her a concerned glance.

She forced strength to her limbs and lifted her head. This was the best day of her life.

Later, after they'd exchanged vows and kissed for the first time as man and wife, she clung to him. "I love you," she whispered as they rushed down the aisle.

His eyes filled with tender amusement. "I know."

* * * * *

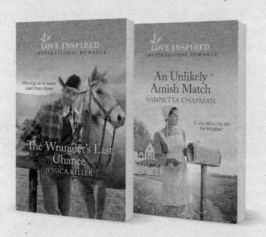

Could this bad-boy newcomer spell trouble for an Amish spinster...or be the answer to her prayers?

Read on for a sneak preview of
An Unlikely Amish Match,
the next book in Vannetta Chapman's miniseries
Indiana Amish Brides.

The sun was low in the western sky by the time Micah Fisher hitched a ride to the edge of town. The driver let him out at a dirt road that led to several Amish farms. He'd never been to visit his grandparents in Indiana before. They always came to Maine. But he had no trouble finding their place.

As he drew close to the lane that led to the farmhouse, he noticed a young woman standing by the mailbox. A little girl was holding her hand and another was hopping up and down. They were all staring at him.

"Howdy," he said.

The woman only nodded, but the two girls whispered, "Hello."

"Can we help you?" the woman asked. "Are you...lost?"

"*Nein.* At least I don't think I am."

"You must be if you're here. This is the end of the road."

Micah pointed to the farm next door. "Abigail and John Fisher live there?"

"They do."

"Then I'm not lost." He snatched off his baseball cap, rubbed the top of his head and then yanked the cap back on.

Micah stepped forward and held out his hand. "I'm Micah— Micah Fisher. Pleased to meet you."

"You're not *Englisch*?"

"Of course I'm not."

"So you're Amish?" She stared pointedly at his clothing—tennis shoes, blue jeans, T-shirt and baseball cap. Pretty much what he wore every day.

"I'm as Plain and simple as they come."

"I somehow doubt that."

"Since we're going to be neighbors, I suppose I should know your name."

"Neighbors?"

"*Ja.* I've come to live with my *daddi* and *mammi*—at least for a few months. My parents think it will straighten me out." He peered down the lane. "I thought the bishop lived next door."

"He does."

"Oh. You're the bishop's *doschder*?"

"We all are," the little girl with freckles cried. "I'm Sharon and that's Shiloh and that is Susannah."

"Nice to meet you, Sharon and Shiloh and Susannah."

Sharon lost interest and squatted to pick up some of the rocks. Shiloh hid behind her *schweschder*'s skirt, and Susannah scowled at him.

"I knew the bishop lived next door, but no one told me he had such pretty *doschdern*."

Susannah's eyes widened even more, but it was Shiloh who said, "He just called you pretty."

"Actually I called you all pretty."

Shiloh ducked back behind Susannah.

Susannah narrowed her eyes as if she was squinting into the sun, only she wasn't. "Do you talk to every girl you meet that way?"

"Not all of them—no."

Don't miss
An Unlikely Amish Match *by Vannetta Chapman,*
available February 2020 wherever
Love Inspired® books and ebooks are sold.

LoveInspired.com

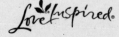